was stretched out, trying to relax after a difficult crosswind landing, when the door opened and Kate walked across to the dressing table, wearing a thin pale-green robe and slim-heeled slippers. She leaned over to the mirror, prodded her hair, and then slipped out of the robe and stood quite still.

I put down my book as she turned around, and despite myself, feasted my eyes on her wonderful assembly of skin, curves, and shadows. We didn't speak...I felt numb at first, no reaction. But eventually that traitorous fold of flesh sensed Kate's urgent writhing, and I clutched her fiercely, eyes tight shut, heart thudding gigantically in my ears, breath whistling in my throat until we hung suspended in a seconds-long limbo that lasted a thousand years.

"A real page-turner... surprise ending."

—*Tulsa World*

About the Author

DAVID GRAHAM served with distinction in the RAF as a fighter pilot during World War II, and later as a flying instructor. He is now a technical writer for an aeronautics firm in Great Britain, and lives in Southampton, England.

Down to a Sunless Sea

A NOVEL BY

David Graham

FAWCETT CREST • NEW YORK

A Fawcett Crest Book
Published by Ballantine Books
Copyright © 1981 by David Graham

Library of Congress Catalog Card Number: 80-25603

ISBN 0-449-21164-9

This edition published by arrangement with Simon
and Schuster

Manufactured in the United States of America

First Fawcett Crest Edition: September 1982
First Ballantine Books Edition: January 1984
Second Printing: September 1986

To Joyce, for thirty-five years
my rod and my staff.

In Xanadu did Kubla Khan
A stately pleasure dome decree:
Where Alph, the sacred river, ran
Through caverns measureless to man
Down to a sunless sea....

Coleridge

Author's Note

Without the generous and unstinting help of British Airways, and additionally of Captain John Race, Pan American World Airways, this book could not have been attempted. Short of allowing me to fly a Boeing 747—a dream which, alas, after fifteen wingless years will never be realized—their efforts to provide authenticity were unremitting and, I venture to remark, more successful than I could have hoped.

I should also like to thank Captain Jan F. Dalby, Chief Information Officer, HQ, 1605th Air Base Wing (MAC), U.S. Air Force, stationed in the Azores, who provided most valuable help with that section of this book.

References within the text to existing aircraft and airlines are incidental, and any resemblance to actual persons is unintentional.

One fascinating and odd fact deserves mention. Through all my life, I have been the epitome of the rabid, outspoken atheist. In writing this book, I thought only of demonstrating that Man is alone in his individual Hell, that he would inevitably sow the seeds of his own destruction, rising and falling in a few hundred millenniums which represent the tiniest fraction of eternity.

Now—damn it all—I'm not so sure.

Bitterne
Southampton
England
1979

1

Flight decks are traumatic places. Memory storages impregnated with sweat, fear, boredom and stress. Somewhere in there, traces of pleasure, satisfaction: nostalgic echoes of vast starry nights like inverted Broadways, snowy peaks jutting through cloud floors in brilliant sunlight, tropical sunsets from a Gauguin canvas. Indescribable things which compensate, ephemerally, for the cruel hours of tense concentration.

Most big jet crews get the hell out almost before the main wheels stop rolling—you could get trampled in the rush, I guess. Assuming, of course, they have somewhere to go, someone to be with, money to spend. Which accounted for my sitting here alone in a silent Delta Tango, staring out at a wet, dimly lit expanse of Kennedy Airport. I blew it on all three counts: nowhere to go, no one to go with—and money was a sick joke in New York, this late October of 1985.

The log lay completed on my lap. I lit a Split, dimmed down the lights a shade. Down back somewhere, the cleanup squad were wrapping it up; Kate and her girls would be clustered at Gate 3 Port, waiting for transport. I slid back the window at my left elbow.

The rain was finished—temporarily, because up there in the blackness above the thinly strung floods, the overcast stretched north to the Canadian border, west to the Lakes and south, for all I knew, all the way to the Gulf.

The Security cordon was stretched thin tonight. Out there, where shadows pressed hard on perimeter lights, the 83rd Airborne stood at four-yard intervals, shiny black helmets over wet, gleaming camouflage slickers. They faced outward, straddle-legged, Armalites cradled in the left elbow joint. Every fourth man carried a machine pistol with sniperscope, and each gun bore sidesaddle a laser sight. The line surrounded Delta Tango, a second 797 with Lufthansa markings, two Varig Brazil Airbuses and five U.S. Army Cargonauts—C5 freighters.

I dragged hard at the Split, pulling it way down deep, slowly exhausting the smoke through my nose, and the fatigue and stiffness seemed a little more bearable. There was a time I had loathed the State-manufactured mix of cannabis with Russian and Armenian tobacco—but when it became the only game in town I wasn't so proud.

I began to think about the way things had turned out, the last few years. Someone once said "man is an infinitely adaptable animal." He was no fool. The big things stood out, of course: abdication and a third King Charles; an eighteen-month Regency before the Coronation; Charles's totally unexpected engagement to a slim American girl. The swift passage of legislation, the crowning of another Victoria from the New World. I remembered with pleasure the stark and beautiful simplicity of the Emergency Measures by which Charles and his Government of Service officers straightened out the chaos of the Dollar Collapse.

I'm the first to admit we were very lucky. We had our oil—and, unlike the Americans, the sense to hang on to it. We had that quite incredible conservation program which soaked up unemployment overnight, taking just a year and a half to insulate every building in Britain. And there was that strange national upsurge of—pride? conscience?—I don't know what it was. So despite the rationing, power restrictions, the single national newspaper and the regression of trade unions into localized bargaining machines, Britain wasn't such a bad place.

But America...I stared out westwards, towards the veiled towers of Manhattan. I could see sparse lights sprinkled along the skyline—crazies who put up with no power, no elevators, no comfort for the sake of a bird's-eye view of a dying city.

I turned. Jerry Chambers came through onto the flight deck, whistling some tune shrilly.

"Hi."

"Jerry. All finished back there?"

My First Officer nodded, slid into the right-hand seat,

offered me a joint. I shook my head. In the gloom, I couldn't see the creaseless trousers, the egg-stained tunic, the soiled shirt—but I knew they were all there. Chambers had only one thing going for him: he was a damned fine pilot. And in my world, that outweighed all the other things: the sloppy dress, the odd walk like a ruptured penguin's, the irritating reluctance to answer a question until he knew the reply was a hundred percent accurate. He was four inches over six feet, thin as a rake, wore his stringy yellow hair long and fascinated strangers, the way his Adam's apple oscillated in his long scrawny throat.

Eventually—

"Nearly." (I had almost forgotten the question.) "The garbage squad finished just now. Kate has half a dozen girls cleaning the galleys—you know how she is."

I knew how Kate was. Finicky. I sniffed. "And?"

"Our tanker 707 is due in from St. John's around six tomorrow night. Full load—they had a lot of snow up there in New Brunswick, or it would have come in around noon. We can finish refueling around nine. No sweat."

"Means a later takeoff."

"Not late—early, Skip. Oh oh thirty Monday morning. You been sitting here for the past hour contemplating your navel?"

"I've filled in the log," I said defensively. "Unwinding" would have been closer, and we both knew it. "What about the weather?"

Chambers sat smoking, staring out of his window. He might have been deaf—but I'd flown with him for six years. I waited patiently.

"Fair—for the time of the year," he said at last. "Big depression over Greenland filling very slowly, almost stationary. We can pass to the south, maybe pick up a jet stream. Full load again, Skipper?"

"Every last damn seat," I told him. "Kate will be pleased. Six hundred and ten, all told. I believe we have some U.N. people, and another batch of homeless kids. The rest mostly repats, I guess."

"It'll never get off the ground," said Chambers pessimistically. "Hauling that number of people off ground at one time is indecent."

I felt the same way. But we had qualified on 797s very early, after four years on 747s; I liked the big jets. People ask me how it feels, pushing 300 tons of aircraft into the air. Did it feel different? Answer: no. I learned years ago, if you fly the front end off the ground successfully, the rest generally follows behind. Regardless of contents.

We had bought up most of the best grounded 747s from Pan Am, TWA, Braniff and American and converted Hurn Airport, near Bournemouth, into one vast factory. They took in a 747, slotted an extra 40 feet into the forward body, fitted a fifth RB 215 into the tail and seats for 620 bodies. All in about ten weeks—I've seen them do it. Air Britain—every British aircraft is in the Company—is almost as big as Bomber Command once was—and we're still overworked. We've hauled the last 100,000 whites out of Rhodesia—Zimbabwe, as it is now; half a million Vietnamese into Australia after China moved in. We've lifted mountains of food and medical supplies into Ethiopia and Pakistan and the other plague spots, flying alongside United Arab Airlines, Iran Air and the rest of OPEC organizations: we won't sell anyone our oil, but we'll fly anyone, anywhere. Including these repatriated Americans. It would take us a long time to whittle down their 200 million to the 80 million a bankrupt country could afford to keep, but the only qualification they needed was a relative, somewhere, who would take them. We came in light from Heathrow, had our fuel flown in from Canada, departed loaded for almost anywhere equipped with fuel storage.

Chambers opened his window, flicked out the butt hastily and closed it again. He stared out through the forward screen, elbows on the control yoke.

"No sign of the crew bus. I could sleep standing up."

"Think yourself lucky," I said shortly, watching a pair of top sergeants moving along the picket line below. "You could be standing out there waiting for trouble."

He got up, stood crouched to see better, an elbow on my seat back. "Not me," he said. "Pacifist—all the way. Besides, I'm a qualified coward; served my time at it. Hey—something's happening down there...."

Something was.

The paras were crouching, heads forward, straining to see through the black night, their shadows long and distorted in the swaying floodlights. I saw a flash from a small group a hundred yards away, and a stark white flare burst several hundred feet above. It caught a small party of indistinct figures, running in wedge formation towards the parked aircraft across a waste of concrete. I heard a bullhorn challenge, incredibly loud, badly distorted: I think it said, "Hold it right there!"

It didn't stop the flying wedge, maybe fifty or sixty strong. What they hoped to achieve I do not know—food, perhaps; maybe even a seat outbound, ahead of a twelve-month waiting list. Guns, certainly; if they reached the picket line, more than one para wouldn't need his gun anymore.

We watched, silent. Chambers breathed through his nose, heavily. The troops let them close to about fifty yards, fired a short burst above their heads. They kept coming, bunching as if for shelter from whining slugs. A noncom bawled an order and the guns flared again. Almost at once, the overhead flare sputtered and died—but it didn't really matter. The troopers got torches going, walked stiff-legged along the straggling line of bodies. Here and there a hand or leg jerked, twisted. It may have been just muscular reflexes, but no one took any chances. It was over very quickly—perhaps sixty seconds at most.

Chambers said thickly, "Jesus...Jesus God. I feel sick."

"Not in here—open your goddamn window, man."

"All of them...They didn't leave one alive," he mumbled. I gave him a Split and held his wrist until he got it in his mouth. He sagged back into his seat, shaking visibly.

"Come on," I said harshly. "You know the score. Prisoners have to eat. And no one gets away with attacks on the Army, even now."

"You're a callous bastard."

"You're a callous bastard, *sir!*" I said.

"You're as bad as those noncoms out there, Skipper. Doesn't it even bother you a little?" I could see his eyes glistening in the half-light.

We sat for long moments in silence. You never really got used to it, I thought. It must have been this way going over the top in World War One.... Nine hours ago we were in an almost normal Britain, with law and order, armed traffic wardens, safe streets after dark, private cars (even if the gas ration was ludicrous). Here, at once-bustling, overcrowded Kennedy, there was death and hunger and darkness and no man could guess how distant the sunrise.

Talk to any American. Ask him what it was like when the sky fell on him, back in January 1983. He'll tell you. He'll tell you they all saw it coming—and did nothing to stop it. They had enormous reserves of oil, right under their feet—and used it, down to the last drop. It wasn't enough. They bought more and more, anywhere they could—and sold it for a few cents a gallon. Among them, Americans used more energy in seven decades than the rest of the world together. They had one gorgeous lifetime of the biggest cars, brightest lights and hottest central heating in Christendom.

And then the oil ran out.

What remained of America's own reserves was earmarked for the Armed Forces. The lack of forward planning, the persistent refusal to implement a conservation policy made the final result certain. Most Americans believed it could never happen—and when it did happen, it was the sheer velocity of collapse that was so appalling. Many factors contributed.

There was the stubborn resistance to conservation by the power companies, a far stronger lobby than the gunmakers ever mustered. When Detroit stopped making gas guzzlers and went for smaller cars, they thought they'd solved it—but their idea of "small" was way off. Heating levels in most buildings remained unhealthily high; Congress repeatedly fought the White House in its efforts to introduce legislation. Alaska came on stream late in 1977, building up to 1½ billion gallons a day—but towards the end they needed a new Alaska every three years, just to maintain 1977 consumption. The U.S.A. started to buy oil overseas, shipping it up the Mississippi for storage in empty salt domes. Brilliant! Soon they had almost 500 billion gallons stashed away, a thousand feet deep. If things got tight, it would last for a while, at least.

At least three months...

And so the dollar began to slide. They tried to fill the gap with coal—but they were twenty years behind in gasoline production from coal. It could not be done overnight.

I stowed the log away in my briefcase, stretched briefly and watched the troopers pulling away loaded handcarts.

Where had I been when the Collapse came? In what used to be Salisbury, Rhodesia. We were bringing out the last few loads of whites, using the makeshift runway they cleared by blasting out the city center. I didn't know the full story—few did—because there were so many other things happening in a crazy world around that time. I was the last aircraft out but one. There was a solid ring of smoke, fire and bloody death not more than a mile from the city center, where an exhausted rear guard was disputing every inch, every second of time...time for one more load of women and children. We flew out nearly 100,000 of them in seventeen days, a sort of airborne Dunkirk—except that the enemy came from Cuba, Libya, Spain and Taiwan.

"Any progress with that cranky inverter?" I looked across at Chambers. He stirred, dragged both palms down his face, stared at me. It worked. He made a grim effort and tried to concentrate.

"Chalky White and Ben Price are still down in the hold, Skip. Shall I give them a buzz?"

I thought for a moment. "Negative. Let them be. When they've fixed it, they'll let us know. How about taking a walk over to the terminal and finding that crew bus? It seems fairly quiet out there now."

"Okay, Skipper. If you're staying here, I can buzz you on Selcall?"

"No." I shook my head slowly. "I'm going down aft—that hooley out there has probably scared the hell out of the stews. I'll see you later."

The copilot nodded, ambled out with that queer gait of his. Like a stork wading in hot water. I got my gear together quickly: small overnight bag, flight briefcase and Portafreeze. The bag was heavy—I had two 15-kilo bags of corn aboard for Charlie Hackett. I wouldn't be without my Portafreeze— suitcase size, made in light plastic; the small battery-driven compressor ran for four days and nights without recharging. Ideal for picnics, camping weekends and New York stopovers, where you haul in your own food—or you don't eat.

I checked the windows shut, closed the flight-deck door behind me and went aft, past the toilet and VIP galley into the upper lounge. The spiral stairs were a drag, fully loaded, but I made it to the main cabin below and off-loaded at Gate 1 Port. Far aft I could hear shrill female argument, but ignored it—Kate Monahan could handle her eighteen girls without help from me. The intercom buzzed.

"Jerry?"

"No, Mr. Scott—Chalky White. What the hell was all that row outside? We thought we heard shooting."

I said as nonchalantly as I could, "No sweat, Chalky. Some intruders—the paras sorted it out. Ben there with you? What was the problem?"

"Ye want blinding with science, Captain? Ah...perhaps

*not. Mr. Price is going to run Number Five in a moment, but
we think we've cracked it. We had a system imbalance on the
AC bus bar which kept throwing the inverter off line, but once
we tracked it down it was easy enough to fix."*

"Good lad. I've left the log at Gate One for you. Mr. Chambers mentioned refueling yet?"

"Aye." The broad Northern accent seemed distorted on the
intercom. *"More bluidy overtime tomorrow night."*

I grinned. "Shove it, Chalky. You're making a fortune on
overtime."

The intercom hissed for a little while. Then—

*"Aye, well . . . we work for it. And nowt to spend it on. Ye
can't even buy a glass of beer over here. Not worth risking
your neck looking for it."*

I asked him if there were any other problems.

*"No—everything checks out, Mr. Scott. She'll be all ready
for you. Do you know takeoff time yet?"*

"Just after midnight tomorrow night," I told him.

He said, *"Bluidy Hell's bells!"* and hung up. I did the same,
turned and found Kate Monahan at my elbow.

My chief stewardess was in what she called her "shore
rig"—she'd served three years as a Wren at Chatham, and
it showed. Trim blue uniform skirt; black turtleneck cash-
mere sweater, filled perfectly with lovely Monahan. Black
suede shoes with old-fashioned flop-over tongues. Red hair
swept back, lashed down with black ribbon.

Our Kate is a fine-looking woman—and she knows it.
They say she's pushing thirty, but I think she can push for
a few years yet. Her legs stop somewhere in her armpits.
She's a natural genius with an eye-level grill, likes motor
hang gliding and slightly blue movies. In my book, a winning
combination. She has that saurian high-cheekbone facial
structure, green eyes, translucent skin which identifies that
odd out-world species called redheads.

She came up to chin level, green eyes staring up at me,
a worry crease cleaving the bridge of her nose.

"Jonah—did you see . . . ?"

"I saw. Rough, wasn't it?" I said quietly.

She bit her lip. "Some of the girls are upset . . . they're
talking about staying aboard until we leave. My regulars are
all right—but some of the new Indian girls were in the aft
door when it happened."

"They'll feel better," I said gently, "when they're safe inside the Nunnery with a hot meal in front of them."

She shivered briefly, and I moved to the door, closed it, locked down the bar.

"It's as cold as a polar bear's bottom out there," she said crossly, "and there'll be no damn heating in that god-awful crew quarter."

"If you hadn't burned all the furniture last winter," I said reasonably, "you could have had open fires."

She sniffed, standing with feet crossed, arms folded under the famed Monahan overhang, an elbow in each palm. "I wondered . . ."

"Yes?" I said. I knew what she was after.

"You know what I mean. Are you going into town?"

What she really meant was "Are *we* going into town?" Our odd relationship survived best on a casual basis; which means that if we were both available, we went together. If not—it was still a free country.

"Are *you*?" I said cautiously.

"Don't give me that crap, Jonah Scott. I'd rather sleep in an empty bus than in that freeze box of a Nunnery—with those cackling bitches!"

That wasn't strictly true. She had her own little room outside the big common dormitory. I thought I would give her just a little more needle.

"Jerry and Ben Price are going into town," I said blandly. "You could go with them."

"No way," she said angrily. "They both have your trouble. All you think about is your stomach and your . . ." She looked down, smiling.

"Charming," I clucked disapprovingly.

"And so are you, Scott. What about it?"

I twisted the knife a little more. "Well—I've got a little steak and a little bottle of wine, and I'm going to eat one and drink the other and sleep for twelve hours."

She stared at me, green-eyed, and stood a little closer. Some 1000 millimeters of resilient Monahan nudged me in the lower chest. Her eyes were unblinking, catlike.

"Ah, now, ye wouldn't be doin' that, now, would yez? An' leavin' ould Monahan to starve by herself entirely?"

I laughed out loud, the sound echoing strangely in the vast tunnel of the 797, and Kate relaxed, blinking slowly. I thought that New York might perhaps be bearable with Kate along. Give the woman her due; she always worked her passage.

"Okay, okay... but you're going to be stuck with the cooking. I still have the key to Ted Radford's apartment. The only problem is getting into town. You sit tight. I want to organize some transport."

Ted Radford... when would we see him again?

Ted had given me the key to the apartment before he moved west. Before he left, five months after the Collapse, he had thrown out the useless electric stove and put in an old wood burner he'd found in a Village antique shop. He'd knocked a hole in the living-room wall and built a real fireplace with a stovepipe out into the back area. It was big enough to roast two Boy Scouts whole.

He had hauled in loads of dead trees, sawn into logs, from Central Park and such places, and maybe if some of them weren't quite dead when he found them, they were sure as hell dead when he left. First time I used the apartment, last year, I'd brought along Ben Price to do the cooking. We'd found the hall and spare bedroom stacked high with sawn lumber, and a saw bench hooked up to a pedal-operated belt drive standing on end in the master bedroom. Before he got organized, Ted had burned most of the furniture, in those bitter early months of darkness, and his visitors—one, two or ten—all slept in the big double bed or on the stack of cushions on the living-room floor. That was New York City.

When I opened Door 1 Port, an icy blast hit me. I changed my mind about going down to ground and made my way back to the flight deck, switched on the Selcall to raise the Air Britain office. A rich Georgia accent on a husky low-pitched voice meant only one thing: Mortensen had changed his girl Friday again. It was strictly a buyer's market—there were probably as many as ten thousand beautiful girls in New York, all looking for a job that rated a private flat in the Reception Building, three meals a day every day and two free trips a year to Europe. Since each dolly bird lasted a week on average, I figured it would take Mortensen two hundred and ten years to clear the decks. Even Mortensen couldn't last that long—but let's hear it for the Mortensens of this screwy world: they never stop trying.

"Go ahead, Delta Tango," said Miss Cottoncandy 1982, sweetly.

"Uh—who's this?" I said.

"Mary Jo Catlin, sir. Do you wish to speak to the Operations Officer?" I said I did and added who I was. With a bit of luck I could get Old Baggy Eyes out of bed—he didn't keep that divan in his office for decoration. Especially not on night duty, which he tended to stick on his number two, Trevor Chapman, while he, Mortensen, exercised his *droit du seigneur*. Dirty old bastard...If the job was vacant when I retired, I might just take a poke at it.

"Yes, Delta Tango?"

"Mort," I said in my best pleading voice (marred by the tongue in my cheek), " can you check with the West Gate if Charlie Hackett is available? You know, Gasbag Charlie?"

There was a long pause, and I heard Mortensen sigh—just loud enough to make sure I heard. *"All right, Delta Tango. Wait one."*

I slid into the engineer's seat, got out my Splits and lit up, waiting for Mortensen to get the lead out.

In the dark silence of the flight deck I began to feel calm and relaxed. I had few friends in New York; let's face it, there weren't many New Yorkers in town. But Charlie Hackett was the best I had. A real character—there's not many of them left. Through all the troubles, he kept his old Yellow Cab going on gasoline until the pumps ran dry. Then he changed to a weird mixture of meths, kerosene, white spirit and wood alcohol. Eventually even the rocket propellant ran out, but that didn't faze Charlie. No, sir. He kept mobile on methane gas, stored in a big plastic bag on the roof and generated in what he called his "shit machine" in the trunk. He kept half a 40-gallon drum full of fowl manure garnered by his four teen-age kids from his rooftop chicken run. They had a full-time job collecting anything the forty or fifty hens would eat that humans couldn't, and believe me, that wasn't a lot. In their spare time, they took turns riding shotgun on the birds with Charlie's old pump gun.

So Charlie was almost the only hackie still serving JFK, a service we treasured beyond price, and we paid invariably in kind. The food we brought in kept his family fed and clothed. Spares cost him nothing—there were ten or eleven thousand abandoned Yellows rusting away all over New York—but already tires were almost impossible to find. For a while last year they were actually used as currency.

The problem was that the Army wouldn't let him on the field for any reason, and he had to park on the open lot outside

the West Gate three miles away—and Delta Tango sat on
the south side near the bay. I know some of the crews helped
him out; true, most of them called him "Chicken Shit
Charlie," which I would never do, but the big Brooklyn hackie
didn't seem to mind.

Anyway, he and I had got to be close friends. I had a lot
of time for Charlie—because he was a survivor if ever I saw
one. He had adjusted better than most to catastrophe (most
of the 'Nam veterans did), and he had not been slow to use
fist, boot, head or gun in coping with the Jacks. I don't know
how the savage homeless looters got the name—maybe we'll
never know. But they formed maybe half the remaining population of the Big Apple—thieves, rapists, hopheads, mug-
gers, stickup and second-story men, all well used to living on
their wits and thriving on chaos.

Charlie had worked out his own ground rules: no exterior
door handles on the cab, no pickups except on main streets
in daylight, a gun on the seat and a spare in the glove locker.
Electrically operated bulletproof glass partition at his back.
And for pickups in the "no-go" areas shunned by the Army
patrols, he carried a friend up front with more artillery.
Things were a little better now, but I believed that when the
good times come round again, Charlie would be right there,
up front, collecting his share—and deserving every cent.

I burned my lip getting the last drag from the Split, put
my foot on the butt and went on thinking about Hackett.

January last year, I helped get him started again by hauling in a box of fertilized eggs. Earlier, he'd lost most of his
birds to the cold and hungry street kids who would eat a
chicken alive if they got the chance. I was glad to help—I
didn't look forward to walking those dark miles into town
from Kennedy. Each time I came in after that, I brought in
one or two sacks of corn, and I had a standing invitation to
his apartment up near Borough Park.

Well, I was not about to get involved that way. When he
walked out from Brooklyn to collect his eggs last winter—
things were real bad around that time—he brought his kids
with him, all those miles, partly to ride herd on those eggs
but really because he wanted me to meet them. The young-
est—could have been boy or girl, name of Jess—was only
thirteen, and the eldest sixteen, with a pair of twins in between. They all wore the cut-down jeans, multiple sweaters
and the long sheath knife strapped to the right thigh just

above the knee. Kids grew up fast in the Troubles or they didn't grow up at all, and it was very plain to me that these kids knew their way around town. All the same, I got a lump in my throat just looking at them; I regard myself as a fairly hard-boiled character, but no kid of sixteen should be as thin as Denny. He may have pushed ninety pounds and five feet, but I doubt it, even with his boots filled with mud.

The Selcall chimed, and I sat up straight.

"Delta Tango?"

Mort sounded angry, and I grinned. Serve the old rooster right.

He said, *"The Gate says Hackett is parked over the road. He's waiting for you, and will you please get the lead out, because his heater's on the blink."*

"Thank you, Mort. You sound more American every day. Is that new bird of yours giving you lessons?"

There was a long silence, broken by the faraway undertone on the Selcall which we could never eliminate completely on this particular aircraft. *"Please observe radio discipline, Delta Tango. Out."* That Mortensen...

I hurried back to the forward steps where Kate and my bags were waiting. It seemed an awfully long way to the ground; I missed the mobiles, with their integral central heating always turned up too high, but they stood abandoned, over by the Airport Vehicles compound. The stairs were still better than sliding down the escape chutes—an exercise I disliked, but had had to tolerate for the first few trips inbound during Year One.

Kate was dozing, legs stretched into the aisle. I nudged her, none too gently.

"Huh...? Oh, Jonah. Are we off?"

"Soon. I think your girls are finished—they're all out there waiting for the crew bus. Got your ditty bag?"

"Yes. Look, that nice Airborne captain's here again. Can't you talk him into running us into town?"

"No way, luv. In any case, it's not me he's interested in. Why don't you take pity on the poor guy sometime and give in gracefully?"

Kate scowled. "Because he's got the opposite of your trouble, Jonah—he's not interested in my body, only what I give him to eat."

"Come on." I nudged her again. "Down we go."

The captain met us at the foot of the stairs, gave Kate a smart salute and a big grin. "Hello, ma'am—nice trip?"

"Yes, Captain."

"Marcovitch—Joe Marcovitch."

"Joe—Jonah—you know each other, don't you?" Kate bubbled.

We knew each other—vaguely. I'd got used to him, rather like seeing a cigar-store Indian every day—big surprise when he actually talked to me. "Sure." I shook hands. "We met last trip but one."

"Right. Say, Miss Monahan, I wondered..." He stopped, looking at Kate with big black eyes full of disappointment. "No?"

"I'm sorry, Joe—really—but we're eating together. Perhaps next trip we can sort something out. Okay?"

"Sure—fine. I'll take a rain check," and he shuffled his feet awkwardly. He was very young.

He looked so sick, I clapped him on the shoulder and said, "I'm sorry too, Joe—I've got an unfair advantage, that's the problem. I've got some steak, couple bottles of wine in this here box."

"Steak?" He shook his head slowly. "I can recall how it looked—saw a picture the other day in an old magazine. But smell...and taste—no way, man. No way."

"Listen, old lad," I said smoothly. "We have to get over to the West Gate to Charlie Hackett. If you could organize wheels of some sort, I reckon we could split the steak three ways. But no booze—that's for us."

He looked around cautiously. The nearest file of paras was a hundred yards away on the perimeter. He grinned.

"You have yourself a deal, sir. Thank you kindly. But let's you and me do this thing quietly, or we get killed in the rush." He turned away and bawled for his top sergeant. The noncom hurried away and came back in a short time with— believe it or not—an electric milk cart converted into a baggage truck. The topkick got out; we got in with the captain and whined off into the dark. The headlights were two degrees brighter than glowworms, but he seemed to know where he was going: we passed through the standing army, cut in between the last two Hercules freighters in the line and trundled on. We passed a big patch of pink-stained sawdust, and I looked away.

We ran into problems cutting the steak en route. None of

us wanted to stop out there in the dark night, but Joe got me to steer and hauled out a very nasty-looking knife from his field boot. It was about a foot long, thin-bladed and sharpened on both sides to a hair. He got the frozen steak onto the lid of the Portafreeze, laid a blade edge tentatively across the slab and waited. I nodded. "Okay, fella. Mind that pig sticker doesn't slip."

He shook his head, and I tried to steer and watch at the same time. He sawed in vain and said, "Goddamn it—I could eat it raw, 'n' I can't even cut the damn thing. Wait a minute..."

I saw him unclip a grenade from his belt, set the knife blade vertical and start hammering with the horrible thing; I shut my eyes and concentrated on keeping my sphincter tight.

"Okay, Captain. All stowed away. Man, am I going to eat or am I going to eat!"

I uncrossed my legs, started breathing again. My chest hurt a little, but I tried it again and it came a little easier. I stared at him, incredulous.

"That thing could have gone off! And you've ruined that knife."

"Shoot," he said, "that little old steak's worth twenty knives. Soon hone her up again. Ever I kin do anything for you—anything at all—just holler. Right?"

I said faintly, "Right."

The cart rattled on over the field, grinding over piles of windblown garbage. I could see the hard profile of his face in the dim light from the dash. He was whistling between his teeth, and I wondered what made such a man tick; half an hour ago, his men had quietly disposed of half a hundred people whose sole crime had been trespass.

"That...incident tonight, Captain..." I hesitated, uncertain of my next words, and he glanced sideways; his eyes looked black and huge under the steel brim of his helmet. His cheeks were sunken, and it seemed to me that he ate as much—or as little—as his men. How could they maintain such discipline on worse than 1200 calories a day?

"Yeah?"

"I mean...does that happen often?" I asked.

"Oh, sure. Most days we have people breaking through the fence patrols—not usually so many in a bunch. You saw it?"

I nodded, speechless.

"Well...don't start thinking we like to do that, sir. We don't. But they have to be stopped—you know?" I made no reply, and he went on: "They try it all ways—singly, in skirmish lines, day, night, sometimes like you saw it. If we rope them in, we have to feed them or take them back to town, and we have no transport for that exercise. Goddamn, I'd rather take 'em on the run like that than have 'em kneel for a bullet in the neck. They're not enemies, you know—they're good Americans just trying to make it on board an airplane. You know what? There were a dozen or more women in that bunch—and the oldest must have been near seventy. That old woman must have run half a mile or more before she caught a slug in the chest."

There was a long silence, and he dropped us, drove away without a backwards glance.

2

The single floodlight over the gate did the best it could, but a solid wall of blackness crowded in close. The heavy rain had stopped, but there was a dank thin drizzle showing as haze in the light, and the west wind was bitter. The guards slid open the gate for us and we walked through. Charlie Hackett emerged into the glare, wearing the same olive-drab flying jacket with fur collar, the mutilated yellow cap with shiny peak.

"Hey—Cap'n Scott—Miss Monahan. Nice to see you again, folks. Here, gimme those bags. This way—over to the parking lot. Say, you got in two hours ago—some kinda trouble over there? I heard shooting."

We hurried along behind him. He kept turning his head, grinning all over his black face, the misshapen cap a size too small perched high on his head. I'm over six feet—and come up to Charlie's shoulders.

"So did we." I didn't want to think about the shooting, even less discuss it. "How are you doing, Charlie? Getting enough to eat?"

"Hell, no, Cap'n. But who is? Seems like I take an extra notch in my belt every week. Wastin' away to a shadow. But I can't grumble—we do better'n most, I figure."

If he was only a shadow of his former self, my mind boggled at the way he had been three years ago.

"Charlie," Kate said breathlessly, "slow down a bit, will you? And have you cut down the perfume in that old thing yet?"

"The what? Oh, shoot, you mean the shit machine—beggin' your pardon, ma'am. Jeez, I don't even notice it now. Honest. Dunno what folks keep bitchin' about; hell, it's better'n walking, right?"

"Right," I said firmly. "Don't upset the man, Kate. Shut up and keep walking."

She had no sense sometimes, that woman. She opened her mouth to have a second prod at Hackett and his Yellow Peril, and I had to give her a bit of elbow in the ribs. She said "Ooof," and we reached the cab before she could push her luck too much.

A row of white teeth in the front seat greeted us. "Hi, Captain. What do you know?"

"Hello there, Denny. Here—point that damn thing someplace else. What with nearly being blown up by a hand grenade and you waving a shotgun around, things are getting damned dangerous around here." I opened the back door, shoved Kate inside and climbed in after her. Charlie dumped the bags and Portafreeze on our laps and we were off, the old yellow Chevy bouncing on the roughly cleared ground once occupied by the offices of an airline catering firm. It seemed to me that Charlie must spike the mix in the chicken machine with beans, the way that engine groaned and boomed its way along, down the Van Wyck Expressway at a steady thirty. We headed out past Richmond Hill, and I struggled to organize things so we could stretch our legs a little. Those place names—Queens, Kew Gardens—always reminded me of home. We were heading for the Midtown Tunnel before Charlie relaxed; we were getting into the light-up area again. Every fourth light on the Expressway, every sixth on the main drags, one light per block out in the jungle.

"Same place again, Mr. Scott?"

"That's it, Charlie. West 75th. How are things? Any better?"

The driver shrugged, broad shoulders silhouetted against the shallow street lights.

"What d'you want me to say, Cap'n? Things are fine? Compared to this time last year, I'd say great. Which means godawful, still."

I said nothing for a while. Then I lit three joints, gave one to Kate, passed over two to Charlie and his son, lit another for myself. After a while, Charlie opened his side window a crack.

I said, "How are the chickens, anyway?"

"Fine," Charlie said quietly, "just fine. We're down to thirty-one now—lost a dozen or more a week or so back, on account of something in the feed the kids brought in. Must have been something bum in there. But there wasn't much of it, and first come, first dead. We could've lost the lot. Lucky, I guess."

I leaned forward. "I have about sixty pounds of corn in that case for you. That's why it's so heavy."

"Hey, hey." He turned, grinned. "Those chickens, they're gonna eat real good tonight. That corn's just what they need. Heavy? I didn't notice."

I scowled. Maybe he hadn't, but I had. Nearly pulled my arm out by the roots. "Don't give the young chicks too much corn, Charlie. You'll lose them too."

"Yeah. Well, maybe I'll stretch a few pounds for Stella— she kin bake some fresh bread for the kids."

And that was Charlie Hackett—looked and talked like a killer, but under that mean sound was a gentle man. Sometimes.

I sat smoking for a while, surveying the slight traffic on the unrepaired streets, ruined stores and warehouses, derelict cars everywhere. Not many people—there were apartments for everyone who wanted one and to spare. I noticed there were more horse-drawn flat carts around this time—all with rubber car wheels on a makeshift chassis. One or two were getting into the cab business—half a dozen passengers sitting with legs adangle, clutching boxes, bundles, bags. I wondered what they used to pay the fare—food, or cigarettes, probably. I had about eighty pounds in sterling on me, worth about $45,000 at current exchange rates (if anyone was foolish enough to want to trade), but I would probably have it all intact going home.

"Charlie, don't you ever feel you'd be better off in the Breakaways?"

"No way, Mr. Scott. Okay, so they eat regular, I hear— sometimes every day. Big deal—I don't like the way they get it. If'n I see one of those foraging parties coming my way, I get this old thing moving the other way and real quick. You know?"

I said I knew.

"Those Muslim brothers," he said—and there was a world of condemnation in his voice—"they have to run things tight, I guess, but it don't seem natural, the way folks have to work in there, twelve hours or more every day, makin' those truck gardens, haulin' water a mile or more. Say, did you hear those mothers wear all black? Even black motorcycle helmets, and that goddamn badge of theirs—"

"Badge?" This was a new one on me.

"Sure—circle with the top half black, bottom half white, red border all around. Linc Tolchard—lives down the block a ways—he says it means black victory over the white man, and the blood spilt in the process. Hell, seems to me a man's got no time for politics if'n he wants to eat regular. Those mothers live off all the other folks in the Breakaways. No, sir—it ain't for me."

We rode silently for a long time.

I could see the Midtown Tunnel coming up. Charlie slowed down, looked round at us. "Look, we have to pay toll here. Bunch o' jerks tryin' to make a livin', but the Army leaves them be—they keep the tunnel safe for folks to use. Time was, you had no more'n a fifty-fifty chance of gettin' through alive, past all the kids used to live down there. Close up your windows, git ready to duck and stay tight, Captain. You got any more of those joints for toll?"

"Yes. Hold it—what do you need?"

The driver leaned forward, car barely moving down the slight incline.

"There's three of'em, sir. You got three packs?"

"Sure. Here—coming up."

"Right. You got a gun?" he said softly.

"No, Charlie. Not with me—there's one in the apartment."

He nodded. "Okay—we'll make out. Get all your stuff onto the floor, put a coat over it. What they can't see they can't grab. Here we go ..."

The cab stopped. The stench of chicken manure welled up from behind the seat, and Kate started coughing and muttering. Outside, I saw a single bearded man, a rifle in the crook of one arm, wearing a gray blanket in which a hole had been cut for his head; in the headlights, light rain sleeted down. Kate caught her breath sharply. Two dirty faces peered in, one each side. I looked into the cold eye of a gaunt skeleton-jawed man, trying not to look at the exposed crater of the missing eye.

Charlie blipped the horn, slid down the left front window an inch, held up the Splits in the yellow glow of the street lamp with his left hand and alongside, the big .45 revolver with the blued barrel. In his huge hand, it looked like a toy. I found myself sweating as usual, and I believe it is always the speed of transition that causes it, every trip. Just over two years ago, America was a pleasant and civilized country still enjoying a degree of law and order, where most people had a job and a home and enough to eat. Now...

Blanket Man walked stiffly up to the cab. Charlie opened the window just enough, dropped the cigarettes out one packet at a time; as the last fell out of sight, the man with the rifle stooped swiftly, scooped them up inside the blanket and moved the rifle round to point at us, sitting quite still in the back seat.

The big black driver grinned, brought up the handgun and rested the end of the barrel on the window frame. "Don't push your luck, fella. You kin eat for a week on those joints."

The engine chugged like a diesel for a long moment. The man in the blanket nodded slowly, waved the rifle muzzle in the direction of the tunnel roadway, and Charlie got the car moving again. We all resumed breathing, and young Denny said proudly, "I knew he wouldn't tangle with my paw. You'd have blown him clean away, Paw—right?"

Charlie Hackett's laugh rumbled deep in his chest. "Sure thing, kid. If'n I had to. No sense in wasting a man tryin' to make out. You see what I mean, Mr. Scott? These damn kids'll grow up into savages, less we get this thing straightened out pretty soon."

We went on through the tunnel and headed uptown, and I began to remember the way all this had started. We had got very good TV reports right up to the time things got out of hand.

It just happened too fast, that's all. Lack of communication. That week, I took a full load in a 747 bound for Singapore and Darwin on the Monday, stopped in at Salisbury, Rhodesia, for that final pickup, got back on Friday about noon—and it was all over.

Right up to the last, they were trying to buy oil. But time was running out—had run out. The previous week, the dollar fell through the floor, despite all the efforts of the International Monetary Fund to plug the leak. The London stock market stopped trading in the dollar when it hit the $50-to-the-pound mark; at that stage no one could even give it away. The President announced emergency measures to support the dollar—and could have saved his breath. Sometime during the weekend, Washington decided on a clampdown. President Langford made a broadcast stating that countries hostile to the U.S. were preparing to take advantage of the stricken American economy, and declared a state of national emergency. The clamps went down tight on mail, telephones, TV, radio, newspapers.

All through Sunday and into Monday morning, the Army threw everything into distributing what gasoline and oil was available on a selective basis. If you saw a gas station closed, you didn't worry too much because the next one would be open. Through Monday, the Senate and the White House argued, fought and got nowhere because the vested interests were dug in deep. The big utilities—oil, gas, electricity—all wanted to go on producing, selling, and full-scale rationing was just a dirty word, even with the country balanced on a razor edge.

The White House clocked up eleven and a half thousand hours of telephone time that last weekend. They talked to anyone who would listen, who had oil to spare. And they got the same answer: Sure! We got oil—but not for dollars.

An aging Senator Edward Kennedy rushed a proposal through channels to release gold from Fort Knox for oil purchase—five billion dollars' worth. And could have saved his breath: it would take three weeks to shift the gold out, ship oil in—and America had two days' supply left.

Sure, there were big reserves—all earmarked for the Army and Air Force and Navy; deep in trouble as they were, not one voice was raised in favor of releasing a gallon of it.

Monday, three-quarters of all U.S. refineries and storage facilities shipped out the last of their gasoline and kerosene and diesel fuel. But the system was cracking: someone forgot to protect the pipelines—and they were overrun.

Tuesday passed without serious trouble, warehouses shipping out remaining stocks of food to the shops and maintaining a semblance of normality; the Army began organizing road convoys for emergency medical supplies, canned milk and children's food, but shops began to run out of most items through Wednesday. Milk stopped flowing early in the game, as the main distributors used their last diesel oil; water, on the other hand, kept flowing for many weeks until the coal-fired pumping stations used their last stocks. The power companies relied almost exclusively upon oil-fired generators, and power in the national grid fell in a six-hour period to less than five percent of normal output. A few of the older stations in Pennsylvania and neighboring states still burned coal, but stopped feeding power into the grid in favor of local distribution.

In Britain, we knew something very ominous was happening across the Atlantic. Every news bulletin concentrated on the plight of the dollar; every commentator introduced interviewees from the stock market, the IMF and the government. When the dollar crashed to 500 to the pound and 350 to the Deutschmark, the EEC convened an emergency meeting of the twelve finance ministers for midnight Wednesday; at noon Thursday they were still locked in discussion.

America could buy no oil with worthless dollars. Dollar holders were selling at any price they could get. The U.S. domestic oil fields were depleted, and most of their production had to keep the Armed Services supplied.

Britain pulled twelve supertankers out of dry dock, fitted them in an emergency nonstop program at Southampton and Milford Haven, but it would be almost two weeks before they reached the Eastern Seaboard of America; and the 20 million tons of crude they carried would need refining and distributing on arrival—five to six weeks, whichever way one looked at it.

Venezuela dispatched its own fleet with naval escort, subject to meeting U.S. officials off Panama with 40 tons of gold specie from Fort Knox—which never arrived, because the Army convoy detailed to ship the gold to Galveston was engulfed in mass riots before it reached the Gulf. Mexico's leftist government prohibited all oil exports to capitalist countries.

Until the satellite ground relay stations in America went off the air, viewers all over Europe and the rest of the world followed the collapse of a nation. Riots spread to Seattle, Dallas, New Orleans and the great cities of the Midwest; that old hellhole Watts erupted into downtown Los Angeles—and the one common denominator was hunger. With food supplies into cities halted, the starving mobs stopped at nothing: warehouses, shops, hotels, bars. . . . There was to be seen the first great schism in the American population: the hungry but still civilized segment of the people began to leave the cities, walking, cycling, but not driving—by Black Friday there was no more gasoline, and every road and avenue was choked with abandoned cars. Those who stayed were used to living by their wits; the homeless, poor, criminal and insane went on the greatest looting spree of all time. It was only when they realized that a suitcase containing a million dollars would not buy one loaf of bread, one can of beans, that they began looting for food, not valuables.

Five million people poured out of New York City over every bridge, through every tunnel, by every available boat and ferry. Where were they heading?

Most of them did not know. They believed, vaguely, that country farms and villages would have food, that starvation was unique to cities. They filled roads and expressways from side to side, pushing along in virtual seas of humanity, and they kept on walking because those who fell never stood up again. The Army cleaned up behind them for almost three weeks, burying, cremating thousands at a time, and a year later, emaciated bodies and skeletons were still being found. The countryside absorbed all those people, somehow. Those who survived found sanctuary where they could. Many died trying to penetrate the makeshift defenses around isolated farms others camped deep in the northern woods, existing on small game, leaves, bark from trees; there were frequent and obviously well-founded rumors of cannibalism.

After Black Friday, the whole free world pitched in. Relief food ships headed west; Argentina got four meat container ships away before noon Sunday. Brazil sent a thousand-truck convoy north on the Pan American Highway, and Britain began flying in medical supplies, drugs.

I was in the first wave; Airbrit had commandeered every spare 747, Tristar and Airbus they could find—but we ran into big problems three hours out from New York. JFK was jammed with refugees hoping for a flight out to anywhere, and the Army said it needed twenty-four hours at least to secure the field. We diverted to Gander, thirty-seven big jets jamming the airfield, and sat it out until Kennedy was secure.

No one had time to take any positive action until it was too late. When things began to settle down and the dust cleared, the racially defined Breakaways were established, and they were there to stay; any attempt to penetrate the no-go areas would have sparked off the civil war everyone feared and which the Army knew it couldn't handle. Of the three million people left in New York, perhaps a third were white, half a million Asians and Latin Americans, and the rest were black, organized, living on their own land, obeying their own leaders.

I lit another cigarette, passed the pack forward to Denny and looked at Kate. She was dozing again, uneasily, head resting on the seat back and rocking with the motion of the car. We began to pass groups of scavengers—mostly teenagers, sex uncertain under the multiple layers of salvaged clothing. They tended to huddle under the lighted street lamps, standing around in the pools of yellow light, crowding round the small foraging patrols as they came in, two or three strong, carrying paper sacks, boxes, cans. It seemed to me that they were all dirty—yet extraordinarily cheerful. The cycles with box trailers were much more numerous, and I was interested to see the first cycle rickshaws—human-powered taxis similar to those which have operated for years in the cities of the Far East—but with two cycles hauling one box seat. It took me a few moments to work that one out: no single rider ate well enough in this town to have enough strength to haul a passenger, and more important, there was safety in numbers. I already knew that only fools walked alone in New York, even in daylight. Incredibly, New Yorkers had developed a quasi-military system of movement in organized parties, with pairs of scouts ahead of and behind the main body, checking side streets for the first indication of ambush.

"See what I mean, Cap'n?" said Charlie, waving a massive hand towards a group of children scratching through a pile of garbage. "Me, I'm kinda glad I'm pushin' sixty, because I figure these kids might be my age before they eat a square meal again."

There was nothing I could say to that. . . . We were getting close; I recognized a landmark here and there, and nudged Kate gently. She sat up, poked a little at her hair and yawned. "Nearly there, Jonah?"

Charlie turned, grinned briefly. "Sure are, Miss Kate. Say, Mr. Scott, better take this." He passed over a heavy handgun. "It's a spare I carry. We're okay when we move, but this here ain't too good an area after dark, not for standin' still 'n unloadin'."

"Yes. All right, Charlie. Look, I'm leaving some things on the back seat for you. Careful with the corn sacks—they tend to burst easily."

"Fine, sir, fine. I'll be careful. Man, if'n I dropped a bag of corn, Stella'd crease me with anythin' light enough to lift."

I grinned, sorted briefly through the Portafreeze. I looked again at the gun—an old Smith & Wesson six-chamber .45 revolver, with a barrel like a sewer main. I'd seen such guns frequently in old TV Westerns, watched the hero whipping them out like a feather duster and blasting away. God, the thing weighed about ten kilos; I'd be lucky to lift it with one hand, let alone fire it. I checked the operation of the safety and had a sudden thought.

"You ever had to use this thing in anger, Charlie?" He chuckled in that deep bass voice. "Why, sure, sir. Just the one time, though. But it worked pretty good."

"How good?" I asked.

"Well, sir," he said slowly, easing the cab round a right turn, "I find a fare down to the U.N. building this time, some kinda foreigner, well dressed, so I figger he's okay. Hell, he tries a stickup right there on Seventh Avenue in broad daylight—waves this here little lady's gun at me. 'Course, he don't see I'm holdin' the old equalizer, and it don't seem like a good time to start an argument, so I let go—and damn near break my wrist. That slug goes right through the door, on out through his guts, and makes some hole in the far wall."

The cab lurched on, and it seemed hot and oppressive, the stench of chicken manure heavy on the air.

"So I stomp on the pedal an' git goin'. I see this guy sort of float across the sidewalk and his back hits the wall, both hands holdin' his belly tight, and then I don't look back no more."

Kate stirred uneasily. "Give me a cigarette, Jonah. All this talk of killing makes me nervous. Surely things are getting better than they were?"

"The way I see it, ma'am," Charlie Hackett said, "what we need is time. These here good ships are coming in most days, and the Army does what it can to see everyone gits a fair shake. We got a big plastic sheet we spread on the roof when it rains, so we got good water to drink mostly. But we have to crack this energy thing—you know? We git power back, we can start the railroad an' factories moving again, farmers cropping all their land—not just the bits they can reach by walkin'. We git TV twice a week, radio most times if you can find batteries. It's a slow job, but we're gittin' there, Cap'n—we're gittin' there."

Kate said, "You always sound cheerful enough, Charlie."

"Hell, no use moanin' all the time—but we git sort of ashamed, I guess. It ain't no fun takin' charity. Time was, America used to feed half the goddamn world..."

I looked up. "That's it, Charlie—other side, beyond that wrecked panel truck. Fifteen Fifty-two. And we have a reception party, folks."

The driver's head swiveled, and he nodded. "Yeah. I see 'em. But they don't look no great risk, Cap'n. Not real Jacks— kids mostly. Just the same, you leave 'em take a peek at ol' Whammy while I git these bags up the steps. You make it okay?"

"I think so, Charlie. Kate—can you take my small kit? I'll get the Portafreeze box."

"Yes, Jonah. Just—don't get too far from me, will you?"

"Okay. Pull up here a moment, Charlie—fine. How're you fixed for tomorrow?"

"What time you thinking of, Cap'n?" He swung round in his seat. I thought quickly. The tanker 707 would be in around 4 P.M. from Canada. Give them, say, two hours to pump the load into Delta Tango. They would probably want to spend the night in town, in which case Charlie might hook another fare back in. I told him we'd be ready about 5 P.M. next day, and why.

"Sounds good, Mr. Scott. Okay—can do. Here we go."

He swung round in a U-turn, got in close to the curb and got out quickly, closed the door and stood with his back to it, face shining with sweat in the street light's glow. The little crowd numbered fifteen, perhaps twenty, with latecomers drifting in from the side streets. They stood around in a semicircle, eyeing the big driver standing with arms folded.

Charlie grinned disarmingly. "Just stand back, folks, and nobody's about to git hurt. These here folks are British, stayin' overnight, an' we don't want 'em upset—right?"

The ring of thin faces moved back slightly, stood ground and stared down at us, still seated in the cab. Charlie reached down, thumped on my side window, and I opened up, passed out the bags. Kate followed me out, and we left Charlie's fare on the floor, out of sight: sacks of corn, a 2-kilo pack of frozen fish, two packs of beef sausage, a half-cooked "U-Bake" loaf and two cans of beans. Young Denny hung over the back seat, staring hungrily.

"Okay," Charlie said. "You first, Mr. Scott. Then Miss

Monahan. Got your key? Fine. Just git up them steps and inside an' don't stop for nobody, nohow. I'll be right here in back of you. All set? Let's go!"

The little ragged mob pressed closer, feet shuffling, hands plucking at our clothes and bags. I lashed out with both feet, moving fast up the steps, and someone bleated in agony. I got the key in, door open, hurled in the freeze box and shoved Kate inside. Charlie hustled indoors, loaded with bags, and I got my shoulder against the door, feeling the press of humanity outside. I shoved the big gun through the aperture, let go two shots skywards, and the pressure on the door slackened. I slammed it and turned, sagging, looking mutely at the smoke curling from the gun muzzle. It was sharp and acrid in my nostrils.

I opened the door a smidgen, took a peek outside. The Welcome Home delegation were in full retreat down the steps, feet clattering on the sidewalk. I closed and locked the door and turned. Charlie and I beamed at each other.

"See?" he said grinning. "Nothin' to it."

I wasn't convinced. And I remembered Denny, out there alone.

"Shoot," Charlie said, unmoved, "I ain't worried none about him. He's got that ol' pump gun on the seat—they won't start nothin'. All okay now—or do you want an assist wit' the bags?"

"No, thanks, Charlie." I shook my head gratefully. "You get on your way—we'll see you tomorrow, around five. I think I left enough in the cab for the round trip, but if you feel hard about it, we can haggle a little."

I gave him back his gun.

"Not me, Mr. Scott," he said reproachfully, and opened the door, took a look round. "You've always been square with me. Take care, now." And he was gone, door slamming hard behind him. I locked up, slid both bolts and relaxed just a little, looking round the dingy hall. Shabbier than I remembered it, a single oxyacetylene lamp burning. Feet thudded on the basement stairs, the door burst open and John Capel came through fast, gun in hand.

"Captain Scott—and Miss Monahan! Well, well. Say, if I'd known you were coming I'd have met you in the street. You catch Hackett's cab at the airport? Was that you doing the shooting?"

I shook hands, offered him a smoke. "Yes. No panic. How are you, John?"

"Fine, fine. I hope you had a nice trip over, sir. These all your bags?"

"That's all. No elevator, John?" I looked at him sideways. It was our usual joke; no elevator had run in the city these last two years or more, except in the U.N. building, which had its own generator. Capel was lucky—his area of responsibility was a building only six floors high. Some downtown building guards covered up to sixteen floors—about as high as most people could walk on 1200 calories a day, the standard relief ration. Capel was a slim gray-haired man in late middle age, wearing a threadbare but clean ex-police shirt and trousers without badges.

We started up the stairs at the slow, deliberate pace all New Yorkers used—it was easier on the leg muscles and heart. I knew a little about Capel: spent three years in Vietnam, came back knowing about forty-'leven ways to kill a man, all very sudden and very painful. No family—he had lost his wife in an auto accident, and that had made him enlist. I knew that when the trouble started, he had moved fast, stocked up his basement flat with food and ammunition, prepared for a long siege. He worked out a pretty good deal with the tenants: from ten at night until seven in the morning, they slept securely while John prowled the building, checking doors, windows, back areas. Twice in the first week intruders ran into Capel and regretted it: the first escaped, the second went out feet first. The word went out; Capel's territory was given a wide berth from that time on.

I must be getting out of condition, I thought: up two floors, three to go and wheezing like an accordion. Capel was up front, hauling the two big cases with deceptive ease, and I got a little comfort watching Kate's shapely rump, level with my eyes; she had stripped off the gabardine raincoat, let her skirt ride high for easier climbing. I looked, dragged my eyes away, concentrated on the stairs.

Capel had rigged makeshift 12-volt lights on each landing, hooked up to old auto batteries. Down in his basement he charged them on a haywire contraption made from half a bicycle, an angle-iron frame and an alternator from an '81 Ford. He claimed he did it for exercise—but I know he took his job as building warden very seriously indeed.

We got to the penultimate flight and stopped, breathing

heavily. There was a fine sheen of sweat on Kate's brow, and I leaned gratefully on the stair rail, breathing hard. I looked at Capel, standing patiently at the foot of the final flight of stairs: he was breathing deeply, but plainly under no pressure. I could only assume that climbing these wooden mountains day after day kept him in shape.

He lifted an eyebrow in interrogation. I groaned. "All right—I know. One more effort. Damned if you don't seem more energetic each time we come, John."

Capel shrugged. "It sure as hell ain't all the steak and lobster I eat, Captain. But I got to keep fit—part of the job."

We started on up, and Capel said over his shoulder, "The door is open, Cap'n Scott. I got in a new load of logs two days ago. Keep it stocked, Mr. Radford told me. Say, I had a parcel from him back in June. Know what he sent? Candles. Whole gross in a box. Shoot, I can get ten, maybe fifteen eggs for a good candle."

"Great," I said. From his point of view it probably was. He dumped the bags at the apartment door, opened up and waited for us to make the last few steps. The door opened up into a wide passageway stacked high along one wall with sawn logs maybe a foot long. The carpet Ted had laid there so carefully was missing, the bare timber boards scuffed and dusty. We went through into the living room, and it was just as stark as I remembered it. There was a long, low coffee table surrounded by piles of cushions and short, thick rolls of hall carpet tied into makeshift seats. The fitted carpet was still deep and soft, but someone had cut out a half-circle round the open fire—probably because of the fire risk from rolling logs—and replaced it with a sheet of zinc, or maybe it was aluminum—whatever.

John carried the bags through to the bedroom, and Kate wandered into the kitchen. I sagged down onto a carpet roll, lit a cigarette and began to enjoy a good cough.

Capel came through into the living room, mopping his brow. "We get to have electricity between nine and midnight tonight. Fires are all laid; plenty of wood, as you can see. If you want a bath, there's a big billy can in the bathroom closet; you can heat maybe five gallons at a time that way. Dirty water out the bathroom window—the pipes are blocked somewhere below and I can't trace it yet. Oh—and I got the house phones working from batteries in the basement; just pick it up and you're through to my room. Can't talk to anyone else yet—not until I get some sort of switchboard figured out. You need me for anything, you call. And lock this door tight at night—hear?"

"Right, John. Sounds good. Hey—how about a drink?" I asked him.

"Hell, no—thanks all the same, Cap'n. You've only just got in. Later, maybe—okay?"

He went out whistling softly beteen his teeth, and I closed the door, slipped on the chain and got rid of my cigarette butt in the fireplace. That door looked like the Bank of England: safety chain, two bolts, a big mortise lock and a Chubb Special Burglarproof. I felt a little better, drew the curtains and went into the kitchen. Kate was standing dead center with hands on hips, nibbling her lower lip and looking at the massive old kitchen range.

"You must be joking," she said witheringly, "if you expect anything cooked tonight, Jonah Scott. I'd need a bath after just getting it lighted!"

"Only dirty people bathe," I pointed out. "Go light the livingroom fire and leave this lot to me. I know how to boil steaks and burn water."

"That I believe. Well...on your head be it. Still—call me when the thing is lit and working."

I started.

The stove smoked, but not too much—and I daresay Kate's sirloin tasted edible, because she cleaned up the last of the gravy with a piece of bread, shoved the plate along the coffee table and fell back among the cushions. She spread out her long legs towards the fire, slipped off her shoes and sighed.

"You did that so well, I'm going to let you do it all the time, Jonah."

"Glutton," I said rudely. I lit two cigarettes, offered her another glass of Riesling. She shook her head. "I'm loaded, Jonah. For a pilot, you're not a bad cook."

I shook my head in sorrow. "You're getting fat and lazy. Not surprising—not with eighteen stews to do all the work."

She protruded an inch of pink tongue. "Why don't you come down to Tourist during a dinner serving sometime? You think we girls have a nice, easy job? I think we should be paid as much as you—or more. After all, what are you? Glorified bus driver?"

I just smiled.

Suddenly, the lights went on. I got up, blew out the candles, leaving a smoky, greasy smell in the air. I wondered what they used to make candles these days—and decided ignorance was bliss. It sure wasn't paraffin wax.

Kate began to clear away the dishes. She said—apropos of nothing—"Jonah, don't you think John Capel has aged a lot since we started coming here? And I'm sure he doesn't get enough to eat. I feel quite guilty after a meal like that. Do any of them really get enough to keep going?"

"That's the name of the game, love," I told her gently. "And don't forget—it's not too long ago since Americans had an obesity problem. Stomachs too big, freezers too full, cars too large—you name it. They really had it good for half a century. Chances are they'll all feel better for losing a little weight."

Kate sniffed. "You're a cynical swine sometimes, Jonah Scott. I don't know why I put up with you. To hear you talk, you're glad to see them down and out."

"Down, maybe, but not out. They keep the Armed Services going: they've still got an army, nuke submarines with Cruise missiles, and a few nuke warships, carriers and the like. All the big aircraft have gone, mostly—no fuel—but they find enough to keep the Harrier-Carrier fleet at sea. It may be years before they start to run down from lack of spares—and things could change a lot by then."

I followed her into the kitchen, started drying the few dishes we had used. Kate hummed an unrecognizable tune under her breath, forearm deep in soapy water.

"I suppose this is the best job Capel can get? Working here, I mean."

"I suppose. Tip that water out and get some fresh—it's all greasy. Why?"

"He seems an educated man, Jonah. Yet he's really just a janitor."

I stacked the dry dishes away in the cupboard on the wall, threw the towel onto the draining board and ran my hand through my hair. My scalp felt itchy, and a bath seemed a good idea. "Capel," I told Kate, "has a master's degree in engineering from M.I.T. He spent two years lecturing on applied mathematics at Fordham University, right here in New York. Maybe when things get started again they'll reopen the schools and colleges—but at the moment, no transport, heating, books, supplies or staff. And nothing but Monopoly money to pay for it. John told me most of the campus buildings are wrecked, anyway."

We went back into the living room and I tended the fire. Kate wandered round the room haphazardly, and I sat on a carpet roll against the wall, watching her. She and I had got to be very close in the past year, which was no problem because the Company no longer frowned on crew/stew fraternization, in line with the relaxed attitudes of the country in general.

I mean, I never told her I loved her. How could I? I didn't know for sure myself. And there was an unwritten agreement in favor of extracurricular activities if either of us felt so inclined. (I'd avoided that problem with success for a long time now, and if Kate did play around, I certainly never got to hear about it.)

In the beginning I daresay there was more than a trace of pity involved by way of getting me back into circulation after Julie's death. Kate had taken the initiative then, and more often than not she still did. I let her, partially from habit and perhaps because it turned me on a little. After all, show me a man who dislikes being raped slowly and enthusiastically by a hotblooded gorgeous Irish colleen, and I'll show you a man with a problem.

Talk to Kate about Women's Lib, and she'll bung something heavy your way. But if she feels like getting loved, a little—and thank the Lord, she frequently does—she's not going to sit around and wait for her trousered partner to start the action. No way. In the early days it embarrassed me if she got in a quiet grope under the table at a party—until it dawned on me that she was only doing what I'd done myself since I was fifteen. Now I think it's kind of a nice compliment, and my Kate is sensible in choosing times and places. We'd never got it together in the air, for instance—although many have. But other places—how about standing up, jammed in the corner next to the piano at a swinging party, surrounded by hordes of happy people? I don't think anyone noticed—and we wouldn't have cared anyway.

Kate stood by the window, looking down at the street.

"What enormous problems they have, Jonah. Do you think they'll ever get back again?"

I thought for quite a while about that. It was a popular topic back home, and the big bookie chains had taken more than a few bets, so we had both heard most of the arguments for and against.

"Long-term," I said finally, "it's all about energy, Kate. We knew—and so did every other nation, fifty years ago—that the oil wouldn't last forever. You can make petrol out of coal, but it costs too much even now to provide fuel for family cars. I think in maybe fifteen, twenty years there won't be a lot of cars left. Unless we come up with a substitute for the petrol engine."

Kate wrinkled her nose. "I'll be sorry to see the end of the car, Jonah. Perhaps I was born fifty years too late. Imagine what it was like between the wars. They had twenty marvelous years of it, from 1919 onwards. All those Bentleys and Pierce Arrows and empty roads and no speed limits..."

We were quiet for quite some time, thinking about the "could have dones" and "might have beens."

"Damn it, Jonah, I'm not going to sit here moping all night. Go get us a drink and I'll get the news on the radio."

"Terrific. Then we can drown our sorrows. There's a bottle of Red Label in my bag, but no ice—have to be water."

Kate fiddled briefly with the battered transistor set on the mantel, finally came up with a Canadian station.

"Latest reports from the Middle East, Israel may be planning early retaliation against the PLO following the poison attack last month on Tel Aviv. Nearly a quarter of a million Israelis died following the poisoning of the city's water supply. The delay is possibly due to the distance involved, since Israel came out of the 1981 conflict occupying all of Syria, Lebanon and Jordan.

The unprecedented merger of Catholic and Protestant churches into the Universal Church of Northern Ireland seems at last to be achieving results. Violence in Ulster against the British military presence continues, but there have been no sectarian killings since the new Church opened its doors to all.

In Britain, the Social Exclusion Act seems to be gaining some support. While the practice of branding convicted criminals on the brow and releasing them subject to virtual total exclusion from society was originally opposed by the rehabilitation lobby, it does seem to be working. Excluded persons are banned from athletic contests, theaters, discotheques, bars and all public places including transport, and may not form or join any group of more than three persons. Latest reports indicate that the rate of recidivism—that is, return to criminal activities—has fallen to extremely low levels.

Reports from New Orleans confirm that the emerging Black America Movement conference proposes that black enclaves in the major American cities shall be evacuated, provided the states of Georgia, Louisiana, North and South Carolina and Mississippi are allowed to secede from the Union as an independent black nation. Washington is studying the proposals carefully, but the final decision will be a difficult one for President Booker T. Langford, the first black occupant of the White House.

Chicago. The Emergency Transport Commission issued an interim report on the progress of the massive redevelopment of steam-powered railroad engines. The first of the new coal-powered locomotives to be built in the ETC Development Complex in Cleveland has completed full reliability and testing evaluation on the route between Chicago and St. Louis, and is now to enter full-scale production in the Detroit automobile factories being converted for the program. Surely good news for transport-starved America.

These new locomotives run on a special powdered-coal injection process, and production of the new fuel is already under way in the anthracite fields of Carbondale, Scranton, Hazelton and Pottsville, in eastern Pennsylvania.

Additionally, it is reported that since the Armed Forces in America are to remain at their present level because of the unsettled international situation, the manpower needed for the new open-cut and deep mines now being opened will be secured by the drafting of all unmarried physically fit men over twenty-five with no family dependents, and from volunteers, whose families will be issued food and clothing at military levels as an incentive.

This is Station CQRB in Canadian Montreal. This program has also been broadcast by our sister station FTKL in Pays-Français Montreal. Now, some music for your enjoyment.

"There you are," I said heavily. "Some good, some bad."

"That announcer"—there was more than a trace of disillusionment in Kate's voice—"actually sounded as if he was enjoying it. Damned ghoul—he's sitting on the outside and he doesn't have a problem."

"True. They say the Mackenzie Bay field will be producing enough by next year—and we're supplying Canada until it does."

Kate nibbled her lip. "There must be a lot of gasoline coming south across the border."

I shook my head.

"No way. That's why most of the Canadian Army is camping out along the line—and why it's a capital offense to export petroleum products from Canada."

She stared. "Capital? You mean...?"

I said gently, "It's a hard life for everyone these days, Kate."

She said nothing, as we sat through a long uncomfortable silence, listening to the wail of synthesizers and the hard tonal harmonic drumming.

Kate retreated into the bathroom, and I sprawled in front of the fire smoking. I tried to read a paperback I'd bought in Heathrow, Main Terminal, but I found myself reading the same page over and over. I rolled on my back, listening to Kate splashing about and singing in that husky voice, and got to thinking about that loveliness stretched out in warm soapy water. So different from Julie—Julie of the lean, lithe figure, schoolgirl breasts, smooth black hair and a penchant for huge theatrical earrings. Kate and Julie—they'd met, just the one time, at a promotion party thrown by a brother officer, and next day Kate had confided to Jerry Chambers that she couldn't figure out who was luckier, Julie or I.

There is no way of knowing why people you love are taken away from you. Sometimes I think it was punishment for things I had done or said or thought; but that doesn't make sense unless you believe in predestination—that every life is preplanned from cradle to grave. If you believed that, you had to believe also that some Planner fed the data into some universal computer, which meant that every second of every life on every inhabited planet from the beginning of time was of equal importance to the Planner.

I preferred to believe that Julie's death—and all life— was a simple accident of nature...she and I had just been unlucky. No question of guilt, or cause, or retribution—we'd had something very, very good going for us, but by the laws of chance a certain number of lives are shattered every year, and we happened to draw the short straw.

I did all the usual things in a mechanical sort of way when Julie was killed in the National Front riots. I went down to identify the body, but they would not let me see her; petrol bombs can make drastic changes in the way people look, and they accepted identification of her rings, her wristwatch and the three-inch gold earrings, distorted and tarnished by the extreme heat.

The Company gave me ample time off—I would have been too high a risk in that mental state—and I went down to see Julie's parents in Esther, taking all her things along. I sold the house and found a service flat in Maidenhead. I put the car in the garage; took a train down to Paignton in Devon, where we'd spent our honeymoon, and got paralytically drunk alone in my hotel room. After three days and five bottles, Jerry Chambers and Kate found me, decided there was still more blood than alcohol in my veins and that it was worth attempting a salvage operation.

Next week I went back to flying, passed a route check and did the 797 conversion course.

I lit another cigarette.

Kate is a very wise woman. She caught on very early to the fact that unless something was done, I would spend the rest of my life soused in memories of a dead woman. She could see—everyone could see, I found out later—that I was really shut down, out, licked and crushed. I did my job well enough, but I'd stopped enjoying it.

Our first session was nothing short of clinical rape. There was a sudden weather clamp at JFK, and we diverted to Gander; they have well-furnished quarters for transient crews, and the beds are good, really comfortable. I was stretched out, smoking without enjoyment, trying to relax after a difficult ILS approach and crosswind landing, when the door opened and Kate walked in. She locked the door carefully, glanced at me and walked across to the dressing table, wearing a thin pale-green robe and slim-heeled slippers. She leaned over to the mirror, prodded her hair a little, slipped out of the robe and stood quite still, looking at me in the mirror. God help me, but I laughed.

I choked off the guffaw and put down my book. She turned round slowly, and despite myself I had to look at that wonderful assembly of skin, curves and shadows. We didn't speak....I lay, silently, watching Kate make the running, and I felt numb at first, no reaction, no excitement. I wondered how in hell I could tell Kate "no way" without offending her—that we were not really on the same frequency at all. I began to understand that Kate was using me, impersonally, in an odd withdrawn context, almost as if I was one of those inflatable sex dolls. She was trying to tell me that there was nothing serious involved in this: she didn't want to be loved or cherished or adored—she just wanted to be alive in bed with as many variations as possible. She wanted only the arousal, the fulfillment, and I wondered why she couldn't simply have gone to bed and masturbated.

At least—that was how it started out.

Towards the end I became involved, brain full of confused thoughts of guilt and remorse and sadness, knowing that Julie (wherever she was) would somehow understand that I had finally lost her. Not completely—I would never forget her as long as I lived; but for the first time, the outside world had forced itself, like some wedge, into my gray world of grief, and nothing would ever be the same again.

I tried. God help me, I tried—but that traitorous fold of flesh sensed Kate's urgent writhing, and I clutched the firm buttocks fiercely, eyes tight shut, heart thudding gigantically in my ears, breath whistling in my throat until we hung suspended in a seconds-long limbo that lasted a thousand years. No sight, no sound, no movement . . . except somewhere in the unbelievably deep liquid universe which surrounded me, a soft tendril of pressure from some enchanted muscle opened a new line of communication.

We lay immobile, utterly spent, Kate a slack dead weight on me, her hair spread over my chest. We rolled over, still interlocked, and I rested on my elbows, looked down into luminous green eyes. If my smile was a little twisted, Kate ignored it, and contented herself with saying lazily, "Hi. Welcome back, Jonah."

Lying there, thinking and remembering, it seemed to me that Julie was very remote from me in time and space; I tried to recall her face, her voice, the way she walked, and it was too hazy, indistinct. More important, it didn't seem to hurt anymore—and without being disloyal to Julie, I knew how much I owed Kate.

3

Kate was still in the bathroom when someone knocked on the door. It was a loud, confident knock—not hesitant, apologetic, as many knocks are. It had a message to give: the knocker was official, had a right to be there and was not to be kept waiting.

I got to my feet as Kate came through in a blue robe, towel round her hair, questions in her face. I shrugged, motioned for her to stay put and went to stand at one side of the door.

"Who is it?"

"Captain Novak, Sergeant James, Military Police. Open up."

Now, that was odd, I thought. After dark, Capel locked that street door up tight and no one got in—but no one. Not even police, the military, or whatever: too many Jacks roamed the city in uniforms stolen or stripped from dead men, coming their way in to unwary victims. Which was why most residential buildings had their Capels, human guard dogs. Besides, the Army withdrew at dusk—left the city to the Jacks and kiddie mobs, because their casualty rate got too high for comfort. So...

"Slide your ID under the door, Captain," I bawled, and didn't wait for an answer. I scooted past Kate into the bedroom, grabbed the telephone and said in an urgent whisper, "John? John Capel? You there?"

"Sir?"

"Ah. John. Jonah Scott. Listen—I can't talk for long. You let anyone in the building in the last thirty minutes?"

The line made a shallow hissing noise as I waited. Then—

"No, sir. No one came in since you got here. You got problems?"

I said slowly, "Could be. Two, maybe more, characters at the door. Say they're military police—but I doubt that."

"Okay. Don't open up that door—I'm on my way. Say, you got that gun handy, Mr. Scott?"

"Yes." I'd been afraid he was going to ask me that. I don't like guns much. "I've got Mr. Radford's old forty-five automatic here."

"Right. Make sure she's loaded, and don't leave that room until I say it's okay. Keep them talking—and if you have to come out, check the safety and come out shooting. Got it?"

"Got it."

The phone clicked. I hung up, knelt on the floor in the corner and levered up a loose board. The gun was wrapped in plastic, with two spare clips. As I stood up, the knocking started up again, incessant and noisy. I closed the door on Kate, went out into the hallway and stood near the door.

"All right, all right—don't make so much noise! Where's that ID?"

"Never mind the ID, buster—open up before we blow away the lock and you with it."

I had the gun out now. I slipped out the clip, checked that a round was showing, replaced it and gave it a little tap with the heel of my palm; I'd seen enough old Humphrey Bogart movies to know what to do. The safety was stiff, but I got it free; stood with my back to the wall, gun at my side, one up the spout.

"Okay...wait one. What do you want, anyway?" I was stalling.

"Open up—for the last time, man. That way you won't get hurt. We can smell that cookin' in there—we figure there's enough for everybody."

Kate tapped my shoulder and I jerked, startled. She had the only bedroom chair, a wooden straight-back, and shoved it towards me. "Under the door handle, Jonah!"

I nodded, jammed it into place and stood to one side. The gun felt heavy; it was an old M1911 automatic, once the property of a real U.S. military cop. I had fired it only once in practice, down in the New Forest back home. And it had scared the crap out of me—not just the noise, which was bad enough, but the way that slug blew away most of the width of a six-inch silver birch without stopping. For all I know, it's still going strong somewhere.

The door shuddered, bent in a little at the top. I wondered how long it would take—and hoped that meant they didn't have any guns. They should have put a couple through the lock by now, and I began to feel a little braver.

They tried again, and again; then silence. I heard a muted whispering. Then Capel, outside, somewhere along the hallway: "All right—*freeze!* Drop those guns!"

In that instant, something strange happened to time. Everything seemed to slow down to half normal speed; the lights seemed brighter; the air seemed to glow. I could hear street sounds far away, the dull roar of a jet high overhead.

It was not unfamiliar, that sensation: at least four times in the past, in some sort of emergency such as losing an engine on takeoff, I have been given this gift, and it is a very wonderful thing. I have, it appears to me, all the time in the world, to pull back the throttle of the failed engine, cut the fuel, hit the fire button and wind on some trim against the unbalanced power. I have time to take a leisurely peek out of the window to check my position, make sure the flaps are coming up, call the airfield on the radio. And it all happens in about one and one-half seconds. Some call it good training. I call it a goddamn miracle.

The first three shots were close, and they were very loud. Two different sounds: a deeper explosion between two lighter cracks. It stood to reason that the middle one was Capel's own .45 Police Special. There were confused shouts, another single heavy boom, and I had the chair out of the way, door open.

A long-faced man with olive skin and exaggerated sideburns below lank black hair was standing spread-eagled against the opposite wall, his head turned to the right, staring at Capel. His gun was at arm's length, a snub-nosed revolver with a very short barrel, a wisp of smoke curling upwards.

A second man in a brown windbreaker lay face down in the hallway, a big ragged-edged hole in the back of his neck, maybe three inches wide. I got a glimpse of what was oozing out of the hole and made a mental note to be sick when I had time.

No one moved.

Sideburns started to bring up his gun hand, head swiveling towards me, slowly, so slowly, as if he was walking in his sleep, and I looked left down the hallway. Capel was at the top of the stairs, on his knees, clutching his left side with both hands. He stared blindly at me, gun five feet away against the wall, out of reach. He turned his eyes to look at the little black hole Sideburns was showing him.

I felt calm and unworried and quite sure what I had to do. There was no need to rush things, because everyone else seemed to be knee-deep in molasses. I even thought about turning, closing the door first, because I didn't want Kate to watch this. I took a single long pace forward, brought up the gun and took some of the weight with my left hand under my right wrist. I lined the barrel up nicely with Sideburns' left ear, shut my eyes tight and clenched both fists. For some strange reason, I never heard the shot. To this very day I cannot recall hearing anything, but I could have been deafened by the previous shots at close range.

And my wrists hurt like the devil—that .45 kicked like a halfback. There was something warm running down my forearm, too—maybe I'd been hit.

Sideburns was sliding slowly floorwards, legs jackknifing at the knees, revealing an egg-shaped red-painted hole in the wall behind him. The hole in his face started where his mouth should have been, taking in most of the throat, so that his head lay back as if very tired, on the pillow of his shoulder. What remained of his face was patched with black, and from the middle of the hole a scarlet jet as thick as my forefinger pumped regularly in a parabola past my left side, with amazing strength: it was his blood that stained my forearms. Mental note number two: work out, some way, the pressure needed to produce a jet of that size and strength. An interesting problem in hydraulics.

Just as his backside hit the floor, Sideburns got his head up a little and looked at me. Maybe his brain got the message, maybe not. But his eyes said it all.... He fell sideways clumsily, coughed up a great welter of blood and lay still. His head hit the floor solidly. Mental note number three: he'd have a hell of a headache in the morning.

I was vaguely surprised that I felt nothing myself. No shock, horror, relief—I just felt a little pleased it was all over. I stepped over the legs wrapped in dirty jeans, dropped the gun and walked stiffly along to Capel, squatted down beside him and supported his back. He eased his legs forward, sat down very gingerly and looked up at me.

I pulled his hands away from his side. There were two patches of blood, each the size of a saucer, about four inches apart, and I tried to figure how he could get hit twice in the same spot.

"Just sit still, John—don't move." I eased him back until he could lean on the wall. Along the hall, two doors opened; frightened faces stared out, withdrew hastily.

I saw Kate stepping over the casualties, robe held high over her knees. John said, "Hell, no sweat, Mr. Scott—only a scratch. Lemme get up."

"You stay right there, John Capel," said Kate very firmly. "Hold his hands, Jonah."

She tore open his blue shirt, hauled it out from under his belt, got a grip on his mesh undershirt and revealed the damage. I took a quick look. Midway between armpit and hipbone, the front hole was round and neat, black at the edges and beginning to exhibit the usual blue bruising caused by the impact of a high-velocity bullet. The second hole—the exit point—was twice as large, ragged, uneven, with little strings of skin and flesh showing. I could see a strand of navy-blue cotton, carried straight through from the entry point. Blood was welling from the bigger hole of the two, but not spurting; I'm no medical wizard, but I figured there were no arteries damaged.

Kate whipped the towel from her head, made a thick pad and laid it in position, told Capel to hold it there with one hand while I got him to his feet. Between us, he walked a little unsteadily to the apartment door, stepping over our friends. He stared down, said something indistinct about "sons of bitches" and went on. I noticed the total lack of sound in the building. Maybe every door concealed frightened people holding their breath—we could have been the only living beings within half a mile. Well, I thought grimly, you can't blame people for wanting to stay clear, safe behind doors. There's no place like home when the shit hits the fan.

Capel sat on the coffee table, clutching his towel in place. Kate found a small basin, some hot water, and I found the remains of my bottle of Red Label. I gave Capel a long pull, took another myself, and we sat grinning foolishly at each other.

"Jesus H. Christ, Mr. Scott—I've seen nothing like that since Vietnam. Where did you learn to blow a man away like that?"

"Just now, John. It hasn't sunk in yet."

"Aw, don't give me no bullshit, fella—I know a pro when I see one. That wrist grip—we always used that in the Army. I tell you, I was scared shitless when you stepped in....I dropped the little guy first shot—bull's-eye. Then the other bastard wings me and I drop my gun—I tell you, I could hear those pearly gates creakin' open for me. Then you stroll out like it's a Saturday-night trip to the movies."

"Here's Kate. Shut up, now, while she has a look at that hole."

It was clear that Capel had been extraordinarily lucky. The slug must have grazed a rib and ricocheted straight out again; Kate thought there was little danger of bone fracture and set to work to clean the torn flesh, first with warm clean water, then with a scrap of linen soaked in Red Label. The flesh between the two holes was blackening and swollen into a hard ridge.

"We have to clean out the hole," she said worriedly. "Jonah, give him another drink, because this is going to hurt. And I want some wire from a coat hanger—straight, about ten inches long."

She sterilized the wire with boiling water, made me twist a small loop in one end. A scrap of clean linen through the loop, like a rifle pull-through, soaked in whiskey, and she sat back, looked at Capel.

"John?"

"Go ahead, Miss Kate. Gotta be done, I guess."

"Yes, that's right. Hold him still, Jonah...."

She slid the wire neatly into the wound, probed briefly until it showed at the bullet exit area. Capel made a heavy animal sound in the back of his throat, and I bore down hard on each shoulder. Kate looked up.

"All right?"

Capel nodded silently, chest heaving. Kate said cheerfully, "Nearly finished. Now...easy does it..."

She withdrew the probe and the blood-soaked pad in one quick motion, cleaned up deftly and applied a prepared pad over the holes. She ran a long bandage torn from a sheet three times round Capel's middle, secured it with a scrap of adhesive plaster and sat back, looking at her work critically. The probe pad told its own story: several strands of blue cotton from Capel's shirt and even a remnant of white string from his undershirt.

Capel gulped down the last of the Red Label and used Kate's towel to wipe away the sweat from his face. Kate got to her feet unsteadily, said, "I think I want to throw up," and walked unsteadily into the bathroom.

I started clearing up.

Capel said, "Say, that's one fine woman, Mr. Scott. How come a nurse gets to be an air hostess?"

"Nurse?" I said, surprised. "Kate's no nurse. Had the usual first-aid training the girls go through on the Cabin Staff Course. But she's nobody's fool, John. That graze should give no trouble, if that's what you're thinking.

"No—'course not. I'm real grateful—to both of you. I got into one or two hassles in Nam, but there was always someone in the platoon to cover you. This thing just now—I must be getting old. There was a time I could have taken two punks like that without creasing my pants."

I lit two Splits and gave him one. "You did fine, John. Listen—how in hell did they get in?"

"I've been wondering about that myself," he said worriedly. "I'll go get myself a clean shirt and take a look around. Probably the roof—I would have heard them coming in on the ground floor."

I wasn't really listening. I was watching my right thigh with fascination. It had started to twitch violently, muscles contracting with a life all their own, and I could do nothing about it. I stood up to flex the leg a little and the room took off in a spin to the left; Capel grabbed my elbow and it stopped, went the other way. I heard Kate crying out, my upper arms were seized forcibly and I found myself kneeling by the toilet pan, trying to recall when I had last been so sick. With ludicrous logic, a corner of my mind sang a lament for a lost steak dinner—hauled across three thousand miles to end up in a New York drain. Thinking about it started me off again, and Capel held my head until the storm passed.

"Easy, fella...easy."

"I was thinking about the mess out there in the hall," I said.

"Well, man, we clean that up ourselves. Let me get squared away and I can handle that. Look, this happens every day in these parts. All we have to do is get them clear of the building."

"You mean we have to drag them downstairs and out into the street?"

"There's an easier way than that. There's a window at the end of the hall. Straight drop into the basement areaway. We can clean up the hallway, get some sleep and shift Macy and Gimbel early in the morning."

The sheer unreality of the situation began to sink in, and I started laughing. I'd killed a man—and it was on the cards there would be no investigation, arrest, trial. We were going to dispose of the evidence and jettison the bodies out of a window—and not twenty-four hours ago, I had driven sedately along an English road listening to Capitol Radio and a commercial about biologically active washing powders. Capel grinned, went downstairs and found a clean shirt. We used two more of Ted's irreplaceable bed sheets to wrap up Sideburns and Co. They weren't heavy—probably because of the quite amazing amount of blood leaked all over the floor. They went out of the window head first, flicking their heels, and I pulled the window down quickly to shut out the unpleasant sound effects from below. Capel went away to check the building security, and I spread a blanket to cover most of the stains in the hallway.

I found Kate curled up on the bed in a tight ball, feet tucked inside her robe, fast asleep. I did not disturb her; sleep was the best thing for her at the moment. Taking my time, I locked and bolted the door, cleaned and reloaded the .45 and wrapped it up in the plastic bag. I splashed my face with cold water, washed the stains from my arms, put on a T-shirt and got the living-room fire stoked up. As long as I kept moving and didn't think too much, I was okay—but as soon as I sat down the shakes hit me.

It started crazily. The events of the last two hours seemed so unreal, impossible... I remembered the way Sideburns slid down the wall, legs every which way—and I thought madly of Pinocchio and the puppet maker. This seemed extraordinarily funny, and I started giggling. After a while I heard someone bellowing with insane laughter and realized that it was I. Gasping, I could not breathe against the stomach convulsions giving birth to the uncontrollable laughter. My cigarette burned my fingers and dropped to the floor. This was too hilarious to believe, and I was down on my knees, chest heaving, stomach muscles aching. The incessant laughter turned to racking coughs, and I was hanging on to Kate desperately, face deep in some warm hollow wet with tears.

I wept, in great choking spasms, whilst her soft woman's voice spoke gently in words I could not understand.

Believe me, shedding tears is no easy feat after thirty-odd years without practice. Nerves, muscles and glands unused since childhood cannot be pressed into service again without penalty. The process, in fact, is extremely painful, damned humiliating and almost impossible to stop, once under way.

I tried. A tiny voice in back of my ears somewhere kept up steady protest, mouthing words like "unmanly," "immature," "childish." To no avail—it had to run its course. I realized that I could no more control the beast than walk on water; I was reduced to helpless dependence on the strength of a woman, a strength which seemed to flow like some warm river from Kate. She knelt like some impregnable castle wall, shielding me from the storm.

How long it lasted God alone knows. Somewhere along the way, the lights had gone out; Kate managed to get a log or two onto the dying fire, and at last I lay exhausted on the cushions. She sat smoking, staring into the flames, silent and totally understanding, and eventually I made it to the bathroom, filled the hand basin from the big aluminum billy can and soaked my head for long healing minutes.

I decided I didn't particularly want to see anyone at that time, especially myself, and carefully avoided the mirror.

There was a big pot of fresh coffee waiting. Halfway through the second cup, I found the first had almost scalded my throat, but no coffee ever tasted like that. Kate had got her hair more or less under control, the robe belted securely; best of all, she didn't look at me directly. There was a small secret smile on her face, it seemed to me, but I figured she wasn't laughing at me.

My watch said fifteen minutes past midnight. My brain said we had been in this place fifteen hundred years—or thereabouts. Kate cleared away the coffee cups and sat down facing the fire, long legs stretched out, bare feet rubbing together luxuriously. She looked up at me and smiled.

"Better?"

I nodded. Couldn't trust myself to say anything. But what was there to say?

She took my hand and squeezed. I slid down beside her, ran my hand gently down the thick red hair, into the nape of her neck, turned her head towards me and kissed her. She sighed, settled down with her head on a cushion, eyes closed.

Her left hand toyed idly with my cigarette lighter on the rug, her right resting lightly on my leg; it tightened into a gentle squeeze, relaxed, and she exhaled a long slow breath through her nostrils. I watched: they flared delightfully. Half her body was in shadow, hair stained with firelight into a deep wine shade and framing the smooth chin, curved cheeks. Kate had lost at last the hard, brassy facade most people knew; now she was soft, dreamy, almost defenseless.

I poked an exploring finger into the neckline, moved south, lifted. She opened her eyes, looked at me, closed them again. The smile hovered around her mouth, lower lip protruding slightly, textured like a ripe berry and moistened by the tip of a mobile tongue. I ran a forefinger down her forehead, nose, over the full lips, into the hollow of the neck to her waist; the robe parted easily, slid aside.

I sat for long moments lost in thought. Kate's chest rose and fell in long slow breaths, and a little pulse blinked visibly in her throat. I leaned forward, blew a fine jet of air onto her right nipple. It stirred, the convolutions vanishing, the dark-brown areola distending, long hard nipple erect, monolithic.

My tongue found the tip, my lips circumscribed the warm tight cone of flesh which bulged, like a breast on a breast, and I laid my hand on the underslope, with gentle pressure.

Time became of no account. Neither she nor I was excited, except that every few moments a shudder, a vibration almost, seemed to flood through her body. The slowness of our journey itself seemed unreal, compared with the lusty initiative of Kate's usual approach, and I knew that something unique and unbelievable could happen to us. Tremble she might—but I knew this new, incredible Kate was treading the same path, and I found a corner of my mind collecting and storing each touch, each movement, each emotional peak in a remote but accessible corner of my memory. I was aware that my heart was beating slowly, ponderously, in a massive pounding cadence.

Kate's hand was cool on my thigh. The pounding moved to my loins as the butterfly fingers ran up my flank, drifted across my belly and began a slow flat penetration through the mass of hair. I knew that I was deeply aroused, more so than I could ever recall, and in such burning heat and tension I cried out incoherently at the first touch. Then I relaxed somewhat; Kate clearly had the situation well in hand. The ordinary world of ordinary people ceased to exist. The room

contracted, diminished into three fragments of the same holo-
gram: searching tongues, breast smooth and nipple rough
under the palm, and the slow, maddening progress of slim
fingers towards a far-distant summit.

Kate began to make odd little glottal sounds, like a weight
lifter taking a first strain, but ending in a sigh, and my hand
slid down her body. She turned slightly to meet it, left knee
rising, toppling slowly sideways; she was moist, cool to the
touch, totally submissive yet actively involved. She opened
her eyes briefly, opened her mouth to my searching tongue
and wove wonderful patterns with a hand suddenly urgent,
gripping me tightly, as one grasps a lifeline, and I went willingly where she pulled, opening and surrounding me tightly.
I paused, fractionally embedded, resting on my elbows, and
looked down at the flushed cheeks, long lashes. Kate's tongue
lay exposed between her lips in intense concentration, eyes
tightly closed. She moved restlessly under me, laid firm warm
hands on the backs of my thighs and pulled me within,
smoothly, almost imperiously, on and on to a final deep universe of dark sensation. We lay breathless, spent, fearful to
move lest the spell be broken, and I felt her relax, her body
softening, sagging with the languor of fulfillment. Somewhere, a million miles away, some small muscle flexed,
tensed, gripped, squeezed with exquisite strength, and I saw
a small secret smile on her face.

The fire was dying in its tracks. I blew out the candles,
went back to the creased battlefield of the rug, and we slept
close, interlocked, through the long private hours of the night.

4

Something prodded my lower ribs.

I rolled over, chewed my tongue, decided it tasted lousy and tried to pick up my dream again. No dice. Which—or whose—bed I was in seemed irrelevant. The prodding started again, and I squirmed into a fetal attitude under the blankets, trying to opt out of the rotten old world.

"Come on, brother...move it!"

It was no use: I was awake. I gave up fighting it, rolled on my back, tasted my tongue again. It had not improved. I got up on my elbows, bleary-eyed.

Kate sat on the bed, forefinger cocked again. She looked disgustingly clean, smug and adorable. If she'd been a cat, I'd have checked out the milk. There was one alleviating factor: coffee in a brown chinaware mug, hot, strong, black and sweet. It cut through the mud around my taste buds like a laser, and suddenly the coffee tasted like coffee. Bottoms up, dregs and all, and hold out the mug for a refill.

"Oh, no, you don't," she nagged. "Get that great belly out of bed and I'll find something to fill it."

A flat gut, at my age, deserved better than that, I thought. I stared at her, suddenly serious.

"Morning. Was that all a dream—or did we have visitors last night?"

"'Twas no dream," she said. "I took a peep into the hallway just now. John Capel and an old black woman were clearing up. Most of the...mess had gone, but he was having trouble getting the wall clean."

My face made a "yeuch" comment, silently. "How is the old coot this morning?"

"A very lucky man, I think. He'll be as stiff as a board for a few days, but he says it's a nice clean wound. He'll live."

"Live?" I said sourly. "Born to be hanged. The old bastard'll see us all out. That was a neat bit of first aid you did. Christ, I never want to go through anything like that again. When I think of how it could have turned out..."

Kate chewed her lip reflectively, nodded. "I know. It was so quick...just a few moments—and two dead men outside, one wounded in here."

"You know," I mused, "this is no place for the likes of you and me. Somehow I've talked myself into accepting things as they are, but sometimes I get to believing we can still go downtown to those little Village restaurants and ride the hansom cabs in Central Park and take the ferry to Staten Island. Then the whole bloody mess blows up in my face and I find I have to shoot some poor bastard because he tries to pinch the grub we bring over."

Kate sniffed, unimpressed. "That wasn't all they were after."

"That's not the point. Look, there'll be no police, no arrest, no trial—nothing. Well, they may have asked for it, but that doesn't change my opinion. Kate, it's a stinking, lousy world, and I only hope the rest of it doesn't go the way New York is going. Now shut up. Either get my breakfast or get back in bed—I'm easy either way."

"Well, I'm not, squire. Besides, I'm dressed," she said quickly—a little too quickly. Well—there'd be other times, and I needed to go to the bathroom.

We splurged on a pot of tea to go with the toast and a can of cranberry jelly we found in Ted's kitchen cupboard. John Capel arrived just after I lit my second cigarette—a Low Tar Special, because I don't touch grass or Splits before 5 P.M. Capel lit up gratefully, refused a cup of tea but settled for an instant coffee. He sat down against the yellow-painted wall, legs asprawl with coffee cup handy, and grinned complacently. I stared at him.

"You look horribly fit, Capel. All this morning exercise I hear you're indulging in."

"Exercise, crap," he said bluntly. "I was up before six, shifting the rubbish. I don't like to see the place cluttered with people like that. Bad enough bleeding all over my upper hallway, without lying around dead and giving the place a bad reputation."

For a moment, I thought he was being facetious—until it dawned on me he was more upset about the mess than about the cause of it. There was more to John Capel than the ability to shoot fast and straight.

"Sounds a reasonable complaint," I agreed. "What are we going to do with our friends?"

"Do?" said Capel, surprised. "I already did it. Found some big plastic sacks in the boiler room, made nice neat bundles and took 'em down to a vacant lot on the corner. Garbage Squad'll pick them up later today."

"Hell, you could have called me," I said in some anger. "You could have torn that hole open again. What happens now? Trouble?"

"No trouble, Jonah. Some of my people in the building, they wanted to know what all the hassle was about, but apart from that, those Jacks won't be missed. Mrs. Simpson—lives next floor down—she helped me clean up. 'Mr. Capel,' she says, 'anytime you want to blow away people like that, you go right ahead.'"

We laughed—couldn't help it: his imitation of an old woman was perfect.

"No joke," he pointed out bleakly. "Mr. Simpson went out one morning last fall looking for grub and never came back. She believes he got it from the same kind of bastards we had here."

Kate stared at Capel, clearly upset. "You mean he just went out and she never saw him again?"

"Right. And Clyde Simpson knew where it was at—damn near as big as Charlie Hackett, and a fast mover. Never carried a gun—he had a length of rubber hose with three inches of lead in one end, and he was a real hard character. Before we lost Clyde, I used to think I would make it okay, but sometimes I wonder." He dropped his cigarette butt in the coffee cup, stretched gingerly inside his bandage.

Kate said softly, "This awful place..."

Capel glanced at her and shook his head. "Aw, goddamn it, Miss Kate, it's not all bad. Mostly we live here because we wouldn't like it someplace else—if we had anywhere else to go. Okay, so it may be three or four years before the Army lets anyone leave the country voluntarily—they ship out anyone of foreign nationality with relatives who'll take them, and the fewer people left here, the more food to go around. Well, maybe we finish up with fifty percent WASPs and fifty percent black, and that's a pretty good formula for disaster on its own. But it sure can't get any worse than it's been the last two years."

I said speculatively, "Would you get out yourself if you could, John?"

"You'd better believe it, fella."

Well, that was what I'd figured. Capel crossed his legs and got his hands into his pants pockets. "Look at it this way," he said: "I got no family, no home, no job, no wages, no future. Oh, sure, I have my room in the basement, and the folks in the building feed me—I get enough to eat more often than not, and that puts me in a small minority in this town. The Big Apple is a mean city these days—you know?"

I said nothing. Capel shrugged. "Well, sir, I don't have to be no Gypsy palm reader or Jesus freak to know that someday, some hopped-up sonofabitch is going to take me like that mother tried last night. So I want to spend my last few years someplace I don't have to lay it on the line every night. That's wrong?"

We said it wasn't wrong. It didn't help Capel, or make him feel better.

Kate caught my eye and said slowly, "Jonah...couldn't we...?"

"No, we couldn't, and you know it," I said flatly.

"But—"

"But nothing. If we ever got him past the Airborne boys at Kennedy, we'd come unstuck at London. Sorry, John lad."

"Don't be," he told me. "I figure lots of people try to get out the hard way and don't make it."

"Check," I said. "At Heathrow we get off quickly, but they take hours with the passengers. Everyone goes through a kind of sieve, what with police, Immigration, medical, Customs—you wouldn't believe it if you saw it."

Kate said indignantly, "And the fine man saving your bacon last night."

"Look, love, no use getting your knickers twisted."

She snorted, stalked off and stared down at the street from the window.

Capel climbed lazily to his feet. "Don't start no shootin' war on my account, Jonah. Jesus, I got it made here—which reminds me, I have folks to check out the front door pretty soon. You leaving soon?"

I nodded. "Charlie Hackett is supposed to collect us around five. We're due out for London just after midnight."

Kate craned her neck. "Think again, Jonah. Guess who just arrived—Charlie. With Jerry Chambers aboard."

"Jerry? Here?" I took a quick look and started for the door. "Come on, John—let's go see."

In the foyer, two middle-aged women waited patiently. A gaunt, pale man with long hair, wearing a long black coat and black beret, stood silently behind them. Capel slid the bolts, worked the big brass key in the old-fashioned lock and eased the door open on the safety chain. He took a long cautious look before opening up all the way.

"Okay, folks. Morning, Mrs. Wallach, Mrs. Klebb. Hi, Joe."

The man in the black coat nodded, opened his coat and steadied the machine pistol against his thigh. He stalked halfway down the front steps, examined the street area, glanced up at the roofs and nodded to his employers. "Right, ladies. Stay close, stay cool."

At the foot of the steps, they passed Charlie Hackett and Chambers on the way up. My copilot was dressed in a gabardine trench coat, cavalry twill trousers, a floppy red scarf and a woolen cap with pompon; he looked more like a football fan than an airline pilot, and I didn't like it. He wasn't alone, either: the creature he hauled along by her right arm was tall, skinny and pallid, with a mane of motley hair jouncing around her shoulders. Her clothes did nothing for her: reading from the base line up, a pair of ragged white sneakers, black stockings featuring ten holes to the square foot, heavy tweed skirt ripped up the right thigh and a floppy wool sweater. There was a pattern knitted into the front panel: a circle with a small cross tacked onto the base—the age-old sign for a woman. Just as well; I'd seen Marines who looked more feminine.

"Mornin'." Charlie produced a huge grin. I stood in the doorway—solidly. The three of them stood there, one happy, one dazed and the third clearly wondering what my reaction would be.

"And who," I said coldly, "had the bright idea for this visit?"

Chambers shifted his feet around a little. "I asked Charlie

if he knew where we could find you, Skipper—we stopped him downtown. Sheer luck, really."

The look I gave Charlie wiped off his grin cleanly. "Well?"

"Well, shoot, Cap'n—I didn't figger it was no state secret—you know?"

"Next time, figure it is, Charlie—or else. Get it?"

"Right, Cap'n. I dig. Sorry."

I relaxed a little. "Well—better come inside. The street stink is worse this morning. Not you, Charles—or have you another fare?"

"Mr. Chambers, he told me to wait, Cap'n."

"Well," I said sourly, "I hope he pays you. You'd better come on up—John Capel doesn't like people hanging around down here."

We started up the stairs, and Chambers began explaining. "This is Nickie—Nicola Bassett. Old friend. Couldn't find her last night—flat empty, no clues at all. Found her early this morning, down the local subway—scared to death. She's in big trouble, Skip. Father and mother got caught in a crossfire three days ago—looting party coming out of a warehouse, Army patrol, shooting up everything moving. Nickie got away somehow, hid for a day or two, went home. Found their flat stripped, burned out. Nowhere to go except down the subway. That's about it."

He stopped, short of breath, as we reached the upper hall-way. Charlie and the girl went on. "Don't know what to do, Jonah. Can't leave her on the streets—she's eaten nothing for three days."

I said, "Do you know what you're getting mixed up in?"

"Mixed up? Jonah, she's my girl! Known her for a year or more."

"Serious?"

He hesitated. "Well—you know how it is. I see her when we're here, but there has never seemed to be anything hard and fast—we just like being together."

"All right," I said finally. "Kate can feed her, clean her up a bit, and we'll see. But I don't know that I can do any more than that."

The flat seemed crowded, even with Capel doing his rounds elsewhere.

Charlie found a strategic spot near the window, leaned against the wall and began chewing a matchstick. The girls disappeared into the kitchen to organize coffee; I hoped our limited supply would stand the load. Chambers slumped down beside me near the fireplace.

"Jonah. I know it's asking a lot, but—what are the chances of getting Nickie home? With us, I mean?"

I shook my head. "No way, son."

"But we could—"

"No. You know who carries the can when she's found at LAP—and I like my job too much to chance it, even for you and Nickie. Look—I'll do what I can. She can stay here for a couple of weeks until we come through again. Capel will keep an eye on her, and you can leave her enough cigarettes and food to get by."

Chambers shook his head glumly. "It's not on, Skip. Christ, you can see how she is—she won't last five minutes by herself. You know what it takes to get by in this place. Survival of the fittest."

Kate came through from the kitchen in time to take it in. "He's right, Jonah. She seems such a nice kid, but frightened out of her skin. She's eaten nothing since Tuesday—I gave her a sandwich and a fresh pot of coffee. She's only a hair from nervous collapse. We have to do something."

I was beginning to get angry: they were both trying to present me with a *fait accompli*, and I wasn't going to have it. Damn it, they had no right even to ask. There must be fifteen million Americans trying to make it from the few ports and airfields still open; those 83rd Airborne boys weren't standing around JFK just for sunshine and fresh air.

I said bluntly, "You know I don't *have* to do anything, Kate. She can stay here for a week or two, and next time through things may be better. You and Jerry know damn well there is no way of jumping the queue, even if the girl could find the fare—which is about fifteen thousand dollars one way."

Chambers stood for a long moment, hands flexing, and I didn't like the look in his eye one little bit. I hoped he wouldn't do anything stupid. Not that I couldn't handle him, but you don't try to work over your captain—not if you want to stay with Air Britain. I wondered what in hell had got into him— a senior pilot, thirty-two years old, in line for his captain's ticket soon, and responsible (with me) for the lives of hundreds of people every time we got a 797 airborne. And here he was, going round the bend for some skinny bird with holes in her socks. I was going to have to file a report about this, back home, and that I didn't like at all.

Kate sniffed, turned away and went off to organize a bath for Nickie; Jerry walked stiffly away and spoke quietly to Charlie Hackett. The big man listened impassively, nodded once or twice, and I went into the bedroom for a new pack of Splits: I needed a lift. I'd run into this kind of problem before, a month or two back with a hard-nosed operator called Calleia who wanted a lift to the U.K. He was loaded with jewelry which was so old-fashioned in setting, the stones so large, they were embarrassing. So much so, I figured they were real—about 55,000 pounds sterling worth. Two years' pay. Nice—but not nice enough: I had too much to lose, and told him so. The important thing was that I spent a little time afterwards thinking about how it *could* have been done, and I came to the conclusion I'd just quoted to Chambers. It couldn't be done.

I went back into the living room. Kate and the girl sailed past without a second glance—bathroom bound, judging by the size of the hot-water pan they carried.

"Still here, Charlie?"

"Just waitin', Cap'n."

"For Mr. Chambers?"

"Yessir."

I nodded. "Okay. What now, Jerry?"

"I'm just going," Chambers said stiffly. "Charlie says he knows where we can pick up some clothes for Nickie. I've got some trade goods in the cab—grub, smokes. Be about an hour. Are we invited for lunch, or do I take Nickie away for a picnic on the local garbage heap?"

I grinned. "Sounds more like the Chambers I know. Sure— we've enough to go round. Charlie, make sure they don't rob him blind, wherever you take him. Right?"

"Right, Cap'n."

"I suppose *you* think we should take this Bassett girl with us too?"

Charlie grinned sheepishly. "Well, sir, it ain't none of my business but there ain't many unattached broads around this town anymore. 'Specially young like that, I mean. If she stays around, she gets round heels or she gets to be dead—there's no other way."

I pointed a forefinger at him. "You're dead right, fella. It isn't any of your business. And while I'm on the subject, I don't want half the staff at Kennedy in here—got it?"

Charlie said he got it. He tramped out behind Chambers, black face sweating slightly and eyes down.

I finished the cigarette, got Capel on his steam-powered house telephone and asked him to come up. He must have finished his rounds early—he made it in just under two minutes. Just for once, he refused a cigarette and listened without interruption. He turned things over in his mind briefly. Then—

"Well, sir, I guess I can help out. Can't stand twenty-four-hour guard, but I guess I could look in frequently. Supplies—no sweat, with a few smokes to trade. Main hang-up as far as I can see is—what in hell is she going to do all day, up here by herself? She can't go out alone—and it won't take the local Jacks more'n a day or two to locate a juicy target like that. I don't want last night every night—you know?"

I knew.

"So—okay. But you tell her, she does like I say and no argument. She opens the door to no one but me. Anyone comes by to see her, I call on the phone first. She keeps that door locked tight, and if she has to go somewhere, she tells me first. Deal?"

"Deal, John. And thanks. You can brief her yourself if you like."

Kate came in from the bathroom rosy-faced and visibly shocked. "She won't say when she had a bath last, Jonah. Ashamed, I think. I threw her clothes out of the window—they were *crawling!* John, could you stoke up the kitchen stove, like an angel?"

He stood up stiffly. "Sure thing."

I shifted uneasily, listening to the distant street noises. A little like Sunday morning back home, I thought—no traffic, occasional sound of footsteps. I found myself listening for the church bells.

Far away, I heard a shot—and another. I thought I heard a scream, too—very faint, echoing in my mind. This was a strange, a savage city; after the Collapse and its seven days of bloodletting, world opinion had given New York a month to survive. It was still living, but it seemed to me that the downwards trend was irreversible. It might just take a little longer than first expected—a New Yorker is as tough and adaptable and resilient as the Cockneys in the Blitz. But a new D-Day? I couldn't see it.

I kept coming back to last night. Recurring Technicolor nightmare. Who was the man I shot? Had he had a name, a home, parents, somewhere? Someone may have married him, loved him. For what? To have his brains spread over a painted wall by half an ounce of lead traveling at 1200 feet a second?

It made no sense.

Chances were, he wasn't born a killer. Maybe he had been an ordinary kid, riding a bike to school, playing baseball on empty lots, smoking in school lavatories, graduating, job hunting. Getting married in some church.

I began to think about churches. Never been involved, myself. Me, I'll go to churches three times. Been twice already—christening, wedding. One more trip to go. I'd always had too much of a logical engineering background to accept things without corroboration, to accept things just on faith. You can try taking off a full-loaded airplane trusting in faith the tanks are full, you have the right flap setting and that all engines are going to work. You can try it—but it won't become a habit. Every pilot craves confirmation—that tanks are full, that altimeter is set right, the speed on landing is correct. Aviation is a logical and prescribed world, subject to natural laws of immense symmetry, beauty and significance, in which nothing is left to chance.

If the winter forecast says "rain," I know there is a cold front around someplace without being psychic. I know because the pressure and temperature are falling and the wind is veering, perhaps from west to north. I know if I stand with my back to the wind in the Northern Hemisphere, there is a low-pressure area on my left, because winds always circulate anticlockwise around a depression north of the Equator. Never clockwise. It has been that way since the beginning of time—and always will be.

With laws like that, belief in facts is ingrained in the pilot. No faith, finger crossing, crystal balls, horoscopes. How can he believe in something that happened two thousand years ago, a story passed on by word of mouth through fifty generations? How could I be expected to believe in a thing like that?

Sometimes I hoped I was wrong—for the sake of the billions who died for their beliefs, the millions who gave up

their lives to enter the priesthood. Because if I was right—
it had all been a hell of a waste of time.

I lit another Low Tar Special.

Besides, I pondered, look at the state of this Garden of
Eden. Nations at war. People being robbed, mugged, mur-
dered. Being talked to death, preached to death, worked to
death. Earthquakes, floods, famine and disease. From Libya
to Nigeria, the Gold Coast to Somalia, not a living human
being. Only locusts—countless billions of them. Last I heard,
they'd eaten all the vegetation and were now eating each
other. And breeding every eight weeks.

Kate came back, carrying a spare uniform skirt and my
best white shirt. I opened my mouth to protest, saw the look
in her eyes and closed it again. She draped the shirt from the
mantel to freshen up, hung the skirt over the coffee table and
went off to find some shoes.

There was one log left. I poked away at the hot embers
with it, made a shallow hole, dropped it in.

Down in the street, an odd grating sound was followed by
a crash of breaking glass. I went to the window, stared down.
The street, as usual, was waist deep in garbage, stacked into
long piles. Down the block, on the far side, half a dozen people
were hauling on a rope tied to a wrecked car, half buried in
a shopfront. Two men were bossing the show, carrying automatic shotguns at the ready; the sound I had heard was the
collapse of the shop-window remnants. The gunners moved
fast; one stood guard; the other moved catlike into the shop.
The scavengers stood around listlessly waiting their turn.
The gunner reappeared, carrying a loaded sack which made
his knees buckle; he nodded to his partner and they walked
away. The mob poured in for the leavings, and I moved away
from the window, depressed and upset.

I began to notice the unnatural quiet: only the whine of
the wind, blowing the garbage into whirling vortices in back
alleys; streets barren of people, birds, animals. Not even a
rat—because the garbage had been sieved long since of anything edible.

5

I felt tired, jaded. I knew I worried too much about things out of my control—it came with the job. In recent years I'd seen plenty of misery and suffering, in a score of countries, and there seemed to be many cracks appearing in the facade of civilization. Rhodesia, and now America. Idi Amin, flying back to Kampala with a hundred pounds of explosives smuggled aboard, spreading his influence around a wide area of Africa—very wide, because they never found so much as a medal. Cuban mercenaries throughout Africa. Uruguayan Red Brigade in Haiti. The Polish Freedom Brigade locked in another Warsaw ghetto. The Chinese in Panama in strength, in Pakistan in milllions and Taiwan by invasion. The Dutch were back in the East Indies by force, using nerve gas to clear millions of square miles of jungle. There were stories of submarine pirate tankers sucking at other people's wells, hunted by killer subs of the oil conglomerates like Shell, Exxon and Mobil.

I stirred restlessly. Dammit, I told myself. Do your job, just keep your nose clean, and quit worrying.

I turned. Nickie came in, feet bare, wrapped in Kate's bathrobe, and made for the fire. The vast hair thatch swung this way and that in the welcome heat, and she slid me a quick shy smile. I took a longer look: she seemed softer, less scrawny, even feminine, and I thought Jerry Chambers was no bad judge of women at that.

"Feeling better, Nickie?"

"Mm-hmm. Thanks. Never thought I'd be clean again—or safe, even for an hour or two. May I call you Jonah?"

I laughed out loud, and it felt good. "Folks generally do," I conceded. "I hear you've had a rough time lately."

"Ah," she said softly, "you know it, you know it. Did Jerry tell you? Well, I'm not complaining, Jonah. People can adapt, you know. To anything. Do you know there is hardly any mental illness around these days? People who can't compensate can't survive . . . so some learn. Maybe it was for the best, the way the sky fell on us."

Surprised, I stared at her, impressed despite myself. "You talk like a shrink."

"Right," she said calmly. "I finished my training four years ago, in psychiatric social work." She smiled at my surprise.

"I'm trying to adjust myself," I said, "to thinking about you as someone not totally helpless. Jerry worries about you—but I think you're a survivor, Nickie. Right?"

"Right." She grinned impishly, throwing her hair back behind slim shoulders. I like a woman I don't have to talk down to; with Nickie barefoot, her head came almost up to my eye level.

I said, "I've arranged for you to stay here for a while. Till you get organized. The gentleman dozing in the corner is John Capel—looks after the building. He is going to keep away salesmen, debt collectors and things that go bump in the night. But you have to do what he says—savvy?"

She stared, breathless. "You mean I can live here—on my own? Till Jerry comes back again?"

"Sure. Think you can cope?"

Nickie came close to me, and I caught the clean, sweet woman smell of her; my breathing gave me a little trouble. She wrapped warm arms round my neck and kissed me with that broad generous mouth and everything she had.

"Jonah Scott," she said firmly, "I want you to know you're a good person and I love you."

"And Jerry?"

"I'm *in* love with Jerry—but I still love you. Thank you, Jonah."

I put that one aside for future reference. Behind me, Kate said explosively:

"Charming!"

I let Nickie go. Reluctantly—she was sort of lean but cuddly, a paradox in a bathrobe.

"I've told Nickie she can stay here, Kate."

"I heard. You staying too?"

"Temper, temper..."

"I don't care, you know," Kate said defiantly. "We don't need you to get home. Jerry can do it, if you want a little holiday."

"Don't push it, honey," Nickie told her. "He's your problem, not mine. And never tell a guy you can get along without him. He might believe you. Mine did, years ago—and went back to Tulsa, Oklahoma."

Kate tried to keep a straight face, failed, and we all laughed. She got the clothes together, draped them over Nickie's arm. "Go change. And don't tell me about pushing my luck when you're hoofing around almost naked and two sex mechanics within ten feet."

"I heard that," said John Capel, "and I'm proud to admit it was once true. Hi, Nickie—we're to be neighbors, they say."

She nodded, gray eyes twinkling, and shook his hand. "Right. May I call you John?"

I decided she used that gambit with all men, because even I got a glow when she worked it on me. Trust a trick cyclist to use loaded questions, I thought.

Capel preened visibly. "Sure you can. Why don't you go dress and we can talk it through?"

Chambers returned soon after that, paid off Charlie Hackett and bought two dozen eggs from him. The girls swooped on the treasure and started on a king-sized omelette; we lay around loose eating it from paper plates looted from Delta Tango, and I sat apart a little, listening to the chatter. Capel and Nickie were discussing security and reminiscing about New York restaurants. Her skirt-and-shirt combination fitted—a little tightly, and in no way did she resemble the ragamuffin we had first seen. Her hair turned out to be a strange natural shade somewhere between blond, auburn and gray.

Had she any future, here in New York? Living alone, between our irregular flights into JFK? She and Jerry kept exchanging glances, brief paragraphs in some silent language; I didn't want to lose a good officer, despite his personal habits, but it was very plain he'd resign rather than leave her here.

What made me do it?

Don't ask. There is no logical simple reason why I began to think about taking chances; but if you figure that I might have found it difficult to live with myself if I hadn't tried to help those kids, you'd be close.

I caught Kate's eye, jerked my head towards the kitchen. She nodded, followed me out. "Shut the door, love. Right. Come here, you jealous bitch..." I could taste the omelette. She relaxed, worked her way in closer and tried it again.

"Listen, Kate." I held her round the waist and she leaned back, eyes wide. "Nickie, out there. Could she get into your uniform?"

"I....Oh, yes. Yes, Jonah dear."

"Never mind the compliments. Okay—she travels back out to the field with us. I'll get Charlie to take us right to the aircraft. It'll be dark by five thirty Eastern Standard Time. Anyone asks, she's one of the new girls from Canada. Her papers are in her bag on board. Once aboard, she's all yours—you keep her hidden and you keep her away from Chambers until we're clear of St. John's. I don't want old Mortensen spotting her—right?"

"Yes, Jonah. Bless you."

"I told you—cut that out. Put her in the compartment behind the glass screen in the VIP lounge until the passengers start boarding. Then up to the flight deck. Got it?"

"Yes, Jonah. Don't worry. Now—what about London?"

"Christ, Kate, I haven't got as far as that yet. I have to walk before I can run."

Kate nodded.

"Now, go get her briefed and dressed—and make sure she looks right."

Kate said tartly, "Don't teach your grandmother to suck eggs, me man. Jonah, this is the nicest thing you've ever done and I won't mess it up for you. You know what? Play your cards right and you could get yourself a bonus—if I can find five minutes to spare."

"Only five minutes?"

"That includes dressing, you ape," she twinkled.

"Huh," I said dourly. "I wouldn't have time to scream for help—or enjoy it."

"You wanna bet?"

I spent a few moments trying to improve our kissing technique—a difficult exercise because Kate started giggling, having spotted John Capel over my shoulder. He stood grinning, carrying a loaded tray of dishes. I thought, What the hell...this man saved my life last night, and I was going to leave him to rot in this cesspit. I looked at Kate and damn me if she wasn't thinking the same thing. I turned to Capel.

"Listen, Wyatt Earp," I said softly, "how would you like a trip on a magic carpet tonight—courtesy of Air Britain?"

He dropped the tray. Heads began poking round the door, and I said, "Get lost, kids. We adults are talking business." Chambers and Nickie withdrew, mystified.

Capel said hoarsely, "Say that again?"

His face was grim, disbelieving, but I could see that it was lighted up inside with joy, and I knew I was doing the right thing. I said very slowly, "John, if we can figure some way to get you on the aircraft, you'll be in London tomorrow morning. Now—passport?"

"Yeah. Right."

"Do you want out—for good?"

"You'd better believe it."

"Can you be ready by five o'clock?"

"Jonah, I'm ready now. There isn't anything I want to take with me."

I stopped to think for a moment. If it would work for Nickie...

"I'll tell you how it might work. In my uniform, at night, we look near enough alike. Same height, same build. You ride in the front with Charlie. Nickie's coming too—in Kate's clothes; they ride in the back. Kate will front for Nickie, but you'll be on your own. Jerry can ride in back with the girls."

Capel nodded. "Understood. But how about you?"

I'd been thinking about that myself. There was one possible answer—and the more I thought about it the more I hesitated...

"No sweat, John," I said at last. "Believe me. Now, let's get this thing on the road. We get together at four P.M. to thrash out the details. Charlie collects us around five, we get to the field about six when it's dark. One thing, John: no one must know. It means leaving your tenants flat, but it can't be helped. One whisper of what's planned and there'll be a queue from here to St. John's. Understood?"

"Right. Listen, Jonah—I got something to say, but I don't know—"

"Don't try. It was all said last night. We'd have been cold mutton but for you."

Capel's eyes traveled from me to Kate and back again. He shook his head, mumbled something about "Goddamn pokerfaced Limeys!" and straightened his shoulders, turned and marched out. I told myself I was all kinds of a bloody fool— but somehow, it did not seem important.

Charlie Hackett's cab had a full load and complained bitterly, bouncing over the hard-packed street rubbish and open potholes. Charlie wasn't too happy about it either, but cheered up when I told him the score. I sat between Charlie and John Capel on the front seat, wearing a shirt, slacks and denim jacket donated by Capel. The old boy looked quite the part: Kate had trimmed his hair, shaded out much of the gray hair with mascara, and my uniform was a reasonable fit, if a little long in the leg.

As we drove out through East 59th Street making for the Queensboro Bridge, I briefed Charlie.

"John here has all my papers, and we are all crew members—Nickie is a stewardess, and she has a cover story ready. Jerry can answer any awkward questions. The Airborne lads on the gate know most of us well enough, and we have a good chance of getting through without trouble. But you have to take us right out to the aircraft, Charlie—Jerry will show you the way. Jerry—you got your story off pat?"

Chambers grinned broadly. He lifted up his right leg. The trouser leg was rolled halfway to the knee and the ankle was bound with white bandage, three times normal size. It had taken the last of Ted's sheets—but it could work, with luck. "I've got a badly sprained ankle, can't walk, and I want to get back home to get it fixed. No medical care available here."

"Right. Once at the aircraft, Kate and Nickie help you inside, John gets the bags."

"You haven't said what *you're* going to do, Jonah," Kate said angrily, "I suppose you're going to wait outside the gates for Charlie to pick you up?"

"No, love. We all go together or not at all. Charlie stops half a mile before we reach the main gate. I climb into the boot—there's plenty of room—and Charlie parks where I showed him—inside the main landing gear, port side, with the car in the shadow. While Jerry goes up the forward steps, I nip out, up into the port undercarriage, and sit tight until everything is quiet."

Kate was horrified. "But—that awful smell, Jonah—you won't be able to breathe!"

"Sure I can. Charlie found me a short length of radiator hose—that's it sticking up through the back luggage shelf. It's plugged at the bottom end at the moment to stop the smell coming through. I'll only be in there five or ten minutes, Kate—I'll survive."

"But why there, Jonah? Of all places?"

"Because the guards all know Charlie's cab—and the smell from the devil's brew in back. They wouldn't go nearer than five yards themselves, and it doesn't make sense that anyone would actually get in there. Simple."

There was plenty of comment—but no alternative suggestions. The only thing I worried about was Charlie—it could be very awkward for him if we ran into trouble.

The big man wasn't worried. "They won't bother me none, Cap'n. I'm just drivin' the hack—what do I know if some knothead decides to climb in the trunk? Besides, you're doing a good thing and I'm happy to help. Don't you fret—I'll make it okay. You let me know when you want to stop."

It was dark now, with a massive buildup of cloud in the west and a cold, damp feel to the night. We sat silently for most of the time, listening to the asthmatic intermittency of the motor, looking out at the wet, deserted streets. Once on Long Island and heading out into the suburbs, the rare street lights became nonexistent, and there were long stretches with not a living person to be seen. Here and there, lighted windows showed, mostly in the upper levels of the buildings: ground-level accommodation was undesirable—high-risk. I saw perhaps half a dozen other vehicles, some cyclists, a single open horse-drawn cheap taxi with shotgun guard alongside the driver, the passengers huddled under coats and makeshift hoods.

I began to work on plans for dealing with the security at Heathrow. John and Nickie would have to stay aboard until the craft was refueled, cleaned, all the postflight checks carried out. I tried to visualize the Flight Program: when was Delta Tango scheduled out again? Airplanes don't earn money standing on the ground, and another crew would be ready to take her over—she'd be on the ground six, maybe eight hours at the most. Then—where? America again, perhaps; Rio; Johannesburg; Beirut en route for Australia; maybe even Hong Kong.

It meant I would have no more than an hour or two to get them out. I could talk to one or two of the ground engineers—but that didn't seem a good idea; it only needed one careless comment to start an investigation. There was only one real possibility; they could hide in the used food containers after the aircraft was provisioned. The big alloy boxes were handled almost wholly by machinery, loaded and off-loaded on pallets and forklifts, moved around on wheels inside the cabins.

Which got John and Nickie as far as the yard of the container depot, where the boxes were cleaned and sterilized before further use. Past that, I got stuck. I felt tired, very insecure and worried out of my wits.

"There she is, folks," Charlie was saying—"JFK." The glow reflected on the low clouds, a mile or two ahead. I gulped, buttoned up the denim jacket.

"Anywhere along here, Charlie. You know what to do?" I asked him, anxiously. The white teeth flashed in the darkened cab. "Sure, Cap'n. Good luck."

"I'll need it," I said quietly. "Play it cool, now—come and lock me in."

We walked round to the back of the car and he lifted the trunk lid. A wave of warm, stinking air hit me in the face, and I staggered back a pace or two.

"Ain't she something?" demanded Charlie proudly. "Wouldn't go back to gasoline if you paid me."

I took a long look in the red glow of the tail lamps. The big fifteen-gallon tank in the right half of the trunk was connected to a small electrical compressor, which forced the methane up to the roof-mounted storage bag; there were masses of spaghetti pipe, the purpose of which escaped me, and a big metal toolbox which Charlie shoved to one side to make room. The plugged end of the radiator hose showed six inches to spare at the hole in the back panel we'd made that afternoon.

I took a deep breath, climbed in, wriggled around until my head was as close to the breather pipe as possible and gave Charlie the thumb. He nodded, grinned and shut down the lid. I had barely enough time to ask myself how in hell I'd got myself into a jam like this when the pump whined, the car jerked forward and I was on my way.

The breather pipe worked fine—which was just as well. I pressed my nose into the end, breathed in slowly and found the stench just about bearable. Better still, I found I could hear conversation very well indeed if I took a breath, held it and got my ear to the pipe.

Charlie: "Just relax, folks...he's fine. There's the gate up ahead. Say—there's an officer there. You know him at all, Miss Kate?"

Kate: "I can't see....Wait a minute....Yes—that's Captain Marcovitch. We're in luck."

I had to take another breath. Then—

Kate: "—me do the talking, Jerry. Here we go...."

Voice: "Okay. Stay loose, folks—routine check. Why, it's Miss Monahan."

Kate: "Hello, Joe. How are you?"

Captain Marcovitch: "Just fine. Just fine. Say—you lost Captain Scott?"

Kate: "No—he's coming out later. You know Captain Chambers?"

Marco: "Sure. What in hell have you done to your leg, sir?"

Another long breath. I came back on the air as Jerry finished saying his piece.

Jerry: "—okay when I get home. Trouble is, I can't walk too far. Charlie here can take me straight out to the aircraft—if that's all right?"

Marco, after a pause: "I don't see why not. I don't believe I know these other folks, Miss Monahan...?"

Kate: "This is Captain John Capel and Miss Bassett—they came into Dulles with one of our tanker aircraft from St. John's and went unserviceable. They came up to New York by road and found us this morning. They're going out on the tanker that brought our fuel in."

I needed two or three long breaths and missed the soldier's reply. It must have been satisfactory because the car started up again, and I knew we were past the first hurdle. A cold, wet wind blew around my feet. My cheek was tingling, and I could see a broad black shape bending over me.

"Cap'n! Mr. Scott—move it, fella! C'mon—hit the deck!"

I clambered out unsteadily, leaned against the open lid of the trunk and stared glassily at Charlie in the shadow of the

797's gear. The gas had really got to me. "I'm all right, Charlie. Must have passed out for a minute. No problems?"

"No, Captain. Everything's just fine. They're all on board safe—but there are some troops the other side of those steps. I gotta go. Good luck, sir. See you next time, okay?"

"Sure. And—thanks, Charlie. Look after yourself."

The big man nodded, grinned and moved away. I got up onto the main gear, up the radius struts into the nacelle, found a comfortable corner against a service hatch and settled down to sweat it out. A dozen times in the next hour, people passed under the wing: ground engineers, catering operators.

Hand-hauled baggage trucks shuttled back and forth, men in rubber slickers cursing the rain as they moved bags into the holds, fore and aft.

When I had heard nothing for ten minutes except the constant beat of rain on the aircraft, the trickle of water onto the concrete, I came down slowly and quietly, crouched in the shadow of the big wheels and checked out the area. Captain Marcovitch had his men out at the hundred-yard perimeter at ten-yard intervals; I saw the sergeants making their rounds. There were four two-man patrols making random walks between Delta Tango and the nearest buildings, and two more soldiers standing under the tail, talking to a ground engineer and looking up at the tail section.

I got aboard in two moves: one to the bottom of the steps, the second straight up into the doorway between seat rows 8 and 9. Kate stood inside the hatch, waiting anxiously.

"All right?"

"Yes, Jonah.... You've been so long..."

"Couldn't be helped, love. God, I stink. What's the situation?"

"Nickie's in back of the VIP lounge. Cold, but okay. Jerry and Capel are on the flight deck."

"Anyone else aboard?"

"No. We've got all the meals stowed away. I sent a message with Chalky White for the girls to be here by eleven. Is that all right?"

I checked my watch. Just after 8:30 ... plenty of time. But with Jerry "lame," I'd have to complete Flight Planning and Clearance myself....

"Super, Kate. There may be a problem down at the back end—I saw one of the engineers doing a visual check just now. As soon as the passengers start to board, give Nickie some hand baggage and get her into the jump seat at Gate 1 Starboard. She's not to talk to anyone—and for God's sake don't let Mortensen see her. I'll try to keep him off the airplane. Okay?"

"I think so. Yes—fine, Jonah."

"All right." I kissed her quickly and went up the spiral stairs to the flight deck. Jerry was in the galley organizing a hot drink. I nodded, grinned and thumped on the toilet door.

"John? It's me—Scott. Open up."

Capel came out, my uniform jacket over his arm. "Problems?"

"No," I said, pleased. "It all went off fine—except for the smell. You're not going to like wearing these togs. . . . I have to clean up, change and get over to Flight Planning. Get stripped off, quick as you can, while I wash."

"Right!"

Chambers stuck his head round the corner of the galley. "I have a spare shirt and trousers which might fit, Skipper. . . . Where's Nickie? Is she all right?"

"Keep your mind on making coffee," I said sternly. "She's okay. Where are these pants?"

"In my bag in the locker—Number Three over there. Help yourself . . . and don't come too close to me: that pong is awful."

I snorted. "I won't have insubordination in my crew. One more word and you wear these things yourself. Where's Ben Price?"

"Our engineer is with Chalky White, Skip. He wasn't too happy about Number Five jet pipe temperatures, remember?" from the galley.

"Ah . . . yes. They were within limits, weren't they?"

Chambers brought out paper cups of steaming coffee just as I got down to my underwear. "I reckon—in steady cruise, anyway. On takeoff and climb they fluctuated a little, red-lined once or twice. Ben thought it could be a faulty instrument, but with duplicated circuitry. Chalky wasn't sure."

"Refueling?"

"All checked out, Skipper. I went over the load sheet with Chalky myself, and Ben has the external check to do when he gets back."

I filled the hand basin, started washing the clinging odor of chicken crap out of my hair. In the gangway, Capel pulled the belt tight on his slacks, hung my uniform jacket on the door peg and found a comb. Ten minutes later, I was clean and dressed and felt very much the better for it. One cigarette with the second cup of coffee and I was ready for the next round. I got my flight bag out, checked it through and met Kate at the forward hatch.

"Well...so far, we've been lucky, Kate. All right down here?"

"Everything's fine, Jonah. And Nickie is so excited...Does she really have to stay in there till we start loading?" Kate said pleadingly.

"Use your head, girl. Anyone can walk in, any minute, and start asking questions. John Capel's safe enough in the flight-deck toilet, and everything seems normal on board. It must stay that way until we're off the ground. Luckily, there's quite a bit of other traffic on the board: our tanker is going back to Canada without a night stop—they're short of aircraft—and Jerry says there are four Army transports going out to the West Coast anytime now. Once we clear Gander Control, I'll call you up front and we can work on London. What about your girls: are you going to put them in the picture?"

Kate nibbled her lip briefly. "I don't think I should. Most of them I can trust, but there are others...I think Nickie should come up to the flight deck as soon as we leave the ground, before the girls start circulating. I'll sit up here for takeoff on the jump seat."

"That sounds good," I agreed. "Well—play it as it comes. I'm going to Planning and Weather—and I want a good look at the passenger list. There may be someone aboard who could help."

She stared at me, mouth trembling a bit. "I never thought you'd take a chance like this, Jonah...it's awfully risky."

"I had to find," I said slowly, "some way of repaying you for—last night. It seemed as good a way as any. Besides...Jerry has the chance of finding something like Julie and I used to have—like you and I have now—and life's too chancy these days to worry about the future. Now...give me a Monahan Special before I go."

Her arms went round my neck. That Special was something *really* special.

The process of flying a big jet across the North Atlantic has changed very much during the last ten years, since I started. In those days, the weather situation was like the poor—always with us—and we simply accepted the conditions that we met along the Great Circle tracks we flew. A great circle is the shortest distance between two points on a globe, and involves changes of heading to cross the meridians of longitude at the angles necessary to make it good. A rhumb line, on the other hand, crosses all meridians of longitude at the same angle, but involves a longer distance over the land (or sea, as the case may be).

Now we feed into a computer the Great Circle tracks and the upper wind speeds and air temperatures. This produces a comprehensive analysis of "best time" tracks from which the captain can make his selection. If, for example, there is a jet stream—a very fast linear air current—to the south of the Great Circle track producing the shortest distance, adding perhaps a hundred knots to the ground speed of the airplane, it makes sense to fly the longer route.

The Meteorological Briefing Room was warm, well lit, and I lit a cigarette while studying the general situation map.

It was typical autumn weather in the North Atlantic. The big depression over Greenland showed the close concentric isobars that signaled very low pressure and strong winds. Across the mid-ocean area a long ridge of higher pressure slanted up towards Scandinavia, with a second large depression over the Low Countries and Germany. That meant cold, blustery northeast winds, low clouds and rain for London, unless the low moved away at high speed. Knowing a little of the habits of depressions, the best I could expect there was something like 25 knots over the ground, which would still place it much too close to the U.K. for comfort when we arrived in less than twelve hours.

The present New York weather came from an occlusion over the Great Lakes, a situation that would not improve until the parent depression over the Midwest moved on through into the Atlantic, for all products of the great depression factory which is North America move eventually eastwards.

So I could look forward to a full load, wet runway, increasingly heavy rain and entry into cloud at less than a thousand feet. No icing risk—not that icing was much of a problem. I would get an updated local weather report over the JFK Control frequency after start-up—the automatic taped broadcast was changed every hour and given a letter of the alphabet for identification.

I watched the flying fingers as the spectacled forecaster fed data into his computer terminal. He passed me a copy of the printout, and I sat down to read.

We would have to climb out to 37,000 feet—Flight Level 370—and allow the altitude to increase, if we wished, as the weight of fuel was consumed. Alternatively, we could elect to allow our cruising speed to increase. At FL 370, we would hitch a ride from the westerly winds below the Greenland depression, stay above the clear air-turbulence layer and make a good fast crossing. That pointed to Track X-Ray, which looped well south of the Great Circle track, giving Delta Tango a total flight time of about seven and a half hours. Not too bad at all.

Every 797 carries three sets of Inertial Navigation Systems, and up to nine "way points" may be fed into the sets at any one time. A way point is simply a geographical position, in latitude and longitude, and when a pilot engages the autopilot, the airplane flies along the track connecting the way points.

This sounds very simple, but anyone who thinks a pilot earns his money easily is very mistaken. Twenty million pounds' worth of airplane and six hundred passengers are at risk if just one of the millions of components in a critical system fails—unless the pilot does what he is trained to do, quickly, correctly and without hesitation. One aircraft, one passenger load saved and the pilot has earned his crust for the whole of his life: and at those prices, 25K to 30K a year is bargain rate.

Ben Price came in as I finished the clearance in Departure Control.

"Hello, Skipper. All clear—we found that electrical fault on Number Five. And we put in a new inverter. Takeoff time?"

"Hi, Ben. Oh oh ten Eastern Standard. What about fuel?"

"We have 177,500 kilos of fuel for a total flight time of nine hours. What's the flight-plan time?"

I checked the clearance and flight plan. "Seven hours ten," I told him. "Alternates Manchester, Gatwick and Paris Charles de Gaulle."

He nodded, satisfied. "That sounds okay, Skipper. Full load as usual, I take it?"

"Check. Passengers 588, crew 27, total 615. We're about ten thousand kilos under maximum permissible weight—

surface wind's only about twenty knots. Passengers start boarding at 23:15, doors closed 23:40, taxi at 23:50, take off 00:10. We may get off early—there's not much traffic out tonight, I understand. Bunch of Army transports going west around eleven, a Varig Airbus at thirty minutes after the hour. A Lufthansa 747 to Bonn due out about our time, and only four inbound flights."

"Okay." I watched the little plump hands writing quickly on his pad. Ben was a good engineer; like all the best ones, he had come up through the ground-engineer network and probably knew as much about the 797 as the Boeing designers. I inherited Ben when we moved onto the Jumbos—and never regretted it.

I thought for a moment, sitting in the deserted Departure Control. "Come and sit down for a minute, Ben. We have a little problem...."

He listened quietly as I told him about John and Nickie— as much as he needed to know. True to form, he made no attempts to criticize—only to help.

"What can I do, Skip?"

"Nothing—yet, Ben. The thing worrying me most is London. And getting them off the aircraft. I can get them out of Heathrow all right—but you know what security is like now."

"Don't I just. It's a hell of a problem. Any ideas?"

I explained about the foot containers. Ben scratched his chin and looked uncertain.

"Offhand, I can't think of anything better, Skipper. I don't like it very much, but—let me work on it a while. I have a very rough idea in mind...."

I knew Ben Price of old. It was more than a rough idea. I felt a surge of confidence.

"Okay, Ben—keep in touch. But I don't want you involved personally, right? If the crunch comes, you know nothing. Now—grab my flight bag and take it back with you. I'm going to Main Reception for a look at the passenger list...there may be someone on board who could help. I'll be back before boarding time."

Ben stood up, a grin splitting his moon face. "Right. You've changed, you know."

"Me? Changed?" I said suspiciously.

"Mm-hmm. More human. Relaxed. We all think so."

"So, little man—you discuss your Captain behind his back?" I accused.

"But of course." He grinned impishly. "Why not? You're public property."

He beat a hasty retreat, and I shook my head despairingly. People, sometimes, made little or no sense.

6

Walt Eisemann in Passenger Control looked up. "Hi, Captain. How are you?"

"Fine. What have you got for us?"

"Full load—you know that?"

"Surprise, surprise," I said sardonically. There hadn't been a spare seat out of Kennedy these last eighteen months. I walked over to the window overlooking the Main Reception Hall. Almost a thousand people, in an area planned for half that number. Many were standing—had been standing for twenty-four hours or more, afraid of losing their places. Half the next aircraft load were allowed to attend in case of cancellations or vacancies. It was a fair-enough system. If your seat number was the same as a cancellation and you were there, you got the empty seat. If you weren't there, the seat went into a draw so all had the same chance.

No holiday crowd, this. Too many shabbily dressed, underfed people, thin-faced, haunted by dreams of new lives in Europe. Scheduled passengers were easily identified: the inner glow of anticipation, ready smile, resigned patience. The others—the backups—rarely looked away from the big digital-readout clock overhead. It told no time: vacant seat numbers came up like an automobile odometer. They called it the Wheel of Fortune, running from 0 to maximum seat capacity—in our case, 588.

It began clicking as I watched, and a sea of faces stared upward. It slowed, stopped on 403; away down the concourse, a small, nondescript man in a long black coat yelled exuberantly, grabbed his bags and began to fight his way to the check-in.

Beside me, Walt Eisemann said, "It always gets to me, Scotty. What happened to the real owner of that seat? Missing? Dead? Or just late? We never know. They get their seat allocation six weeks before flight time—and they still miss it. I've seen them get here five minutes too late.... God, I couldn't take it myself."

"You and me both," I admitted. "But it's a fair system, Walt. We're all gamblers."

"Yeah." He scowled, walking back to his desk. "Only we're all losers here."

I cocked my head on one side, "Aw, come off it, Walt. Don't cry on this shoulder—it's wet. Try this one...."

He laughed, a little forced and rueful. "Okay, okay...goddamn Brits. What can I do for you, anyway?"

I told him I wanted a sight of the passenger list. He got out a copy, punched his computer terminal, made an alteration at No. 403, fed it into the terminal and gave me a printout. I sat on the edge of his desk, ran my fingers down the list. Zone L First—the VIP deck. Twelve seats: four Russians (probably U.N. personnel going home via London). I looked at the booking date—two days ago. Someone was in a hurry. The Thunderman—I recognized the name. Pop star extraordinary, complete with girl Friday. A bunch of eggheads—Professor this, Dr. that. What else? I found a block booking for sixty seats through Zone Z amidships—down to UKMOD. What in hell was the Ministry of Defense doing with sixty civil seats—had Strike Command run out of transports? I checked it out with Eisemann.

"Oh—that bunch. Company of your Special Air Service boys. Been over here for eight weeks training the National Guard conscripts in street fighting."

"Well, they should know how," I commented. "They've spent plenty of time in Northern Ireland."

"Right. They'll be glad to get home, I guess. I hear they lost several guys cleaning up those Filipinos in Queens. Molotov cocktails from rooftops."

Apropos of nothing, I said, "Where do they get the gas?"

Eisemann shook his head. "Who knows? They won't tell. The SAS boys scratched them all. They were very annoyed, I hear tell."

"I'm not surprised," I said flatly. I turned back to the window, watching the teeming throng below. It was a stinking world, I thought. Dirty, stinking rotten cesspool. You could fly over the ground ten miles below, in the clean bright air, and it all seemed remote and peaceful. Lift up the skin of civilization...and the maggots and the stench were unbearable. This Earth could have been a paradise...all any man needed was a home, a little security and a family to love. I started in thinking about Julie again, and wrenched my traitor mind away violently.

Just who in hell, I thought, gave all these people the right to start wars, cause food shortages, ferment industrial action? Who licensed the polluters, the killers, the thieves and the hooligans?

Human values were crazily inverted. Crime paid. The 500,000-pound embezzler got two years, suspended; the hungry shoplifter, five years. The violator was encouraged, "rehabilitated"—but no one gave a damn for the victim.

There were times when I was so damned ashamed, just being a himan being.

"Captain?"

"Huh?" I swung round. Eisemann was looking at me with an odd expression on his face. "Oh—Walt. Sorry—I was miles away. Be with you in a moment."

I got back to the passenger list. These people in the VIP lounge...Dr. Moshe Rabin? Dr. Sven Olaffsen, Dr. K. G. Waldheim, Prof. Karl Volkel? That last one rang a bell.... Of course—not medical doctors. They were scientists and geologists from the Emergency World Conference on Alternative Power Sources in Washington, called by President Langford. I hoped they had achieved something—but I doubted it.

There was a second block booking in Zone D, aft of the SAS detachment—eighty-two seats for IRC? Oh, yes. We had a similar load two flights back—International Red Cross, with a party of eight adults and seventy-four homeless kids. Ages six to eleven, I noted. There were probably another hundred children among the emigrants—Kate would be real busy.

"More kids than usual," I commented, passing the list back to Eisemann.

"Yeah. Expecting trouble?"

"None we can't handle," I told him drily. "Besides, those SAS boys'll keep 'em quiet. Got the manifests ready?"

He nodded. "Sure. Speedbird Flight 626, Kennedy to London Heathrow direct. Not much freight; those SAS troops have some gear in the hold—ammunition and the like. Security's cleared it under seal."

I didn't like the sound of "ammunition" very much. I dumped the butt of my Split in Walt's ashtray, saw his lugubrious expression and gave him the half-pack remaining.

"Thanks, Scotty. Never thought I'd be happy smoking grass—it started my kids on the hard stuff. But I'm beginning to see things their way—it makes this shitty world smell a mite better. Temporarily."

I nodded. "And no hangover. Got to go—take care of that cough, Walt."

"Sure thing. Good luck, Scotty. Watch the weather, right?"

"Right. So long."

I went out, down the stairs and down the long, dimly lit corridor to Main Reception. I passed one or two security officers in 83rd Airborne olive-green drab, and two gorgeous Lufthansa stewardesses who didn't even glance when I walked by. So up yours too, Frauleins....

At the check-in desk, Rosie Van Heusen had tangled with an Armenian-American family. Only the five-year-old grandson spoke English—of a sort. She was having a hard time, but eventually got them squared away. I checked the time...10:38 EST. They would start boarding in about twenty minutes. I said cheerfully, "Hello, my darling!"

She let loose a big smile.

"Any VIPs in the lounge, Rosie?"

Despite her surname, our Rosie is as English as her Christian name—with a fruity Birmingham accent to prove it. Heart of gold, generous to a fault and quite unflappable—except when someone made a pass. Despite the invariable success which rewarded the prospectors (see above under "generous"), she still got flustered and blushed with every new proposition. Besides, it was good for business—and certainly good for Rosie, who bloomed more each day.

"Ah—Captain Scott. I was going to have you paged. Yes—about a dozen. Are you going to see them?"

"I'd thought about it." Correction—I'd thought about giving it a miss; but Airbrit rules were strict on etiquette.

"Fine," Rosie gushed. "And could you call back here before boarding? I'm having trouble with these soldiers."

"Why, Rosie," I said reproachfully. "And there's only about

sixty of them...." She screamed—but not too loud. "You're an awful man, Captain Scott. Not that way; I'm having trouble getting them in here. Their officer says they will sit outside in the American Army transports until they go aboard."

I couldn't see anything difficult about that, and said so. "Have you seen Mr. Mortensen around?"

"No, Mr. Scott. He doesn't answer his telephone—that yucky American takes messages for him. They say such awful things about him and I wonder at times like this if they are true. He should be here, you know."

I knew—but that was Morty, every time. I patted Rosie sympathetically on the rump, grinned at her grateful squeal and worked my way through the crowd to the VIP lounge upstairs.

It was spacious and reasonably clean; the standby generator was doing well, and the indirect lighting brought up the sheen on the red carpet. About half the big leather easy chairs were occupied, and a small group of people stood round the bar in the corner. The barmaid was new to me—five feet plus of black skirt, white see-through blouse and no bra, with nipples outlined European style in orange fluorescent paint. A gold nose ring, too, by God! This little bird was really flying. No chromed teeth as yet, however: that was still too far out for Airbrit.

"Well, Captain Scott?"

I swung round. "Morty, you old bastard. Your little girl on the desk is going spare looking for you."

"I have every confidence in Miss Van Heusen's ability to cope with emergencies," he said loftily.

I said, "What you mean is, you don't want to know and you're going to let her sweat it out. What's wrong, Morty—did she say 'no'?"

He flushed angrily. "I happen to be the Senior Officer at Kennedy, Captain, and you should watch your manners."

I looked him up and down. Uniform too tight at the waist, shiny gold braid on the sleeves, immaculate shirt, shiny bald head and horn-rimmed glasses. His nose was huge, beaky, Romanesque—and with a distinctly red end. In short, Morty was a real gone character. Sex Mechanic Grade 1—and a first-class shit, too.

"Oh, sure, Morty. Will do. Surprised about Rosie, though—she's usually very cooperative."

"Captain!"

"Okay, okay. Relax. Who do we have here—anyone I should know?"

I walked over and asked the goddess for a coffee. She smiled, and I saw teeth like a graveyard in the moonlight. Morty stayed at my heels, yapping away; I ignored him and took a look at the VIPs.

"...returning home from Washington, Captain," Morty burbled on. "They came up from Dulles in an Army flight. That is Dr. Olaffsen, tall chap with a beard. And Professor Volkel in the gray suit. The lady in the fur coat—Dr. Waldheim, Swiss geologist. They say she has an IQ of 168...."

I watched the woman for a moment. About forty, and stoutish.

"Come along, Morty," I said. "Introduce me."

We shook hands. Karen Waldheim's hand was warm, strong and vital. Her eyes were black and very penetrating.

"Are we to have a good flight, Captain?" she asked briskly.

"I think so," I said. "Weather fair, winds in our favor. Just over seven hours."

"Good," she said, smiling. "It seems a very large airplane, Captain. You have many passengers?"

"Full load—almost six hundred. Yes, she's big—big is beautiful when it comes to economy, you know. The relevant factor is kilograms of fuel per passenger-mile. The less we use, the happier I am. Until we find an alternative source of power."

"Such as atomic power?" Dr. Rabin's accent was thick Middle European. The manifest had him down as Israeli, but I would have placed him somewhere along the Adriatic coast—perhaps Albania?

"Such as atomic power, Dr. Rabin," I agreed. "Matter of fact, a friend of mine is working on nuclear-powered aircraft out West at Seattle—the Spruce Goose Two program."

Karen said quickly, "Not Ted Radford, surely?"

"That's the one." I grinned. "Do you know him?"

There was general laughter. "Your friend was also at the Washington Conference," Sven Olaffsen told me, "and spent his time pumping us for information."

"That sounds like Ted. I almost hate to ask—how did he make out?"

The woman eyed me steadily. "He didn't, Captain."

"Yes...point taken, Doctor. Well—see you good people on

board. I see Mr. Mortensen is getting things moving. Nice to talk to you."

The VIPs were moving out slowly, picking up bags and coats. I met some of the others briefly and went back through the concourse to give Rosie the sailor's farewell. A square man in camouflage jacket and black beret stood at her desk. Square—because he was almost as broad as he was tall. His jaw was underhung like the bow of a supertanker, his face tanned by many suns, eyes set far apart under a lined brow. He must have been forty years old, and I thought he could probably take care of himself, within reason. He carried a new Sterling on one shoulder, a .45 automatic in a thigh holster, four grenades on his lapels, and the haft of a knife showed in each ankle boot. The nearest thing to a mobile arsenal I'd seen for years.

"Captain—thank goodness you've come. Have you seen Mr. Mortensen?"

"I have, Rosie love. He's herding the VIPs around—said he was too busy to stop by, but he has every confidence in you."

"The beast," she said fiercely, "just when I needed him. This is Major Brand—Captain Scott."

"Major."

"Captain!"

We laughed together. He had a deep, chesty laugh, pleasant to hear. He said, "I gather you're taking us home, Captain. Will you tell this young lady it is in order for my men to board independently? I don't want sixty armed men wandering around—might make the passengers nervous."

"Not only the passengers, Major," I said cheerfully. "Okay, Rosie—I'll take full responsibility. Come on, Major—I'll take your party out to the aircraft. Now, Rosie, hold the fort and behave while I'm away. If you can't, go right ahead and enjoy yourself."

She giggled deliciously. "You are terrible, really. Take care, now. Have a good trip. Goodbye, Major."

Brand nodded. "Goodbye. Good luck." He picked up a small pack, settled his armament more comfortably and looked at me expectantly. I led the way out into the foyer, down the side corridor lined with telephone booths as obsolete as the hansom cab, through double glass doors into the rear vehicle yard. His men piled out of the two Army trucks, and the CSM reported all present and correct.

"Thank you, Sar'nt Major. Where are the officers?"

"Just gone to the bog, sir. Back in a jiffy, they said. Sir!"

Brand glanced at me and smiled. "Loyalty, Captain, is a priceless virtue. All right, Sar'nt Major—send a man for them and get the rest aboard."

"Sir!"

I walked out with Brand through the cordon of U.S. paras, which opened to let us through. Behind us the group of soldiers marched to the aft stairway, boots splashing in the pools of water. Joe Marcovitch met us at the front stairway.

"Hello, Joe. Everything okay?" I said casually.

"No problems, Captain. Major Brand—on your way, eh? Sorry to see you go. The boys in the Guard say you did a fine job."

"Thanks, Joe," Brand said, nodding. "We did what we came to do. Left four of our lads behind, but it's all in the game."

The U.S. captain grinned, pushed back his steel helmet. "Some game. It gets kind of busy around here sometimes. Like last night."

"I heard. Sticky, wasn't it?"

"Some. It's not easy, shooting down unarmed people."

Brand nodded. "I know. Good luck, Joe. See you." He started up the steps. We watched him go up, enter the aircraft. The oval of light from the cabin shone down on Marcovitch's face, and I saw the deep lines, too deep for such a young face.

"Didn't see you with the rest of the crew, Captain," he said quietly.

"That's right," I said. "I came out later."

"Seen Captain Chambers recently?"

"No—not since we went into town. Why?" I didn't like the way he looked at me sideways.

"Think his leg will be okay for flying?"

"Oh, sure. You can fly a 797 on trim alone if you—" I knew I'd boobed even before his expression changed.

"What is going on, Captain? You know your man twisted an ankle early today—but you haven't seen him since last night. So how come? And where's that Canadian crew who came in today?"

I stared at him in the flickering floodlights. A great crocodile of passengers was approaching, and I knew I was in the clutch.

"This is strictly private, Joe. Don't ask."

"It's my job to ask. I'm asking."

"None of your business, Joe."

"Yeah? If you're taking someone out, it's my business, Captain. Something pops the other end, I get reamed here— but good. Level with me."

"It's not like you think, Joe." I told him.

"How do I think?"

"That I'm taking money for it. I'm not. Listen…" and I told him the truth in a few brief phrases. Passengers were flooding past me, impatient to be aboard, and he stood in silence, staring at me with dark hooded eyes. Then—

"I forgot to tell you, Captain…"

"Tell me what, Joe?"

"It was a real nice steak." He stuck out a horny hand. "Luck, Captain."

I shook his hand, slapped his arm with my free hand, shook my head in baffled wonder and went aboard. At the top of the stairs, I turned, saluted. He gravely returned the compliment. It didn't seem out of place.

7

The flight deck was comfortably warm, quiet save for the intermittent flurry of raindrops on Delta Tango's metal hide and the buzz of conversation and movement on the main deck below. I stripped off my jacket, hung it in the recess aft of my command seat, draped my necktie over one shoulder. A clean tissue, a long, pleasurable nose blow, a quick trip into the lavatory and I was all ready to start work. The sequence was wholly automatic, and rooted in superstition, like the football manager's lucky suit, the rally driver's "noddy dog" on the back shelf.

I glanced round. John Capel sat upon a stack of holdalls in the emergency-escape-chute recess behind the copilot's seat. He glanced up, winked and grinned.

"Okay, John?"

"Sure. No sweat, Captain. Thanks."

I nodded. "Fine. We'll get together later on, with Nickie, to work out something for Heathrow. Don't touch anything. If you have problems, talk to Ben here."

Chambers sat hunched forward in his seat, going through the Radio Checklist. I left him to it; he was a good copilot and needed no one riding herd on him. Ben Price sat facing the vast array of instruments, gauges and controls on his panels—so intricate and involved that he could monitor them only by using the special sequence scanning pattern which ensured that every instrument was checked every thirty minutes during flight. Nickie was in the VIP galley, under the wing of Jill Stewart, the VIP Lounge hostess.

I sat down, got comfortable and settled the micro headset in place, throat mike comfortable and snug. Thirty feet below me, the ground chief stood at the nose, attached to Delta Tango by his own umbilical communication cord.

"Captain to ground—okay for starting?"

"All clear, sir. Standing by."

I glanced across at Chambers. "Radio checklist, Jerry?"

"Complete, Skipper."

"All right. Check INS."

Chambers bent over the central console. "Okay, Skipper. Present position confirmed as Way Point One. Way Point Two inserted."

I sneaked a quick glance. The indicator on the center Inertial Navigation System showed the latitude and longitude of JFK. The apparatus, connected to the Automatic Pilot, would fly us accurately to Way Point Two—and Three, up to a maximum of nine checkpoints. Still more could be fed in along the route, and our current position would be indicated at all times, clicking up in the small electronic window of the gauge.

"Okay, Jerry. Overhead Panel Guards?"

"All down, except Auto Skid and Body Gear Steering," he confirmed. After 20,000 hours on big jets, mistakes could still happen. The guards gave insurance against operating the wrong switch—and there were plenty to choose from: the overhead panel was about a yard square.

"Fine," I said. "Check all cabin warning signs on, Jerry?"

"No Smoking, Seat Belts, Exit lights—all okay, Skipper."

"We're getting there, we're getting there. Let's keep it tight, fellas. Okay—external lights?"

"All set."

"Flight instruments, transmitter switches?"

"All guards down." Chambers pulled up his trouser leg, idly scratched a bug bite; I frowned but let it go. What a sloppy character—for such a good pilot. The checks were almost through.

"Altimeters?"

"On and checked," said Chambers. He sounded happy, relaxed, on top of the job. Well, I expected no less, after rescuing him and his girl at great personal inconvenience. I stopped briefly to consider what form the inconvenience would take if we bought it at London Heathrow—and hurried on.

"Clocks, Jerry?"

"Set to GMT and servoed," he came back. We would use Greenwich time—coded "Zulu"—throughout the flight. It was already ten minutes to five in the London morning, five hours ahead of Kennedy. We went on with the checks. Oxygen, interphone and equipment checked. Ben Price confirmed his checks complete. We set the takeoff bugs on radio and pressure altimeter to 800 feet and ground level; the airspeed-indicator bugs would advise us unmistakably when we reached takeoff speeds.

"Almost there, fellas. INS Mode, Jerry?"

"Selected to NAV, Skipper."

"O-kay," I said, satisfied. I called up the ground chief.

"Captain to ground—blocks in—ready to start?"

Chalky White came through loud and clear. *"Okay, Captain. All clear for start."*

"Turning Number One..."

Ben Price: "Number One turning, Skipper. Start valve open...oil pressure is okay...coming up to 15 percent power...acceleration normal...exhaust-gas temperature fluctuating slightly—settling down now. Start valve closed...pressure light out. Okay, Skipper—Number One stabilized at 60 percent of N2 power."

"Thank you, Ben. Turning Two..."

I watched the other engines start up, recalling the early days, with only a revolution counter and exhaust temperature to watch. Now, with the two-stage compressor in Delta Tango's engines, we measured maximum power as a ratio—the EPR. I remembered that some pilots had had difficulty adjusting to the new situation, but the end result was the same, I thought. You opened up to 1.42 EPR and you got takeoff power, no matter what the gauge said.

The exhaust-gas temperature checked in at about 850°C, well below the redline emergency mark at 920°C—a good safety margin.

Safety...a two-edged sword. I remembered a crazy philosophy used by pilots on multiengined aircraft, when landing with an engine out. You took your normal landing speed...and added 5 knots for the wind, 5 knots for the wife and 10 for your pension. Another 5 knots for luck—and you ended up coming in at excessive speed, overshooting the runway and making a loud, expensive noise in the fields beyond.

I jerked myself back to attention. All five fans were turning satisfactorily.

Chalky came back on the phone, below. *"All set, Captain. Landing-gear pins out. Clear to taxi when ready. Have a nice trip."*

"I will that, Chalky," I said cheerfully. "Bring you back a stick of Blackpool Rock."

"Don't you dare," he said laughing. *"They put very rude four-letter words in that rock, these days. But I'll settle for a bottle of Black and White, or a crate of Newcastle Brown Ale."*

"Okay, Chalky. Can do. Out."

For a brief moment I sat musing, but my brain was ticking over in high gear. This stage of a flight resembled finishing off a jigsaw puzzle...the last pieces were falling into place, the picture taking shape. I called up Kate, got her first time.

"Have we still got an airplane back there, Kate?"

"Of course. Bulging at the seams, but ready to go."

"No empty seats, Kate?" I asked.

"You must be joking," she snorted. *"We had three missing bodies at final check-in, and had to use these soldier boys to stop the rush. Anyway, Jonah...cabin secure, documents briefcase aboard and checked. All staff present and accounted for and all doors on Auto."*

"Thanks, my love. Go get strapped in."

"I hear and obey, O master."

I grinned, switched back to Tower frequency. Chambers checked the door lights: all were closed, as we were ready to roll.

I stared out of the darkened flight deck, past the banks of softly glowing instruments, over the darkness of JFK to the Manhattan skyline, barely visible under the driving low cloud. I could see occasional lights on the Tower blocks...not many, and very dim. In other days, the glare of downtown New York could be seen twenty miles out on final approach.

"Okay, fellers, here we go. Jerry, check anti-icing and trims, please. Kennedy Ground, this is Speedbird Flight 626 at Gate Two. We are heavy for London, we have Romeo departure information and we are ready to taxi."

"Six two six, Kennedy Ground. Roger. Taxi to Runway 22 Right via Alpha and Runway 13 Left, wind southwest at 10, altimeter 28.65. Clear to Sardi 2, Flight Level 360 to Hampton, altimeter 29.54."

I boosted all four forward engines until the aircraft moved, pulled back on the starboard throttles and let her swing gently forward on the turn, moving at a steady ten knots over the wet concrete desert. The big bird taxis easily on her nose-wheel tiller, and the great secret is to keep moving: a great deal of thrust, energy and fuel is required to move more than three hundred tons of aircraft, fuel that might be needed in an emergency later in the flight. I began to think about the trip ahead.... We carried about 180,000 kilos of fuel in the massive main tanks—about a sixth of our all-up weight of 800,000 kilos. This would reduce, of course, as fuel was consumed in flight, but initially we could not hope to achieve our cleared cruise altitude of 39,000 feet—flight Level 390. We were, in real terms, "heavy" for London. I took a quick glance at the computer flight-plan printout and then concentrated on negotiating a taxiway corner; the swept wings of the 797 have an uncomfortable tendency to extend outwards in a turn, and the aircraft needs plenty of ground maneuver room. Let me see...we could make 36,000 feet—Flight Level 360—initially. By the time we passed St. John's, we should be able to make 39,000. We hoped. It was a long haul to LAP, and while we carried a 10-percent fuel margin to make our alternative airport at London Gatwick, it did not seem so much, sitting here on the ground.

The Tower frequency burst into occasional life as we progressed.

"Army Flight Code Seven holding."

"Roger, Code Seven, Kennedy Ground. Change to Departure Control Frequency when airborne. Line up and hold."

"Code Seven, roger." The ripe Middle West drawl brought to mind an instant picture of Rock Hudson sitting with eyes crinkled at the corners, indecently relaxed and secretly amused.

"Kennedy Ground, Mideast Flight 124 to 22. Right, holding."

"Okay, 126. When Code Seven ahead is clear, enter the active and hold."

"Flight 124, roger."

It was time to say my own little piece to the passengers back there.

"Good evening, ladies and gentlemen, this is your captain. Welcome to Speedbird Flight 626. We are cleared directly to London at an altitude of 39,000 feet. We shall be flying at a Mach number of .84 and our flight time is seven hours and sixteen minutes estimated. We shall be showing a film during the flight, and your stewardesses are available at all times. Please enjoy the flight. Thank you."

Ben Price came to stand at my shoulder, scanning the forward panels.

"All checks complete, Ben?"

"All clear, Skipper."

"O-kay. Jerry, takeoff checks, please."

Chambers nodded. We referred to the checklists—no matter how often these checks were completed, the lists were used every time. You get no second chances.

"Transponder and DMEs?"

"On code, DMEs set to Norm," said Jerry.

"Signs and Lights?"

"All set."

"Engine Checklist?"

"Complete."

Chambers paused, passed over the list to the engineer for cross-check. I dialed up the automatic Departure Information broadcast.

"Kennedy Departure Information Service." The recorded voice tended to gabble. *"Sierra time 0450 Zulu. Depart Runway 22 Right, wind 240 and 20, altimeter setting issued by Ground Control. Temperature 44, Departure Control Frequency 121.1. Do not change to that frequency until instructed. VFR departures advise Clearance Delivery of route of flight and whether you request to remain in the Terminal Control Area beyond 8 miles. All departures advise clearance delivery. You have received information Oscar."*

I watched the aircraft ahead roll and accelerate, jets hurling spray behind, wide body glistening in the runway lights. She rotated, nosing upwards, lifted and skimmed out of sight into the night sky. I jumped the gun, started rolling, and the Tower said, "Flight 626, line up and hold."

Gently, I coaxed Delta Tango onto the vast runway, lined up on center, checked the aircraft heading against runway direction. Crosswind of about twenty knots...no problem for the power steering.

She sat monumentally on runway's end, singing to herself. To the layman, a huge and complicated piece of machinery— but ask any pilot, and he will tell you that the airplane becomes alive, a primitive intelligence, just before takeoff, as if it knows that soon it will return to the place for which it was designed, made and destined.

"Clear to go, 626!"

"Thank you, Kennedy, 626 is rolling."

I opened up all engines to 100 percent power. Flaps were at twenty degrees...she rolled straight and true. The throttles jiggled slightly as Ben adjusted a balanced power, and Jerry began calling off speeds.

"Fifty knots...

"Sixty..."

Ben Price cut in: "EPR good at 1.42. Exhaust temperatures 820 degrees and steady."

I moved the tiller slightly, holding her straight down the white line.

"Ninety knots...V-One, Skipper. We could still abandon takeoff, if necessary," Ben said quickly. "All engines good on 1.42. Number Five Exhaust Gas Temperature fluctuating slightly...."

"Rotate." I moved the yoke back firmly, and Delta Tango reared skywards.

"V-Two."

"Gear up, Jerry."

"Gear coming up, Skip."

"Check positive climb."

"Climb established. Airspeed 160 knots...170 knots... V-Two plus ten."

"Fine." I settled back in my seat, breathing deeply, adrenaline flooding. Everything sounded good. I told Jerry to take flaps up to ten degrees, and Ben Price set rated power. I glanced out of the window: we were passing 800 feet, and Delta Tango slid through the dark sky above New York, turning towards the east and home. We went into cloud and I got back to the instruments.

"Kennedy Departure, 626 airborne, passing 2300 feet."

"Roger, 626. Turn left heading 130 degrees."

I started the turn. "Kennedy, am I cleared to 5000 feet?"

"Negative. We have other traffic."

I scowled, slowed down the climb.

"Six two six, clear to 5000 feet, call New York Center on 134.45. Good night." We settled into the climb, conversing briefly with New York Center. Jill brought us our first coffee, and we made contact with Boston Center on 133.45.

"Six two six from Boston. Understand you are passing Flight Level 220 for 330, turning to heading 110 degrees. We

*have you identified on radar contact. Contact Moncton Center
on 133.6. Good night and good luck."*

"Thank you, Boston." I meant it: it is a long haul across
to Europe, and we needed all the good wishes we could get.

Moncton handed us over to Gander Center, and we got out
Oceanic Clearance around the time sufficient fuel burned off
to let us make 39,000 feet—Flight Level 390. I locked in the
auto-pilot, handed over to Jerry.

"You have control, Jerry. Way points for Track X-Ray set
in INS. Maintain 390—I'm going aft for an hour or so. Okay?"

He nodded, settled down lower in his seat. The flight-deck
lights were dim, the instrument banks shining in ghostly
ultra-violet; the cloud tops lay ten thousand feet below, and
we were a small isolated community, a speck in the starry
vault of eternity.

Only the beginning and the end of flight are spiced with
danger. On takeoff, the airplane is heavier than at any other
time, and more vulnerable; major failure close to the ground
means almost certain disaster, and the anxiety load on the
crew is correspondingly heavy. On landing, perhaps in bad
weather, after a long flight, the crew may be fatigued, fuel
state low, mechanical failure more possible after a long flight.
Only in steady cruise is the enjoyment greater than the stress.

I sat for a while, enjoying the feeling of release, before
going aft. I would have to make my rounds shortly, but for
now I was content to let the peace and splendor of the night
penetrate my weary body and brain. At Mach .85 the sound
of the engines was a muted hiss; I thought I could hear the
dashboard clock ticking and smiled, remembering the Rolls-
Royce. Outside, the temperature was forty, fifty degrees below zero, but the stars were brilliant. I leaned forward, identifying many old friends from my early days in Celestial
Navigation. We seemed not to be moving—suspended in
limbo over the unseen cloud layer below, and it seemed hard
to believe we were covering some 600 nautical miles each
hour.

Standing up, I stretched, lit a cigarette and put on my
jacket and peaked cap. Time to go visiting.

The Selcall chimed. At this stage of the flight, this was
not only improbable—it was unique. Chambers and I exchanged glances. He switched the Selcall onto Speaker,

picked up the telephone and said, "Speedbird 626, Delta Tango. Go ahead."

Ben chuckled. "Probably a wrong number, Skipper."

He could be right, I thought. Through a chain of repeater stations and satellites, any Company office could dial the call sign of any aircraft, exactly like a telephone call—but the chances against a wrong number were astronomical; people don't make errors of that magnitude.

"Flight 626, from Airbrit Kennedy. Do you read?"

I slid into my seat, took the telephone from Chambers. "Six two six. This is the Captain. Go ahead."

"Six two six, are you on intercom only? Check your PA system is inoperative." I checked: it was. "Okay, Morty—what the hell is going on? Over."

"Six two six, this is an Armada signal. Are you ready to copy?"

I heard Chambers suck in his breath sharply. Behind, Ben Price said softly, "Christ Almighty..." John Capel came forward in the dim light and said, "Scotty? What is it? What's wrong?"

Price said heavily, "The end of the world. That's all."

I said angrily, "Shut up, Ben. Pass your message, Morty."

"Roger, 626. I will read you the signal received from LAP eight—no—ten minutes ago. Cairo, Beirut, Damascus attacked simultaneously at 0200 GMT by nuclear ground-to-ground missiles launched, it is believed, from Israeli warships in the eastern Mediterranean. All contact lost with cities and with area approximately ten-mile radius around each. Seismological stations in Turkey, Persian Gulf, East Africa report disturbances Strength Six on Richter Scale.

"No other information at this time. AP reports possible loss of life sixteen, one six, million minimum.

"All Speedbird aircraft to continue flights as briefed. Flight Director LAP has assumed personal control of all flights. Captains are instructed at this time to open sealed Armada instructions and implement up to Condition Red Two. Repeat, Red Two.

"Following message from the Chairman is repeated to all transit aircraft. Quote. There is no reason to believe, at this time, that this catastrophe will escalate. No other powers are involved, including Britain. However, captains at this time will assume full responsibility and authority to land their aircraft at the nearest safe location compatible with landing

weight, taking into consideration fuel states and present positions.

"We trust and pray that sanity and tolerance will prevail. We commend all crews and passengers in transit to the mercy and love of Almighty God, this night of Armageddon. Message ends."

Mortensen's voice echoed in my head for long moments. I found myself listening to the small, inconsequential human sounds—whispered curses from Ben Price; Capel breathing heavily through his nose; Chambers saying helplessly "No...no...no..." over and over again.

I felt numb. My mouth was dry, and a vein in my forehead throbbed painfully and very fast. My hand gripped the telephone so hard I groaned from the pain.

"Six two six...626 to Kennedy. Roger. We copy. Christ, that was a body blow. No reason to believe the reports were false? Over."

"Negative, Scotty. Negative. We are listening to news reports round the world. The U.N. Security Council is in emergency session. Commentators point out that Israel's withdrawal from the U.N. last year, after failing to gain support for their U.N. Middle East Army proposals, means that no U.N. decision can be binding on Israel. Scotty, I would advise against releasing this to your passengers as yet. I have your manifest here, and there are a number of Jews and Arabs aboard."

"That is roger, Mort. Two exceptions. I have several scientists aboard from the Washington Power Conference. Also SAS company under Major Brand. Both may be able to help."

"Yes, Scotty." Mortensen's voice was unsteady, hesitant. *"Agreed. Suggest you open Armada instructions now and contact London on Company channel. Wait one...news flash just in. Russian and Chinese delegates have vetoed Canadian resolution in Security Council that no U.N. member country should support Israel or the Arab nations in this emergency. Mr. Kanikov, leader U.S.S.R. delegation, accused America of supplying the nuclear warheads used by Israel. Russia reserves right to support victims of terrorist attacks and is holding urgent discussions with surviving political representatives. CBS reports U.N. supported unanimously censure motion against U.S.S.R. and China, warning that free nations of the world will not stand by and watch genocide committed. End of report. Did you copy that, Scotty?"*

I acknowledged. Sat frozen in my seat, locked in cold

sweating panic. The flight deck was silent; no spoken comment could start to express what each of us was feeling. I was aware only of the leaden sick feeling in my guts, the involuntary contraction of sphincter muscles, and my sheer inability to stop the crazy swirling roundabout of images flashing through my mind—a kaleidoscope of fireballs, surrealistic mushrooms, stark brilliant white flashes—and behind it all the quite unbelievable concept that I would soon be dead.

At last—

"Six two six to Kennedy. Mort—I still can't believe it.... We have a nice ride going here; smooth air, clear skies, the stars...Dear God, how are they taking it back there in New York?"

"Not good, Scotty." Mortensen's tones were flat, neutral; he seemed to have gotten a firm grip on his nerves, and my estimation of him rose several notches. *"General opinion— America almost certain to be dragged in. We have local TV channel going at the moment—they pushed up the power network to maximum as soon as the news broke. Most commentators believe, given time, it may be possible to prove Israel made the damned things herself. Few believe we will be given the time."*

"Understood, Morty. What's happening in New York?"

"We think many people are trying to leave the city, Scotty. With lack of transport, movement is slow—all bridges over Hudson jammed tight, many people walking upstate in belief prevailing northwest winds will carry fallout away to sea. Wait—another news flash..."

We waited in mute shock; the Selcall hissed softly, the channel still open, and I heard faint movement noises, remote echoes of voices and superimposed, the noise of an aircraft on takeoff run.

"Six two six. The President has just made a short broadcast. Four points. One—stay cool, stay home, stay by the radio. Two—State of Emergency, martial law, Condition Red announced. I think that's Air Attack Imminent, Scotty, God help us. Three—U.S. would never, even in this grave crisis, make any move to escalate the conflict but would use all available means of defense if attacked. Four—he confirmed U.S. had not supplied Israeli warheads, asked for time through the U.N. to prove his case. He confirmed Middle East war now two hours old had caused in excess of 18 million casualties already.

*He asked every civilized nation to appeal directly to U.S.S.R.
and China. Ended asking every human being listening to him
to unite in prayer for the survival of mankind. Message ends."*

"Thank you, Morty. We have all that on the tape. I think
we are all working on that last request right now. Over."

*"That is roger, Scotty. Same here. What are your inten-
tions?"*

"Unchanged as of this time, Morty. I want to talk to London—with luck we can complete flight plan to Heathrow. I
will come back to you later. Over."

"Okay, Scotty. Good luck to captain and crew."

I got up, handed over to Chambers, got out my flight briefcase. I unlocked it, slid open the concealed panel in the side
section, took out the envelope that had remained undisturbed
for almost two years, since the Instructions were last amended.

I looked up. "Ben, organize some coffee, will you? And ask
Jill for a few miniature brandies—we all need a lift. And
listen—all of you. I want no comment, discussion, talk of any
kind outside this flight deck. That means to passengers or
stews alike. And I want absolute quiet while I read this thing.
Right?"

They nodded dumbly—Chambers, Price, Capel.

The envelope was black—a nice touch, I thought bitterly—with the single word ARMADA printed in yellow in
the top right corner. It was sealed with red wax and the
Airbrit cipher. It held a single sheet on Air Britain letterhead,
signed by the Chairman and Operations Director. I reached
up, switched on the convenience light and began to read.

This Instruction was drafted in the hope and belief that
worldwide nuclear conflict would never happen. That you are
now reading it is tragic proof that we have failed. The outbreak of hostilities leaves captains of aircraft in transit with
but a few options.

First, this Instruction is issued only to captains of inter-
continental flights. Intercity and local flights will be recalled,
diverted or grounded on the outbreak of hostilities.

Second, your choice of options will depend upon the location and extent of the conflict. As of now, you may act independently to take whatever action you may consider necessary to achieve the survival of crew and passengers.
Preservation of the aircraft is totally irrelevant. The options
are three in number.

If your destination is under nuclear attack, you will consider any alternate which offers the best chance of survival. This will include return to your departure airport, fuel permitting. Next, the choice of alternates cannot be influenced by considerations of politics in any way: the paramount requirement is survival. Lastly, if no suitable alternates can be established, you must make your own decision on a choice of location for forced landing or ditching.

You are advised to restrict the passage of information to your passengers as a means of reducing possible panic and rioting. Further, the Company has provided for your protection a supply of firearms and ammunition, which will be found by removing the back of the aftermost crew locker on the flight deck. It will be necessary to scrape away the concealing paint to reveal the countersunk screws.

We can do little more for you, except to wish you a safe and successful landing. Lastly, we join in a prayer for the safe return of your own and all other aircraft in flight, at this time of danger, when Lucifer is rampant and his shadow is over the face of the Earth. We commend our souls to the mercy of the Lord Jesus Christ, in the knowledge of everlasting salvation. Amen.

8

Later, I found that Ben Price had taken the document from my hand, read it and passed it round to Capel and Chambers. For long moments, I had withdrawn into myself, as if to blot out the hideous imagery pouring into my mind. I learned that the terrible burden of responsibility for more than six hundred people became in part an actual physical load which seemed to press down upon the nape of my neck; I sat with head bowed, shoulders slumped, oblivious to everything but the refined tortures of my own private hell.

"Jonah?"

"Huh?"

Chambers stared at me with an expressionless face. "Gander Center on 125.9, Skipper."

I straightened up, aware that several pairs of eyes were watching with painful intensity, as if waiting for me to perform a miracle. I slipped on the headset, adjusted the throat microphone.

"Flight 626 to Gander. Go ahead."

"Six two six from Gander. I read you. Are you aware of the international situation?"

"That is roger, Gander," I said heavily. "I have been briefed on Company channel."

There was a long pause. I sat listening to the pounding in my ears.

"Six two six, I have information for you. Is it your intention to return to Kennedy?"

"Negative, Gander."

The deep Canadian voice said, "Roger, 626. *Advise that Kennedy has now closed down indefinitely due to military aircraft movements. Further advise Shannon will accept no further movements under State of Emergency declared by the Government of Ireland at eight minutes past the hour. Shannon advises heavy movements of military aircraft in progress from Cuba and West Indies, possibly fifty plus aircraft. Do you copy?"*

I checked. The four-hour tape was still running.

"Affirmative, Gander."

"Roger, 626. Your alternates still Manchester, Gatwick, Paris de Gaulle, but confirm when in direct contact with London Heathrow. Overfly Shannon at Flight Level 390 and do not contact Shannon Center. Over."

I gave him a roger, slipped off the set and nodded to Chambers.

"Okay, Jerry. You heard the man."

Jill Stewart came forward with coffee and brandy; she glanced around curiously in the subdued light, raised her eyebrows slightly and went out again. The brief flood of light from aft took its toll on our night vision, and I lit a cigarette, deep in thought. The drink dispersed to some extent the chill in my lower guts, and I found it a little easier to think straight.

Chambers said carefully, "No one ever ditched a 797 before, Skipper."

"No one's going to ditch this one," I told him. "I'm going to take this airplane into Heathrow all in one piece—and I want no goddamn argument. Ben—fuel state?"

"Okay, Skipper. Nearly six hours' flying time left."

"John, I want you to help Nickie and Jill in the VIP galley. Keep your ears open for any indication the passengers have caught on—someone may have a portable radio going. But first, go down and put Kate in the picture. Quietly, mind you. I don't even want the cabin staff involved at the moment."

"Okay." Capel nodded, moved away.

I laid a hand on Chambers' shoulder. "Jerry, I'm going aft—if there is anyone who can help with advice at the moment, it's those eggheads. Now—get on the intercom and get hold of Major Brand. I'd like him to come up to the VIP lounge right away. Questions?"

"Plenty," he said glumly, "but they'll keep."

I nodded, went aft past the lavatory and galley into the

VIP lounge. Three rows of double seats were located down the port side as far as the aft bulkhead, which was decorated in opaque plastic sheet in a "knight and dragons" motif. The first four seats were occupied by the Russian party; I wondered briefly why their trip home was so urgent they couldn't wait for a Concordeski. It was even money they'd known something was in the wind.

Behind the Russian diplomats in the forward double, two black-suited men with large toe-capped boots and cropped hair sat stolidly, a briefcase on their laps supporting a chessboard, presently being scrutinized by the man nearest the window. His partner stared blankly at me and looked down again. I figured them for KGB escorts for the U.N. representatives. Tough, dedicated, ruthless.

In total contrast, the rear seat accommodated the latest crap-rock star and girlfriend. They were indistinguishable from each other, in filthy jeans, black sweaters, leather jackets and greasy long hair. Both were clean-faced (beardless) and dirty-faced (hygienically). They sucked incessantly on the twin pipes from their hash hookah bubbling in the aisle. Thunderman, I knew, was not quite nineteen years old, knew not one note of music notation, used a row of four beautiful nude girl drummers behind neo-lit outfits and earned around nine million pounds a year. According to his passport, he was named Ernest Winterbottom, born in Widnes, Lancashire, and he was homeward bound from a six-week engagement in Hawaii, where accommodation was restricted to standing room only on the nearest beach for anyone earning less than six million dollars a year.

I recalled reading about Thunderman's act. A deafening musical background around 130 decibels, above which he could be heard yowling unintelligibly. Audiences received printed sheets of the lyrics, largely hard porn of the worst sort, which they read in time with the music. This paid lip service to the latest U.S. pornography laws, which prohibited oral and broadcast hard porn but set no limits on printed words and visual effects. Thunderman, it was rumored, had spent a quarter of a million pounds on plastic surgery to equip him with impedimenta any stallion would be proud to own, and on which (as a grand finale) one of his girls sat unsupported. I guessed his worst problem would be bruised knees....

The small bar in the starboard aft corner was self-service,

because it was all free. The veterans of the Washington Conference were grouped nearby.

Their seats around the coffee table were low and comfortable; ashtrays were full to repletion, but the forced ventilation kept the air clean. Olaffsen saw me first, got up and nodded.

"Ah—Captain. Taking a short break from routine?" He clutched a tall vodka-and-tonic which had been severely ill-treated. The almost-empty bottle on the bar hadn't got that way accidentally, either.

"Dr. Olaffsen. Celebrating?"

There was some laughter, during which Major Brand arrived, minus cap and most of his personal armory. He admitted, during introductions, to answering to the name of Mike; I left him chatting with Rabin and Professor Volkel, and met Kate and Nickie at the top of the stairs. Both girls were very pale and nervous, and their eyes mirrored the heavy load of fear.

"Take it easy, you two," I said gently. "We're all right at the moment. In a few hours we'll be on the ground at Heathrow. Listen, Kate—which one of those is the head man?" I gestured towards the Russian party.

She hesitated, pushing back a stray lock of hair. "That one, I think—in the front seat, Nabokov."

"Okay. Look, go help Jill organize coffee. And one of you start getting rid of the booze lying around—I don't want drunks making things difficult. Then stay out of sight in the galley until I want you."

They were both uneasy, but did as they were bid: it made a difference having something to do. I could feel my own confidence returning. I went over to the Russian diplomat, who seemed to be asleep. In the row behind, the muscle sat up straight, watching keenly.

"Mr. Nabokov—sir? Do you understand English?" I asked slowly.

He blinked, sat up straight and blinked once or twice. "Yes, I speak a little. Captain Scott, is right?"

"Yes, sir. Look—I have received a very important message which concerns all of us aboard the airplane. I would value your advice before I speak to the passengers. Will you join us for a few moments? Just yourself, sir?"

He stared at me with eyes full of suspicion. "What have you to say that you cannot say also to my First Secretary?"

"When you hear what I have to say, sir, you will understand. Would you like some coffee?"

"Please. Black, with sugar, slice of lemon."

I called Kate and gave the order. "Leave the rest of us for the moment, Kate. I have to talk to them."

We gathered at the bar—the four scientists, the soldier in the camouflage jacket (strangely out of place), the Russian and myself. I got my back to the bar, rested my elbows and told them the situation in plain unvarnished terms. I used every way I knew to keep the profile low: I emphasized that the conflict was still, as far as I knew, local in scope; that the U.N. was working full blast to stem the tide. I told them I would welcome any comments and suggestions, particularly on their assessment of probable future trends. I said I thought politics should be left out completely—I was only interested in getting the aircraft safely on the ground, in which respect I had full and free scope of action.

I went on, "We're all human beings. Threatened with final destruction. I want to forget racial and national aspects, language difficulties. I am interested in only one thing: survival. My own and that of every passenger. No—don't speak just yet. I think we should all break for coffee and devote a few moments to considering the problem in the way I have suggested."

No coffee for me...I fixed myself a straight tonic water and watched the girls serving the coffee.

The reactions were extremely interesting. Olaffsen was clearly shocked but intrigued from a technical viewpoint, scribbling madly on the back of a paperback novel. Professor Volkel lit a cigarette, declined coffee and turned, leaned on the bar, lost in thought. The older gray-haired stubby man, Rabin, walked unsteadily to a seat, leaned forward and put his head in his hands. Karen Waldheim stood immobile in silent shock, hands writhing together like two frenzied animals.

Olaffsen found a well-worn pipe in a side pocket, jammed it unlit into his mouth and sat back in his seat, glanced around. "So," he said calmly, "it has happened. Well...it is no great surprise. That is all you know at present, Captain? What you have said?"

"Yes. You know all I know, sir. They'll call me if anything develops. We are in contact with our company and with Oceanic Control at Gander."

I explained about the Selcall. How the system of satellites and repeaters enabled ground operators to contact aircraft anywhere on the globe.

Professor Volkel said, "I think you were very wise to call this meeting, Captain. It can do no good at this stage to involve the rest of the passengers. Wouldn't you agree, Mr. Nabokov?"

The Russian had taken the news calmly. Too calmly, I thought. He was smoking a pale cigar and looked very relaxed. He was a burly red-faced man, dressed immaculately, with iron-gray hair cropped very short, so that it stood erect upon his head. His eyes were dull slate gray, and I had noticed his fingers at once: very long, strong but with square, almost spatulate ends and broad, flat nails.

"Professor," he said flatly, "I am grateful that the Captain has included me in this party, but I know you will understand I cannot make any comment without first consulting my superiors in Moscow. In any case, it is my own personal opinion that the United States has committed the criminal act of supplying nuclear explosives to the Zionist murderers. The Soviet Union can only condemn such depraved actions."

Brand swung round violently. "America? Jesus, man— look at America! Out of oil, food; industry closed down; riots; mass emigration...does *that* sound like a nation bent on making war?"

Nabokov smiled indulgently. "Do not believe all you hear or read, Major. We would be foolish to believe that this is the true state of affairs in America today."

"You don't really believe that," the SAS officer said bluntly. "Let me tell you this, sir—I brought sixty of my men over to teach the National Guard conscripts the basics of street fighting and mob control. Fighting street guerrillas. I left four of my men dead in New York—and you try to tell me it's all a hoax?"

Karen Waldheim laid a hand on Brand's arm. "Gently, Major. Make allowances for Mr. Nabokov—he can't change his script at will; he must toe the Party line. May I ask a question, Mr. Nabokov?"

"Certainly."

"Other than America, what other country could possibly gain from supplying Israel with these weapons? Well?"

Nabokov pulled at his cigar. "A very good question, Doctor.

There is certainly a good answer—but then, I am sure you are going to tell us anyway."

"As Mr. Brand says, America is in serious trouble, and you well know it. There are only eight other nuclear powers—Russia, France, China, Japan, India, Brazil, Canada and Britain. Correct?"

"Go on, please," the Russian said smoothly.

"Only Russia, of the eight, has any interests in the Middle East. But she has consistently supported the Arab bloc; I cannot see her supplying the warheads to Israel."

"So?"

"So—Israel can only have made them for themselves. She has said so, publicly. Why, then, should Russia and China accuse America? Because, Mr. Nabokov, she is a sitting duck. There has never before been such a wonderful opportunity to strike a final blow at the old enemy, and China will consider it seriously because with America gone, she will have only Russia to contend with. Russia will consider it because she is the only crazy schizophrenic collection of lunatics capable of believing that there can be a winner and a loser in such a fight. You have been waiting sixty years for the chance...and you won't let it slip."

The low growl of approval clearly annoyed the Russian. Seasoned campaigner, he brooded upon his reply for long moments. Then—

"Captain, I think I must ask to be excused from further discussion. It is clear to me that all these—people have a distorted viewpoint. But let me say this to you: Russia will not be the first to use her nuclear strength, but if we are attacked, I assure you it will not be without instant retaliation. We shall defend Mother Russia to the last drop of blood."

"Yours? Or everybody's?" Brand said through his teeth. "I tell you this, Mr. What's-your-name...no one will get away with this one. It's like a forest fire—once started, it takes a hell of a lot of stopping. We had only one chance, up to yesterday—and that was to drop every last damned atomic bomb into the Atlantic. That was yesterday. Now it's too bloody late. By forty years."

"Gentlemen." It was Moshe Rabin, straggly white hair surrounding a bald pate, gold-rimmed glasses shielding watery blue eyes. "I have something to say. I have attended the Washington Conference as a specialist in solar research.

What you do not know, perhaps, is that for four years I worked in the Negev, on the Israeli Nuclear Research Project. Six months ago, when I left Tel Aviv, I believed we were two years away from our own bomb. Two months ago, in Montreal, I learned we had exploded a nuclear device on a secret underground test site in Uruguay, on the estate of a wealthy Jewish family."

He stopped briefly, eyes fixed on something far distant in space and time.

"Soon after that, the Tel Aviv slaughter—two hundred thousand of my people dying in agony from poisoned water. Before that, I fought against the use of nuclear weapons. Afterwards, I could not wait for the news of today."

We listened in silence.

"I tell you this, Nabokov, Major Brand. Israel alone is responsible. No other nation is involved. And now the Arabs have learned their lesson....There will be lasting peace in our land."

The little rotund man turned back to the table, sat down, laid his arms on the table and bowed his head. The Russian stood as if made of stone, and Volkel, the Austrian geologist, touched my arm nervously.

"Captain, we must try to understand that Moshe is not personally involved. And our Russian friend here is limited in what he can say. If the emergency passes and he has said too much...Siberia is a cold land."

I said, "Go on, Professor."

"There are a number of possibilities, but only a few probabilities. From these we can compute the worst that can happen to us, and the best. Bear in mind, Captain, we are not politicians. Such men often think and act very illogically, rather like a compulsive gambler. You understand what I am saying, yes?"

"I think so. Go ahead."

"Right. Such people do not compute the risk to their country by going to war, because if they lose, they will be dead like everyone else. They compute only their chances of getting away with it. And they have an insane belief that only their own computations are correct. Remember Hitler? Germany was at full strength a year before he invaded Poland—but he waited because the time was not ripe. Three years later, he invaded Russia, and this time the timing was wrong. But he did not hesitate."

He paused, thinking the sequence through.

"Of course, they compute their own personal risk carefully. They safeguard their families, their fortunes, their loot. Personal aircraft, Swiss bank accounts, residences in other countries. No politician is stupid enough to get himself killed *during* a war. He may be tried and executed afterwards, or even commit suicide, if he has not scuttled in time.

"Lastly, to enter a war, he must have the total support of his people. Democratic nations receive this support voluntarily from patriotic citizens. Totalitarian nations—like Hitler's Germany—exact total support by threats. And that is why, I believe, only Russia could even contemplate entering this conflict. If she wins—as she believes she can—she will share the world with China, but not for long. And her leaders believe they cannot lose. This friend Nabokov believes also—even if he cannot admit it."

"I am not to stand here to be insulted," the diplomat said angrily. "I tell you Mother Russia will never move first against America. I swear this, on my mother's grave."

A general argument started, out of my control. Thunderman awoke, heard the news and collapsed in hysterics; his lady friend just smiled vacantly and stayed with her hash machine. In the middle of it all, Ben Price called me urgently from the flight-deck door. I moved fast, stowed my glass and went forward. The Selcall chimed again as I reached my seat.

"Station calling Flight 626—say again."

"Six two six, this is Airbrit London Heathrow. Captain Scott, this is Harvey, Operations Director. Have you passed point of no return?"

I stared at Chambers. There was a point where it was farther to turn round and go back than it was to continue to destination; I had not heard the term for years. Chambers nodded, held up ten fingers.

"That is roger, London. Six two six passed that position ten minutes ago. But Kennedy is accepting no traffic. Over."

"Understood, 626. Scotty, it was announced a few moments ago that a continuous airlift of Cuban troops has begun into Southern Ireland through Shannon, and that a Liberian freighter which docked at Cork yesterday is unloading military vehicles and supplies. The Irish Government of the People announce that the Cuban force, with Irish elements, intends to—quote—'liberate Northern Ireland from the yoke of the oppressor'—unquote. A statement from Buckingham Palace

and Downing Street less than an hour ago says thet the Regency will take all necessary steps to ensure the Cuban forces are not permitted to mobilize near the border, and that the only cure for infection is cauterization. Charles's name does not appear on the communiqué—it is signed by the acting Prime Minister, Air Marshal Holdenberg. Did you copy that, 626?"

"Affirmative, Harvey. Go ahead."

"Roger, 626. There is a full curfew here, air-defense warning Condition Red One. Everyone not required for civil defense ordered to shelter. Immediate call-up of all males between eighteen and sixty. All military and police leave stopped. All oil exports frozen. No one seems to know what action the Regency intends, Scotty. The only way they can stop the Cubans from walking into Belfast is by air attack—and you know what that means. Over."

"We understand, Harvey. God, things are winding up fast. Is London still receiving aircraft? We're about four hours out."

"Yes, as of fifteen minutes ago, Scotty. But all incoming flights are being advised to ... we ... My God, Scotty ... flash— Christ, it's—"

There was a brief howl of high-frequency feedback—and silence. I stared at the set, looked across at Chambers, afraid to speak, almost afraid to think. I switched to London Center on 116.1.

"London Center, Flight 626. Do you read?"

Nothing.

"London, Flight 626. Do you read me?"

Faintly, we heard: *"Six two six ... this is Luton Tower. ... Jesus Christ Almighty ... Six two six, London has gone ... God help us. ... David Thomas was looking directly at the flash ... blind, blind as a bat. ... I was in the radar booth ... red ball ... It looks so close, but miles away ... boiling. Clouds red, like blood ... I can't ... can't—"*

The voice became indistinct, and I could hear someone behind me sobbing. Over the open channel, I could hear faint noises from the airport, forty miles from London. Soon there came an odd sound, a rumble as from some underground train approaching a station, swelling, booming, roaring ... and transmission shut off abruptly.

I sat there dazed, not quite comprehending what I had heard. Behind me, Nickie and Kate were crying openly, and

Chambers got up awkwardly, face stiff and pale, to take Nickie aft. Capel was swearing monotonously, repeating some phrase again and again, and Ben Price sat at his console, face buried in his hands.

9

Time passed. I was fighting an inward battle on several fronts, and I knew that I must not go insane. If I had had only myself to think about, it would have been so easy to relax pressure on the lid of the pressure cooker that was my brain. There was a sensation of being balanced upon the very knife-edge of sanity, that to relax for an instant would start me on the long slippery slide with no ending. I ground my teeth together, concentrating on just staying sane long enough to concentrate for another few seconds. Once or twice, I relaxed—just an infinitely small sagging of the structure of my being—and my mind lurched sickeningly into chaos.

I became aware that I was gripping the control yoke with maniacal strength, as if to squeeze the very juice from the steel and plastic tubing. The autopilot was still functioning; my forearms followed through on the minute movements of the control column.

Options...options...I shut my eyes tight and forced away into the back of my mind the loathsome image of London as it must be now; I locked away tightly the images, the memories of faces I once knew and whom I would never see again, of streets and parks destroyed forever. It seemed unreal, impossible.

We had passed the point of no return—it came to mind that we had all passed that point when those missiles were launched. Three Middle East cities—London—how many more? And why London? We weren't involved in this damned war, as far as I knew. God, help me to silence that scream on the brink of eruption and let me think straight, just for a moment. Alternates . . . Gatwick? If "it" had been a big one—and judging from Luton, it was—Gatwick would be within the destruction area. And I was so desperately afraid to call Gatwick, in case there was no answer.

I knew I was in no shape to talk to anyone yet. I knew what severe tension can do to voices, and there was this tightness and aching sensation in my throat. We would have to go North—into the Midlands, perhaps even to Scotland. There was Paris—but suppose some sixty-foot titanium thunderbolt had the name of Paris on it? Home was home; if I was going to die, I preferred it to be in my own country—I would be in good company.

Eventually, I faced up to the real question: how far had this thing spread? I had to know, sooner or later. This little private world of mine had not changed; Delta Tango still hissed eastwards at 39,000 feet through a starry night, and the vast crowd of passengers would be mostly asleep, dreaming of new lives, new places. How many had hoped to go to London? How many were bereaved? The five big engines still burned their tons of fuel each hour, blasting astern the microscopic debris of combustion, water, hydrocarbons. The glowing green panorama of instruments told a tale of normality.

I became aware that John Capel was in the copilot's seat: Chambers would be aft somewhere with Nickie. I didn't blame him. Ben Price crouched motionless over his desk, conjuring up streams of meaningless digits from his calculator.

Gander Center would know. . . . I went to 125.9.

"Gander from Speedbird 626."

There seemed to be much static and interference on the normally clear waveband. I guessed the possible cause and balked like a startled horse: the connotation was too frightening to accept.

"Gander to 626"—the voice was flat, curiously neutral in tone.

"Gander . . ." I had trouble working out what to say; "we have the situation in London. We have to think about alternates. Are you working other aircraft at this time? Over."

"Affirmative, 626. We have about ten aircraft under Oceanic Control. Most are working other frequencies at this time. We have an inbound flight from Buenos Aires to London which has declared a diversion to Paris. We . . . we are receiving re-

ports via shortwave, but reception is very bad. We are trying to remain calm and provide a service but...Wait one, 626..."

The flight deck was very quiet. I turned. Chambers, Nickie, Kate and Mike Brand were standing behind my seat, listening intently. I lit a cigarette with shaking hands, dragged hungrily upon it, exhaled a long, slim column of smoke.

"Six two six from Gander. Sorry about that...personnel trouble...we have lost—two of the staff by...They had families in London. Latest information on U.K. as follows. Five detonations reported. All seem to be very big. Targets London, Manchester, Sheffield, Glasgow, Belfast. Situation confused, reports mostly from Service aircraft transmitting in plain language. Do you copy?"

"Affirmative."

"Your U.K. alternates are all shot. What are your intentions?"

"We had Paris de Gualle as second alternate, Gander."

We had to wait nearly two minutes for the next transmission. My mouth was dry.

"Six two six advise all contact lost with Paris thirteen—no, fourteen minutes ago."

I absorbed this blow without reaction, because it was no more than I had expected. I thought more about the way the Gander controller was doing his job. I thought he was doing a fantastic job—only in the past few moments a tremor had crept into his voice.

"Gander from 626...we are so glad we have contact with you.... We want you to know we appreciate the way you are coping. Can you perhaps give us the full picture? We have about four hours' fuel left. Over."

"Thank you, 626. I'm just pleased I have a job to do. Keep my mind off—two of our off-duty controllers couldn't take it after London—we found them a little while back. Shotgun. We can hardly believe this—this god-awful thing is really happening. No signs of anything unusual—that's what makes it so weird. We have lost contact in the past hour with the following: Kennedy. Washington. Chicago. St. Louis. Montreal. New Orleans. San Franscisco—in North America. In Europe—Paris, Rome, Berlin, Brussels, Vienna. Overseas— Bahrein. Aden. Delhi. Tokyo. Wait one—we have a flash coming in on a teleprinter...."

Kate tapped my elbow. I gratefully accepted the coffee she

produced; it was so hot it burned the lips, but I gulped thirstily. I glanced at her in the dim light; tears were flowing freely, but she was still doing her job. She brushed them away quickly. "Sorry, Jonah...can't seem to...stop."

"I know. I know. All quiet aft, so far?"

She nodded, not trusting her voice. Listlessly, she walked back through the door, carrying the empty tray. Jerry came forward and Capel vacated the copilot's seat.

I said quietly, "Nickie okay?"

"Yes, Skip. Kate's looking after her. What's the score?"

I told him. It didn't take long. I asked Ben Price about the fuel state. It seemed to be going fast.

"Okay, Ben. Set up for maximum endurance. Compute the weight, find our best altitude. Jerry, take her down when you're ready. Lose height slowly down to optimum. I want her setting up to give me maximum time in the air—we aren't going anyplace, it seems, but let's keep her out of the drink as long as we can."

I sat immobile at the controls, leaning forward and staring eastwards, where the sun would rise. There was no horizon, and nothing to see: no brilliant flashes, surging fireballs. It was crazy to expect to see anything: we were still a thousand miles from Europe, as near as dammit in the middle of the Atlantic.

"Six two six, Gander."

"Go ahead, Gander."

"This is Gander. Following message received five minutes ago. The Acting President of the U.S.A, Mr. James Mc-Cracken, speaking from an undisclosed location, but assumed to be an underground complex, said America had been devastated by a preemptive strike without warning. The aggressors were even now paying the penalty for this crime against humanity. A retaliatory strike has been launched against both Russia and China, since satellite monitoring channels show missiles directed against the West Coast were launched from Chungking province on the Chinese mainland. The East Coast attack, first detected by the satellite net, came from offshore submarines, which were immediately attacked by U.S. Navy units. Did you copy, 626?"

"Affirmative, Gander. We wish we hadn't."

"Yes...we are finding it hard to continue. We now have four suicides in the control staff here. The medics are handing out tranquilizers, and we are all doped up to hell and gone.

We couldn't make it any other way. We aim to keep in contact as long as possible. Have you an amended flight plan? Over."

"Gander," I said thinly, "I would give my next year's salary for a flight plan. We are maintaining easterly heading 087 degrees and flying for maximum endurance along Track X-ray. We are making flight level 220. Can you suggest any military or civil fields in Spain we can try?"

"Negative, 626. We have no contact with Madrid or Barcelona on radio or land line. Sorry."

"Okay."

The ring was tightening around us. Down at 22,000 feet there was considerably more turbulence, and we passed occasionally through the tops of heavy cumulus which obscured the stars fleetingly. It could wake up a few of the passengers, but there was no way round it. Sure enough—Kate came through on intercom to advise cabin lights were going on, activity increasing. I made a short broadcast.

"This is the Captain. We are descending on course to avoid turbulence at higher levels. Our flight time will be extended slightly and you will be advised. Thank you."

It wasn't true—or even logical—and the more knowledgeable stews would catch on immediately that something was wrong: you don't give away precious altitude in mid-Atlantic.

Ben Price reported, "Skipper, at these settings we can stretch it to eight hours and forty minutes, leaving enough for a straight-in approach with no overshoot. We can pull another forty minutes by dumping baggage. We have about 60,000 kilos on board; much of it Army equipment."

"Thanks, Ben. When is our next way point, Jerry?"

"Twenty-one minutes, Jonah."

"Right." I pondered for a moment, then left my seat.

"Jerry, I want you to work Gander and anyone else you can. I'll take any field within range. If it's too short, I'll dump her on her belly—but we have to have a piece of solid ground very soon. I'm going back to talk to the eggheads again. Call me—right?"

"I understand, Skip."

"And keep your eyes open—report anything you see. Lights, UFOs—anything happens, I want to know. One more thing: get onto Gander and check on shipping between here and Europe. If we have to swim, I'd like a ship somewhere nearby."

* * *

In the VIP lounge, I found an odd atmosphere of anger and resignation. There seemed to be a strange smell drifting around, which I couldn't identify immediately. It was sweat...the human stink of raw fear. The Russians were in a huddle in their seats, arguing, gesturing, faces pale and moist. Thunderman and partner? They were locked together, feeding themselves straight bourbon and happy pills. At the bar, the Washington delegation and Mike Brand were waiting in strained silence.

Olaffsen spoke for them all. "Well, Captain? You have news?"

"I have," I said grimly. "All bad. Look, the lid has blown off everything. Hang on a moment."

Nabokov looked up as I approached. He had unfastened his necktie; the round jovial face was strained, with an odd gray tint. He looked—and was—a very worried man. Who wasn't? I asked myself wryly.

"Mr. Nabokov, you had better come and listen to what I have to say. All hell has broken loose. Very soon, I shall need your help. Will you come?"

He nodded shortly, and we went back to the bar. I told them all I knew, and I did not mince words. They took it quietly, almost resignedly, as if they had expected it—and maybe they had.

I concluded, "...and the critical problem is finding somewhere to land. All usual diversion airfields are out. No military base will receive us, and radio communication is getting difficult. I think we have to accept the fact that we have very few options."

Karen said, "Are we in immediate danger?"

"No. We can stay in the air more than eight hours yet. We are checking every possible landing point. But it must be obvious to you all that this may be the end of everything we know today. We may have to put down in the sea—and you know there can only be one end to that sort of exercise. I would not normally discuss my actions with passengers, but this situation is far outside my normal experience. I need expert advice—and I'm not proud where it comes from."

The Russian, Nabokov, had stood impassively, chewing an unlit cigar, as we talked. Now he spoke.

"Captain, I am not totally certain that this is not a hoax by the Americans to bring the Soviet Union into the Middle

East conflict. I demand that I am allowed to contact my government by radio immediately."

Incredibly, Professor Volkel laughed. "My dear fellow," he said scornfully, "you do not appear to understand what the Captain has said. There is no Soviet Government. There is no Soviet Union. Like the rest of the world, it is being ground into heaps of radioactive ashes."

The Russian eyed him with hostility. "You think is good joke, da?"

"How can I deny it?" Volkel said with a certain amount of satisfaction. "I think Russia has reaped the whirlwind. You have pushed it and pushed it, and now you have pushed a little too hard. And all the billions of rubles, pounds and dollars spent on armaments are totally wasted—money that could have turned this old world into a paradise. I think you got exactly what you have been asking for since World War Two. And we collect the overspill."

The diplomat's face was black with anger. I stepped in quickly.

"That's enough—both of you. Listen. I have authority over everyone in this airplane, and no one is going to stop me getting her down safely if it is at all possible. Major Brand, can I rely on you and your men to keep the passengers under control?"

The soldier nodded.

"Okay. Fine. Our present heading for Europe will be maintained until we locate a suitable diversion."

Brand agreed. "There must be plenty of airfields still open in the U.K. And I have to get my men back where they can do the most good."

Dr. Rabin intervened. "No good, Captain. You must forget Britain now. She has had five heavy-yield bombs, almost certainly hydrogen heads. Within days, the fallout will cover every inch of land. What are the winds overland at present?"

I dragged my memory back to the Met briefing at Kennedy.

"There's a ridge of high pressure...winds light and variable. Why?"

"Don't you see? The fallout will not be blown out to sea. It will circulate, disperse, spread out into huge areas. Landing in the sea would be preferable, Captain. As far as I am concerned."

Brand shook his head, stunned. "What about America? Can we make it back?"

I told him the truth, and an uncomfortable silence descended. Nabokov excused himself, began talking animatedly to his three companions. "Any more ideas?" I asked tiredly.

Olaffsen said slowly, "We are all in God's hand, Captain. One thing I know: they will not stop down there, those madmen, until every bomb is dropped, every missile fired. Listen—can we make Scandinavia, possibly?"

I thought not. Too far.

"Spain? Portugal?"

"Sorry, Karen," I mumbled. "No radio contact. And we can't just go, hoping for the best. We have to find a positive answer—an open airport, even a piece of flat land a mile long."

Nabokov and one of his heavies came over and stood close, the big, hard-eyed man in the blue suit on my right; I felt something hard grinding into my left armpit, in the thin flesh over the ribs. The diplomat spoke very quietly. "Serge here has a very good reason why you should listen to me carefully." His mouth was close to my face, and I got the full benefit of vodka on bad breath.

"We will walk slowly back to your seat, Captain, and turn this airplane round. We are going to Cuba or Jamaica, ladies and gentlemen. Without argument or resistance...Serge would dislike having to hurt your captain."

I think everyone froze. I dug my fingers into my palms, calf muscles knotting.

Olaffsen rumbled, "Nabokov..."

"Quiet. Move, Captain. Slowly..."

Behind me, I heard a fierce grunt of exertion, a sickening thud. The KGB man sagged forward, knees buckling, between Nabokov and myself. The gun dropped. I was pushed sideways and saw Brand's knife flash from his boot, sliding up into Nabokov's chest under the ribs, through clothing and flesh as if through butter. The Russian coughed, choked and coughed again; a flood of bright scarlet stained his chin and shirt. Capel reeled into view, half-crouched, moving very fast towards the two remaining Russians erupting from their seats. Capel swung the fire axe wide and low, meeting the lead KGB man and slicing obliquely across the upper arm into the chest. I saw Brand scooping up the flat automatic, and I screamed, "No guns—no guns!" Even at 22,000 feet, decompression could be fatal.

I shoved the falling Nabokov clear, went in low for the

fourth Russian. My man went backwards, one hand full of my hair, between seat rows. I heard a woman's scream, glasses breaking. My left arm was underneath, trapped, but the right was free, thank God. His hand ripped away a handful of hair; I ignored the pain, got my hand across his face, my thumb in his eyes. I bore down heavily, feeling soft, warm wetness, and he screamed like a stuck pig, grabbed my wrist and scratched deeply. I got the hand away, smashed it down on the bridge of his nose. It stopped the screaming, and felt good. I thought I would try it again, and did. He lay still.

Capel helped me up. My legs felt numb. Kate got a stiff drink into me fast, and I stared around, feeling my new bald patch gingerly. Nabokov lay on the floor, face up, staring at a ceiling through eyes which could not see. Brand was wiping his knife and whistling contentedly under his breath. The KGB man, Serge, lay face down.... Capel's axe had taken him almost horizontally across the nape of the neck, severing the spine— he was dead long before he hit the deck. Capel's second target lay slumped against the bar, watching with strange detachment the blood spouting from an almost-severed left arm. His head twitched crazily every few seconds. I thought he did not look too good at all.

Brand looked at Capel approvingly. "Nice work. Army?"

"Yeah. 'Nam."

"Ah, yes, Vietnam. If you'd learned to fight a little dirtier a little earlier, you could have won that one." Brand's eyes glittered. I guess he just liked killing people....

Me, I was feeling sick. I finished the whiskey Kate gave me. I had to stop this drinking in flight....

We began to clean up the mess; Brand produced a couple of men, who rolled the three Russians in blankets and stowed them behind the bulkhead. The fourth received attention from Dr. Rabin, who had some medical qualifications, and we stowed him back in his chair.

John Capel was sitting on the arm of a seat, cigarette burning unheeded in fingers that tremored occasionally, spilling ash. He stared down at his empty glass, up into my face.

"All right, John?"

"Sure. You're a walking disaster area, Captain—you know? Everywhere you go, people keep getting blown away. We were lucky again—I came through from the flight deck, saw what was going on. The axe was in a bulkhead clamp, right there at my elbow."

"You're a big fella, Capel," Brand said drily. "Don't know your own strength. Birds of a feather, if you ask me, Captain. That character you sorted out—not often you see a man killed with a facial blow. Stove his forehead in—did you know?"

I shook my head. "I know my wrist hurts—but he was pulling out my hair in handfuls. Look...."

Brand grinned widely. "I know. Bit drastic, though, wasn't it?"

I changed the subject abruptly. "What about that last one? He looks poorly."

Brand grimaced. "Rabin says he'll lose that arm; not that it makes much odds—he's lost too much blood. I'll lose no sleep over him."

"Yes." I got up, straightened my jacket, felt my bald patch again.... It was going to take some time to grow again. Rabin had bandaged my wrist scratches, and I thought it was time to get back to the office. "Any reactions from the main deck yet, Mike?"

"Not so far—but you can hear something's stirring down there. They must have heard part of the damned performance."

"I'll see what I can do. Hold the fort?"

"Sure. Go ahead."

I went back to my seat, slipped off my jacket, glanced at Chambers, sitting with headset on, working the radio. He saw my unspoken question, turned a thumb down. Well...what would be would be. I activated the PA system.

"Ladies and gentlemen. This is the Captain. There has been a disturbance in the upper lounge, but everything is under control. I have an important announcement to make shortly; will you please ensure everyone is awake. Thank you."

Chambers leaned over. "Okay, Skipper? What the hell went on back there?"

"Someone wanted to go to Cuba. We didn't. Forget it.... What have you got?"

He said slowly, "Not much, Skipper. No joy with Portugal, Spain. Raised Stanstead and Hurn, but they wouldn't talk—trying to get down dozens of diverted aircraft. Gander reports the thing is way out of control. Russia hit Japan—that was no surprise. Australia broadcast a declaration of neutrality half an hour ago and got hit almost immediately—Sydney, Melbourne, Darwin, Perth. It's like some crazy free-for-all bar brawl, Skipper."

"Yes. The goddamn fools have really done it this time. Can't you raise anyone in U.K.?" I said worriedly.

"I got something very faintly on 116.1, Skip. May have been Preston Center. Something about heavy fallout from Manchester. Sorry, but going off the air—every man for himself. Oh—they said Strike Command hit the Cubans at Shannon and Cork with something heavy. That'll teach the IRA to fart in church," he said bitterly.

"What about overseas? Nothing else?"

"Wait one—I have it on my clipboard. Malta news broadcast. Said the Pope was halfway through a world broadcast asking for peace when Rome got it. They said they thought more than a hundred king-size H-bombs had been used in the Northern Hemisphere alone, that they knew of—maybe many more. He mentioned the Royal Family, Jonah...they were nearly all in London, except Charles—he may have escaped. They were trying to fly Prince Michael back from Vancouver—he may have got out before they got it."

His voice died away, and he stared blindly out into the night sky.

Ben Price, behind me, said tightly, "Why prolong the agony, Jonah? Shove the nose down and let's call it a day."

I looked at him sharply. "No way, Ben. I'm buggered if I'm going to lose this airplane without trying. We have more than seven hours' flying time left. There's plenty we can do. For Christ's sake, snap out of it. Get the damned charts out and start looking: there has to be somewhere we can put down."

The engineer produced a half-ashamed grin and turned back to his desk.

Chambers said quickly, "I have something on UHF, Channel 18."

"Put him on loudspeaker. Call him."

"Check. Flight 626 calling aircraft on this frequency. Do you read?"

"Six two six, I read you...." The voice was faint, indistinct. The background interference was loud, mushy. *"This is Air Force Code Zebra Three. Go ahead."*

"Zebra Three, 626. We are en route New York-Heathrow, about halfway over. We need an alternate very badly. Can you assist?"

"Six two six, we wish we could help. We are an E4A AFCP on station north of Calgary about six hundred miles, near the ice cap. Guess the sky really fell on us today. Over."

I stared at Chambers. "AFCP?"

"Advanced Flying Command Post. Must be about the only one left. They used modified 747s with big radar assemblies."

"Six two six to Zebra Three. Understand. We have six hundred plus aboard. We cannot raise Gander for the last fifteen minutes. Are there any bases still open you know about? Over."

"Six two six, we reckon you can scratch Gander...we saw a big red balloon maybe ten minutes ago. Distance and bearing confirm Gander. Could have been a Soviet submarine missile—we have nothing more coming over the Pole now. Over."

"Thank you, Zebra Three. We figure we're in the last round. What is your status? Over."

"Well...we believe you can scratch us pretty soon too. We've been on station eighteen hours. Our KC135 tanker is one hour overdue and no contact. We think he never made it out of Dover Air Force Base. The brass on board say it makes no odds...we have no contact with any ground control. We have about thirty minutes of fuel left. Over."

My throat was aching dully to go with the pain in my scalp. Would I be able to talk that way—voice normal, no overtones of panic—when we were down to half an hour of life? That E4A pilot was really something....

"Six two six to Zebra Three. Understand...wish we could help."

"Thank you, sir, We appreciate that. But we have things straight enough here. Marion, the kids and I—we live on Rhode Island. Biggest old farmhouse you ever saw, with a cellar I'm turning into a rumpus room. Me, I'm going home. Me and the rest of the guys. We're sitting up here at 30,000 feet going round in circles. We have maybe forty people on board and we just got through taking a vote. We're going to wind up on full forward trim, open up the taps and get going on down home. I got a bet with Colonel Hawkins here, we get this old bird past Mach 1 on the way down. Well...good luck, fella. Wherever you decide to go. Zebra Three out."

We sat for a long time, listening to the faint hiss of static.

Delta Tango cruised eastwards through the dome of night, altimeters showing 22,000 feet, Machmeter settled on .72M— the settings that would guarantee maximum flight time. Life time. Visibility was better; several times, we saw the lights of shipping far below.

The Ocean Control Frequency 125.9...Gander would speak to us no more, but we heard isolated snatches of conversation between aircraft scattered over the far oceans. No needless chatter; least of all any tendency to comment, brood upon the whole tragic mess. Pilots gave advice, encouragement, help where possible in the cool, detached way of the professional; occasionally we spoke to other aircraft, reporting weather, sky, wind states. Without exception, all were faced with the same basic problem: finding an open field within their fuel range. Some succeeded, leaving the frequency after a brief, casual departure call to all who could hear. It seemed to me that in the absence of Oceanic Control, the aircrews followed strict procedure as if Gander were only temporarily off the air, and this was the only epitaph those faithful ghosts would know.

I said heavily, "What options have we got? Get the charts out and get that gray matter working. I want to know every possible airfield within our radius of action."

Chambers looked at me sharply. "All?"

"No, you damned fool," I said viciously. "Use your stupid head, for God's sake. Nothing north is going to be any good:

Gander bought it, and you can bet your ass Thule and all the northern bases would get it too."

"And the mainland doesn't look too healthy," said Price.

"Right," I agreed. "So—what's left? Jerry?"

Chambers spread the Atlantic chart over the central console, turned up the overhead light. "Anything north of Gib. would be suspect, Skipper. I heard Nice a while back, on 116.1, but they were swamped with diversions from all over Europe. And interference is bad—that channel's just about shot. But I could make out that Paris, Brussels, Rome, Milan, Geneva—none of them were answering calls."

I said sharply, "Geneva? You mean, Switzerland—?"

"Looks that way. Too close to Italy, I guess. When the northern cities in the manufacturing belt got it—Turin, Milan—"

I stared at the map again, chewed at my lip. "Malta...we could make it—just. And Luqa is long enough to get this thing down. Have you called them, Jerry?"

He nodded, passed over a short handwritten list. "No contact with these, Skipper. Anyway—if the U.S. Sixth Fleet did its job, Malta is probably just a hole in the Med. now. Remember, Casca—the guy who succeeded Mintoff—did a deal with the Russkies. Grand Harbor, full of Soviet shipping, would be a juicy target...."

I was running out of ideas. It was beginning to dawn on me that there were a number of one-way streets opening up and I didn't like the way they were running. North—into whatever remained of Gander and Thule—held no attraction for me. Northeast was worse: the British Isles, France, the Netherlands, Spain, Portugal—death traps. Any airport near a military base had a life expectancy of about five minutes; those orbiting MIRV hell bombs could carry forty or fifty small missiles, each of which would take out bases such as Toulon, Gib., Casablanca, Algiers...and I had an uncomfortable feeling that aircraft approaching any shore at this time would have to parley with a SAM missile, rather than a controller.

I turned to the Azores. Two chances...a dog's chance and no chance. I had Chambers start calling the main air base, Lajes, on the island of Terceira. It was manned jointly by the Portuguese and U.S. air forces—a major NATO base and mid-Atlantic refueling stop. He called on all the frequencies listed in the Air Pilot, but I knew it was no use...Soviet tacticians weren't going to pass up a juicy one like that.

"No go, Skipper."

"Okay, Jerry. Thanks. Check on that other airport down there—Santo Aro. It's on San Miguel, I think."

"Wait one...yes, I have it, Skipper. Uh-oh..."

"Well?"

"It's only a small municipal strip, Skipper. Caters to interisland traffic and some flights from the mainland. About 4000 feet, longest runway. We'd need about an 80-mile gale to stop this thing in that distance."

"Check the airfield plan. Any flat land around the airfield we could belly-land on?"

He shook his head. "Negative. Scratch the Azores."

"Come on, Jerry," I said angrily, "...there must be somewhere down there we could put down."

"Not if we can find anywhere else. It's volcanic—rocky as hell, hilly."

"Sod it," I exploded, "Find me a piece of land, will you? All I need is two miles."

Ben Price leaned forward between us, stared at the chart. "It's a long haul, Skipper—but what about the Madeiras? Southeast, about 1700 nautical miles—take us about two hours forty-five."

I sat up sharply. "Good lad, Ben. What about the Canary Islands? Bit farther on, but there are several airfields in the group."

"Too far, I think," Chambers put in. "Let's run it through the computer, Ben. But we've lost a lot of fuel coming down to 22,000 feet..."

"Autopilot out, Jerry," I said decisively. "I have control. Turning onto 150 degrees and climbing back to 39,000 feet. I want an ETA and fuel calculation as soon as possible. I'm going to start calling. What's the name of that airport—Funchal?"

"That's it, Skip. Here's the information sheet on it—they have about eight frequencies." Chambers handed me a sheet and joined Price at the engineer's desk. I racked my seat up forward a notch, turned down the cockpit lights and worked Delta Tango round in a climbing turn to starboard; it was a feeling of relief almost like sexual orgasm, to be able to do something positive, after the stresses of the past hours. It was more than possible—virtually certain—that we would find disappointment at the end of the new southeast course on which we were now flying, the big engines whining audibly as they hauled several hundred tons of aircraft, fuel and passengers back up to best cruising altitude. But it did not seem to matter....I sat relaxed, humming some forgotten tune under my breath, staring out at the great curtain of stars.

I locked on the autopilot, checked on the Funchal sheet and started calling. Interference on most channels was worse than I had ever known it...dull roaring and hissing, backed by a cacophony of weird noises composed, I thought, of screams, sobs, hysterical babbling....It was my imagination, I told myself, but there were times when I seemed to be tuned in to a direct channel to Hell, and all the souls of the millions of freshly dead gibbering at those lucky—or unlucky— enough to be still alive.

And finally, on 116.1 megacycles, I made contact. The faint reply through the static was almost unreadable, but the voice undoubtedly said, *"Flight 626, this is Funchal, pass your message—"* and I screeched with joy. Just to talk to another human being on the ground, not some other Flying Dutchman in limbo. I took a deep breath, calmed down a little. I told myself soberly that simply getting on contact meant nothing....Then—

"Funchal. Flight 626. Flight 626. We are a Speedbird flight en route Kennedy International to Heathrow, position approximately 47 degrees north, 45 degrees west, about one seven zero zero nautical miles from you, heading one five zero degrees, flight level 390. We have six hundred plus on board, including three dead. We have enough fuel to reach you with no reserve for diversion. All our alternates are out. We urgently request diversion to Funchal. We have no other viable alternate. Over."

"Stand by, 626." The voice was fainter than ever, distorted; but at least, thank God, we had a chance....If they said they couldn't take us, I knew I would finally cave in. Never had I known such pressure....I looked round at Chambers and Price.

"Fuel okay, Skipper—flight time three hours forty-one minutes. We shall have about ten minutes' fuel left on landing."

"Okay...now tell me the bad news: can they take a 797?" I said.

"Sure." Chambers nodded, grinning. "They take 747s all the time—remember they had that bad accident a few years back?"

Funchal came back on the air, and I choked off the comment half-formed in my brain. But there was some nagging memory just under the surface that I could not solidify, identify.

"Go ahead, Funchal," I said nervously. Had any radio message ever meant so much to me before? I wondered.

"Six two six from Funchal. We can accept you but advise that there are no facilities for passengers, crew or refueling. We have landed more than thirty civil and military aircraft in distress in the past hour, with more than a thousand people on board. Our facilities cannot cope. All we can offer is a runway and a parking area. Is that understood, 626? Over."

"Funchal," I said thankfully, "we'll take your kind offer. Thank you. I didn't fancy ditching...and we have about two hundred children on board. Over."

"That is roger, 626. Call me at one hundred miles inbound and stay off this frequency...we are very busy. Out."

"Thank you, Funchal. From all on board. Six two six out." I took off the headset, draped it over the yoke, found my cigarettes and lit up luxuriously. I watched Chambers feeding the coordinates of Funchal into the INS, and I set up the autopilot to allow Delta Tango to climb gently as we used fuel, to obtain maximum miles for every gallon. We had been flying for more than four hours, and the big jet was beginning to tremble and lurch as upper-air turbulence increased. A brilliant crescent moon was rising. How many holocausts had those cold, airless peaks seen? Were those massive craters really meteor impact points—or the fading scars of some vast prehistoric nuclear conflict, when the moon was young and green and inhabited, circling round an Earth hidden under volcanic clouds of dust and steam?

I remembered with sick horror the four-man U.S./Canadian team in Mare Imbrium, living in their inflated plastic dome, their main module still in a sixty-mile orbit above. Their lunar lander was ready—but how could they return, with only the shipboard computer to guide them home? No Houston Control, no carriers and helicopters to snatch them from the seas...Brother, I told myself, you don't even start to have problems, compared with those poor bastards up there. What kind of God would give them a ringside seat at the last Big Fight? How would I feel, watching helplessly as the world destroyed itself?

I buzzed Jill Stewart in the VIP lounge.

"Capel there, Jill?"

"Yes, sir. Talking to Miss Bassett—Nickie."

"Get him up here quick," I told her, "and organize some coffee. We're going to be busy."

Capel ambled onto the flight deck, stood at my elbow. "What's with the turn, Captain? I saw the stars moving round."

"Jerry here'll put you in the picture, John. I want you to sit here and use your eyes. Don't touch a damn thing—and do what Jerry tells you. I want you to watch the sky, the sea—report anything you see. Right?"

"Right." A man of few words, Capel.

"Good. Jerry, I'm going aft for a while, but I want to talk to Brand. Ask Kate to get him up here, will you?"

The SAS man eased in through the door, closed it quickly, a few moments later. He knew a bit about night vision and the effects of too much light. His shoulders seemed broader than ever and his face was blurred in the subdued lighting.

"Captain Scott?"

I moved to the back of the deck, taking him with me, out of Ben Price's way. I gave him a cigarette and we stood smoking in silence, while I got my thoughts together. Then—

"I want to give it to you straight, Mike. U.K. is out. Had it. Finished."

"Ah..." It was more of a sigh than an exclamation, and I realized that this tough little man had already prepared himself for such news. Then he said quietly, "Now what? Ditch?"

"Not quite, if we're lucky. We managed to contact Funchal, in the Madeira Islands. They'll take us. It's a long haul—nearly four hours, and we won't have much fuel left when we get there."

"Still—that's great." His teeth flashed.

"Wait...there's more," I went on grimly. "They're overloaded already with aircraft—the overspill out of Europe, other people like us. They've no food, no fuel, no accommodation. It's a small island, not geared up to feed thousands of strange people. All they can offer is a runway to use and a patch of real estate to park on. And we're damned lucky to get that...they could have turned us away."

"I see." His cigarette glowed, and I saw the hard set of his chin, the narrowed eyes. "It could be real rough. Am I thinking what you're thinking? That we might have to spend the rest of our lives there?"

"Check."

"Um," he said thoughtfully. "In which case my lot might come in handy. I mean—if it's every man for himself."

I stared at him. "After they stick out their necks to help us, Mike? That's a bit hard."

"Captain," he said slowly, "you're a nice guy but a naive fool. In the sort of world we'll have to live in, only the ruthless can survive. And the nice guys go to the wall. If there's only enough food on that island to feed our six hundred...we eat or we die. And I'm too young and beautiful to die."

There was not much I could say to that. I said quickly, "Well...we're on our way. And I have to tell the people something. What do you think?"

"Captain," the soldier said diffidently, "I have a confession to make. I spread it around that there had been a hijack attempt, that we had the situation under control, and that you'd make an announcement when you had time."

I dragged at my cigarette and stared at him.

"You old bastard. Good. They are okay so far, then?"

"Sure. But most of your grog has gone," he said.

"Oh, damn the grog." I was feeling better already. "Look, they won't feel so good when they hear what I've got to say. What I really want is to use your mob to control things. But we can't afford any shooting—we have to keep altitude to make Funchal, and one loose round'll ruin cabin pressure—and us."

"No problem," Brand said firmly. "How long can you give me to set it up?"

"Ten minutes?" I hazarded.

"Ample, Captain. I'd like my officers and Sergeant Major Hockey up here for briefing. Can you lay that on?"

I said I could lay it on.

Three minutes later, five of us were crushed into the galley, with Kate standing sentry at the top of the steps. I listened to Brand's briefing.

It took him a few brief moments to explain the situation. I found it hard to believe: these men took it almost unmovingly, as if they already knew the situation. Their reactions were those I would have expected from professional soldiers:

Captain Lemaistre, slim, immaculate. Harrow accent, cultured moustache, licked his lips and contented himself with an "I say..." Lieutenant Bond—Hamish to everyone except his tailor, to whom he apparently owed his next two years' salary—said something very quickly in Gaelic and crossed himself, a paradox which I noted but immediately forgot.

The sergeant-major got to the nub of the situation. "We're on our own, then."

Brand nodded. "Right. If we are to survive—at least until we land—the passengers must be controlled. We have about five minutes to get into position and brief our platoons. What time do you have, Captain?"

I hesitated. They were unlikely to be using GMT. Some would have New York time; others might already have reset to the local time zone, but that was improbable. "Look—check your watch time now, everyone—go."

We all checked. "Right," I said flatly. "I shall go downstairs and speak to them from the forward-entrance intercom in exactly eight minutes from now."

The major got down to business. "Right. George, Hamish—brief your platoon leaders. They are to prime the men. As soon as the Captain starts speaking, I want every man to walk slowly, calmly into position, spread out along each gangway. No weapons. Each man to handle his own immediate area. No rough stuff, unless someone gets hysterical. Ten men, family men, to deal with the children. Plus most of your stewardesses, Captain?"

"I agree. All right, Kate?"

She turned, nodded. It seemed to me that she had aged visibly in the past hours.

"All right," Brand went on briskly. "Sar'nt Major, stand by with the medical orderly. Have tranquilizers ready—injections if need be. One last point—remember these people are due for a very big shock; make allowances. They will need help, not bullying. But jump hard at any signs of panic—it spreads very easily. Questions?"

There were none.

"Right. Five minutes. Move!"

They moved—but Kate was way ahead of them, down the stairs to the main deck. Perhaps that was all she really needed—something positive to do.

I made a few notes on paper. How in hell could I tell these people they might die very soon? Could I lie to them? Reassure

them? I debated telling the passengers we were diverting
because of mechanical trouble—but it wouldn't wash. They
knew something was going on, all right.

Downstairs, the main deck was half-lit; people were stirring, looking round with startled eyes. All the main lights
came on, and I picked up the PA microphone at Gate 1 Port.

"This is the Captain. I want you to listen carefully. It is
not good news, and you may be deeply disturbed by it. But
you must keep firm control of yourself. I want no disturbances, and everyone is to stay in their seat. There is no immediate danger, and I believe we shall make a successful
landing—but not at London. Major Brand has placed his men
at my disposal, to ensure order will be kept. Lastly, there are
some people who do not understand English—please translate."

The SAS men strolled casually into position down the
length of the aircraft, and the hubbub of conversation grew
louder.

"Quiet!" I bawled. The noise stopped as if by magic: I'd
forgotten I was using the PA loudspeaker system. I told them
what they had to be told, as simply and unemotionally as I
could. Afterwards, in those faces I could see, the reaction was
totally unanticipated; I had half-expected to be swamped in
screams, hysterics, tears. True, there were bowed heads here
and there, handkerchiefs and tissues in evidence—and every
face, without exception, white and strained. But aside from
the quiet weeping here and there, they sat with their heads
high, watching my face.

"So—that is the situation, as of now. There are few places
where, at the best of times, we could make a safe landing—
this is a large, heavy aircraft. But I can tell you we have
made successful contact with Funchal in the Madeira Islands,
and they will accept us. We are due there in a little over three
hours, and we have ample fuel. You must try to forget where
you were going, what you were going to do. If we are lucky,
we will find safe haven in those islands—the climate is good,
and if we are prepared to work, we can help to support ourselves.

"Now, I will tolerate no actions which endanger the safety
of this aircraft, and Major Brand's men will ensure peace is
kept. Next—conserve all food supplies you carry with you.
Many aircraft have already diverted to Funchal, and food
will be very short. There will be no further food issues aboard,

except to children. One point I want to stress: I want no
segregation or withdrawal of groups of various nationalities.
It is nationalism which has brought us to this extreme; I want
no more of it. We are all in one category only: human beings.
I want us all to qualify for a second: survivors. With your
help, we can do it. Thank you."

I switched off, walked slowly forward to the flight-deck
stairs. Behind—a stunned silence. Topside, Kate waited,
with Ben Price. We looked at each other wordlessly, and I
hunched my shoulders apologetically.

"I'm sorry—what else could I say? There was no way to
break this thing gently," I said tiredly.

"Jonah," Kate whispered, "no one could have done it half
so well."

Ben Price nodded. "She's right, Skipper. You'll see—there
will be no...Listen to that, will you?"

Below, in deep, moving harmony, they were singing
"Abide with Me."

On the flight deck, Chambers swung round in his seat. "Just
going to call you, Skipper. Look."

He pointed out into the night sky to starboard. About
thirty degrees above the unseen horizon, a spherical luminous
cloud, perhaps the size of a tennis ball held at arm's length.
It could have been 50, 500 or 5000 miles away. It was dull
orange in the center, green around the periphery, glowing in
a nightmarish way like some phosphorescent fungus in a
black rain forest. It seemed to pulsate, irregularly, as if alive.

"What in Christ's name," I whispered, "is that?"

Chambers' voice was unsteady. Perhaps, as I had done up
to this moment, he had cherished the belief that this might
be only a bad dream, a gigantic hoax.

"It—just happened, Skipper," he said thickly. "John here
thinks a laser may have detonated an orbital bomb."

"Whatever it was," Capel said, "it was big. I figure that
is maybe a hundred miles away, forty, fifty miles up. I—uh-
oh."

"What is it?" I said tensely.

"Take a look at this." Capel got out of my seat. I slid in
and he pointed forward and towards the northeast. The night
was still black and starry, a crescent moon riding high and
brilliant on the starboard bow; that damned artificial floodlight away to the south extended our vision enormously. Far

out on the horizon, I saw a dim irregular profile, almost saw-toothed...a distant cloud bank, close to the horizon, silhouetted against a glowing amber arc of sky, fading upwards into the blue-and-green end of the spectrum. Almost twenty degrees of the horizon azimuth—in the direction of northern France. Which, I calculated quickly, was more than 900 miles away. I tried to imagine the magnitude of explosion required to throw fireballs that high...25, maybe 30 miles, to the very boundaries of space.

"Take a good look," I said thinly. "That's all you'll ever see of France."

"Great God..." Capel said.

Chambers said bitterly, "I don't think you can count on Him being around. Not if He's any sense."

"All right, all right," I said. Despite myself, I sounded harsh, brutal, but maybe it was what they needed. "We have a job to do. John, we could do with a hot drink. Some soup, maybe? Jerry, let me have an ETA to letdown point for Funchal. Ben—fuel check. I am holding 39,000, airspeed Mach .85. Let's go."

Lighting another Low Tar, I thought I was smoking too much, but I sure as hell wasn't going to die of lung cancer, the way things looked. I blew smoke in a long funnel towards the instrument panel. Maybe it was wrong, but I felt happy, more relaxed: maybe we'd get into Funchal, maybe we wouldn't. I could get Delta Tango down okay....The rest was in the lap of the gods.

Maybe Funchal wouldn't be too bad...sunshine, tropical beach, swimming; with Kate along, retirement might not be so bad. It hardly seemed possible that this would be my last flight....My thoughts drifted back to other trips, other days, other places.

The Funchal frequency, 116.1, was busy when I switched over.

"Funchal, El Al Flight 83, eight miles, final approach."

"Eight three roger, call Funchal Ground on 134.45."

"Funchal, Funchal, Varig Flight 514 en route São Paulo Paris, urgently request diversion. Position 400 miles west of Funchal. Casualties on board. Fourteen dead, thirty plus injured, following hijack attempt. We are depressurized 12,000 feet, very low on fuel. Over."

"This is Funchal, 514. We will help all we can, but situation

critical. We have taken forty-three aircraft unscheduled, eleven others inbound. Airfield congested. We are taxiing aircraft into sea to make room. We have no food or accommodation. State of Emergency declared by local military commander. Our orders are to accept no more aircraft. Over."

"Funchal from 514. I say again—we have casualties and low on fuel."

"There are many casualties in the world tonight. We cannot help further. Advise you ditch as close to shore as possible. We will advise Coast Guard. Out."

"Funchal, Air India Flight 149. We are 440 miles southwest on flight to Madrid-Athens-Bombay. We cannot reach Funchal ... we will ditch about 80 miles out. Can you advise any shipping in this area? Over."

"Funchal to 149. Sorry. We have no information on shipping for last four hours. We have a report from a Middle East Airlines flight inbound an hour ago. Some kind of sea battle was seen off Madrid at that time. Captain reported several nuclear explosions, apparently underwater. Area between Madeira and mainland probably affected by heavy radiation. We have had two very big tidal waves. Over."

"Funchal, Air India 149—we have many passengers on board including children—there must be a ship somewhere near us...."

"One four nine, I wish I could help you. I have many other aircraft in emergency. I can only do my best. I have no information on shipping. Sorry."

Chambers got up, stood between our seats, face milk-white in the reflected lights of the panel. "I—have to go aft, Skipper."

"Okay—make it fast. And ask Brand to come up here— I want to know how things are down below."

"Check."

I looked at the dashboard clock. It would be getting light soon, and dawn could not come quickly enough for me. We had been airborne less than four hours—such a short time in which to destroy a world. I could not adjust to the paradox of Delta Tango flying normally through a starlit night, functioning perfectly; apart from that hellish fireball to the south, we had seen nothing. I leaned forward, staring eastwards; the skyline was dark, those grim fires faded from sight, and I could not assess if that was bad, or good. I took a closer look, turning down the panel lights' dimmer control. The horizon—

the plane above which I could see stars—had moved upwards; there was dense blackness a third of the way up to the zenith. It was possibly ordinary cloud formations...but I felt uneasy.

"Ben, look up sunrise time in this longitude."

"Wait one....Ten or eleven minutes from now, Skipper. Should be getting light in the east now."

"That's what I thought. Take a look." I gestured towards the windscreen, port side.

"My God..."

"Mm. What do you make of that cloud bank, Ben?"

"God knows. Nothing makes sense anymore, Skipper," he said tensely. He was right.

"Funchal, Flight 626. Estimate you in about two hours....I hope to God you can still take us. We are in sight of very heavy cloud concentration to the northeast. Sun apparently obscured. Have you any information? Over."

"Six two six—affirmative. We can accept eight more aircraft...you are number five to land. We are investigating cloud report...."

A strange voice cut in. *"Funchal, Air France 882 inbound to you from Casablanca...we are in that area. Expected dawn ten minutes ago...sky totally obscured, very heavy turbulence. Cloud formation very high...we estimate up to 20 miles or more. We think cloud is nuclear debris coming down from British Isles. Over."*

The channel was totally silent for long minutes.... Frightened men sat in lonely cockpits over the autumn sea wastes, trying to absorb the meaning of death.

I looked at Price and said heavily, "We're not going to get much of a suntan in Madeira, I reckon."

He just stared at me, slumped back in his seat. It was a lousy joke anyway. Chambers came back moments later, climbed wearily into his seat.

"All okay, Skipper. Except—that last Russian snuffed it."

"Snuffed it?"

"Kicked the bucket. The guy Capel hit with an axe."

It didn't seem important. "What have they done with him?" I said dully.

"Rolled all four in carpet and shoved them down into the hold. Oh, and that pop star—what's his name—and his girl are on the way, I think. Too many pills. Doc Rabin says they're in a coma. Good riddance."

"That's as may be," I said. "Our problem is to get this thing down in one piece. What about Funchal?"

"I'll check, but I seem to remember a single runway, about 9000 feet. They had a bad crash a few years back; two 747s collided on the runway."

"Was that at Funchal? It means each arrival has to taxi back up the runway—and they are overcrowded to hell, Jerry."

"I know. God, I'll be glad to see the end of all this."

I got them started on the en route checks. Mike Brand came forward and reported. The passengers were reasonably quiet. Sven Olaffsen was out cold, with most of a bottle of vodka inside him. Rabin, he said, was under severe strain—refused any drink or stimulant and had violent shivering fits every few moments. Kate was looking after him. I asked how Karen Waldheim was taking it.

"Sitting in her seat, quite calm."

The radio suddenly came to life. Chambers answered Funchal's call. They came back.

"Funchal calling all inbound aircraft, all inbound aircraft. Do not land. I say again, do not land. We have an emergency. No landings till further notice."

Chambers said furiously, "Jesus H. Christ!"

"Shut up!" I said violently.

"Funchal to all aircraft. No further aircraft can be accepted at this airport. Runway obstructed. Runway obstructed. We have a ground collision between El Al Flight 83 and an un-identified aircraft which attempted a landing without lights. Both aircraft burning. Other aircraft alongside runway also on fire. Fire is spreading quickly...further landings impossible. I have to advise that we cannot accept further trans-missions and this airport is closing down. Out."

In spite of the problems which now beset us, I felt enormous pity and admiration for the Funchal controller. He had coped magnificently for many hours, and the final catastrophe was none of his making: many hundreds of people would probably die because some criminal idiot had tried to jump the queue, and I hoped to God he had burned in the wreck, because he would undoubtedly fry in Hell for his crime.

We were all, I believe, past making effective comment in Delta Tango. Personally, I just sat back and let the great flood of numb despair wash over me; you keep trying and fighting, coping with each obstacle as it appears, and as long as a chink of light can be seen at tunnel end, you keep on going. But there comes a time when you fetch up against a brick wall, of infinite length, height and thickness, when the basic urge to continue the fight fades and dies.

Without a word, I got up, made my way to the VIP bar, poured half a tumblerful of Red Label and got it down in a single burning swallow. I was aware of figures staring, Kate walking towards me, and I turned my back, got in a second attack on the bottle and set the glass down shakily. I fumbled for a cigarette, and Kate was there.

"Jonah? What are you doing? Jonah?" Her hand gripped my upper arm, and I shrugged her off angrily. The bottle wasn't there anymore when I reached for it, and I moved my head round through a right angle to scowl at her. "My bottle... where's my—"

"Jonah... Oh, God, Mike, what's wrong with him? Has he gone mad?"

I snorted with laughter. "Dear ol' Mike... he knows the score—don't you? Why don't you tell her we won't be home tonight... because there's never gonna be another day.... Sun should have come up by now.... Funchal's out and we can't land. Know what, Kate, old girl? We'll just have to stay put up here until they send a relief crew. Where's the relief crew, Mike? Huh?"

Things became very confused very quickly. I was suddenly more than tired, and the carpet underfoot suddenly got up on end like a wall, and I leaned my forehead on it; something was hurting my upper arms, and I started complaining, and my toes were dragging along the carpet.

In the lavatory, someone (Mike Brand, I found, later) stuck two fingers so far down my throat I almost choked to death and I got angry; I just wanted to sleep.

After a long time and unpleasant upheavals, I found I was back in my seat, head aching like a devil and a sore throat to boot. Two fingers gripped my nose. I opened my mouth to protest and gagged on the hot, sweet coffee. It seemed to help, and I grabbed the cup, drained it. I stared blearily at Chambers when he retrieved the cup.

"Okay, Skipper?" he said anxiously.

"Yes. All right... stop fussing. Let me think."

They stood around in a silent group—Brand, Kate, Capel, and Karen Waldheim, who also seemed to have become involved. What were they staring at? Waiting for a bleeding miracle! I wasn't in the mood for miracles.

Chambers was checking the INS with the Funchal coordinates set in. I leaned forward gingerly, stared ahead and down towards the sea. Was the sky imperceptibly lighter? I thought I could see the Atlantic, far below. Ahead of us, perhaps a hundred miles, the Azores—the damned useless Azores. And 700 miles farther on, Funchal, a small island turned into a gigantic funeral pyre by some damned selfish...

The altimeter still said 39,000 feet.... Delta Tango hummed onwards. She would do just that—until the fuel ran dry. How much longer? I did not know, and I asked Ben Price almost humbly for a readout.

Just over two hours, he reported. Christ, had I been out as long as that? I shuddered and fumbled out a cigarette; Karen leaned over, lit it for me. Land...all we needed was a square mile of God's good earth: it was not too much to ask, surely. Spain? We'd never make it now. We had been committed to Funchal for more than ninety minutes, and I screamed mentally at the thought of the precious tons of fuel wasted. Even now, we were cruising into the southeast, where the sun would soon rise, and it seemed pointless to me, in that moment, to change this situation: we weren't going any place. I thought, ludicrously, that maybe we were better off up here...I did not envy anyone on the ground at Funchal this morning.

"Jonah?"

I turned. Kate looked shattered—hair all over the place, face stained with tears, uniform creased; there was a sharp whiff of stale vomit from her, and I squirmed in shame.

"Finish," I said. "Kaput. End of road."

"But—"

"Don't push him, Kate. He's done all he could," Ben Price told her, as if I weren't sitting there beside them. "More than anyone else could have done. We've simply worked out all our options, and our only chance—a remote one—is to go down and look for shipping. Otherwise, we stay up here waiting for the fuel to run out."

Chambers got up stiffly. "I have to talk to Nickie, Skipper. You okay now?"

"Sure, Jerry. Go ahead. And—"

"Yes?"

"Sorry."

His grin was a little twisted. "Forget it, Skip."

I said, "Best not say anything back there. That goes for you too, Karen. I'll have to tell them something eventually, but I need time. Time to think. Ben—take them all aft for a drink. I'll be okay. Just—leave me alone for a while."

When the door closed behind them, I sat there quietly in the gray half-light of morning. I could see now that the great solid wall of overcast to the east had crept a little closer to the overhead position; the remainder of the sky was an unhealthy milky color, like the underside of toadstools. I stared at it for a long time. I didn't like what I saw.

Somewhere ahead, Funchal, a silent funeral pyre, burned unseen.

Time crept by in a colorless limbo. I sat numbly at the controls, fingers moving restlessly over the throttle levers, the yoke, feeling the delicate, haunting touch of the autopilot making the minute changes in control setting necessary to maintain heading, altitude and attitude. I was dimly aware of activity behind me. Chambers moved from his seat to Price's desk and back again; they spoke briefly in quiet voices, and finally Chambers returned to his seat. He started once more to work his way carefully through one frequency band after another; twice he asked Price to change crystals in one of the VHF or UHF sets, reaching fresh and untried communications bands.

I was trapped in a stasis, the unholy paralysis of nightmare. I knew there were still things to do, needing to be done, but brain and limbs alike were shocked into immobility.

We flew on steadily, into the gray twilight, our course taking us farther into the shadow of that immensely high overcast; I looked up at it and began to think, slowly and laboriously. The detritus of nuclear war lay not only upon the land but upon the face of heaven; it might have been "Guesstimation," but that spreading cancer of gray-black smoke could top 20 miles or more. No one, I told myself, had ever been able to forecast accurately what a really big H-bomb would do, when detonated over a city at ground zero: all previous tests had been on deserted Pacific islands, or underground in sparsely populated country. And that was a thought.

"Ben?"

"Yes, Skipper—feeling better?" he asked anxiously.

I ignored the question. "Get one or two of those eggheads—those scientists—up here. I want them to take a look at this stuff."

"Right."

They came in diffidently, eyeing me with half-concealed misgivings.

I waved them forward. "Take a look up there. What do you think?" They craned their necks to see. Karen looked tired, but calm as usual. Olaffsen was clearly still in his cups but could speak clearly, albeit slowly and with exaggerated care. He coughed into his palm and said, "Interesting. Most unusual."

I said irritably, "All right—so it's unusual. So are nuclear wars. How long is that muck going to hang around?"

Karen Waldheim shook her head. "Impossible to say, Captain. If we knew what caused it—the extent—"

"I know what damn well caused it," I said grimly. "Flaming nuclear bombs caused it. Lots of them. Now—why is it so high? Must be fifteen, twenty miles up. And spreading—we won't see much of the sun today—it's spreading faster than the daylight line."

Karen nodded, eyes focused on the vast gray cloud layer above.

"Of course," she said stiffly, "you realize that it is also very lethal—we are already breathing radioactive particles on the fringe of that cloud. Eventually, it will all drop into the lower levels—and the roentgen count will be calculated not in terms of 'fatal' but in multiples of the lethal level. But we shall all be dead long before that happens."

Volkel shifted uncomfortably. "I'm not so sure, Karen. The dispersion factor—"

She looked at him piercingly. "You know better than that, Professor. From what we already know, we can assume that enough nuclear weapons have been used to kill every man, woman and child on the Earth ten times over. It is not a case of how many shall survive—but how soon the last will go."

Ben Price said in a hollow voice, "That's goddamn marvelous. This is one time I could do without expert opinion. Isn't there anyone with some better ideas than that?"

Chambers looked back from his seat.

"Skipper—"

"Yes, Jerry?"

"I'm getting something...it's very faint, not an aircraft—
on the HF ham radio band. Hang on—I'll cut in the speaker."

He leaned over, flicked a switch, spoke again.

"This is Speedbird Flight 626, Flight 626, transmitting....Come in any station, any station, do you read?
Over."

The static sounded like some distant train roaring through
a tunnel. But in the middle of it, we all heard the faint voice.

*"Six two six, this is Lima Bravo Kilo, Lima Bravo Kilo,
location Pôrto Delgado on São Miguel in the Azores. Do you
read me? I am receiving you faint and distorted. Over."*

"Lima Bravo Kilo, Flight 626, we copy you. Are you an
airport? Over."

The reply came back after a brief wait. *"Bravo Kilo to 626.
No, senhor, I am sorry, this is Juan Silva Santos. I live in
Pôrto Delgado and I am on holiday from Lisbon University.
I have transmitting license—you understand?"*

Jerry stared at me, indecisive.

I said quickly, "I'll take it. Bravo Kilo, Bravo Kilo, this
is 626. We are about two hundred miles northwest of you,
heading for the Azores. We must find a landing place without
delay. Do you know what has been happening during the
night, Juan?"

The radio hissed steadily. Then—

*"Six two six from Juan Silva. Yes, senhor, I know. I have
two friends with me. We have been listening all night. Many
airplanes have crashed—so many we cannot count. Now, not
so many are left. Over."*

I said slowly and distinctly, "Juan, this is important. What
is the nearest airport to you?"

*"Juan to 626—we think Santo Aro—on the north side of
San Miguel. But we do not think you can land, senhor. Many
airplanes come to Santo Aro during the night from the mainland, but an hour ago we hear on the police radio that one has
crashed. The airfield—it is too small, they say."*

"All right, Juan. You are doing fine," I told him. "Now—
we cannot contact anyone on radio—can you telephone the
Airport Control?"

*"Juan to 626—we do not think is so good an idea, 626. We
think the airplane has—hit Control Tower. We do not hear
them anymore ourselves. Over."*

I was really angry now. These things may have been sent
to try us—and someone was trying too damned hard. Well,

I wasn't finished yet...no way. I waved impatiently for
Chambers to hand me the Atlantic chart. Where in hell was
Lajes? I racked my brains to recall what I knew about the
flaming place....I looked at the chart again. That big island—Terceira—that was it.

"Juan, this is 626. All right. Listen carefully now. There
is one other place we can land. The USAF base at Lagens—
we call it Lajes. Do you know it?" We had to wait a long time
for the reply.

*"Juan to 626. Senhor, I do not know how to say this for
you. We cannot see Lagens from my house. But we know where
it lies. In the middle of the night there was a big—fire? Noise
like a very big gun—"*

"Explosion?" I prompted.

*"Yes, senhor. Many windows are broken in Pôrto Delgado.
We run quickly to the cliff at the edge of the sea. It is—high
up, you understand?"*

"Yes, Juan. Go ahead."

*"Senhor. We look over the sea. There is very bright light—
like sunlight. It lights up the sky and all the land, like the
middle day. Soon, there is the big noise, the hurrying wind,
we are...knocked to the ground. It is very bad for hearing
afterwards—and we have the red stain from the light on our
skin. The skin, it peels itself in some places. Senhor, I swear
it is true."*

I had to ask the question. "And that was near Lajes, Juan?"

"Not near. Above. Senhor."

"All right, Juan. Thank you. I will talk to you again in a
moment. Out."

Well, I thought, that was it. Bingo. I knew they were all
watching me, and I avoided the accusing eyes. I groped for
a cigarette, found only an empty pack. Chambers lit one for
me, passed it over, and I took a deep, steadying pull. I began
thinking aloud.

"Okay. We can write off the airports, then. But we can
make the islands. We'll have plenty of fuel for a precautionary
circuit, a belly landing. Somewhere in those islands, there
has to be a mile or two of flat land. Give us the length and
we'll do the job. Brush up on the emergency procedures...use
up the last of our fuel before we go in, keep the fire risk low.
All children back into the tail...best place for them. Kate
can handle that."

I got back to the radio. Thank God we'd found a kid who could not only work his own set—but speak good English.

"Six two six to Juan. Do you read?"

"Yes, senhor. Go ahead, 626."

"Okay, Juan." I spoke as slowly and as clearly as I could. Much depended on his answer. "Now, this is a big airplane and I am going to have to make an emergency landing with wheels up. Do you understand? Over."

"Yes, senhor. I understand. Go ahead."

"Fine, Juan. Just concentrate on what I say. We need to find a section of flat land about...three kilometers long. With no hills at each end. Farmland, grass—anything like that. I want you to think carefully and tell me where we can find such a place. Over."

"It will take a little time, senhor. I will call you again. Stand by."

I made good use of the time.

"Right...let's get this thing organized, if possible. Kate?"

"Yes, Jonah. I'm here."

"Good girl. Take Capel with you. Get all your girls together aft, and go over the emergency landing drill carefully. I'm banking on the Portuguese kid finding somewhere we can land. If we have to think again, I'm going for belly landing on the best beach I can find, or in shallow water near a beach. All right so far?"

She nodded.

"Okay. I want all passengers briefed. Don't hide anything—tell them why we've lost Funchal. Tell them it's going to be rough, whichever option we take—but we're going to make it. All kids to the back of the airplane. You have plenty of time—more than an hour. Get rid of all loose gear—stack it in the galleys, anywhere; I want no gash bags floating around. Elderly people forward of the kids, odds and sods farther forward and Brand's boys in the front. They can handle the impact better than any civilian. If Brand argues, send him up here. Check with me frequently and let me know how things are going. Got all that?"

"We got it, Captain. I'll help all I can." Capel's face was set but confident. "We're not licked yet."

"I hope you're right, John," I said quickly. "Ben—how about an update on fuel at destination? And Jerry, how long to go?"

"Stand by, Skip. Ah—I make it thirty minutes to the

northern island of the group. Another seven minutes to San Miguel. I figure we have a tail wind—quite a respectable one."

"Thanks, Jerry. Ben?"

"On that basis," Price said slowly, "we will have about half an hour flying time left, to get down to maximum landing weight. We'll have to burn off fuel."

I nodded, satisfied. "I'd rather have it that way than run short, Ben. Except that we don't have to worry about maximum weight. I'll put this old girl down any damned weight we happen to be, in these circumstances—but in case of fire, we'd better have as little left as possible."

It was a nice problem. I looked at it from all ways, and it seemed to me that it was the end of the line. But we could take a good long look at the situation when we got there...maybe there was a nice long beach I could use. But I had flown into the Azores years previously, into the little Santo Aro field, delivering a Jet Islander to the Bahamas, on a busman's holiday, and I had dim memories of incredibly rocky coasts, huge Atlantic rollers and white surf a quarter of a mile wide.

But the Silva kid—he might know something. It was so little to ask...two miles of flat land...I had a mind-flash of Delta Tango sliding interminably through underbush, and I sat up.

"Ben?"

"Skipper?"

"I want you to go down to the cargo bays. Take Brand and a couple of his lads with you. Can you leave your board for a while?"

"I guess so, Skip. How long before letdown, Jerry?"

Chambers checked his clipboard. "Anytime. Sooner we get down, sooner we burn off spare fuel."

"Okay. Ben, I don't know what we have stowed away down there—apart from our Russian friends. But I want anything that resembles food or drink brought up into the main cabin. Get down there as quietly as you can—use the hatch in Zone L. Don't leave anything down there we can use."

Price nodded. "Leave it to me, Skip."

I managed a grin. My face was stiff, and it hurt. "We may be a long time in the sunny Azores."

"Sunny, balls," Ben growled. He sounded quite sassy...we

were getting on top of this thing. Slowly. "Flaming sun forgot to come up this morning."

"It's there, all right," I told him. "Probably that light patch farther south. Go on—get going."

He got.

Five minutes later, the kid came up on the air. Louder, clearer. We were getting close. *"Senhor,"* he said. *"We have three possible places for you. All on San Miguel. You are ready?"*

Chambers nodded, clipboard on his knee.

"Go ahead, Juan."

"Yes, senhor. These places are all between the mountains and the sea. I have the map here—how can I say the places to you?"

That was a reasonable question. I thought for a moment.

"Where is Pôrto Delgado, Juan? On the island, I mean. Over."

"We are on the south coast, senhor. The island lies in the sea like a whale—facing to the east. We are on the belly, nearer to the tail of the fish. Do you understand? Over."

I grinned. He was using his head, that boy. "Yes, Juan. Good. We understand. Now—give us the position in two ways. First, the distance along the coast until you would be south of the landing point. Is that clear?"

"Yes. Yes, I understand, 626."

"Okay. Fine. Then you tell me how far north to go. Do you use kilometers?"

The boy said hesitantly, *"Yes. But—I do not know how far it is to go, senhor."*

Oh, God, I thought. Now—a geography lesson.

"Look at the map again, Juan. It will show somewhere a little line marked off in kilometers. It is called the scale, in English. Tell me when you find it."

Silence. Then—excitedly—

"Yes, senhor. Yes—I have it."

"All right, Juan. Take a piece of paper. Mark along the edges a scale, from the map. Place the paper on the map and it will tell you how far to go. Over."

"Yes, senhor. Wait. Wait...yes. It is good, very good. Eight kilometers."

"All right, Juan," I said soothingly. "All right. Now—we have plenty of time. Tell me first about each place, and then where it is. Over."

He had three possible landing areas in mind, all within ten kilometers of the town in which he lived. Two were tea plantations, which sounded good. The third was, of all things, a pineapple plantation—I could almost taste the juice.

"Six two six to Juan. That's very good. Very good. Well done. We are all very grateful. We are still about half an hour away from you. I want you to tell me about the weather. We need to know about the cloud, and about the wind on the ground. The direction the wind is coming from, and how hard it is blowing. I do not want you to try to guess the speed—tell me if it is a little breeze, a strong breeze, a little wind or a big wind. And the direction. Over."

Juan came back strongly. *"Yes, senhor. I will do this. You will wait?"*

I said wryly, "We have nothing else to do, Juan. Go ahead."

About five minutes later, we heard him again. He sounded worried.

"Juan to 626. Senhor, we are very afraid. We have not looked at the sky this morning until you made us look for cloud. The sky—it does not look good."

I said patiently, "Yes, Juan. We know about that. Can you tell us what it looks like from the ground? Over."

He said slowly, *"I have never seen a sky like this before, senhor. It is morning, the sun should be shining and it is still very dark. There is a line across the sky, almost overhead. To the east of the line, the sky is dark—almost black. That is where the sun should be, senhor."* His voice broke a little. He could not be more than seventeen or eighteen—and he was clearly very frightened.

"All right, Juan. This is 626. Take it easy...you know that many bombs have dropped, that many people are dead. The darkness you see is just a cloud—a very high cloud, of debris—of smoke and little pieces thrown up by the bombs. The wind carries it southwest from the mainland. Do not be frightened of it. Do you understand what I have said?"

"Senhor," he said slowly, *"I understand some of the things you tell us. I also understand that all the people here are in the churches—something I have never seen before. Not some of them—all of them. They are all praying, senhor—are we all to die?"*

I was not at all sure how I was going to answer that one. I didn't know myself.

"Juan from 626. No, of course not. Many people have died,

in the cities. Perhaps more have died on Terceira, because Lajes was an American base and a natural target. Understand?"

A small voice said, *"Yes, senhor."*

"All right," I went on. "Now—can you see any low cloud? Below the overcast?"

"No, senhor. The sky is clear, but—I do not know the word, but it means not very light. The wind is from the northwest. More than a breeze but not a very strong wind. Over."

That did not sound too bad. At least two of the possible landing areas favored a landing from the southeast to the northwest, with a run-in over the sea. I yawned and stretched mightily; my back was aching like the devil.

All at once there was a muffled cheer behind me. Kate and Nickie were there, with Capel and Brand—all grinning madly. Ben must have briefed them.

Jerry Chambers turned to beam at his girl, Kate was hugging Nickie and Brand was pounding a fist into the other palm, grinning foolishly and saying over again, "I don't believe it ... I just don't believe it."

It was time to spread the news. I called out to Kate:

"How are things back there, Kate?"

She nodded—and I saw there were tears in her eyes. "Fine, Jonah. Fine. We have them all moved, all settled down. Ben is still down in the cargo bay."

I nodded, turned back to stare out of the forward window, as if I could see the Azores far ahead. That dreadful overcast had scared the crap out of me when I first saw it—and it still did. But the mind adjusts to almost anything in time, and I found myself passing long minutes without glancing up at the death-laden ceiling. I spent a moment or two in thought before getting on the public-address system.

"This is the Captain. I have good news, for a change. Please listen carefully. We are about twenty-five minutes' flying time from the Azores and the island of San Miguel. We have ample fuel. There is no airport open which we can use, at this time. However, we have identified at least three areas where we can make a safe landing without wheels. We are also in contact with people on the ground who are helping. This is a very large and very strong airplane, and given a reasonable area, we have an excellent chance of making a successful landing.

"Shortly, you will receive a final briefing on what to do.

You should do exactly as you are told and not move until we have stopped. You will find the soldiers have opened the emergency doors. There, you will find a long canvas chute down which you can slide safely to the ground. Take your time, do not panic and all will be well. The danger of fire is small—we shall fly around to use all our fuel before we come in to land. I want the children passed up first to the chutes, and a soldier out of each one first to catch them. Listen carefully to the stewardesses. Good luck to you all—I will advise you of progress all along the line. Thank you."

There was an odd noise from below, I turned irritably to Chambers.

"What the hell is all that row about?"

He grinned. "They are clapping and cheering, Skip."

"They must be round the goddamn bend," I said. "Take over for ten minutes—I want to see what Ben's up to."

"Okay, Skip. I have control."

In the VIP lounge, I was stopped in my tracks. Karen Waldheim came over, took my hand in both of hers. When she let go at last, she rested her hands on my shoulders and smiled twistedly. "Bless you, Captain. If you only knew..."

"I know we're not out of the woods yet, lady. But we have a fifty-fifty chance now, which is a hell of a lot more than we had an hour ago. No one ever put a 797 down without wheels before; there's always a first time.

"Good grief" —I stared around the once-immaculate lounge—"looks as if a bomb went off in here."

The seat once occupied by Nabokov was bent, twisted: it occurred to me that I could have done that during the argument—accounting for my backache. Thunderman and escort were still in their seats. I walked over for a closer look: he was sagging in the corner, head on the ledge of the window, the skin of his face an odd beige color and glistening with sweat. His breathing was shallow and fast. I lifted up an eyelid gently and gasped. His eyes were swiveled upwards so that almost all white showed, a thing I had not thought possible.

"He is not good, that one," Dr. Rabin said at my back. "Overdose plus alcohol."

"Can't we do anything?" I questioned.

"What is to do? He needs hospitalization. He needs stomach pump, stimulants to counteract the barbiturates he has taken by the bottle. More, he needs much psychiatric treatment. We have none of those things."

I frowned. "Will he make it?"

Rabin shook his head. "I think not, Captain. If he survives the landing—oh, yes, I know the risks, but I am an old man and not afraid—I would say two, three hours."

"I see. And the girl?" I felt a wave of nausea, looking at her...she had vomited and, from the stench, had lost bowel control altogether. The face was young-old...hardly out of her teens and the lines of a raddled hag.

The fat little man leaned forward, held her wrist, checked his watch. "She is not so bad, Captain. Mostly dead drunk."

"Okay. I'll have the girls take her forward and clean her up a little. Everyone else seems to be bearing up?"

He nodded. Volkel sat at the coffee table, writing steadily; Olaffsen had woken up, cleaned up and was working chess problems on the Russians' board.

I buzzed for Kate, got her started on cleaning up the lounge a little, and detailed Jill Stewart and another stewardess to clean up Thunderman's girl. There was a large ominous stain on the deck, where the carpet had been stripped, and I decided there was no point in touching it.

My pack of Splits was empty; I went into the galley store, found another, told myself it was time I gave up the habit and grinned. Within weeks, everyone was going to give up, willy-nilly.

The joint tasted good, for all that. Back in the lounge, I found an empty seat and sat down heavily. It had been a very long night...nearly nine hours in the air. Just half an hour more, and I would have to go up front and tackle the landing; but for now, I could relax. The seat back was soft against my cheek.

That landing...that was going to be something. I wasn't frightened—I couldn't identify the emotion I was feeling right now, but it wasn't fear. Anticipation? Impatience? I was kidding myself. I wasn't scared—I was just plain damn terrified...six hundred people...300 tons of aircraft...nothing but a row of tea bushes to stop us. Picture of 797 sliding over a cliff into the sea. Picture of Brand throwing out anchors from side doors...pictures...pictures...

12

"Come on, Skipper!"

"Huh?"

Ben Price shook me again, not too gently. "Wakey-wakey, Jonah. Jerry says we are down to twelve thousand feet and getting close."

I sat up straight with an effort, checked my watch and yawned. Big deal—I'd slept all of ten minutes. My neck ached and my mouth tasted like a Chinese wrestler's jock strap.

"Jeez, I could have slept for a week. Okay, Ben—be right there. Get me a drink of cold water, would you?"

"Sure." I drank slow and deep, drank again and screwed up the paper cup. The crud taste was less noticeable—but nothing was going to improve the stiff neck. Apart from that, I felt fine; the scratched hand still itched and my scalp was sore—but these were minor problems.

I went forward, slid into the seat, found my headset.

"Okay, Jerry—what's the situation?"

"Well—I make it about 40 plus miles to go, Skipper. The visibility is worse, if anything. I'm going to level off at 10,000 feet—give us a better chance. The INS seems to be acting up a little."

I leaned forward, checked the high dark-gray blanket which extended now from the far eastern horizon to port, through the zenith and a third of the way to the western horizon. The coverage was uneven. In some areas there were seams and patches of silver gray, where the sun tried desperately to penetrate the gloom. But there were places, too, where it seemed much thicker: there, it was the rich dark slate gray of the underside of thunderclouds, impenetrable and menacing. Worst of all, the sky still visible to the west, beyond the irregular northwest-southeast terminator line, had lost the faint blue content we had seen earlier; it was a uniform silvery gray, darkening down towards the southwest.

I gave up trying to imagine what tracery of upper winds and currents existed at those levels—there was little enough air up there to support the radioactive cloud, which had risen of its own heat. Soon, I knew, it would cool and sink, and cover almost every square inch of the green Earth.

"Right, Jerry. Keep her at this height; start getting the speed back to about Mach .75. Leave her on autopilot—she'll find her own way."

I watched him for a moment, working with Ben to set engine power to the lower figure.

"Now—what have we got on the Azores? Anything?"

Chambers said, "Stand by," reaching for his clipboard, rubbed a forefinger along his nose reflectively and said, "Here we are. About seven major islands in the group, Skipper. San Miguel—where the kid lives—lies well to the southeast of the main group. I'm not surprised they didn't actually see Lajes get it, but the coastline of San Miguel points almost directly to Terceira—they'd see the fireball, all right. Our heading takes us almost over the top. Do we dogleg around, or do we want to take a look?"

I thought for a moment. "It's been some time, Jerry. The fallout will have blown well clear by now. We should be safe enough at 10,000 feet."

"I think you're probably right, Skipper. I may be morbid—but I'd like to see what we missed."

I said sourly, "Don't kid yourself we've missed anything, Jerry. Someone may still have the odd bit of nastiness left up his sleeve. And once that lot up there starts to come down..."

"Don't say it. I don't even want to think about it. Should I give the Silva kid a call?"

"Go ahead."

Chambers keyed the radio.

"Six two six to Silva. Come in, Juan."

The boy must have been sitting with his fist on the transmit key. He came through instantly. *"Juan to 626. I hear you, senhor. Is all well?"*

"Six two six to Juan. Yes—so far. We are about ten minutes' flying time away. We have descended. Have you any further news? Over."

Juan said, *"Yes, senhor. My father, he has come from church and he is here. He says he can help. Stand by."*

"Senhor—you hear?" the Portuguese accent was pronounced, the English difficult to follow. I signaled to Jerry and took over.

"Six two six to Mr. Silva—yes, we hear. Speak slowly and clearly. Go ahead."

"Yes, senhor. Juan, he say the airplane must fall on the land. The land must be flat. Is so?"

"Yes, Mr. Silva. At least two kilometers long. Over."

The old man's voice was uncertain, hesitant. *"Senhor, we live in Pôrto Delgado, Rua de Santa Clara. Is near the sea. West of Pôrto Delgado is Parque Diniz Mota. Is very big park, little trees but no hill. Is possible to come from sea with big petrol tanks on right, west end of Pôrto Delgado. Is understood?"*

"Yes, Mr. Silva. Very good. We understand. Listen, please. We need doctors, ambulances, fire engines. Doctors, ambulances, fire engines. Do you understand? Over."

"Sim, senhor. Is understand. I ask for these to be at my house. The airplane falls near to sea—is near to my house. Is good?"

"Very good," I said—and meant it. "We will fly around before we land. We have fuel left. We can look at the park first. Thank you. Please call Juan. Please call Juan. Over."

The kid came back on, obviously full of his importance.

"Six two six to Juan," I said into the microphone, "how is the light? And is the wind still blowing from the Terceira?"

"Juan to 626. Senhor, I do not see how you know the wind is blowing this way, but is true. Wind faster than before. Makes trees move. Light is bad—like early morning before sun comes. Also, many people from north of island who are close to Terceira when the big light comes have come to the hospital in the Avenida Roberto Ivens—the Hospital São José. They have the red skin which peels like a grape, and great sickness. Some are blind. We think maybe the world has gone crazy, senhor."

"Yes. Yes, I think it did, Juan. Go ahead."

"Yes, senhor. I have spent vacation on Terceira. Is very nice place. Many small farmers for tobacco, wine, oranges. Now...who can say? Meu padre—my father says tomorrow,

maybe, boats go to Terceira, to see who is alive and who is dead."

I said quickly, "No, Juan. Tell your father no one must go to Terceira. Tell him the bomb has poisoned the air and the land. If they go near, they will all die."

There was no reply for a long time. Then—

"Juan to 626. All right, senhor. But some have families on Terceira and say they will go anyway. But we understand. Thank you."

Delta Tango was in steady cruise at 10,000 feet. We did not know the correct altimeter setting—and it would not have been much help in any case, with no airfield on which to land. I had Jerry set in the International Standard setting of 29.92 inches; it would serve as well as any. I got on the intercom to Kate, now hard at work below. I told her we were approaching the Azores, fuel okay, and we would circle a few times to check on the landing sites.

"That sounds good, Jonah. I know we're going to be all right. How are you? It's been a long flight," she said anxiously.

"Me? You know me, love. Endless energy. I could do with a good sleep—say, a week or more—but I'm fine, really. How are your girls taking things?"

"You wouldn't believe it," she said quickly. *"All really pulling their weight—even the Asian girls. I know they're going to cave in after we land, and I can't blame them—almost all of them have lost their families in London and other places. I swear at them all the time, Jonah, but if they knew how proud I am . . ."*

"Sure. Sure you are. Okay—look, I'll give you ample warning, Kate; and don't come steaming up here after we land— your job is to get everyone out in one piece. And I mean everyone. Has Mike Brand organized the Army to go down the chutes first?"

"Yes, Jonah. It's all working like clockwork. You should see those soldiers joking with the children about sliding down chutes—I think they're all looking forward to it."

"Right," I said cheerfully, "best part of the trip. Thank God they don't know yet what sort of world we've left them. See you later, love. Out."

Ben Price came forward, leaned across the center console and peered forward and down, squinting his eyes.

"There—see it, Skip? The egg-shaped island—Terceira. That mountain is about three thousand feet high. The long island to the right is São Jorge, with the steep cliffs. Pico is just behind and to the right—and that's Falal, on the far right."

I took a long look. "I can't see São Miguel, Ben."

"You won't, just yet," he said flatly. "Much farther on and to port—about eleven o'clock. They're all volcanic islands. I wish I had some binoculars—see what shape Lajes is in. Still—another five minutes or so..."

I said, "Where is Lajes—on the island, I mean?"

Jerry said, "I've found an information sheet, Skipper. Lajes is on the northeast corner of the island. One long runway— 160 degrees and 340 degrees—nearly 11,000 feet long. If only...that would have done us fine. Short runway 110 degrees—290 degrees—only about 6000 feet. The airfield is right on the coast."

I nodded absently. No good chewing on the "might have been" and "could have done." We'd see shortly what a really big H-bomb could do. It must have been a cookie in the hundred-megaton range, to be seen 150 kilometers away on São Miguel. I checked the altimeter against the radio altimeter: it wasn't far off, but that made sense—we were into the long-standing Azores high-pressure area.

Terceira expanded in the forward windscreen. I remembered pictures of Hiroshima—and that was a Chinese firecracker compared with modern sophisticated weapons. Let's face it—I was surprised the island itself was still there. Probably an air burst.

"Take her down a little lower, Jerry. There's a strong wind down there."

Chambers said in an odd voice, "Skipper? Do you see what I see?" I got half out of my seat for a better look—and didn't believe what I saw.

"Jesus Christ!" I said, stunned.

We were well below seven thousand feet; in the half-light from the west we could see reasonably well—and what we saw was an intact airfield. One or two aircraft still burned on the ground. There were scattered fires among the airport buildings, but the massive hangars still stood intact. I could see the long flat, empty runway, running parallel to the coast, the low wooded hills on the right and the cluster of buildings between runway and beach. I spotted the high control tower, well down towards the far end of the runway, and the short secondary runway at the north end of the field.

I pulled out the autopilot, settled back in my seat, got a firm grip on the yoke.

"Let's not get excited, fellas," I said quietly. "There has to be a good reason for this. Ben, give me power for about 200 knots. Jerry, flaps to ten—I'm going to orbit at 2000 feet for a good look-see. Where's Capel?"

Ben said, "Back with Nickie in the galley, Skip."

"All right. Ben, I'll set up the power. Go back to the lounge—I want Rabin and the Waldheim woman up here on the double. Move!"

Ben moved, leaving the door swinging. I brought the old girl gently up to level flight, nose pointing towards the starboard side of the airfield. I began checking the ground systematically. The grass was an odd color—but that could be natural. Sort of metallic brown. Glistening. I could see eight—no, nine big USAF transports at all angles on the concrete apron, with the usual refueling tankers, jeeps, mobile generators clustered around. The long-range radar aerial near the control tower wasn't turning—already, question after question churning in my mind. Easy...easy. I took Delta Tango into a standard turn to port, a mile or so out, circling the field.

There was something...Christ, why hadn't I seen it before? Ground movement is always difficult to assess from a fast-moving aircraft: one sometimes has to do a double take to make sure cars are actually traveling, people really walking. But no car was traveling on the ground of Lajes. Nor was anyone walking—because the field was almost deserted. I spotted only a handful of people on the airfield—and they were all lying still, legs and arms a-sprawl.

Rabin said hoarsely, "Captain? What is it?"

"Take a look, Doc. During the night we heard that Lajes was hit by a bomb—a big one. Seen 150 kilometers away in São Miguel. Well—that's Lajes Air Base. What do you think?"

He took off his horn-rimmed spectacles, crowded close to the window behind my seat, stared down for long minutes. Karen Waldheim stood between the pilots' seats, leaning down to see. She had washed and cleaned up recently—I could smell the sweetness of her, and for some strange reason it refreshed me like a cool beer on a hot day. It brought back a little of my lost humanity, dispersed a little of the shame I felt.

The scientist stood up straight. He took out a handkerchief, polished the lenses of his glasses, set them carefully on the bridge of his nose. He watched Karen until she too stepped back.

"Dr. Waldheim?" he queried. They were professionals, consulting one another.

"I find it hard to believe," she said slowly, "but it is the only explanation. Note the grass. Note the trees to the landward side—stripped of leaves. Little or no damage to buildings. The fires—too few, too widespread—probably caused by electrical failure, heaters knocked over. Finally—the people. You agree?"

"I do." Rabin nodded, eyes shining. "Everything points to it. Captain—we believe we are looking at the first neutron bombing in history. It exploded at altitude—perhaps two or three miles. Negligible blast effect, minimum damage. Tell me—this air base—is it unusually important for some reason?"

I was still trying to absorb the meaning of his assessment. "Eh? Lajes? Oh . . . why, yes. Yes—it is the only large staging airfield between Europe and America. Two or three thousand people, I suppose."

"Exactly," said Karen Waldheim. "If you want to use a strategic air base, you don't destroy it. You use a neutron bomb, which leaves the base intact."

I was afraid to ask the question—and had no choice.

"And—the people?"

"Dead," she said coolly. "All dead—from radiation."

13

"Let me understand you correctly," I said harshly. "This—thing destroys life—and nothing else?"

"Yes."

"But—the place itself must be saturated—it could be years before it becomes usable again."

Rabin shook his head positively. "Not so. It was originally designed as a tactical weapon for battlefield use. It is possible to destroy an entire tank regiment and open up a three-mile wide salient through which your own armor can advance. The advance troops might have to wear protective clothing, breathing masks for a few hours—but the area will have no residual radioactivity after a short period."

I turned Delta Tango left again, cruised up the shoreline, staring hungrily at that beautiful long, clear runway. I had to make up my mind very quickly. We had barely enough fuel to make São Miguel from here—but if the background radiation here was too high, I could be sentencing six hundred people to a very nasty death. There were other factors....

I started a slow left turn round the north end of the field, thinking very hard. A wheels-down landing on a runway is infinitely preferable to a belly landing on unknown terrain. More important—if we found the hazard below was really serious, we could refuel and press on elsewhere—perhaps when they had the São Miguel runway clear at the Santo Aro airport. Staring down at Lajes, I could see more bodies now—tucked away in corners, beside vehicles, in the shade of buildings.

That figure—there...it moved, I thought crazily. I stared down, holding the airplane in a steady standard turn....The man waved frenziedly, ran a dozen paces into the open space inland from the Control Tower.

That did it.

"Right—Jerry, Ben—stand by for landing. We're going in. Jerry—get onto young Juan on São Miguel—tell him we'll try to contact him from the ground. Ben—landing checks. Karen—will you go back to the VIP lounge and ask Jill to see everyone is strapped in."

I rolled Delta Tango out of the turn, onto a southwest heading, throttled back a shade to initiate a steady descent down to a thousand feet. There was no sunlight, just the twilight haze to which we had become accustomed. The sea was a steel blue-green, disturbed by long, slow swells. I keyed the PA system.

"This is the Captain. The airfield below is a NATO base, Lajes, in the Azores. We are going in to land. Please fasten your seat belts, no smoking. Now—listen carefully, please. The airfield was hit during the night by a neutron bomb—which kills people but leaves buildings undamaged. The runway is clear, but there may still be radiation. We have no fuel left to go elsewhere. Now, I am going to land—and you must all stay in your seats until we check if it is safe. I have seen at least one person alive on the ground—he may be able to advise. Please follow the instructions given by the stewardesses. Thank you."

The intercom buzzed. Kate.

"Jonah...how marvelous!"

"Don't count chickens, love. You may end up with them fried. Jill has everything under control here; check back when you're all squared away for landing. Got it?"

She laughed, richly, and closed the connection.

"All-rightee," I said brusquely. "All set, Jerry? Ben?"

They checked in. I leveled out at 1000 feet on the radio altimeter, still going downwind to the southwest.

"We'll make a straight-in from about 4 miles, standard approach. No missed-approach procedure: it's shit or bust on the first approach—no fuel to go milling around the sky. We may have to try for São Miguel after all, if—"

Price said quietly, "We wouldn't make it, Skip. Not 150 kilometers."

"Okay," I said, "we'll leave full-flap very late. Jerry, check brakes and get the gear down. Check me three green lights."

"Roger. Gear down...we have three greens."

"Roger. Ben—power for V-Prog. What do you make it?"

"Wait one, Skip...140 knots threshold speed. Add ten for wind shear—final approach speed 150 knots, flaps ten degrees. Setting throttles now."

I turned my head to stare out of the window, craned my neck back to check the position of the field. It was lurking nicely about the seven-o'clock position, over the port wing. Left wing down, nice steady turn onto finals. I set the runway heading on the flight director—three four zero degrees, landing into the northwest. It was years since I had done a visual circuit and landing; congested airfields demanded straight-in monitored approaches from holding points, and the first we saw of an airport was generally the outer approach lighting, yellow sodiums glaring up like lion's eyes.

Airspeed 190 round the turn...falling off slightly to 180—just about right. The runway drifted into the top left corner of my windshield, rotated slightly, and came to rest dead center. On the starboard side of the runway, north of the tower, some aircraft was still burning, smoke drifting straight towards Delta Tango. I judged it was not more than 20 degrees off the runway line. I racked on a couple of degrees' correction to the right, eased back in my seat and got her steady.

The intercom...

"Cabin to Captain—passengers briefed and belted. All loose articles stowed. All doors on Automatic."

"Very good, Kate. Get in your seat and belt up."

"Manners..." she murmured, and switched off. I grinned. Kate back to Square One—for sure.

"Flaps twenty, Jerry, please."

"Flaps twenty, Skip."

About three miles to go; I corrected a shade more starboard, got her back on center.

"Nine hundred feet, one seven zero knots," Jerry reported.

"Check."

Ben Price cut in. "Fuel warning light starboard main tank. May be the electrics—no, she's slowing down, Skipper! Number Three!"

"Close her down. Open cross feeds. Close down Number Two. Increase power on Number Five. I want to hold 170 minimum."

"Roger."

"Eight hundred feet, 165 increasing."

"Okay, Jerry."

"One seven zero knots...seven hundred. Approaching minimums."

"Shove your minimums, Chambers. Stand by for full flap."

"Five hundred feet...four-fifty...about a mile to go..."

"Full flap!"

"Full flap coming down." Chambers slammed the flap lever down without taking his eyes off the airspeed.

"Three hundred...one-sixty...two-fifty feet...one-fifty knots..."

"Shade more power, Ben."

"Coming up...."

We slid in over the grass undershoot, the runway threshold expanding on either side of the nose. There was a massive area of black scars—rubber tread burned from hundreds of tires, contacting the ground at nearly two hundred miles an hour.

"Power back to sixty percent!" I said tightly. The controls were a shade sloppy, and I made big, harsh corrections to keep her level. Back on the yoke—she was barely ten feet from the ground, sinking slowly, nose coming gently up, airspeed falling, and I heard the faraway "keek-keek" of maingear touchdown. The nose went forward and I got on the rubber, keeping her rolling straight and true.

"Chop throttles...in reverse...open up!" I bawled.

Jerry cut in the reverse thrust, shoved open the throttles, and the three live engines roared out a fanfare of brute strength. Some giant hand pushed invisibly at the airplane, holding her back with incredible strength. I was losing bite on the rubber. I shifted to the tiller, kept her straight, speed falling fast now, with almost a third of the runway left. Brakes on now, feet bearing down ever harder, stabbing intermittently to release pressure and avoid overheating.

"Power off," I said tightly.

"Off."

We ground to a halt in a near-silence of stunning intensity. I put on the parking brake, let go the control column and found my hands wet with sweat, throat dry, eyes blinking uncontrollably. Perhaps there had been other times when I'd been more pleased to be on the ground, but for the life of me, I couldn't think of one.

I stirred in my seat at last. Jerry was mopping his brow, Ben Price coming forward to slap my back, beaming.

"That was some landing," he said jubilantly. "Wouldn't have cracked an egg."

I nodded absently, shut down the two remaining forward engines, and that left us Number Five up in the tail only, for taxiing in. There was a dull roaring sound from somewhere aft. Ben opened the door of the flight deck, and a great wave of cheering came swelling up—cheering, clapping, shouting, even crying. I stared uncomprehending at Ben, who grinned and said, "I guess they like you, Skip."

I said roughly, "Balls. You know better than that. It took all of us to get this thing down on the ground—stews as well. Go down and tell them to belt up."

Ben said primly, "Rather not, old boy. Never gone in for politics—and I reckon if they want a Prime Minister of Lajes, you're it."

I slung a clipboard at him and got back to work.

Jerry got the flaps up, unlocked Number Five throttle, and I gave her the gun, releasing the brakes. It took all I could get out of the tail engine to get her moving, and the noise subdued the jollifications aft for a while. But she moved, slowly at first, and I took her forward to the runway intersection, turned right on the tiller and started down the short runway, heading for the taxi track and the parking area in front of the Tower.

The door opened. Mike Brand came up forward, leaned down to get a view of the airport. "Instructions, Jonah?"

"Oh—Mike. Hi. Yes—no one off the aircraft until I say so. I'd like one of your men to go down the forward chute with me, armed if possible. Don't think we'll need him, but..."

"I'll go myself. With you in a jiff. Here—who the hell is that?" He pointed a stubby forefinger forward, down the taxiway. We could see him clearly now...a figure in blue tunic and trousers, hatless, running helter-skelter towards us, arms going like pissed windmills.

"Dunno—looks like the only survivor. And he won't last long if he doesn't get out of the way," I grumbled. Not seriously...I felt too good to grumble at anyone. For the moment, anyway.

Two of the eight U.S. military aircraft on the parking area were burned out; all the rest showed serious scorch damage—tires flat, paint peeling from upper wing and fuselage surfaces, windows misshapen drools of plastic. The grass, I saw, was a dull copper brown, with yellow patches... if not already dead, it was sickening from something, for sure.

The running man veered off to my left under the nose, skidded round and began to run back, with seemingly inexhaustible energy. He wore USAF blues, with sergeant's stripes and a chestful of Technicolor rubbish. He still had all his hair—what there was of it—and favored the semi-crew cut popular with aircrew the world over. His face was split like a cut melon by a compulsive grin.

I got Delta Tango pointed for a clear stretch of concrete only just in time... the tail engine quit, and we coasted to a stop in virtual silence.

"Parking brake on. Fuel off. Clear your board, Ben. We've arrived... and to prove it—we're here."

It was not much of a textbook block check—but it didn't seem important to go by the book anymore. I couldn't quite believe it yet, but we seemed to have finished with the book—and with flying. Well... my last landing hadn't been bad. We would all walk away from it, anyway.

I got up stiffly, stretched and found my jacket.

"Ben, lad—open up that locker and find me something that goes bang, will you? Jerry, how about getting that emergency chute open?" I struggled into the coat.

"Christ," Chambers said explosively, "that thing hasn't been opened since Pontius was a pilot. I've probably forgotten how to operate it."

"Well," I said encouragingly, "the instructions are written nicely on the thing. You can read, I take it?"

"And balls to you too," said Mr. Chambers rudely. In fact, it took him only a moment or two to get the door open, the chute deployed. The long canvas tube stretched down to ground level and length to spare.... I stared down and saw the airman grab hold, steady it.

"All set." Mike Brand stood behind me, looking out across the vista of scorched buildings, damaged aircraft. He carried an Armalite rifle, several spare magazines, a Browning automatic in his right hand. And I guessed those two lethal knives were tucked into his boots.

Ben nudged me, handed over a Smith & Wesson .38, a cardboard box of ammunition. "She's loaded, one up the spout, safety on," he said carefully.

"Check. All right—as soon as I hit the ground, chute back

in, door closed. I want as little as possible of this air into the aircraft. Not till we check."

Brand went into the chute first, disappeared. I went after him, fell sickeningly for six feet, hit the downslope and decelerated gently into the open air. Mike helped me up, and the chute was jerked up out of sight.

Brand stalked off round the airplane, checking out the local area. I found the U.S. airman beside me, hand outstretched. If he grins much wider, I thought, his head will fall off.

"Hi, sir. Sergeant Burns—call me Eddie. Jesus, am I glad to see you fellas."

I shook his hand solemnly. "Eddie. You all right?"

"Me? Sure—just fine. You know what happened here, sir?" he said at last.

"I know we're very lucky to be alive. Is there anyone else . . . ?"

The airman shook his head, frowned. "Not that I can find— so far. I—I was on duty last night in the Secret Documents Registry—in the basement of the Operations Building over there. Two of us—me and Sergeant Kovacs. First we knew, there was a hell of a bang and the ceiling fell on us. I mean— the whole goddamn ceiling just let go and fell on us. Bernie caught it bad—he's still down there. Piece of junk weighing maybe a hundred pounds fell on him—took half his head and one ear with it. I got into the corridor, found it blocked. Took most of two hours to dig a way into the elevator—and I find the fuggin thing's bust. I got out through the emergency tunnel—maybe half an hour ago—and find this . . . this . . ."

His voice broke into a fit of coughing, which wasn't altogether responsible for the tears in his eyes. He was only a kid—early twenties. I gripped his shoulder, laid some pressure on.

"Come on, lad. Easy. Don't you know anything about last night?"

He blew his nose into a huge blue handkerchief, shook his head. "Not a damn thing," he insisted. "What in hell hit this place? And how come *you* are here?"

I told him, slowly and gently, during the next five minutes, bit by shocking bit. I didn't dare ask him from what part of the U.S.A. he came. I reeled off quickly the names of the American cities with which Gander had lost contact . . . and he turned away, broken, when I said "San Francisco."

Brand came back, boots echoing on the dusty concrete.

"Well, no dice so far, Jonah. Plenty of bodies if you look for them. Who's this?"

"Eddie Burns. I'd leave him alone for a while, Mike. He knew nothing about this...shambles until I told him. His folks live in San Francisco—or did. What do you think? Is it all right?"

He shrugged his shoulders; the gun over one shoulder bounced jauntily. "I don't know, Jonah. This blasted radiation...It looks all right—even smells all right. Except those bodies are going to get a bit high later on."

I nodded somberly. "Right. It could be all round, of course—you can't smell it, or taste. What we need is a Geiger counter—but where in hell are we going to get one?"

He considered the question briefly. "Not by standing here talking, old boy. And we aren't going anywhere else, are we?"

"I guess not."

"All right, then. This is what I suggest: let me get my men out and started on a search for other survivors—and your Geiger counter. I have an idea we might find something measuring radiation in the local base hospital—in the X-ray department. The passengers—I'd let them out for a stretch, Jonah. Keep them nearby—maybe start the men on wrapping up the dead, ready to move. There are forty or fifty I found—probably lots more."

It made sense. But I had to do something about those damned chutes. I looked up suddenly. Every window was jammed with white faces, wide eyes, waiting. I turned slowly, spotted what I was looking for.

"Right, Mike—let's get started. Look, if you can get a dozen of your lads down, they can bring that mobile ramp over—it's heavy, but it will move. Get it up to the forward door on the port side."

"Got it. Uh-oh—how in hell do we communicate with them from down here?"

I walked round to the nose, opened the quick-release panel, found the spare headset for the ground phone, plugged it in. "Jerry?"

"No, Skip. Ben—Jerry's back with Nickie. What gives?"

"Listen, Ben—get the sergeant major and a dozen men down here now. No arms—there's work to be done. They are going to haul round a mobile stairway to Number One door. We have no choice but to take a chance. You can open all doors and windows now—if we're going to breathe hot air, so be it. Oh—one more thing: get Kate to ask for volunteers among the men. They have a rotten job to do—clearing away the casualties. But it has to be done."

"Right, Skipper. What about food? They are all hungry—me too."

"Ben," I said tiredly, "you are all going to have to wait. We can't touch anything on the ground until we know it is all right. We won't know that until we find a Geiger counter—and that's a job for the rest of the troops. Now get them moving, will you?"

Slowly, things began to happen. I watched Brand briefing his men, squad by squad; saw Jerry and Ben come down the forward steps, followed by Kate and several of the girls. I walked over to Eddie Burns. He was standing quite still, and alone, eyes staring blindly at infinity.

"Come on, Eddie," I said softly. "There is nothing you can do for them now...and there is a great deal you can do for us. Okay?"

He turned slowly, eyes dry but red-rimmed. He seemed to have aged fifteen years in the space of a few breaths....I could do little about that, but at least I could keep him busy.

"Look, lad—we need transport very badly. How were you doing for petrol—gas—the last few weeks? Are there any cars or trucks we can use?"

I had to ask the question twice. Finally—

"Yeah...I guess there is—maybe down in the pool. Transport Pool."

"Where is that, Eddie?" I asked patiently.

"Over that way—past the Tower." He pointed. I noticed his hand shook, like that of a very old man.

"All right. Fine. Come on—I want you to go with Major Brand....Mike—Eddie here thinks there are serviceable vehicles of some sort over in the Transport Pool. Can you spare a bunch of lads to go with him? We need something to get around in."

"Right. And I'll send Corporal Mellor, my medical bloke—he can take a jeep or something and dig out the hospital. He'll know what to look for."

I agreed. "Good. Look, why not send old Rabin with him? He's the nearest thing we have to a nuclear expert."

"Good scheme. Look, Jonah, feeding these people is going

to be a big priority. We have nearly two hundred kids back there."

We discussed the situation briefly, while his parties got started on their allotted tasks. I saw Karen Waldheim come down the steps in the first rush, mobilize a squad of a dozen volunteers and move off towards the hangars on the north side of the taxiway. Mike had his priorities virtually fixed by that time—transport first, followed by the radiation check on food supplies, and accommodation a slow third.

Ben Price and I walked over to the nearest aircraft, a C5 Galaxy, and helped ourselves to the wheel chocks. I didn't want to see Delta Tango neglected in any way: that old bird had brought us through a particularly vicious species of hell, faultlessly. Apart from almost-empty tanks, and the lack of any place to go, she was quite serviceable. Ben climbed back on board, released the parking brake, and threw down my small valise. I stripped off there and then, changed my shirt. The soiled one was drenched with sweat. The air of the Azores was warm and humid; I judged it was in the high seventies Fahrenheit—warm indeed for early November. The sky was now totally obscured with the familiar but loathsome gray-black overcast; at ground level the air was still reasonably clear, but a thin layer of gray-white dust overlay everything, rising in delicate swirls beneath the feet. What I had mistaken as dust under Mike Brand's boots was in fact a fine patina of atomic ash. We were breathing the stuff, without option.... I wondered how long it would be before they found a Geiger. I had that much longer to live—because it would give a very simple verdict on the big question: life or death. I would feel much better when I knew, one way or the other; all this waiting and indecision was likely to give me indigestion or an ulcer. Come to think of it, I wouldn't mind an ulcer—they took as much as three months to grow, and this sounded an attractive proposition to me.

14

We had trouble finding a suitable venue for a meeting, but the conference room just off the Operations Center in the Tower seemed as good a place as any. It was only just short of crowded now—I checked around, and everyone seemed to be there. Karen Waldheim, Rabin, Volkel and Sven Olaffsen sat in the front row of seats, leaning across one another to speak; Mike Brand sat composedly, smoking that battered black pipe he used alternately with cigarettes, his subordinates either side of him. Captain Lemaistre toyed absently with his moustache, legs crossed and quite relaxed, as if entertaining at some coffee party. Hamish Bond sat with arms folded, staring straight ahead, lost in thought. Hockey, the tough-looking senior NCO, sat some little distance away, talking in a low voice to Corporal Mellor. The medical orderly looked pale, obviously disturbed.

Farther back, the crew clustered together—Kate and her hostesses, Ben, Jerry Chambers sitting very close to Nickie, and John Capel listening with head bowed to Jill, the VIP stewardess.

The shades were drawn, lights on. It lacked a few minutes to ten in the morning, but the sky outside had the gray of winter twilight; lights were essential, and none of us wanted to look at the gray-black overcast. It seemed to give the oddly frightening reaction I remembered from watching a total eclipse of the sun in Australia: a feeling that perhaps the laws of nature were not completely fixed and irreversible.

I walked slowly up onto the dais, jammed my hands into

my pockets because I was afraid I couldn't keep them still and unoccupied.

"We all seem to be here. I'm going to keep my part in this as short as possible because we have a lot to get through. Briefly, the situation is this: we got everyone fed and bedded down last night. So far, only one survivor here—Ed Burns over there."

Burns glanced round briefly, nodded at me.

"I have discussed the situation with Dr. Rabin, who is qualified in nuclear physics. He will tell you what he knows, but everything seems to point to a neutron-bomb detonation at about fifteen thousand feet, centered accurately on the base, about one A.M. yesterday morning. There was a fireball which started ground fires, but not to any serious degree. There was little or no blast damage. The device emitted very strong radiation, which penetrated almost every building and as far as ten feet into the ground. It killed off everything— even down to worms, birds, flies. Ed Burns here escaped only because he was sixty feet belowground in a secure basement."

I stopped for a moment to light a cigarette.

"By the nature of the beast, there is very little residual radiation—the lethal effects apparently appear at the time of detonation only. We have been lucky in finding two Geiger counters, which tell us that the canned and frozen food here is edible. We have a scouting party out in the local area, but we think the island has been almost cleared of life, except possibly in the far western corner."

The absolute silence in the room was unnerving. I went on:

"I spent some time with Dr. Rabin and others, deciding what we can do—but before I go into that, a word from the doc himself."

Rabin got up slowly, shambled onto the platform, and I stood down. His clothes were creased and clearly slept in. He had not shaved—his chin and upper lip were blue-black— and his hair was unkempt. But his eyes behind the spectacles were alert, his voice clear, and he handled the thing like a university seminar.

"Thank you, Captain Scott. I have been asked to describe our situation briefly, in words of one syllable"—he glanced slyly at me—"which is a difficult problem when dealing with nuclear, thermonuclear and neutronic detonations."

A little stir of attention drifted through the audience.

"So. What I have to tell you is not good. But—we are all adult people, and there is no point trying to avoid the issue because the issue is all we have left. First...

"I do not know how many bombs it took. I cannot even guess. My own belief is that they passed into the 'overkill' phase in the first half-hour.

"Mr. Price worked on the Tower radio equipment, putting up a new antenna. In two hours of searching, he found three stations still transmitting: Cape Town; Tananarive, Madagascar; and Hobart, Tasmania. We could not contact them—all the relay satellites seem to have been destroyed or put out of action—but they were transmitting at high output.

"I do not have to dwell on the point. There may be—there almost certainly are—many small groups of people sufficiently isolated from major impact points to survive—and unable to communicate because of lack of power supplies.

"But being alive at this time is an academic point—if one looks at the sky this black morning. To us, a high opaque haze—but to most other parts of the world, an impenetrable black curtain. Let me tell you why.

"Over the Azores, there is very often a high-pressure area—an anticyclone. It is almost a permanent feature. So. The flow of air is from high pressure to low—away from the Azores, in a clockwise rotation. This, I believe, is holding back the main layers of radiation.

"In areas of low pressure, the overcast will be lower—down to ground level in many cases. That is to say, a situation of permanent fallout. For that overcast is composed of the debris from countless thousands of nuclear explosions—carried by thermal updrafts as high as fifteen or twenty miles. Here in the Azores, we have constant rise of warm air, so that the contaminated air all around us cannot penetrate, is carried up and away, leaving only the overcast which hides the sun from us."

The old scientist fumbled in his pocket for a handkerchief, mopped his face. Even with ventilation fans running, the temperature was in the eighties Fahrenheit.

"You observe," he said with irony, "one of the first results—the 'greenhouse' effect. It is warm; soon it will become hot, very hot."

John Capel looked up. "Say, Doc—how long will this mess take to clear away? I mean, before the sun comes out again?"

Rabin took off his spectacles, pressed a forefinger and thumb into tired eyes and shook his head.

"Mr. Capel," he said apologetically, "you do not seem to understand. The sun will not come out again. Not in our time. When the volcano Krakatoa exploded many years ago, it had less than the force of one small atom bomb. But it blew millions of tons of debris into the sky, which was obscured for many months. Now we have not only debris, but the radioactive water vapor from undersea bombs—and God alone knows how many bombs in total."

From where I stood, at the side of the room, perhaps about half of those present understood exactly what Rabin meant. Most of the stewardesses, Nickie, the Army corporal simply stared blankly. But the men knew, all right. I saw Jerry slide his arm round Nickie's shoulders in a gesture of protection—and caught a glimpse of Kate's face: shocked and colorless.

"So"—Rabin placed his spectacles carefully back in position—"what is to happen now? I will try to explain. In most places, there will be no survivors at all. Those who escaped the bombing will meet the radiation. But here, we have just a little time. As long as the high pressure holds, until the contaminated air begins to press inwards, the present roentgen count—the ambient radioactivity—will stay well below fatal 500 level. But none of us can afford to be exposed too long even to low levels of radiation: it adds up, like small bills, until we are bankrupt.

"How long? I do not know. The Captain and crew—they believe no more than a week or two. But I will let him tell you about that."

Mike Brand said slowly, "Is there anything we can do to cut down radiation risk? I mean, like wearing masks?"

Rabin hesitated for a moment. "No, Mr. Brand—in the long term, it will make no difference. All we can do is monitor the daily background radiation—and tell you what it means."

Brand nodded.

"And the water—it's all right, so far, to drink?" Kate wanted to know.

"Yes, Miss Monahan," Rabin said. "So far, it is good."

I got up onto the dais again as the old man sat down heavily.

"Any further questions at the moment?" I asked.

I believe for the most part they were too stunned to think clearly. It is one thing to face sudden death, when flying, because such situations are determined so quickly that one has little time to be afraid before it comes. And it is this which makes a quick death acceptable and preferable. It is another thing altogether to face the fact that one is going to die not immediately, but very soon—in the next week or two. It is this stark knowledge, of course, and the terror it produces, which forms the real deterrent in the death sentence—not the rope, poison gas or electric chair. That is relatively short and quick—humanely so. But sitting around for weeks waiting for a specific date to come round—that is the tough part.

"All right," I said harshly. "Now you know. But only you. The rest of the passengers don't—they think they have escaped by the skin of their teeth, that when things quiet down a little they can climb back aboard some airplane and fly home.

"Sooner or later," I told them, "they are going to have to accept the fact that home doesn't exist anymore. That they must stay here for the rest of their lives. And that may be measured in just weeks. Now—the reason I have asked you to be here is that there is just one small chance. A very small chance—and not for everyone. Dr. Rabin and Dr. Olaffsen came to me with the idea, and it checks out to a fifty-fifty chance. Listen carefully."

They waited, eyes fixed on me. Outside, far away over the airfield, I heard a truck start up, stall and start again. It sounded very loud, in a silence so dense it could be tasted.

"We believe more than 95 percent of the bombs used were aimed at targets in the Northern Hemisphere. And that's where the bulk of the fallout is concentrated. There is only one way to go to avoid it: south. Some of you may remember a novel years ago by Nevil Shute—*On the Beach*—where people in an Australian town waited for the fallout to come down from the north. Well, we have a similar situation—but a thousand times worse than Shute could ever have imagined.

"Survival from this thing depends on two factors. One—getting as far south as possible—and I don't mean Australia; I mean all the way to the South Pole, if necessary. And two—surviving until the radiation falls to an acceptable level. Let's look at that one first. The doc here tells me that the half-life of the radioactive materials used could be anything from 50 to 7500 years or more, for the cobalt bombs and the really big H-bombs. We might have to sit it out in the Far South for eight or ten years—but eventually, we would be able to come back to a foothold in the Falklands or Tasmania or South Africa.

"This is where things get complicated. I think I can get the airplane down there all right—we'll look at that in a moment. But survival means food—a lot of it, in those latitudes. You need food to keep warm. There may be food stocks down there somewhere, but we won't be able to roam around checking out each possible spot. So—we have to take food and supplies with us. And I am talking about tons of food for every person who goes. Do I make myself clear?"

It seemed that I did. Capel coughed briefly, Hamish Bond shuffled his feet restively; but there were no questions.

"Right. Taking it to ridiculous extremes, we can fill every seat, take no food at all and lose everyone within days. At the other end of the scale, if four or five go, with an airplane filled with food and fuel, they will survive almost indefinitely.

"Somewhere in between—and I don't know the answer to the sum yet—somewhere in between, there is an optimum number of passengers, leaving room and weight-carrying capacity for enough supplies to last them, say, eight years.

"I have asked all the crew to be here, because they will be needed to operate the airplane. Mr. Capel and our Army friends because they are the only effective police force we have. And our scientist party here, because in this situation we need all the specialist advice we can find.

"Well—there it is. I'm going to discuss the technical problems involved in a moment—but first, we have to get over this problem of selection: who goes, who stays."

The wave of sound came forward like a tidal wave—everyone talking at once, everyone shouting to be heard. I tried to stop it—and failed. Couldn't even hear myself yelling.

Mike Brand got slowly to his feet, took out the Browning automatic from its holster, worked the mechanism and pointed it at the white-painted ceiling. That stopped them.

"Let us," he said coaxingly, "have a little hush for the Captain, shall we?"

They gave a little hush.

I grinned. Some policeman...I told them that Professor Volkel and Dr. Olaffsen had done a great deal of work the previous day on the whole project. The big Scandinavian shambled forward, a few penciled notes in his hand.

"Thank you. Well, this is the situation. The Antarctic,

since 1961, has been used exclusively for peaceful purposes. Twelve nations signed the treaty, including the U.S.S.R., United States, Australia, France and Norway. By the middle '60s there were many stations there, mostly meteorological and geological research projects. We broke into the USO club reference library this morning and found one or two books which may help. I also found this map of the Antarctic continent...." I helped Olaffsen to pin it to the back wall.

"Although we found nearly a hundred past and existing stations," the Scandinavian went on, "we had to eliminate most of them at once. We need to get as far south as possible, and you see that at only one point—the Ross Sea—do the coastline and ice barrier approach close to the Pole itself. There are no permanently occupied bases south of the 80th parallel—not since the U.S.A. abandoned all its bases, including Amundsen-Scott, near the Pole, early last year. This, as you may know, was due to financial difficulties connected with the value of the dollar."

He stood silent for long moments, staring at the map, his back to the crowd. Then—

"So we have to look at the Ross Sea, therefore, because only there will we find a base far enough south—and one recently used. There are difficulties—the area is on the far side of the Pole and involves a flight of nearly eight and a half thousand miles. Captain Scott tells me we can do it—but only by carrying much spare fuel; and that reduces the number of passengers we can take."

"But if we use the American base," Mike Brand said quickly, "surely there will be plenty of supplies there?"

"Would you like to risk your life on a gamble, Mike?" I said drily. "Sure, it's almost certain they would leave most of their supplies behind—but we can't be positive. With their balance-of-payments problems, they could have hoarded every last can of beans—and loaded their return ship to the gunwales."

Brand looked unconvinced.

"All right—you could be right, Jonah—but suppose we hauled everyone down there and flew back here for supplies?"

"I take it," I said, "that you are assuming we'll make a normal landing there?"

"Sure—why not?" He looked puzzled.

"I'll tell you why not," I said dourly. "When the Americans used their base—at McMurdo Sound, right here—they made their landing strip out on the sea ice. About three kilometers out, where the ice was thirty to sixty feet thick, in the summer season from September through to March. They used a 'pulvimixer'—a machine that chips off the ice surface and leaves a layer of fine ice fragments which are spread by a drag to make a three-inch carpet on the runway. Of course, the surface snow had to be bulldozed away first, into banks either side of the runway, twenty feet high and a hundred feet wide. So much snow that it makes the sea ice sag at the side, hump in the middle of the runway, causing a long crack.

"Seems the boys at the air base—Williams Naval Air Facility—had the thing really weighed off: all the buildings were on sledges, ready to be towed onto the shore when the ice broke up. But we'll have no runway, Mike. And I'm not going to use that sea ice—we will have close to three hundred tons of aircraft putting down, and I want solid snow, ice and land under me for that. Besides, we need to come in as close to the base as possible—even in summer, the temperature is close to freezing, the winds pretty strong.

"No, Mike—it's strictly a one-way trip. We take everything we need—and we don't come back until things have cooled down."

Captain Lemaistre held up a languid hand. "I say, old chap—a small point. How *do* we get back? When the time comes, that is?"

I'd figured someone would ask that one.

"Well—I hadn't got as far as that yet. But there'll be plenty of time to build a boat of sorts. It's a bit irrelevant, though— the immediate problem is survival."

Lemaistre nodded agreement. "True—but we could be getting involved with frying pans and fire, Captain—what?"

"I think," Olaffsen said heavily, "the Captain is right. If there is a chance to survive—no matter how or where..."

"Look," I said flatly, "let's get down to the nitty-gritty. Sven, you did some calculations on the weight. But let's look at the load we can take first. Ben—how about it?"

Ben stood up diffidently.

"Jerry here, and myself—we did some sums on the aircraft computer, Jonah. I have the results listed here. Item—from here to McMurdo is nearly 8500 miles. Using the best track, altitude and speed, about eighteen hours nonstop. Unless we can pick up fuel en route, it means carrying an additional 35 to 40 tons of fuel in 40-gallon drums on board. We've worked out a scheme for hand-pumping fuel into the main tanks—there are difficulties with fumes, fire risk and so on, but it can be done; we need about eight hours' work on the aircraft system."

"Fine. What else, Ben?"

"Well...we looked at this question of maximum all-up weight for takeoff, Jonah. We can take most of the seats out, strip out furnishings, equipment—we can pick up maybe 7 or 8 tons that way. We've also found ample supplies of the new plastic 100-liter storage drums, which are lighter than the old steel drums. Lastly, there is the question of takeoff power. Jonah—this is the last flight the old girl will ever make—right?"

I agreed.

"Well...we take off, with all available power, on a maximum exhaust-gas temperature of 820 degrees Celsius, usually. The red line—maximum permissible—is about 920. We can override the power stop to give us about an extra 12 percent on takeoff. It will be a hell of a strain on the engines, and we have to accept the risk of losing one or more—but it means a hell of an extra load on takeoff."

Ben had sketched in the outline—but there was far more to it than that. Every additional kilo I could get off the ground meant either one more life saved—or maybe an extra month of life, at the other end, for someone else. But what was that against losing an engine, and possibly the whole aircraft, a thousand miles short of McMurdo? Could I take the risk with lives? Should I play it safe, keep the numbers and the weight down for safety's sake—or take a chance and get every possible body away? It was a difficult situation—and complicated by the side issues. Should the children go, without question? Or should I follow the historic precedent of the *Titanic* and other ships—"women and children first"? Hardly—how could any party survive with a preponderance of dependents and nonproducers?

I lit another cigarette, oblivious to the argument and discussion going on around me. I had begun some time ago to accept the fact that whoever went south might perhaps be the last survivors. And despite the long history of science-fiction stories about worldwide disasters, I was going to have to think very carefully about the qualities that might be desirable in a successful candidate. Somewhere I had once read that a species needed a minimum number for survival—

some question of genes and inbreeding. Again—what about children? We needed them for survival of the race—but only if they could contribute something. It was obviously out of the question to produce offspring ourselves for the next few years: God alone knew what genetic results might arise from conception in areas of high radiation. It might be eight or ten years before it would be safe enough to take a chance. Which meant that we had to look at a maximum age of no more than thirty—and preferably a lot less.

I held up both hands and finally got at least a temporary hush.

"I see you are all thinking along the same lines as myself," I said quietly. "Well, I think that is the right thing to do. It stands out that we have to be very careful in choosing who goes and who stays. More important, we have to decide *who* decides—I am only the pilot of the aircraft, and frankly, it is a responsibility I would not want."

Brand looked up. "So what do you suggest, Jonah?"

"Just this. I want to be left alone to figure out how we can get this airplane off the ground. Which means finding someone else to do the choosing. Don't ask me how to do it—I wouldn't know. We haven't time to hold elections, that's for sure. If this trip is going at all, it's going soon—within three days. Maybe you want to hang around waiting for that lot to fall on your heads"—I gestured skyward—"but not me."

Karen Waldheim said, "We have to be very careful, I think, in how we go about this thing. I mean, if five hundred are to stay and a hundred go—those who have to stay are going to have something to say about it. Can't we start by making a list of the essentials? Those people who must go?"

"Better still"—Hamish Bond got unexpectedly to his feet—"a list of those prepared to stay?"

I stared at him. "Hamish?"

He said patiently, "Look, mon—ye only want people with qualifications, skills that will be valuable. Doctors, teachers, food producers—ye know? Well, *my* only qualification is killing people. I ken how tae do it—and do it well. But there's no need for more killing. I'm thinking there's been too much already. I'll be more use—with the major's permission—keeping things under control here. Besides...I don't like snow and ice. I was brought up in it—but I'd rather spend the rest of my life here, where it's warm."

"Damme, Hamish," complained Lemaistre, "just what I was going to say myself."

"There you are, Karen," I said, relieved. "It's a start. Okay—Hamish—will you concentrate on isolating the people who don't want to go further? Here, first—and then among the rest of the people."

"Aye. Will do, Captain."

"Fine. Now—regarding the crew. We need the two pilots— it's going to be a long haul—and Ben Price, our engineer. Cabin crew—Kate to run the stews, a proportionate number to cope with the passengers we take. I mean—with a half load, nine stews; with two hundred or less, six, and so on. Hamish to find who wants to go, who wants to stay—after that, we have to draw lots, I guess."

Mike Brand said, "Yes, I agree. But I also think our Brains Department should go without question—Miss Waldheim and her friends."

"No," Professor Volkel said. "Not if we have the choice— and I think we should have that. I am an old man, and my specialty—geology and oil-bearing rocks—is of no use to such an expedition. Besides...I have some ideas on filtration and radiation protection I would like to try out—and it appears that I may have excellent conditions for experimenting."

"It seems," I said, "many people have different reasons for going and staying. I would like to put this suggestion. Perhaps Mike and John Capel can organize a systematic briefing of our passengers. Interview them in small groups, keep those you have seen separate from those to come. Form your lists— the goers and the stayers. Meanwhile, Ben and Jerry and I will work out the maximum load we can carry. After that, we have to convert the answer into passengers and supplies. Karen—could you and one or two others start working on basic food scales to give a survival ration—say, about 2000 to 2500 calories a day? We need at least that—depending on how warm we can keep the people."

"Yes, Captain. Of course."

"Fine. Well—we have something to work on. Mike—I would suggest the passengers are told nothing of this until you have your briefing program ready. Oh—and one more thing: children. I don't know how all you people feel about it, but I think they ought to go—they only weigh as much as fifty adults, and I can't help feeling our future may be wrapped up in those kids. Have a word with the Red Cross party—Madame Ferrière, I think it is."

The congregation began drifting into small groups, and I jerked my head towards the door, looking at Ben and Jerry. Outside, we instinctively looked up at the gray overcast. Towards the east, it deepened in hue, through a steel gray-blue into a deep charcoal, so that we could not see the horizon.

Ben sucked in his breath. "Christ...I've heard about the end of the world, but this is ridiculous." He shivered, despite the muggy heat.

"Stow it, Ben," said Chambers irritably. "I'm trying desperately to stay sane enough to think clearly, without comments like that. Jonah—I know you have a lot on your plate—but what about Nickie?"

"What about her?"

"Hell, Skip, I can't leave her behind here. Not after all we've been—"

"You won't have to," I cut in quickly. "Look, we won't split families, dependents, whatever we do. You're as married as you're ever going to be, even if you and Nickie survive to a hundred—I don't believe we have a preacher man among us."

He grinned, shamefaced but enormously relieved. "Thanks, Skip!"

"For nothing. Jerry, nip in and have a quick word with her—and then let her alone for the rest of the day. Go find Mike Brand—I want a working party from him, for refueling, foraging and stripping out the aircraft. Move, lad!"

Sergeant Hockey came out, said "Whew" and stripped off his battle tunic. I had a long talk with him, telling him exactly what I wanted. I said I wanted all the seats and carpets and lockers stripped out of Delta Tango—Ben would be in overall charge. I wanted the aircraft lightened of every damned bit of light alloy, steel and fabric that could be spared. I wanted it filled absolutely full of fuel, and I wanted a refueling tanker out at the end of the runway for a last-minute top-up before takeoff. I wanted several hundred of the plastic 100-liter drums made ready for filling, and I said Ben would work closely with him in arranging means of refueling from within the airplane in flight.

Hockey took it all in, made a few brief notes, slipped the pad into a shirt pocket. I looked at him, curious. He was, I judged, from the East End of London—he had served long enough in the Army to lose the broader Cockney accent—and I wondered if he considered himself a goer or a stayer.

"Me, sir? Well...I reckon I'll stay here, sir. I've got—friendly with Carol—the girl from the aft lounge? Yes, that's her. She doesn't want to fly again; I think she had enough yesterday—what with the things that went on upstairs, according to Major Brand."

"Yes." I could only agree with him. "Things got very rough. You—realize what will happen if you stay?"

"Sure." He stared at me defiantly. "I know. And I knew from the time I joined up I'd have to suck it and see, one day. Well, it could be worse. I've been shot at in Belfast, bombed in London and almost knifed in New York. Carol lived in Highbury with her folks, and my mother is in Deptford. I don't think we're ever going home again—and you never know—it could work out pretty well here."

Impulsively, I stuck out my hand. "You're a nice fella, Sergeant. Good luck."

He grinned, saluted. "Thanks. Same to you. Better get started—see you in a little while."

We watched him march off along the concrete path, under the flowering trees sprouting from the clumps of rhododendron. Far away across the airfield to the west, we could see the long sloping hills covered with orange orchards, stone walls. Beyond them the forest-clad slopes of the Cordilheira de Santa Barbara, climbing more than three thousand feet towards the stained sky.

"You know," Ben said softly, "there are going to be a lot of people around we might call heroes in the next few days, Skip. The real ones. I mean, not the type who charge enemy trenches, but people like Hockey there. That bit about Carol—goddamn hooey, of course. What he really meant was that he's ready to stand down just to get all those kids aboard."

"I think you're right."

"Yes. Well—we'd better get started."

We walked slowly out to the aircraft. I glanced up at the Tower and saw Ed Burns framed in the open window. He had a radio headset on, and waved briefly before moving out of sight. I knew he was still trying desperately to make contact with America—hoping against hope.

"What about these engine settings, Skip?" Ben said tentatively.

"Yes. I've been wondering about that, Ben. First things

first—let's get a flight plan out, run it through the computer, see what we have."

The flight deck was uncomfortably warm; we stripped off jackets and ties. Ben had found a serviceable mobile generator in the workshops, and it stood beneath the nose, diesel engine thudding away to manufacture 230-volt power for the airplane systems.

An hour later, I stood up, stretched and stared at Ben.

"That's it—other than winds. The best prediction I can make is that they should be light and variable once past the Equator. In still air, we make it not quite 8500 nautical miles, cruising at 34,000 feet and climbing to 39,000 as fuel is used. True airspeed 475 knots—giving us a flight time of 18 hours and 5 minutes. Christ, we're going to need some fuel for that, Ben."

"You said it, Skip. But I think it is on. Remember, we allow nothing for diversions, and we're stripping a great deal out of her. I make it we'll have to carry an extra 50,000 kilos of fuel—five hundred drums. They weigh about 4 kilos each—nearly two tons of drums. We can dump them en route by breaking them up and depressurizing the cargo hold each hour. They'll go out of the garbage dump box—I can use an oxygen mask while I do it. That two tons'll come in handy."

It sounded all right—except the depressurizing bit. I would have to think a bit more about that one, because depressurization at 35,000 feet can be most unpleasant, even with oxygen. I didn't mention the bends specifically, but I knew Ben was thinking along the same lines.

The next big problem was fuel transfer.

"I can easily rig hand pumps," said Ben, "to pass fuel into the main tanks; I'll have to make a hole through the main deck into the cargo hold, and that may give us problems with dumping empty drums. But the only worry is fumes—no matter how careful we are, the place is going to reek like a gas station before we get there."

I considered for a moment. "What about knocking up a light wooden partition? We can use oxygen when transferring, and keep the area sealed off."

"Not worth the extra weight, Skip. Unless—I could organize something out of lightweight clear polythene sheeting, if I can find any."

"Anything you want, you tell Brand or Hockey," I said.

"They're there to do the running, Ben. The important thing is—what do you make the payload?"

"Nearly 90 tons, Skip—92,000 kilos."

"What did you take the average passenger weight to be?"

"A hundred twenty pounds—about 55 kilos—excluding personal baggage," he said.

"There'll be damned little of that aboard," I said firmly. "All right—that gives us something to go on. Now—supplies. How in hell are we going to work that one out?"

"I would think," Ben said thoughtfully, "it has to be done two ways, Skip. We need to know the weight of equipment we need—vital things, like heating stoves, oil, that sort of thing. The remaining weight we can split up among passengers. But if you reckon a man needs, say, 4 pounds of food daily—28 pounds a week, about 1500 pounds a year—plus his own weight, making near enough three-quarters of a ton; give him what—five years? Right—we are working on about 4 tons per person. Allow about 10 tons of equipment, bedding, fuel oil—it looks like no more than twenty people, Skip."

We stared at each other.

"Is that all, Ben? Jesus—how can we ever pick twenty out of all the people who will want to go? We can't even take all the kids...."

I walked blindly from the flight deck, down the long empty cabin, bumping into seats, swearing in a steady flow of filth and invective dredged up from schoolboy memories. Far aft, I sat down heavily in a seat, got my head down into my palms and tried with all my strength to think clearly and lucidly.

Suppose we carried half load. Three hundred people—about 18 tons. And carried supplies to make up the load. We could manage, probably, about six months on that calculation—and run out of food in the depths of the Antarctic winter.

The permutations kept running through my brain, and I was still groping for a solution when Hockey brought a dozen of his men aboard and started stripping out seats. Ben Price hovered around.

"Leave about a hundred seats in, Sarge. Mostly at the back—safest place in a belly landing. Don't forget there are about a dozen seats up top—count them in. Heave the rest out of the hatches; you can open all the doors—here, I'll show you how."

I shoved my cap on, slipped it to the back of my head and

went down the main steps forward, heading towards the north end of the field, hands in trouser pockets and deep in thought.

Only twenty people, for God's sake ... twenty—out of all the world.

15

Half an hour of hard walking brought me out of the base, up the two-lane tarmac road from the Operations Center, thick, lush vegetation on my left and a long white-painted fence on the right. Beyond lay the wide grass plains and scattered buildings; halfway up the hill, I could see Praia far off to the right, half-hidden in the smoky haze.

Outside a small white building at an intersection, I found a Portuguese guard, uniformed, caught in the open by the millisecond flash. He was lying face down, the backs of his hands pinky-red and peeling; I walked on by, hardened already to the face of death. Away to the left, the green and red roofs of the main support area; there there would be bodies—many more bodies—and I stumbled blindly on to the east, down the road between the cottages on the left and the long row of terraced houses on the right. All were plaster-finished, painted in brilliant colors. The houses to the right seemed to be American living quarters: almost every house had the parked car, the standard blue mailbox on a post by the gate.

Soon the road petered out into a dirt track, pounded hard by many wheels. As far as my eyes could see, the farmland stretched away, seamed with the volcanic rock walls which enclosed small garden and field alike. Everywhere, the remains of animals . . . cattle, tied to stakes with legs hobbled, felled where they stood by the hammerblow. Birds beyond number, heaped pathetically around the shrubs and bushes in which they had made their last roost. Every parked vehicle bore the stigmata of the bomb—burned, peeling paint, still smoldering; but surprisingly few had caught fire: perhaps the blast wave that followed the neutron flash had extinguished many outbreaks. There was an acrid smell of burned paint mingled with burned flesh, and I began to retch, mouth filling with bile, horror piling upon horror. The children...

I lurched on, away from the charnelhouses into the clean, deserted countryside. My footsteps made little noise on the hard dirt road, and I found the utter silence depressing; somewhere far away I would hear the surf breaking on some rocky shore, but no crickets chirped, no birds sang, no dog barked.

Slowly, the exertion and mindless exercise began to ease the tensions and strains in neck and shoulder muscles; a warm glow spread through me, and I went on, passing occasional vehicles. A white Volkswagen stood askew at the end of long skid marks, both doors open; a young lad, barely out of his teens, in a neat dark suit, white shirt, lay face down, one arm extended towards the girl who crouched on frozen knees, head buried beneath a swirl of brown hair, remnants of a scorched evening dress about shoulders festooned with strips of peeled skin. The speed with which the thing had killed was frightening: I knew that it caused, among other things, massive degeneration of the blood cells, releasing the oxygen content, starving brains, nerves, muscles of the fuel of life. But I could not be unhappy about the speed with which these people had died: they had suffered terribly, but very briefly.

Now I heard the surf, louder, the air full of driving spray. I followed the road as it turned south again, along the line of a steep, almost vertical cliff. I stood for long moments on the brink, watching the huge Atlantic rollers surging against jagged volcanic rocks below. The surf boiled, a wide milky sea of foam hundreds of yards out from shore; among the rocks, lethal tide races and whirlpools would suck down anyone foolish enough to fall in. For a timeless instant, the temptation was there, strong and demanding...it would be so easy to sink into the creaming white foam. I teetered dizzily on the brink and breathed heavily through my nose. No way, Scott, I told myself. You don't get away with it so easy.

I walked back to the road, stumbling, and my legs trembled as if under enormous loading. The cigarette I lit tasted stale and foul, and I threw it away unsmoked.

The town was closer now. I began to seek ways of avoiding

it, or circling back to the base. Human bodies I could take—but it was hard to meet the accusing stares of the animals...so many beloved pets—dogs, cats—each lying in an attitude of extreme agony. They seemed to have lived marginally longer than their masters, I thought; perhaps the fur afforded some slight protection. But all bore the same bare patches of skin whence fur and hair had fallen; eyes were clouded and milky, and they bled from every orifice.

Rabin had said that death would come quickly under the massive neutron radiation. Blood cells, nerve tissues, muscle fiber and brain networks would be distorted and shattered. The brain, starved of oxygen, stunned by the tragic glare as bright as the sun, would retreat instantly into unconsciousness. Moreover, he believed, the damaged nerves might not be able to transmit the message of pain to the brain...death would be like sleep.

Well, Doc—you have your ideas and I have mine, I thought grimly. All these people, all these animals were united in death by one common denominator: they had taken brief minutes to die—but death had come as a blessed relief.

As I lurched on through the gloomy half-light, I repeated my blasphemous litany.

I cursed to the far corners of Hell the crazy, inhuman bastards who had triggered off this nightmare. I wasted no time praying...I figured any God who had ever existed was sitting in some remote corner of another universe, trying to figure out what had gone wrong with the Grand Design. If He existed, I thought, He was much too far away—and just too damn disappointed—to be listening in to the particular frequency on which I might be praying.

But one little thought, prayer, desire I did launch, to Providence or Justice or whatever. I prayed that the men who pushed the first button had survived a long time. So that they would go down knowing what they had done, and in knowing, they would fry for a million years and die every second of it.

Soon I was walking back through the main gate, glancing briefly at the fused glass of the sentry box in which one Portuguese guard sat immobile, one hand grasping the telephone to make a call which would last through Eternity. A second lay spread-eagled nearby, one arm flung across his face as if to protect it, and I was glad I could not see his blind eyes. The two men on duty at flashpoint time might have been recognizable to their mothers...but I doubted it.

"Jonah!"

I stopped, looked around, startled. Kate Monahan trotted down the road from the Tower, legs flashing under short blue skirt, breasts bouncing rhythmically under the white shirt. I walked towards her.

"Jonah..." She fought for breath, hanging on to me desperately, gulping down great drafts of air.

I said, "Easy, now, love. Easy. What's the panic?"

"Ed Burns, in the Tower..." Her eyes were glowing. "He went down to try the teleprinter machines, Jonah. And he made contact—he's talking to someone in Brazil, and someone else in the Falkland Islands. Come on!"

I made for the Tower, fast, Kate trotting alongside. The teleprinters...how could I have forgotten them? The radios might have failed, the satellites blasted from orbit, but the teleprinters, with their buried landlines, submarine cables...there must be people everywhere with access to the telex network.

The TP room was three floors below the surface, under the Operations Center. I followed Kate down the echoing stairs, along a short green-painted passageway and through an open glass door. Ed Burns sat at a chattering machine, watching a message coming through. He turned, grinned hugely and nodded.

"Tried some overseas numbers at random," he said, "and bingo!"

He waited till the machine stopped for breath, ripped off a quarto-sized sheet and gave it to me.

KVA5416 TO ANY STATION. KVA5416 TO ANY STATION.

I READ YOU KVA5416. WHO ARE YOU?

KVA5416 RECEIVING. BURNS HERE. LAJES BASE AZORES. WHERE ARE YOU?

PPF4320 TO BURNS. I DO NOT RECOGNIZE CODE IDENT BUT SO GLAD TO MAKE CONTACT. I AM CARLOS VARGAS, BRAZILIAN NATIONAL BANKING CORPORATION BRASILIA. I HAVE BEEN TRYING ALL DAY TO FIND SOMEONE STILL ALIVE. IS ALL THE WORLD DEAD, MY FRIEND?

Burns' reply was brutal and to the point.

BURNS HERE. I GUESS SO CARLOS. I AM ONLY SURVIVOR ON
LAJES BASE, BUT BRITISH AIRLINER LANDED HERE
YESTERDAY WITH 600 PLUS ABOARD. WHAT IS YOUR
SITUATION, CARLOS?

WISH WE COULD HAVE MET BETTER CIRCUMSTANCES FRIEND
BURNS. I AM HEAD OF NORTH AMERICAN DIVISION. ON DUTY
IN BANK VAULT PARAMATRA 40 MILES WEST BRASILIA WHEN
IT HAPPENED. VERY LARGE EXPLOSION. WENT UPSTAIRS TO
SEE. FOUR FIREBALLS. TWO VERY CLOSE, TWO FAR AWAY.
ONE IN DIRECTION BRASILIA. AIR VERY BAD AFTER HALF AN
HOUR. CAME DOWN AGAIN.

Burns had asked gently:

UNDERSTAND, CARLOS. ARE YOU OKAY?

TO TELL TRUTH FRIEND BURNS, I DO NOT FEEL TOO GOOD AT
ALL. WHEN AM LOOKING AT THE FIREBALLS I AM
FEELING...NEEDLES AND PINS, YES? FOR TWO HOURS I HAVE
BEEN VERY SICK AND I AM BLEEDING FROM PLACES I WOULD
NOT SHOW MY WIFE.

Ed Burns looked at me. His eyes were wet, and he shook
his head. "That brave, crazy Spic," he said, "down in some
hole bleeding his live away and he can joke about it..."

I put my hand on his shoulder. "We can all find that bit
of courage, Ed, when the chips are down. You too. We've all
lost families, friends—even our homes and our countries."

He looked at me with eyes full of pain. "Yeah...we're
suckers for punishment, all right."

I went back to the printout. I said slowly, "Ed—can you
call him back and ask him if he has contacted anyone else?"

"Sure." The airman sat down at the keyboard.

BURNS TO CARLOS. WE ARE ALL PULLING FOR YOU. HAVE YOU
MADE CONTACT WITH ANYONE ELSE?

THANK YOU. NOW I HAVE SOMEONE TO TALK TO, I DON'T
FEEL SO BAD. NEGATIVE YOUR QUESTION. THERE WAS A
SHORT MESSAGE DURING THE NIGHT FROM PANAMA. SOME US
NAVY OFFICER. UNREADABLE AFTER FEW MINUTES. YOU CAN

GUESS WHY. TELL ME, FRIEND BURNS...WHY DID THIS
HAPPEN? I WILL NEVER SEE MY EVA AND MY CHILDREN
AGAIN...I THINK I HAVE TO GO. I WILL CALL AGAIN IF I CAN.
GOOD LUCK MY FRIENDS.

Burns bit his lip, staring at me with an unspoken question
on his face: I nodded, and he turned back to teleprinter keyboard.

CARLOS FROM ED BURNS AND ALL HERE. OKAY. DON'T
LOSE CONTACT. WE ARE STANDING BY HERE. HAVE YOU
ANY DRUGS WHICH MIGHT HELP?

Five very long minutes went by. Then the machine burst
into life again.

FALKLANDS CALLING LAJES. FALKLANDS CALLING LAJES.
ARE YOU STILL RECEIVING?

Burns said quickly, "That was the first contact. Before
Carlos. I tried getting back to them, but they didn't give code.
Till they do, I can't answer."
We waited. Ten minutes went by.

ZNR2338 FALKLANDS. ZNR2338 FALKLANDS, CALLING KVA5416
LAJES.

Burns said quietly, "Now they're thinking straight. Here
we go." He dialed up.

KVA5416 LAJES TO FALKLANDS. WE HAVE CONTACT NOW. GO
AHEAD.

LAJES FROM FALKLANDS. THANK GOD. WE HAVE BEEN
CALLING ATLANTIC ISLANDS HOPING FOR CONTACT...WE ARE
FIVE. SEALED IN BASEMENT ROOM UNDER GOVERNMENT
BUILDING FOR PAST THREE HOURS. ALL TELEPHONES OUT.
CAN YOU TELL US WHAT HAPPENED?

ED BURNS HERE. LAJES AIR BASE AZORES. SOMEONE PULLED
THE PLUG, I GUESS. NUCLEAR WAR. WHOLE DAMNED WORLD
INVOLVED AS FAR AS WE CAN SEE. WHAT HAPPENED YOUR
END?

He shook his head, puzzled. "They sound bomb-happy, Cap'n. Must be bad—I don't like the sound of that 'sealed' business. But—the Falklands—Jesus, that's way down in the South Atlantic. Who in hell would want to hit a remote place like that?"

I did not know. But we soon found out. While we waited, the big old-fashioned white-faced clock on the wall filled the silence with a deep, resonant "chonk-chonk"..."chonk-chonk" noise of movement. We looked at it without interest. Time had lost all meaning.

ED BURNS TO FALKLANDS. ARE YOU STILL RECEIVING?

The machine ticked over, talking quietly to itself and poised for action, the printer jacked up and paper clean and clear. Waiting. Suddenly—

FALKLANDS TO BURNS. SORRY. WE HAVE...[the printer hesitated, clicking] PROBLEMS. WE DO NOT KNOW HOW LONG WE CAN HOLD OUT. AIR IS GETTING BAD. WHAT IS YOUR SITUATION? ARE YOU ALONE?

Burns answered:

NEGATIVE, FALKLANDS. BRITISH AIRLINER LANDED YESTERDAY WITH 600 PLUS ON BOARD. MANY CHILDREN. ALL IS NOT LOST.

THAT IS GOOD TO HEAR, ED. WE STILL CANNOT YET TAKE IT ALL IN. HAVE YOU ANY NEWS OF ENGLAND?

Burns stared at me. I said slowly. "He has to know, Ed. Send this as I dictate:"

CAPTAIN SCOTT, AIR BRITAIN 797 DELTA TANGO. WE WERE EN ROUTE KENNEDY HEATHROW WHEN BALLOON WENT UP. LUCKY TO LAND HERE. ONLY ONE SURVIVOR OF NEUTRON BOMB SO FAR. I THINK I MUST TELL YOU THAT UK HAS GONE. AT LEAST FIVE MAJOR HITS AND PROBABLY MANY SMALLER ON MILITARY BASES. MOST MAJOR CITIES IN NORTHERN HEMISPHERE HAVE BEEN HIT. WE CANNOT UNDERSTAND WHY YOU CAUGHT IT.

The reply took a long time. I could understand why.

WHAT A HELL OF A MESS SCOTT. LT REDFERN RN HERE. WAS
LIAISON OFFICER ON NUKESUB USS APPOMATTOX ON FLAG
SHOWING VISIT. LEFT SHIP TO JOIN CAVE EXPLORATION
PARTY. SAW MAJOR EXPLOSION TEN MILES NORTH, THOUGHT
APPOMATTOX HAD EXPLODED BUT NOW KNOW MUST HAVE
BEEN ENEMY ACTION WHILE SHIP WAS ON LOCAL CRUISE
WITH GOVT OFFICIALS. RETURNED TO GOVT HOUSE BUT
FALLOUT ALREADY VERY BAD. STAFF EVACUATED BUT SELF
AND FOUR TYPISTS CAME DOWN TO BASEMENT TP ROOM. AIR
IS GETTING VERY BAD. ESTIMATE WE HAVE ONLY A FEW
HOURS BEFORE WE MUST BREAK CELLOTAPE SEALS ON DOOR.
TALK ABOUT HOBSONS CHOICE...FRY OR SUFFOCATE.

We read through this poignant message again, and a feeling of deep pity and sorrow welled over me, not only for the faraway Redfern fighting for breath in some cellar, but for the human race itself. Bad things we had done in plenty—and we had polluted the earth, such that a thousand years of rain would not wash away a millionth part of the poison. I thought how we had dragged ourselves up from the mud and the slime and the wet cave in the menacing night. Huddled together, listening to the prowling beasts beyond the flickering fire.

Over the centuries, we had devised, invented, improved, and our footsteps would stand in the dust of the moon for eternity. Yet by our self-inflicted wounds we lay dying in cellars, scorched and maimed in Red Square and Times Square and Trafalgar Square. Or drifted in the high upper winds as poisonous radioactive products of combustion.

I whispered to myself, "Dear God...we did not deserve all this"...but I knew we did.

I spoke with Burns, and he made a few notes.

SCOTT TO REDFERN. WHAT CAN WE SAY THAT WILL HELP?
ONLY THAT WE WISH WE COULD BE WITH YOU. WE ARE
CONSIDERING FLYING SOUTH TO ANTARCTICA TO AVOID
RADIATION. WE CAN DIVERT TO FALKLANDS IF YOU CAN HELP
WITH FUEL. HAVE YOU FACILITY TO TAKE VERY LARGE
AIRCRAFT?

SORRY OLD BOY. LIGHT AIRCRAFT LANDING STRIP ONLY. IF
YOU CAME YOU WOULD HAVE TO STAY PUT. GREAT PITY. I
WOULD HAVE HITCHED A RIDE.

YOU WOULD BE WELCOME, SORRY WE CAN'T DROP IN. ARE THERE ANY OTHERS NEAR YOU?

NEGATIVE. INTERNAL PHONES OUT. RADIATION LEVEL MUST BE VERY HIGH. EXPLOSION I SAW WAS VERY BIG. DIVED DOWN HOLE QUICK. NOT A FIT NIGHT OUT FOR MAN NOR BEAST. HOW IS WEATHER WITH YOU?

NOT TOO GOOD. HEAVY OVERCAST. AZORES HIGH IS HOLDING BACK RADIATION BUT WE HAVE TO MOVE SOON. DO YOU KNOW IF MCMURDO BASE ANTARCTICA STILL OCCUPIED? SUGGESTED DESTINATION. CAN YOU HELP?

WAIT.

REDFERN HERE. WE HAVE SECRETARY CHIEF MET OFFICER FALKLANDS IN THIS BUILDING. ADVISED HE HAS SHORTWAVE BATTERY/MAINS SET AND SPEAKS REGULARLY TO MCMURDO WILLIAMS AIR FACILITY. I CAN HANDLE SET BUT MEANS BREAKING SEALS WITH UNPLEASANT RESULTS. WHAT DO YOU NEED TO KNOW URGENTLY?

I tried to make our requirements clear—and brief. Time was running out.

I CAN HAUL PASSENGERS OR SUPPLIES BUT NOT BOTH. IF SUPPLIES IN QUANTITY AVAILABLE MCMURDO CAN AIRLIFT ALL AZORES SURVIVORS OUT. IF NO SUPPLIES AVAILABLE, MAXIMUM AIRLIFT ONLY TWENTY HEAD, REPEAT TWENTY HEAD, ESSENTIAL WE MOVE QUICKLY, RADIATION HERE SOON. SCOTT.

Much time passed. Kate went upstairs, organized a tray of coffee and some whole-meal biscuits. Ten minutes...fifteen. I lit a Split to cool my jangling nerves. Kate looked at me as if to speak, and I made a "hold it" face at her. I knew what she had in mind—and it wasn't going to do anyone any good. I had more than six hundred people on my back, with a 50-50 chance of making it, against four people in a cellar far away. People who would soon die anyway, no matter what I did. I wondered about this Redfern character. A two-ringer on liaison to the U.S. nuke-sub fleet was no amateur oarsman, for sure.

Burns sat tapping a pencil on the desk, watching the TP

machine. Kate went back upstairs with the coffee and things. The tension was getting to her; rather than face a breakdown, she got away from the kitchen, because things had suddenly become too hot. I would have liked to escape myself. So much depended on the reply coming up—if there was one. I started thinking about Redfern not making it, and the shakes started all over again.

REDFERN HERE. SORRY FOR BREAK. I SEE YOUR POINT, OLD CHAP...WE CHEWED IT OVER AWHILE. ONE OF GIRLS VERY ILL. I DON'T SEE MUCH FUTURE HANGING ABOUT HERE. WILL HAVE A STAB AT IT. CAN I BORROW YOUR UMBRELLA, OLD SPORT. WEATHER HERE A BIT OFF.

Goddamn it all...he hadn't even tried yet! I swallowed my impatience; I would never know what had taken place in the past twenty minutes, but I could guess. For the four people in the Falklands, it was a simple choice on the face of it: a quick death or a lingering one. Not so simple when you had to make the choice...

We sent:

SCOTT TO REDFERN. ANYTIME, ANYTIME. DON'T SPEAK TO ANY STRANGE MEN. GOOD LUCK.

Ed Burns sat back, flexing his fingers to relieve the cramp. I said, "Fine job, Ed. This is your usual job? I mean..."
He smiled crookedly.
"Hell, no, Cap'n. I run the Confidential Mail Office—or, I did. Just down the hall. But I had to type memos sometimes, so I taught myself to type, on night duty. Say, that's some guy down there. No way you'd find me leavin' a sealed room, the way he's fixed. You know?"
"Ed," I said gently, "you know you would. And he knows he's only a few hours left—and how much it means to us. A little luck—and a man like Redfern around when you need him—that's all we need."
"Yeah. Well...anyway, I don't believe I'll be coming with you, Captain, if it's all the same to you. Seems to me I'm the senior man around here, and someone has to mind the shop until the relief gets here. Besides, my buddies are all here— how can I shove off and leave things be? Huh?"

"Eddie, lad…Eddie," I said softly. He was close to breaking.

"No, no," he insisted irritably. "I've made up my mind. I'm staying, with your permission, sir."

He stood there, straight and smart and young…and I let him go.

"Okay, Eddie. Okay. If that's the way you want it."

"Captain! Captain Scott—!"

The call drifted down three flights of stairs, faint but clear. I started for the door on the double, slowed enough to say, "Ed—sit tight. Wait for Redfern—it's vital. Okay?"

"Okay, sir. Will do."

I went up the stairs three at a time, met Kate on the way down and doglegged round her. At the swing doors to the main ground floor, Sergeant Hockey waited.

"What is it?" I said, breathing hard.

"Another aircraft, sir. About fifteen miles away. We got the standby generator running, and Mr. Price, up in the tower, got the airfield surveillance radar working—it has a standby antenna on the roof."

The stairs to the Tower seemed endless; my legs were leaden when I burst into the once glass-walled room, now open to the air. Price sat at the console on the right of the door, fingers gently moving controls.

"What have you got, Ben?"

"Skipper? Ah…yes, look. About twelve miles now. Traveling fairly slowly—I don't think it's a jet. Ground speed about two hundred. Coming in from the northeast. What in hell can it be, Jonah?"

"I don't know—and I don't like it. Not from that direction. Is the PA system still working?"

"Dunno." He flicked a switch, tapped the microphone with a forefinger. We heard a distant booming noise. "You're on, Skip."

I said urgently, "Attention everyone. Captain Scott. An unidentified aircraft is approaching us from the northeast. Everyone take cover at once—out of sight. Move! Major Brand to the Operations Center. All Army personnel within five minutes of the Tower—get here fast. If you can't, stay out of sight. I don't want anyone to move—or make a sound—until they get an All Clear signal on this system." I switched off.

"Stay up here, Ben, but out of sight. Can they see that antenna rotating from the air? No? Good. How far away now?"

"Nine miles, closing. That is a fat old blip, Skipper. It's big, all right."

I went down the stairs faster than I'd come up, met Brand and his two officers at the door. Hockey was directing the SAS boys into cover as they arrived.

"We have about five minutes, Mike—maximum. Take over?"

"Sure." He grinned savagely. "It's about time these lay-abouts earned their keep. How many, Sergeant?"

"Forty-two," Hockey said, "all armed, sir. Ten men still on the aircraft—I have four others taking their arms out to them and they'll stay put. Sir!"

Brand nodded, satisfied. "All right. We have to assume this is a hostile until otherwise proved. Lemaistre, take a dozen men, get in among those aircraft. The only logical place for this chappie to park is over there—and I want him boxed in. No action till I signal. How many radios?"

"Six," Hamish said. "One at the aircraft, two with foraging parties now here, plus our three."

"Right. Johnny—take this one, get started—not much time. We'll stay here as an assault force. Call when in position."

The little group of men left at a dead run, and I moved inside the Tower building, walked through the ground-floor offices to an open window facing northeast. The afternoon was already hot and humid, the light deteriorating quickly— I could barely see the far side of the airfield to the north. I watched the sky steadily.

At first a vague blob against the overcast, the strange aircraft expanded and sprouted wings; identification was difficult because it was flying directly towards me, but the puzzle began to fit itself together: high wings, four propellers, bulging pregnant fuselage with wheel pods...a C-133 U.S. freighter—or an Antonov AN-10. Which?

It started a smooth turn to starboard, coming in over the airfield at around a thousand feet, engines throttled well back. I saw the big vertical stabilizer, the black paint and the red star—and started running back to the main hall.

"Mike—it's Russian. AN-10—freighter!"

"Cornbread to Weasel—it's hostile. I want no action until I give the word. Cornbread to Satchell—did you get that?"

"Satchell—we copy."

"Cornbread to Whitehall in Delta Tango—remain out of sight and observe. Wait instructions. Out."

The big Soviet job droned directly overhead, very low, and I watched from the door as it swung into a turn to the left, heading downwind on Runway 34, just as we had done—was it only yesterday?

"Mike?" I nudged the soldier in the ribs, feeling a little naked and unarmed, with possible excitement in prospect.

"Yes?"

"What's the plan?" I said urgently.

Brand stared at me. "Buggered if I know, Jonah. What can we do but wait and see? There could be two hundred armed troops aboard that thing."

"And if there are?" I was almost afraid to ask.

"We don't want 'em around, Squire," said the major calmly. "We ask them to leave peacefully—without getting out, if possible."

"Maybe they won't like that."

"More than possible, old boy. In that case, things are likely to get a little warm around here. But we'll manage, never fear."

The entire airfield was silent—how they were keeping all those kids quiet in the PX building, I couldn't imagine—and the Russian's engines were only a whistle and a rumble several miles out. It started a turn inbound, coming in over the town of Praia to line up with the runway. The big landing flaps came down, and the massive airplane drifted in over the threshold. I wondered how far it had come. If I remembered correctly, those beasts had a phenomenal range—nearly 8,000 miles. A big cigar fuel tank showed on each wing.

It touched, floated, touched again and stayed down. The nose dropped 3 feet to the runway, and the propellers roared in reverse pitch as she passed us, going from left to right up the runway. The AN stopped easily, short of the runway intersection, cleaned up the flaps and began to taxi in slowly. I could see nothing of the crew or occupants. Beside me, Mike Brand breathed deeply and slowly, eyes never leaving the big airplane.

There must have been a hundred hidden eyes watching as it entered the parking area, swung and stopped. All four engines cut simultaneously, the propeller disks slowly dissolving into four-bladed assemblies running slowly and interminably.

After three or four minutes, a side hatch opened, an extending ladder came out into position and a figure in black coveralls came wearily down the steps to the ground. A second followed. Both took off what appeared to be leather flying helmets and shook their heads. Long hair drifted and swirled.

Brand said, astonished, "They're women! For Christ's sake, they're women pilots!"

"And not bad, either, from where I stand," I said, amused.

"Yes. Well—damn thing could still be full of troops," Brand grumbled. "I think we'd better wait." He reached for his radio. "Cornbread to all stations. Wait."

We watched. One of the girls walked stiffly to the aft of the airplane, touched a spot on the fuselage, and the big hatch forming the underside of the tail began to hinge down to ground level, forming an exit ramp. People began to pour down it, carrying bags, holdalls, bundles. They were mostly women—many with children, but among them many trim girls in green uniforms and forage caps. A few old men stumbled down the ramp.

Brand said softly, "I don't believe it. Women!"

"Come on." I hauled him out into the open air, and we started walking towards the Russians.

Brand bawled into his radio, "No shooting—keep those arms out of sight! Cornbread to all sections—stand fast. Captain Lemaistre, Lieutenant Bond, Sergeant Hockey—proceed to the Russian aircraft. Don't run—we don't want any panic."

He turned to me, shaking his head, baffled. "Women...Well, I'll be...Come on—let's go see what the hell they are doing here."

We walked slowly out into the half-light, towards the big Antonov. The navigation lights were still on, flashing intermittently, and we could see the interior, dimly lit by small bulbs, stacked with bags and boxes in untidy heaps and revealed as the passengers gradually cleared the airplane.

The girls in black coveralls—clearly the crew—stood by the nose of the transport, waiting. They were both tall, slim creatures, with long fair hair shoved back untidily from their faces, and I saw that their faces were stained and marked with the seams of oxygen masks.

Hockey arrived.

"Sergeant," Brand snapped, "get some men together and

stop these people wandering around. And keep our own people away from them for the moment."

"Sir!"

I stopped in front of the women, moved my uniform cap to the back of my head and stuck out my hand.

"Captain Scott—Air Britain pilot. Do you speak English?"

The smaller of the two—she must have been five feet eight inches tall—took my hand shyly.

"I speak a little, Captain. Valentina Borofsky, Lieutenant, Soviet Air Force. This is Lieutenant Elena Zoloty."

We stared at each other, with a very odd mixture of curiosity, suspicion and genuine pleasure, because it dawned on me that we were as big a surprise to them as they were to us. Particularly since they might well have believed that they were the remnants of the human race—mostly female except for a proportion of the younger children, who would certainly be male, and one or two old men. I could see half a dozen boys in the ring of curious faces surrounding us.

I said, "Why are you here, Valentina?"

"For the same reason you are here, Captain," she said bluntly, looking at Delta Tango. "We have come from Sukhumi, on the Black Sea. When the bombs come, we are flying from Sverdlovsk to Odessa after taking soldiers to the North. We are two hours from Odessa when...it happened. I take the airplane away to Sukhumi, the home of my family. I land on the road near my town. We find fuel in Army store. I take all my family and all people from my village. I tell them in a little time no one will be alive in Russia. We have two hundred people—maybe more, maybe less."

"That was a long flight, Valentina."

"Yes. It was very long. Fourteen hours, Captain. I am sorry—but—have you food? There was not much to bring with us. The people have not eaten for more than a day."

I looked at Mike Brand.

"Hell, yes, Jonah—why not? These people are no threat to us. And we have plenty. While they are eating, I will see what we can do about bedding them down."

"Fine," I said. "Valentina—it is all right to call you Valentina?" She flashed a tired smile. "Of course, Captain."

"Right. Your English is very good."

"I spend six years in university in Volgograd. At first it is very hard. But now I think it will grow better. Yes?"

"Sure." I nodded. "Look—I want you to tell your people

that you are welcome. They are safe for the moment. But they must stay near the airplane until we are ready—you understand."

"I understand."

"Good. We will feed them and find them a place to sleep. How many children are there?"

She turned, spoke in fast Russian to a group of flat-faced pleasant-looking women who were listening with fascination—and without understanding a word. They went into a huddle, came up with a figure.

"They think about forty, Captain," Valentina reported.

"Right. Does—Elena here speak English?" I asked hopefully.

"No. I alone speak. I am sorry."

"Hell, Valentina, don't be sorry—it could have been worse. We have to talk now. Can you leave Elena here with Major Brand to see the people stay near the airplane?"

"Yes. You are Brand?" she said in a businesslike way. It was plain that she considered Mike her equal, as another military body—or maybe just a little inferior. Mike grinned good-naturedly.

"Yes. Call me Mike. Please tell Elena I think we shall work well together."

I gave him a hard look. "You're working pretty well already, matey. Détente is a good thing—but not too quickly—follow me?"

Brand nodded. "All the way, friend—all the way."

I took Valentina by the arm and walked away from the airplane. She gave Elena her leather helmet and pulled out an American baseball-style cap with broad peak, in bright red. It suited her.

"Valentina, I am going to the Control Tower first. I want to tell our people what has happened—they are all hiding."

"From us?"

"Let's face it, girl—you could have been loaded with soldiers—armed to the teeth," I pointed out reasonably.

She frowned. "Captain, I think the time for all fighting has ended. We did not think anyone else was left alive. We called many places on the radio. We talk to people in India—and soon they stop speaking. We talked to other people in Cyprus and Egypt—and they too stopped after a time. For five hours, we have no one to talk with us. It has been very bad."

It may have been her English—but for sheer understatement that took some beating. We started up the stairs to the Control Room. On the way, she offered me a Russian cigarette. It was smooth, faintly scented and cool—like her.

We found Ben Price in Control, standing at the window watching the great throng of people around the Antonov. He turned, eyebrows elevating half an inch when he saw the woman pilot.

"Switch on the PA, Ben. This is Lieutenant Boro—oh, call her Valentina. This is my engineer."

They shook hands gingerly. The girl grinned and said, "I too am engineer. I have degree from Volgograd University for aviation engineer."

I left them to talk shop and flicked the Transmit switch. I heard my voice booming and echoing around the field.

"This is Captain Scott. The Russian party consists mainly of women and children. They are unarmed. We are going to feed them and find them sleeping quarters. Please stay away for the time being—they are very tired and afraid, as we were when we got here. I want volunteers from you to help with cooking and serving; please report to Madame Ferrière of the Red Cross, who will be in charge. Only one of the party speaks English; if anyone of you can speak Russian, please report to Madame Ferrière. Thank you."

I looked at the girl in the black coveralls. "All right?"

"All right, Captain. Thank you."

"Call me Jonah," I told her. "Now—something to eat? Drink?"

"Later, thank you. Jo-nah? It is a strange name. Wait— I have heard it before, I think. There was a man which was eaten of a fish and lived a thousand years in the stomach. Is correct?"

"Near enough," I said, amused. "Near enough. Tell me, Valentina—why come here?"

"There was nowhere else," she said simply. "I knew it was important to go away from all places where bombs fall. We go first to Lisbon, to find fuel, to cross to South America. Elena says we must go to small countries south of Rio de Janeiro—it will be safe for us. But first we must find fuel. And we fly to Lisbon—but there is no Lisbon. Only darkness and much burning."

Ben said, "So you came here—you had enough fuel?"

"Enough," she said lightly—"enough for five, six minutes more, maybe."

I caught Ben's eye, and we laughed. "Snap!" we said together. She looked puzzled until I explained.

"We were just the same." I took a last regretful pull at her Russian cigarette and trod on the butt. "Enough for perhaps thirty more minutes."

She nodded solemnly. I felt a sudden rapport, a knowingness, a togetherness beyond mere friendship.... Each knew what the other felt, and uniforms, nationality mean very little, in the long run, between pilots.

The telephone rang—and shocked us all. It had not occurred to me that the Tower might have the usual battery-operated emergency network. I picked up the handset nearest me—a black one, probably the house phone. It was.

"Captain?"

"Yes. Who's that—Ed?"

"Yes. Can you get down here fast? Falklands on the line."

"On my way." I hung up. "Ben—put Valentina in the picture, will you? And get hold of Kate—ask her to find beds for the pilots. And organize some coffee—all right?"

I didn't wait for his answer. Going downstairs was a hell of a lot easier than coming up, and I took just under a minute to reach the teleprinter room. Ed was waiting, beaming, a strip of paper in hand. I grabbed it.

FALKLANDS TO SCOTT. FALKLANDS TO SCOTT.

BURNS HERE. SCOTT ON WAY. PASS YOUR MESSAGE.

LT REDFERN BACK...THIS IS JEAN CAREY, SECRETARY...WE HAVE SEALED UP AGAIN BUT AIR CONTAMINATED...REDFERN TOO ILL TO MOVE...I HAVE HIS MESSAGE...AS FOLLOWS.

CONTACT MADE CDR ELKINS IN CHARGE WILLIAMS NAVAL AIR FACILITY MCMURDO. BASE HOLDING PARTY NUMBERS ONE SIX, SIXTEEN. ALL SAILORS AND MARINES. ADVISES LARGE QUANTITY SUPPLIES AVAILABLE IN STORE AFTER BASE EVACUATED LAST YEAR, ESTIMATES SUFFICIENT FOR THOUSAND PEOPLE SEVEN YEARS...ALSO BELIEVES FURTHER SUPPLIES CAPE BYRD NEW ZEALAND BASE ACROSS MCMURDO SOUND...PERSONAL MESSAGE FROM COMMANDING OFFICER...DON'T MARRY OFF ALL THE GIRLS BEFORE YOU

GET HERE...NUCLEAR POWER STATION GUARANTEES WARM
RECEPTION. ELKINS.

I read the message again, looked at Ed Burns and started
laughing. It felt good, and I let it come, full and free. Those
crazy goddamn Americans...they'd known for only a day
that there weren't many other people left—and they were
thinking about girls. I thought a bit about that—and decided
I would have done the same thing if I'd been stranded for
keeps with fifteen men at the South Pole.

"Ain't that something, Captain?" Ed Burns said wonder-
ingly.

"It certainly is," I said slowly. "Ed, I want to thank that
gutsy character down in the Falklands—push this out for
me, will you?"

"Sure thing. Go ahead."

SCOTT TO REDFERN...SCOTT TO REDFERN...HOW CAN WE
THANK YOU...WE CAN ALL MAKE IT NOW. BUT DAMNED
SORRY YOU CAN'T BE WITH US. I AM SPEAKING FOR ALL HERE
IN THE AZORES WHEN I SAY OUR PRAYERS WILL INCLUDE
YOU FOR MANY YEARS TO COME. GOD BLESS YOU AND GIVE
YOU QUICK RELEASE. SCOTT.

When Burns typed it out it looked as trite as it sounded—
but I guess they knew at the other end how we felt. Soon
afterwards, they came through for the last time.

JEAN CAREY HERE. THANK YOU CAPTAIN SCOTT. REGRET LT
REDFERN DIED FEW MOMENTS AGO BUT NOT BEFORE HE
HEARD YOUR MESSAGE. COULD NOT SPEAK BUT NODDED. WE
THINK HE KNEW WHAT IT MEANT WHEN HE WENT UPSTAIRS.
HE WAS A VERY BRAVE MAN...WE ARE CLOSING DOWN HERE
NOW AND AFTER A PRAYER WE ARE GOING UPSTAIRS FOR A
LAST LOOK AT THE SKY. WE WISH YOU SAFE JOURNEY AND
BELIEVE THAT A BETTER WORLD WILL RISE FROM THE ASHES.
GOD BLESS YOU ALL. MESSAGE ENDS

I was standing there a few minutes later, alone, when
Kate came down with Valentina. Ed Burns had mumbled
something, blown his nose into his huge blue handkerchief
and stumbled out.

"Jonah?"

I gave her the teleprinter sheet, walked over to the machine and switched it off. I took out the roll of paper, wiped the keyboard and plastic shields with a tissue from the box on the desk. It was just a piece of machinery—but if I could have found a glass case to put it in, I would have worshiped that printer for the rest of my life.

I turned to face the girls, swallowed once or twice.

"Sometimes you get good news," I said huskily, "and sometimes you get bad. And sometimes they come together. I tell you, Kate, religion is not for me and never has been—but if they're not shouting Redfern's name at the Pearly Gates right now... 'and all the trumpets sounded for him on the other side'..."

"Yes, Jonah," she said gently. "I know you're an outright heathen and always will be—but I know that some of us are meant to come through. Like Valentina here, and John Capel, and Nickie and Madame Ferrière—we are all being sieved out and selected and sorted and kept safe because it was never intended we should all die."

The Russian girl was crying unashamedly with Kate, their arms round each other, and I knew if I didn't make a move, I was likely to follow suit.

"Come on." I shoved them gently towards the door. "We have work to do. All of us. Valentina—we have to talk about that airplane of yours, once things are moving. It won't be very pleasant, down there in the Far South—but it's all the home we've got—and we're going to make it."

We went up into the evening twilight. Mike Brand's boys had got the standby generator working, and lighted windows were shining through the dusk. The black lid of the sky was still there, but it seemed a little less menacing now.

Half an hour later, Lajes was beginning to quiet down.... The Russians (I made a mental note that we had to find a different name for them—that one held too many memories, too much suspicion, and after all, there was no Soviet Union anymore—or anywhere else for that matter)—the newcomers were sitting down to a meal of fried chicken, French-fried potatoes (another new name to be invented?), greens and apple pie. Mike Brand and his officers were deep in discussion with Ben Price and Jerry Chambers on reinstalling the seating in Delta Tango, and working on the refueling.

In the conference room, Kate had set up a small coffee

production line with an electric kettle, canned milk and instant granules; it tasted very good to me. Valentina and Elena were there, talking to Karen Waldheim—who could speak fluent Russian, a fact which she had kept very much to herself. Valentina had brought along two or three of the older women, at my request, and I found myself once again in the position of unelected chairman. One thing for sure: as soon as we got to journey's end, I was going to be plain Mr. Scott, with just one aim in mind—finding an unoccupied bed big enough for two. Suddenly, the prospect of being grounded for good became very attractive. I remembered that the polar nights lasted six months...I was all for that.

I looked around the room. Kate had brought half a dozen of her girls along, because this was going to be in the way of a briefing; Ed Burns had sauntered in, talking to Jill Stewart. Their heads were close together, and I began to harbor a suspicion that Ed might change his mind about staying after all.

"Okay...let's settle down."

I waited until everyone found a seat. Nickie was there; if she couldn't be with Jerry, she stayed pretty close to John Capel, with whom she got on very well—hardly surprising, since they were ex-New Yorkers together. Sven Olaffsen had come along, with Volkel and Karen, but Doc Rabin was busy—two of the Russian women were in labor. He was content to work as a medical doctor again, and I believe he was enjoying it.

"Right. First, let me welcome our new friends on behalf of us all. I am no politician—in fact, I guess we're going to have to get along without them in the future"—a slight but unmistakable chuckle from most of my listeners—"but I am only saying what we all think: that we must forget about nationalities from now on. We are survivors—for the moment—and I believe we are friends. On that basis, I want to make it clear that you have as much say in what goes on, Valentina, as anyone else. If you disagree with anything, or you can see a better way of doing things—we all want you to speak up. Right, folks?"

They left me—and the Russian girls—in no doubt. Valentina flushed, smiled and spoke quickly to Elena. The other girl nodded, and Valentina stood up self-consciously.

"You will excuse my English that I learn in university,"

she said hesitantly. "I want to say that we are very happy to be here. And very lucky."

Laughter—and applause.

"We have talked, myself and my friend Elena," she said diffidently, "about what has happened since we have come here. We think that your Captain Scott is correct. It is to do no good to anyone that we talk about what has been done to the world. We are not to...to think too much of the people who have died. We are better to think about living. Living together. Let me say this to you. We have no hate for anyone. We are women like your women—and when our children grow to men, they will be men as your men. We will work together in love. Is good?"

I found myself applauding like the rest. "Working together in love"—I thought we could go along with that.

"Thank you, Valentina. And welcome. Now—down to business. Please translate as we go along, if you will.

"You all know the wonderful news we got from McMurdo Base. Someday, I want to tell you how we got that news— and about the very brave man who made it possible. We know that there are ample supplies at McMurdo for all of us. We believe there is also power—the Americans have had a nuclear power station there for years, and we shall not have problems coping with the cold.

"Because we do not have to take supplies, we can take everyone who wishes to come. You have all been briefed on the situation here—that within a very short time fallout will start, and build up to lethal levels within days. We have to move out quickly.

"So far, only a few people have opted to stay. I hope they will change their minds, because I think they did so in the belief that they were helping other people survive. We have been able to work out how to modify the airplane to take the extra fuel we need. And here, I have to tell you that the flight itself is not going to be easy. I want to be honest with you: to get off the ground with a full load of passengers and fuel, we have to push the airplane to the limit.

"Now—there is still an unknown quantity: Valentina's aircraft." I walked over to the pilot. "Valentina, I need to know some things about the Antonov. Is it possible to reach McMurdo Base? It is 8500 miles—about 13,500 kilometers. Can you make it in one flight?"

She bit her lip, thinking furiously.

"Wait, please...." She began talking to Elena very quickly. The copilot searched through her coverall pockets for pencil and paper; I offered my clipboard and ballpoint, and collected a broad smile from Elena. That in itself was a relief, because the copilot had been quiet and reserved from the beginning. It was not only the language problem—there seemed to be a deep gulf of misunderstanding and distrust, shown vividly in the way she had stood aloof from discussions, speaking only when spoken to. Well... it would have to work itself out.

Valentina looked up.

"Captain..." She saw the look in my eye and laughed out loud. "Jo-nah—I am sorry. Yes, we can do this. My Anti is fitted for in-flight refueling tanker and carries fuel tanks for this. With our own fuel, we fly three-quarters of the way. With the other tanks filled, we go all the way. We must find a way to feed the fuel into our engines; but Elena says yes, she can do."

"Okay. Fine. Now—what about load? Are you fully loaded with the passengers you have aboard?"

Another consultation—a little longer this time. She checked again the figures on the clipboard paper.

"With the fuel we have to add," she said at last, "we are almost at full weight. We have ten, fifteen thousand kilos to spare—no more."

"At full power?"

"Yes, Jo-nah. And flaps."

It seemed so odd, becoming involved in technical discussions about flying with a slip of a girl no more than twenty-five years old. But she knew her stuff.

"Two things, Valentina. You can make the airplane lighter, I think, as we are doing. Take out all unwanted things. The people must take as little as possible. Second— we are setting our engines to make maximum power for take-off, for this last flight. It means taking a chance—a risk. Can you do this—and perhaps take some of our people? Thirty or forty?"

She hesitated, talked to Elena for a while.

The copilot took out a small pocket calculator, ran through several series of computations. Then—

"Yes, Jo-nah. Elena and me—we think perhaps thirty, but we need more time to check. Is good?"

"Is very good, Valentina. Thank you. How soon can you have your airplane ready?" I pushed her a little harder.

"When you are ready to go, Jo-nah, we will be ready also. We need five, six hours—and perhaps your strong men can help with filling of the fuel?"

"Of course. Look: it is seven o'clock—nineteen hundred hours—local time. I had planned to leave tomorrow afternoon, to land about noon next day. Eighteen hours—a little more, maybe. Have you any idea of the flight time you need?"

They worked the answer to that one out very quickly.

"If there is no wind, we take twenty-one hours. We fly at true speed 650 kilometers an hour, but is better as fuel is used. What do you know of winds, Jo-nah, please?" she inquired.

"The most I can tell you is that they should be light and variable at this time of year. This is summertime at the South Pole, you know."

She chuckled. "Is true—except that it is all the time like Siberia in winter. So—is all right, I think. We go first—or after you have gone, tomorrow?"

I thought about that one. Options...options.

"I think we should go first, to get weather reports for you, and winds. We can overfly most of it: we cruise around 40,000 feet—about 12,000 meters. How about you?"

"Not so high. Jo-nah, my friend. Ten thousand meters. And we must check on our radios—to have the same... same..."

"Frequency?"

"*Da*—yes—is right."

"Okay. Very good."

I turned to the rest of the crowd, half-expecting them to complain about being bored and neglected. Far from it—they were following the proceedings intently.

"Well," I said quietly, "you heard. We've a damn good chance of making it—but it means working most of the night. As for the other end—I am not too worried about it. The landing, I mean. It means a belly landing, in deep snow—nice and soft, and 3000 miles of ice cap available. I want those of you with specific jobs to stay behind. The girls had better start on flight meals right away—an eighteen-hour haul means two meals for everyone and plenty to drink. There will be about a hundred seats short, to make room for the fuel drums. Kate, I want you to sort out the forty or so people going with Valentina—mix in some of Mike Brand's troops, to make the women feel a little more secure. Nickie—help

Kate all you can. John, I'd be grateful if you would stay with Karen here, and work with Valentina's people—Karen to translate, you to do the running round for whatever they want. Take a jeep out from Mike Brand. Right?"

"Can do, Jonah."

Christ, so many things to think about...

"Valentina, will you work on a 1500-hours local time take-off; we'll go off at noon. Will that give you enough time? We can take care of the refueling for you—there is plenty of it here."

She nodded briefly. "Yes. We will be ready."

Kate stood up with a very determined look on her face.

"Jonah, we may have to work all night—we don't mind. But you and Jerry and Ben have to fly that airplane tomorrow—and it is a hell of a long flight. Bed for you—quick."

There was a roar of laughter, and I glared at her. Then I saw the sense in her words—and grinned. "Yes, ma'am. Certainly, ma'am."

Valentina Borofsky stood up and nodded.

"Is good thinking. We sleep also. Tomorrow, we fly again— for the last time—but we fly together. Is good."

After they had all gone, I sat for a long time, drinking a final cup of coffee and looking at that unfamiliar chart on the wall. The great irregular mass of the Antarctic continent ...what would it hold for us? Sanctuary?

I looked around the paradoxical normality of the conference room: scattered chairs, overflowing ashtrays, bright overhead lights, depleted water carafes. It would be many long years before the next conference assembled here....

16

Base Officers Quarters at Lajes were unexpectedly comfortable, once Brand's boys revived the electricity supplies. With ample hot water, we lacked for nothing, and we had a room each: privacy, unadulterated luxury. I had been in constant contact with people, it seemed, for two solid days, apart from intermittent and hasty calls of nature. My electric razor would not adapt to the base 110-volt supply, and I thought of Jerry Chambers' safety razor and aerosol cream. I wandered in, half an hour after my cold shower, and found him and Nickie, still fully dressed, sharing the wide single bed in sheer exhaustion, and fast asleep.

I could see no strong reason for disturbing them—although I guessed Jerry would think differently. He had managed two buttons on Nickie's borrowed Airbrit shirt before sleep knocked him out for the count. I found a spare regulation-issue blanket in a closet, threw it over them, pulled off their shoes and left them to it—after pinching said shaving gear.

John Capel called in briefly about nine thirty with a bottle of bourbon and two glasses, stayed for a quickie and an interim progress report.

"It's fuggin bedlam out there, Jonah," he said wryly, "but I guess it will sort itself out. Ben Price is working on the fuel-transfer system—there are a couple of good boys in Brand's bunch, and he's shown them what to do. We have most of the seats back, with room left for the fuel drums. Those people to fly with the girls—all fixed. Ben says he'll finish around midnight; he needs two, maybe three hours to fix the engine power overrides in the morning."

I sat quietly, trying to take it all in. So much going on; if I hadn't known there were many capable people doing what they knew best, I would have been more worried.

"It all sounds fine, John. No—no more for me: this looks like my last trip tomorrow for a long time to come, and I don't want anything working against me. I need to be around fairly early—six thirty or seven. Are you sleeping in this block?"

"Yessir," he said. "Right down the hall. Kate is doubling up with Nickie—I sort of hinted that she should make sure Jerry gets a good sleep.... What are you grinning at?"

"Go take a look across the hall," I said smugly.

He came back a moment later, wearing a look of utter disbelief. "Well, I'll be a ring-tailed son of a—say, I bet he's real mad when he wakes up. You gonna let them sleep?"

I said, "They deserve it, John. We've all had a hard time. Yet...you know what puzzles me? People aren't talking about it. It's almost as if they were all born yesterday—and yet not one of them hasn't lost family. Even you and I, John. How the hell can you explain a thing like that?"

He accepted the Split I offered, sucked smoke deep into his lungs.

"I don't know, Jonah, and that's the truth of it. I had nothing much to do on the way, and I had time to think about it myself. I figure most people did what I did, when they got the chance—got into a corner, shed a tear or two and said 'What the hell.' You know?"

"I know," I said. "I got hold of half a pint of whiskey from somewhere—Mike made me throw it all up, but it seemed to get me over the hump.

"I've been thinking quite a bit about this thing, John. You know, when something bad happens to you—like being raped, or being in an automobile accident—the brain kind of switches off. I know people who can remember nothing about their accident or whatever—it seems as if the brain deliberately erases a length of tape because it would overload the system if played over and over again. I expect this sounds completely crazy...."

"No—I'm with you," he insisted. "You mean maybe we're all under a kind of amnesia?"

"Right, John. Listen—try it. Try to think back—remember what New York was like. Well?"

"Goddamn," he breathed, "I don't believe it... but it's sort of—dreamlike, hazy. I can picture the streets and parks... but it's not real. Like watching a silent movie. As if New York never really existed at all. That what you mean?"

"That's it, John. You know, given a few weeks, I'm going to have trouble remembering what things were like at all. And maybe that's good therapy."

He sat for a while, smoking quietly, on the edge of the bed, legs swinging to and fro, doodling ash into the glass dish on the locker. He seemed to me to have aged noticeably in the last twenty-four hours—the gray in his hair was nearer white, the creases in the brown face a little deeper, the eyes sunk a shade deeper into the dark-rimmed sockets. At length, he stood up.

"Life's a strange thing, Jonah. If you hadn't known Ted Radford, we'd never have met. If your man Chambers hadn't brought along his girl, you wouldn't have got the idea of taking anyone out. And if I had stayed in New York..."

"Don't go religious on me now, fella," I said uncomfortably.

He smiled. "No way... only I just figure I got lucky, and I hope it lasts. Give it to me straight, now—are we going to make it tomorrow?"

"We'll make it—all the way."

"And when we get there—then what?" he persisted.

I stood up and stretched. "John, all I know is, there are supplies in plenty, accommodation for everyone and piped heat from a nuclear power station good for maybe a hundred years of running. Sure, it's going to be cold, and rough, and it's going to last a long time—eight or ten years maybe. We're going to have problems getting back to civilized parts when the time comes; we may even have to build a smaller airplane from the remains of that old bitch sitting out there on the airfield. But it all simmers down to this, doesn't it—that no matter how bad it may be, it is a hell of a sight better than melting like butter in an oven and counting your fingers and toes every morning to see what dropped off in the night. Now get to hell out of here and let me get some sleep."

"Okay." He made for the door and stopped short. "You know what? You think you have problems now? Wait till you start running a bunch of women like ours and those Russkies—because you'll be top man, and any broad that gets alongside you gets to be Number Two. I tell you, Jonah, you're gonna have to beat 'em off with a big stick!"

The door closed before I could work up something really special in reply. I stubbed out the butt, capped the bottle and left it standing on the bedside table. The sheets felt cool and slightly damp—but oh, so good. With the light out, and curtains drawn over the window to keep out the lights and noise from the airfield, the room was black as a goat's ear in a coal mine. I lay on my back, naked, cool and relaxed, hands tucked behind my head.

How long I slept will remain a mystery—but I hadn't moved an inch. For long moments I had no real idea of where I was, even what day it was. I wondered what had woken me—and the knock came again softly.

"Who is it?"

The door opened, light from the corridor silhouetting a tall figure in trousers. I yawned. "Come in—shut the door. Let me get this light."

Valentina Borofsky's voice was soft, husky. "No light, please, Captain. I want to talk for a little time—is all right?"

"Sure—but..."

She came quietly toward me in the faint light filtering through the window drapes. My sight had adjusted—but not enough to see her face. Only her hand, stretched out in a gesture of admonition. She sat down on the bed, shoulders back, one straight arm bridging my legs to give her support, the other resting on her thigh. I could make out the long straight hair, sleek and combed, glistening and smooth.

"Valentina—what is it?" I thought, almost in a panic, that something had gone wrong with her aircraft—and said so.

"No. Is all right, Jo-nah." She dragged out the syllables deliciously, like no one ever made my name sound before. "I wake you up?"

"I guess so. No matter. I thought you had gone to bed—you and Elena."

She shook her head, hair swirling. "Elena is at the airplane. She works to make it ready, until six of the morning—is correct? Ah—six o'clock. Yes. Then she sleeps, and I go to the airplane."

"Then you should be in bed, girl."

She nodded. "Yes. Is true. But first I come to thank you, Jo-nah. Since we are coming here I have not spoken to you alone. But is important. You know and I know that...my country and yours perhaps destroyed each one the other. You are understanding?"

"I understand, Val. But you don't have to—"

"Yes. This I must do—because I want to do. When we come, you spoke like friend, not enemy. You give us to eat, and sleep. And you say we are your friends. How can this be—so soon? Is only one day, two, since the bombs come, and...and..." Her voice choked up, and she had both hands over her face, the bed shaking. She was fighting to hold back the tears. I sat up, leaned forward, found her hands and brought them away from her face, held them tight.

Somehow, I was holding her close, feeling wet cheeks on my shoulder, locking my arms tight to control the shudders ravaging her body. I ran my hand down her hair lightly, again and again, mumbling quite stupid things. Her hair smelled clean and sweet, and was slightly damp; I could smell soap and a musky woman-odor.

Her weight was heavy on my legs. I relaxed back onto the pillow, her head in the crook of my left arm, long legs stretched beside me, waiting until the storm of emotion passed. I found a corner of the bed sheet, touched her eyes delicately to dry the corners and the damp tunnels down the high cheekbones.

"Val? All right?"

After two attempts...

"Yes. All right. I am so sorry, Jo-nah." She sniffed like a little girl, brushed a hand ineffectually across her nose. I leaned over, found a tissue on the locker top, centered it and said coaxingly, "Blow!"

She blew, laughed unsteadily, her face deep in the mass of hair falling over my arm. I bent slowly, found the wide, generous mouth. She twitched, startled, then slid her arms round my neck. Slowly, almost reluctantly, her lips opened, and I felt the birdlike flutter of her tongue along my lips.

"Val...Val..."

"Jo-nah. Help me. I cannot be alone. I have much fright. Jo-nah...do not send me away. Please."

I blew gently on each eyelid until it closed, sealed each eye with a kiss.

"I will not send you away, Valentina. Relax. Sleep."

She sighed—a remote childlike exhalation. "Soon. Soon I will sleep. Jo-nah...you have wife?"

I said woodenly, "No, Valentina. She died. In London. No—not from the bombs. Long ago."

"I am sad for you."

"No need. It was a long time past."

"Jo-nah..."

"Yes, Val."

"I have husband. He is major, in the Soviet Air Force. He is in the Academy of Aviation in Moscow. Is instructor."

"Don't talk, Valentina. Go to sleep."

"Soon. You know...he is dead. Yesterday, when we fly, I do not believe it. I say myself, is not true...is not dead. Today, I know. Is dead."

"Did you love him very much, Valentina?" I asked her.

"Yes. Very much. Will love forever, Jo-nah...will forget him soon, but love forever."

"I know. Don't talk now. We must sleep."

"Yes, Jo-nah. I...you tell, is bathroom here?"

I grinned in the darkness of the room. "Sure. Over there— the left-hand door."

She moved silently across the room, and I could no longer see her. The bathroom door opened, closed, and a thin line of light appeared along the floor. I lay there thinking about her. It occurred to me that like everyone else, she was ridden by nervous tension, fighting to hold back the screaming panic, bearing down hard to erase persistent thoughts of death, mutilation, injury. I knew I liked her very much; but there was much else mixed with the liking—pity, sympathy, a desire to protect her, even admiration for the way she handled her professional job. In many ways, she was so like Kate— honest, forthright and in no way devious. I stretched, turned on my side. Tomorrow...tomorrow could look after itself.... When Val got back from the bathroom, I would have to do something about fixing a spare bed...problem, because I didn't want to spend the night in a chair...spend...

Valentina Borofsky turned back the covers, slid in beside me and flattened her long body close to me. She pushed her head down into the hollow of my shoulder, slid an arm around me and lay motionless. I felt the cool air of the night along my shoulder, drew up the sheet behind her smooth back; she was naked, and the skin was smooth and soft along the curve of her spine.

"Val...For God's sake—you don't have to—"

She stirred. "Not to talk, Jo-nah. Not to think. Only to work in love together."

"Yes...oh, yes, Val darling. Together." Our searching mouths met and savaged each other, tongues touching, parting, plunging, caressing. Inch by inch, she relaxed, until she lay supine beside me, fingers moving in tender exploration over my back. I thought fleetingly that I could spend all my life willingly trapped in the sweetness of her mouth. My palm traversed the scenic route from shoulder to elbow, and the soft curve of her breast lay under my arm. My hand encircled it and found it full, firm, warm, the nipple hard and erect. Valentina slipped the sheet aside. I bent my head and kissed, opened my mouth to engulf the aroused nipple, and she made a small hissing sound. My tongue rolled round the nipple, toying, pulling, sucking.

He lay across her flat belly, a dead weight, a throbbing, an ache verging on sheer agony, and I could not control the forward grinding movement of my loins, until her cool slim fingers enveloped him, lifted him, traversed the length of him, encompassed the girth of him. She gripped tight, and I felt, rather than heard, the faint whisper in my ear.

"Slowly, my Jo-nah...This one night for us...is all. Tomorrow, we will be dead...or in the ice and wind. Tonight ...slowly...with love together. Is good?"

I said shakily, "Yes, Valentina. Yes."

"I know nothing of you, Jo-nah. Is not matter. Is enough to know you...let me know you, my English captain...."

Once, in the remote secret hours of the night, we woke again to renew the urgent sweet battle. Somewhere outside the room, the great base lay dark and silent, save for the rustling of garbage, the sigh of the poisoned wind. But within, there was a mutual search for solace, reassurance, comfort, from each one to the other. When I woke around seven, local time, she was gone—as if she had never been there. But the primitive smell of her was within the bed and upon my body.

17

Exodus Day was the mixture as before: an obscured sky, increasing humidity, hot erratic winds, visibility noticeably worse than the day before. Outside the BOQ block, lighting my first cigarette, I stared around the arc of sky. It was darker by two full shades—a steel-gray flat umbrella from horizon to horizon, with a lighter patch no greater than ten degrees of arc a little above the eastern panorama of stark buildings, occasional trees, stretching towards the shoreline a mile away.

I walked slowly across to the USO canteen we were using as a dining hall, joining the crocodile of people lining the concrete path. I wore a uniform shirt and trousers, without cap; the last possible thing I could have imagined was that these people would recognize me—yet the buzz of comment ran fast ahead of me, and they began clapping. I was embarrassed more than I could describe, to the point of actual pain, and walked past quickly, shaking my head. Women here and there stepped out, found my hand and tried to kiss it, and I shook them off as politely as I could.

Kate, John Capel and Nickie came to the door as I got there, attracted by the noise. I dived in between them like a startled rabbit.

"For Pete's sake, tell them to pack it in, Kate," I said angrily. "That sort of thing is not on. What the hell do they think I am, anyway? Some kind of tin-pot hero? Damned stupid. Stupid."

They followed me into the hall. There were perhaps fifty

small tables, most of them full, and a dozen motherly types behind the hot plates, serving. They damned well started again, standing up, no less, and I went under the counter flap bent double, finishing up round the corner of the kitchen next to the freezers.

Kate came through more slowly, laughing so hard it must have hurt. From the main hall, a rhythmic stomping: *"We want the Cap-tain—we want the Cap-tain."*

"You'll have to say something to them, Jonah," Kate said. For some ridiculous reason her eyes were shining, and I believe she was almost in tears.

"I don't understand," I said dazedly, "what the hell is it all about."

"Jonah, you darlin' knucklehead, don't you realize that we all owe you our lives? That what you did yesterday was so incredible that some of these people actually believe God was riding on the flight deck?"

"Rubbish!" I said harshly. "Load of balls. We'd never have got here without Jerry and Ben helping to fly the aircraft. It took John Capel and Mike Brand to sort out those Russians.... My God, Kate—are they still down in the hold wrapped in carpet?"

She shook her head. "Of course not. When we started clearing the bodies from the airfield yesterday—when you went on that hike of yours—Brand's men got them out and took them away."

The thundering went on. I decided I had to do something about it, and went out, climbed on a chair near the servery and held up both hands. Eventually, they became quiet; many sat down.

"It's all very well," I said defensively, "but I haven't even had a cup of coffee yet."

There was a gale of laughter. Someone bawled, "Give him some champagne!"

"No—seriously." I looked round at the hundreds of beaming faces. "It makes no sense, going on like that. All right—we brought you here safely; but we were very lucky, and I had a fine crew helping me. So do me a favor: no more of that. Tell me—have we any Russian families here? *Russki? Da?*"

A stout red-faced woman in a check shirt and jeans waved a hand. "I think so, Captain. I speak a little Russian. Wait ..."

She spoke briefly. Little groups of people shyly stood up, women and children, and I nodded slowly, smiled and waved.

Gradually, in twos and threes, people began to sit down, resume eating, and I was able to eat a quick breakfast of coffee, toast and canned butter.

Half an hour later, Kate, John Capel and I walked down the airfield. Three big yellow refueling tankers were unloading—one for the Antonov and two for Delta Tango; Ben Price was moving around, supervising the filling of the main tanks and the filling and sealing of layer after layer of big bottle-green plastic containers. A sweating crew of soldiers, hounded on by Sergeant Hockey, shoved and heaved the drums into position, stacked in rows eight deep across the cleared deck of the 797. I saw Ed Burns piloting a jeep around, with Jill Stewart riding second dickey, shifting load after load of packed meals from the USO building to each aircraft.

I asked Kate where all the bread came from.

"Thank the Russian girl—Elena—when you see her, Jonah. We found plenty of flour and packaged yeast. After working on the Antonov, she worked through most of the night with the older women—ours and theirs—baking nonstop. A thousand fresh loaves—and plenty of rolls."

"Fantastic. You must have been late to bed, Kate," I said.

"Mm-hmm. About one in the morning," she admitted. "I didn't disturb you, Jonah—you need your sleep more than anyone."

I decided some things were better left undiscussed, and we went over for a closer look at the Antonov. It was a solid workmanlike assembly of light alloy skin, but with perhaps a rougher finish to joints than those I had become accustomed to seeing on British aircraft. The big propjets reminded me strongly of the old Britannia, and each propeller must have been twenty feet in diameter, with broad paddle blades of polished steel.

I climbed up the ladder, looking back at Kate. "Coming up for a look-see?"

"Not just now, Jonah—too much to do. I can see Ben waving like mad. See you later." She strode away across the expanse of concrete under the dark sky.

Inside the Antonov, I peered around, adjusting to the gloom. A few interior lights were on, down the long rectangular-section hold. A group of Air Force girls in fatigues were cleaning up, tidying, stacking loose baggage and clearing away the debris of a long flight; they looked up, smiled and nodded—some with frightened, solemn faces, but holding themselves rigidly under control. Behind me, a short flight of steps on the port side of the aircraft led up to the flight deck. I clambered up, and found Valentina working at the engineer's seat, back in her flight coveralls.

"Morning, Valentina."

She looked up, the ready smile full of untold secrets. "Good morning, Jo-nah. You sleep very well? I hope!"

I grinned, leaned over and kissed her hard on the mouth. "You're a hard case, Borofsky. A very hard case. I don't know why I love you so much."

She said distantly, "What is this 'love'? You say nothing of love last night, Captain."

"No," I admitted. "Of course, I didn't have much time to say anything. Fighting for my honor."

"Perhaps you did not fight hard enough, Jo-nah...." Her eyes twinkled.

"Maybe—but the way I feel this morning, I must have gone fifteen rounds with the world champion," I grumbled good-naturedly. "What are you doing?"

"This is Antonov engineering book." She showed me the manual, and I was impressed: it was well printed on glossy paper, beautifully illustrated so that even I could absorb a remarkable amount of information. Valentina showed me the problem.

"This is fuel system, Jo-nah. This is to supply our own engines, from tanks—here, and here. We carry fuel for other airplanes in wing tanks—here and here. Is necessary to fill all tanks, and fix—what you say?"

"Pipes?" I suggested.

"*Da*—pipes. Is good. Elena has made the drawing on paper for the pipes, and your friend—Jerry? Yes, Jerry—he is working with other men to fix pipe in workshop."

"Sounds good, Valentina. You will be ready in time?"

"Yes, Jo-nah. Ready to go before"—she checked her watch—"fifteen hundred. Is correct?"

"Yes, Val—correct. How many are you taking?" I asked.

"Our people...two hundred and nine. With Elena and me—two one one. And forty of your people."

I laid my hand on her shoulder. She looked very beautiful and fresh, sitting before the massed ranks of instruments, and I thought absently that it might have been a hell of a trip getting here—but it had been worth every mile. My heart ached, thinking of the separation in time and space to come, before we could be together again. Loving her had become a simple part of living, like breathing and walking, and I could not wait to tell her. Kate...Kate was a more-than-friend, a less-than-lover, comrade, colleague, consoler and comforter, to whom I would ever be in debt for more reasons than I could list in a century.

"Val...we have to stop talking of my people and your people...we are one people now. Think of it as a new nation—for we are all emigrants to a world we have never seen before. Where we may stay for all our lives—and I am no longer British...you are not a Russian. We will be—people. Nothing else. Just people. Do you understand?"

"Yes. Yes....It will not be easy, I think. We speak Russian, you speak English. What we teach the children to speak? You see, my Jo-nah, Russia is gone, but we are still Russians. Tell me true. If I say to you that all English people must speak Russian, they will not. They will say they are speaking English and will not speak Russian. So. Is same for us. *Da?*"

She was right, I told myself bleakly. There was going to be no easy way to make two nations live together—but a way had to be found. It might take three, maybe four generations before all the kids spoke a common tongue—and it would not be one or the other, but a bastard mixture of both. What matter?—the important thing was that eventually we would be a single people, with a single tongue, the same customs, manners, dress. So that when the time came to venture out into the cleansed world, there would never again be differing languages, customs, frontiers. Our nation would live in peace, and repopulate the earth as one family.

I left Valentina deeply involved with her mechanical problems and visited Delta Tango, collected the chart bag and found a quiet corner in the VIP lounge to work.

I drew the track on the charts; laid them out on the floor of the lounge, over the brown patches where perhaps the last Russian blood had been spilled; and stood back, appalled. There was no way, I told myself, that an overloaded 797 was going to make that staggering journey almost a third of the way round the underside of the world. The line moved south, always south, intersecting the 30°W meridian at a fine angle and crossing it somewhere east of Salvador, in Brazil. It was over the sea all the way, until we hit the Antarctic continent, south of the Weddell Sea. I followed the line down, skirting the Cape Verde Islands, making the nearest approach to land passing Recife, on the eastern tip of Brazil. Then the long haul down the South Atlantic, overflying the Falkland Islands Dependencies and the Weddell Sea. No land diversions, only small and rare islands en route. I began to worry about hitting mechanical troubles along that huge leg, and suddenly realized that there was nothing really I could do about them anyway. If anything went wrong—we went into the drink. It was as simple as that. No lucky breaks. No second chances.

I felt the sweat breaking out in the roots of my hair, welling out over forehead and cheeks. I was crazy to think it could be done, insane for listening to those damned eggheads....Eighteen hours? We had to carry almost as much fuel in drums as the entire internal tanks would hold; and even flying at most economical speed, there was going to be damn all to spare. Worse—we had no idea of winds. They told me that all the reference books seemed to indicate light and variable winds in the Antarctic summer—but how could they expect me to risk the lives of nearly a thousand people on what they'd read in some school textbook?

I went back to the flight deck and the on-board computer. I began to work on options. Suppose we found adverse upper winds?...If we were no farther south than the Tropic of Capricorn, twenty or so degrees south of the Equator, we would have plenty of fuel to go almost anywhere in Brazil—but where? And why go at all, with the world ankle-deep in radioactive ash?

I lit a cigarette with trembling hands—one of a precious stock of American Pall Malls and Lucky Strikes, still in bond in Lajes two years after the factories topped production in mainland America.

I decided the time had come to dump any heroic ideas of going anywhere—except south. I would do what I could— make sure we hit every checkpoint, although the autopilot would do that without any help from me; even the vagaries of the Magnetic Poles had no effect on the INS systems. You start off with an instant position and lock in a series of gyroscopes. Thereafter, the aircraft maintains itself only in relation to a point of inertia in space, every turn and climb and dive being directly related to that first position. No, I had no worries about navigation.

The same applied, in fact, to the mechanics of flying the aircraft exactly along the correct course, and at the right speed, to hit the next way point dead on the nose: the INS told the autopilot, and George wiggled the controls, worked the throttles.

I used to wonder just what in hell they needed a pilot for. The answer at one time was for takeoff and landing only—except now it could all be automated. Well, I told myself, it was going to take some autopilot to put Delta Tango down in thirty feet of clean snow and ice at the other end. No, brother: this one was my last, and by God, I would do it my way.

I ran through a zero-wind flight plan, at the utterly ridiculous all-up weight they were going to ask me to move. Eighteen hours, give or take a minute or two. I began to think about the global-weather-situation effects on a flight of this length. I could run clean through half a dozen depressions and highs on the way, with winds from all directions; there might be a fair chance that they could all cancel out.

The charts went back into the flight bag, power to the computer off, and I went back down the spiral stairs onto the main deck, making the best of my Lucky Strike.

Ben and Jerry were at the forward gate.

"Hello, Jerry."

"Skipper. Sleep okay?" said the copilot.

"Never better," I said, "But I'm having real bloody nightmares about this trip."

"Don't," Ben complained. "That'll only make me more nervous."

I stared down the cavern of the fuselage, watching Brand's boys lashing down the last few drums of fuel. I didn't want to meet anyone's eyes at the moment—especially crew members who could scent lack of confidence a mile away.

Jerry Chambers spoke confidently. "I felt the same way, Skip, until Ben and I ran it through the computer this morning. We should make it with maybe an hour's fuel left, assuming light winds."

"Then you made a boob on the machine, Jerry. I just ran a check on it—eighteen hours dead, and not a drop to spare."

There was a pregnant silence. Then—

"You know the Russian girls are taking forty of our lot?" Ben ventured. Christ—so they were. I felt sick. If I could forget an item like that... Nearly 5000 glorious kilos to the good—damn it, Valentina had told me too, and it had slipped clean away.

I shook my head, and they laughed. "See? It's a doddle," Jerry said comfortably. "Progress report, Skip. Fuel—all tanks filled. All drums filled. Three hand pumps on board for fuel transfer. We've been working with Mike Brand and Hockey, and they say they can cope—all we have to do is tell them when to transfer, which tanks and how much. Have a look at this." He led the way to an open hatch in the port gangway. "We've rigged up a transfer pipe and filler point here, at the hatch. There is a small access panel we can use in the cargo bay to bleed off air very slowly; that gives us a positive airflow into the lower hold—no fumes. Okay?"

"Keep talking. I'm listening," I said.

"Kate says the flight meals are in hand. We've even found some movies to show the kids—cartoons. We thought it best not to show any ordinary films...might get people thinking about—about—"

"I get the point. Go on."

"Right, Skip. We have a tanker ready out at the end of the runway to top us off before takeoff—"

"Wait a minute," I said harshly: "someone's got to drive that thing—and we are leaving no one behind—right?"

"Right." Jerry nodded. "Ed Burns and Capel are handling it. As soon as they finish, they abandon the tanker, get aboard quickly. Mike Brand has a squad laid on with ropes and a simple wood seat—we'll have them aboard so quick you wouldn't believe it. Did a dummy run early this morning. By the time you wind up to full power, we'll be all sealed up."

"Which reminds me"—I began to get nervous again—"Ben—what about those engines?"

He looked at my face, put on his "nothing to fear" expression and used his bedside-manner voice. "Everything's fine, Skip. No sweat. We shifted the locks to allow takeoff revs right up to the red line—915 degress on the tailpipe temperatures. I figure they'll stand it for five minutes maximum—and we worked it out that we'll be at 800 feet three minutes after takeoff."

"And if we lose one?" I said quietly.

Jerry grinned. "Number Two survival drill. Close the eyes. Place hands together in front of the chest, and say slowly after me, 'Our Father...'"

"Funnee." I was in no mood for bad jokes. It was after ten, local time—which was the time we'd be using all the way. "What time are we starting to load?"

"I haven't settled that yet, Skip," Ben said uncertainly. "Everyone was warned to be ready to move at eleven A.M. We only have the one boarding ladder serviceable; I think it will take all of forty minutes to get everyone aboard and settled in."

I thought about that one. "Yes—I'll go along with that, Ben. No earlier—they are going to get sick of the sight of the airplane after eighteen hours, but we can't help that. You two got all your stuff aboard?"

"All we're taking," Jerry said lightly. "All the warm clothes we could find, a bottle of Johnnie Walker and plenty of cigarettes—they don't weigh much. I got Nickie some things together, too."

"How's she bearing up?"

"Surprisingly well, Skipper. Like everyone else, I reckon—starting a new life and determined to forget all that's happened."

I clapped him on the shoulder. "Fine. I'm going back to the BOQ, get my stuff together. Kate said she'd look after anything else I need. I'll see you back here at oh eleven: I want to be here when they start boarding. One last thing, Ben—how about starting up?"

"Same drill, Skipper. Ed Burns and Capel are hauling away the power mobile, clearing the blocks, before they go for the tanker."

"Good. You know, it seems you fellers have done all the work while I was sleeping."

"Sleeping?" said Ben innocently. I caught the beginnings of a grin on his face—and Jerry was ostentatiously staring up at the overcast, his face working. The bastards...they'd known all the time about Valentina—and never let on!

"Get the hell out of it, you couple of..." And then we were all laughing. I suppose it was funny—and kind of naive on my part: I should have known that nothing much goes on in aircrew billets that isn't public knowledge. A sudden thought struck me.

"Here—does Kate know?" I asked anxiously.

"Of course," said Ben. "Why not?"

"God," I said heavily, "I bet she was spitting blood."

"On the contrary," Jerry commented, "she was like a dog with two tails. No kidding—genuinely pleased, Skipper."

"We all were," Ben put in. "She seems a fine woman, that

Valentina. And they are bloody good pilots, too—that Elena knows her onions."

I was still puzzled. "It doesn't figure," I said. "I thought Kate would have been as jealous as hell. It's a bit disappointing, in a way."

They hooted with laughter.

Finally—

"Look, Skip. You want to know why? Ask Kate. She'll tell you. She thinks the sun shines out of your pants, but she's never considered herself attached in any way. I think she looks on herself as ship's comforts—like coffee, flight sweet issue and using the best hotels."

"Well..." I was still dubious.

"Skipper—she brought you back from the dead, a year or two back, didn't she?" Ben demanded.

"Yes."

"Well—she's helped all of us, one time or another. Right, Jerry?"

"Check. One of the boys, is Kate. Never known her turn a guy down." And that was the nub of it, of course... wonderful, generous Kate—I just hoped, somewhere south, there was a lonely Marine or sailor for her.

18

Boarding had been in progress for fifteen or twenty minutes when Ben Price arrived, with Professor Volkel and Sven Olaffsen in tow. They hurried past the long crocodile of passengers, stretching almost two hundred yards across the flat concrete; past the family groups, singletons, the mass of children aged from five to fifteen shepherded along by Madame Ferrière and her team of Red Cross people. For the most part, they queued quietly and patiently, moving along inch by inch, carrying their meager suitcases, holdalls, even rolls of blankets. Everything there was available for the taking, yet few I saw had indulged themselves at the jewelry counters of the PX store. Money and precious stones had no meaning now, nor were they likely to regain value at any time I could imagine; the valuable items now were shoes, underclothing, bedding, warm outercoats. I stood in the forward doorway, helping the infirm and aged, the children; almost invariably, I received a smile, a salute—more than once, a kiss.

Ben and the boffins came up the stairs, each loaded with items peculiar to their needs: Volkel and Olaffsen carried a few books, instruments—no weight problem: well within the ten kilos we allowed every passenger.

Ben said, "Guess what I've got."

"Go on—surprise me."

"Spent half an hour in the Meteorological Office," he said smugly, "with the Prof. here. We found a supply of balloons and gas, and a theodolite—and got an upper-wind reading."

That was really something. "And—?" I said.

"Good news and bad," he said cautiously. "The upper winds are round to the southeast; the high-pressure area is beginning to drift eastwards, towards Europe. Maximum wind speed about 40 knots at 12,000 meters. The bad news is that we lost the balloon after about half an hour—in the overcast, at around 3000 feet. That's about 10,000 meters. It's coming down fast, Jonah—no doubt about it."

"Rabin was with us," Volkel said, "taking readings on that damned Geiger counter of his. He will be here soon—but with bad news also. The radiation count has doubled in the last twelve hours, Captain."

"Can you put that into words of one syllable for me, Prof.?" I said apologetically.

"Ah. Yes—we are breathing air contaminated to almost half the lethal level: 250 roentgens. If we continue to do so, within a few days we shall have absorbed a deadly dose. In a week, exposure to the air will be certainly fatal. I would not recommend staying around here too long."

"I'll drink to that," I said grimly. "Keep that little gem to yourself, Professor—these people have enough on their plates without that. Although they must have an idea," I said worriedly, staring up at the cloud of gray-black filth overhead. There was no sign of the sun, not even a lighter patch by which we could orient ourselves—and the diffused light over the airfield was much worse. We had all possible lights going; when Valentina took off three hours after us, they would leave everything burning. There would be no one left to worry about them, and it meant a little of humanity would still be left when we were all winging southwards.

Once again, the question burned bright in my mind: how thick was that overcast? Would we be able to soar above it? Or were we doomed to spend eighteen hours breathing in death in a particularly nasty form? There was no possibility of flying beneath the "hot" overcast—we needed every scrap of height we could gain, for the jet airplane flies farther on less fuel the higher it climbs. No use asking Ben—he had watched his yellow balloon rise into the crud layer, but had no means of telling how high it must climb to reach the bright sunlight above. Sunlight...how long since I had seen old Sol? Three days? Or was it four?

I bit my lip, went towards the door.

"Going over to see Valentina," I told Ben. "Be about five minutes. What do you make it now? Eleven twenty-five?"

"Check."

Around the Antonov, vehicles were unloading boxed meals, blankets, bags. Rabin was there, stumbling around nervously watching a group of Russian girls loading half our entire medical supplies; we had split vital consignments, such as vaccines, blood plasma and the like, between the two airplanes. We told ourselves—a hundred times—that nothing was going to go wrong—but if it did, we would at least salvage half of most things.

Rabin nodded, his once-white shirt soiled with patches of sweat; it was now uncomfortably warm.

"Hello, Doc. I got your message about radiation levels. Guaranteed to cheer everyone up—like hell." I said drily.

He was not amused. "We shall be well advised to move out quickly," he told me. "The level is rising fast. I was coming to see you—I do not think it wise to delay this airplane for three hours."

"Okay. Say no more." I walked round to the nose of the airplane, found Valentina and Elena loading their own gear aboard.

"Valentina—"

"Ah, Jo-nah. You are going now?" Her face showed unmistakable signs of strain.

"Soon. Hello, Elena."

The other girl grinned widely and winked. I started to get a bit annoyed—seemed everyone and his sister knew about Val and me.

I turned back to Valentina.

"Val, Dr. Rabin says the radiation count is going up fast. I want you off the ground as soon as you can. Can you ask Elena to pass the word fast?"

"Yes. I am telling her now." She spent a moment or two briefing Elena, and the copilot nodded, frowning, before hurrying away.

"There is something else," I said bluntly. "The overcast is much lower—about 7500 meters. If you get away quickly, you may be able to stay under it. But you know, if you cannot, you must fly in radioactive cloud all the way?"

She stared at me, eyes afraid but steady. "I understand, Jonah. Yes, we must go soon. We have radio?"

I understood what she meant. "Yes, Val. Call me on 121.5 Hertz as soon as you get off the ground—understand?"

"Yes. Jo-nah...if—if we do not..." She faltered. Then,

"If we do not meet again, I want you to know that I am loving you very much. You will take care?"

"I will take care, dearest Valentina. You too—yes?"

She came to me, kissed me very hard, just once, and pushed me away. "Go now—or all our children will have two heads." She produced a grin, incredibly, but tears filled the corner of each eye.

I walked away, ever more quickly, towards Delta Tango, not looking back.

"Captain to passenger deck. Report."

"Jonah, everything is fine. All seated, all doors closed and on Auto. No documents aboard—I threw them all away to save weight."

"Okay," I said slowly. "Kate—do something for me?"

"Sure. Name it."

"This is our last time—you know? I'd like everything to be right—not strictly to the book, but let's do it all the right way. Please?"

"Sure. I understand. You're right. Let's show 'em we can really do it."

"Fine. Come up once we're airborne, Kate, and let me know the situation. Captain to deck—out."

I looked down onto the ground from the window on the left of my seat. Ed Burns and John Capel were waiting beside the mobile generator throbbing away under the nose; Jerry Chambers had briefed them well on the starting procedures. John was wearing the headset, plugged via his umbilical cord into the intercom system.

"Captain to Ground—all clear for starting?"

"All clear, Captain."

"Stand by. Copilot, starting checks, please."

Jerry Chambers had the clipboard ready; Ben sat behind us going through his own checklist. The flight-deck door was closed, shutting out the constant buzz of conversation from below. We had kept the VIP-deck seats clear for our own group—Ed Burns, John Capel, Nickie, our four tame scientists, Kate and Jill Stewart.

As for Thunderman and Girl Friday—I did not know and I did not want to know.

We moved quickly and competently through the checks, until all five engines were whining away steadily a hundred

feet aft of the flight deck. I heard the "click" as Capel un-
plugged the ground-link telephone, and checked with Ben.

"How does it look, Engineer?"

"I have a green board, Captain. No unserviceabilities, all
generators on line, all systems on and checked."

"Right, Ben. Fine. Jerry, what do you estimate the surface
wind?"

"The last check we did in Control, Skipper, 270 degrees,
30 knots."

I frowned. We would have a crosswind component, with
the takeoff wind effectively about 10 knots. We would need
every inch of runway.

"Okay...here we go." I checked to each side and ahead,
in the gathering gloom. I saw Valentina, all ready in flight
clothes, waving, smiling; Ed Burns and Capel had moved the
generator clear and were running for the tanker waiting
nearby—they knew the need for haste. I released the parking
brake, opened the four forward engine throttles and waited
for her to move. Nothing. Had I forgotten to have the blocks
taken away? No—I'd checked that myself. I got them open
to half-throttle, a storm of noise washing over the flight deck.
She trembled, moved a little, hesitated. Christ, she was
heavy! I shoved them open all the way, the whole airplane
shaking, and she gave way, lurching forward. I believed she
knew, poor old cow, what she was in for....

Delta Tango moved majestically towards the taxiway,
passing the Antonov on the starboard side; I noted in passing
that she was being loaded at top speed, people walking
straight onto the loading ramp as they arrived. Val and Elena
were at the entrance hatch in the nose, turning for a last
wave, and the final glimpse of Valentina was of those slim
strong hips swinging aboard her airplane.

Ahead of us, Ed Burns pushed the massive 5000-gallon
tanker hard, making for the end of the runway. I knew we
were taking an unwarranted risk in topping up fuel with
engines running—but we needed every last thimbleful we
could carry.

We finished the takeoff checks without any delays: at least
that fantastic old bird was giving us an easy time mechan-
ically. Close to the runway threshold, I was able to take a
long clear look at the situation. There was, thank God, a long
grass undershoot—it must have been 600 feet long—between
the perimeter fence and the runway proper. I began to feel

a little better; in fact, I was no longer actually terrified...only scared shitless....

I brought her round very slowly, staying on the concrete until I had her centered squarely on the white line.

"Okay, Jerry. I'm going to back her slowly down to the hedge. I think the undershoot area will take it all right—it's there to cope with undershooting aircraft. In any case—we have no choice. We need every inch. Now...select reverse thrust."

"Thrust reversed, all engines."

"Ben—get your head out of Jerry's window, make sure we go straight. I'll take this side; Jerry, handle the throttles. Brakes coming off...open her up. More. More. Hit her hard.... Okay, she's moving. Keep her straight...tail to starboard slightly...center...hold it. Throttle back. Good....A shade more, Jerry—about 50 yards...good—right. Brakes on."

The 797 sat with her tail actually over the 6-foot-high wire fence around the airport, main gear down 6 inches or more in the topsoil—but I could wear that. The tanker swung round the nose into position.

"Ben—cut the inboards. We can restart on batteries, with the rest running, and there's no point taking too many chances."

"Right. Shutting down Two and Three. Did you say taking too many chances, Skip?"

I leaned out of the window, signaled Burns and Capel to go ahead with topping up, and turned to Ben. "Yes—why?"

He grinned impishly. "We have an overloaded aircraft, 40 tons of fuel stacked in back, no diversions or alternates and a belly landing when we get there. Who the hell worries about taking chances?"

It got a laugh, of course, and we began to feel tension easing. It might be rough—but we were doing the job we were trained for. I said a silent prayer for the souls of those Rolls-Royce engineers buried in the slag heap that had once been Britain.

I could see the fat back of the tanker dimly below, in the yellow approach lights; it moved back, turned and rolled clear of the runway. Burns and Capel raced back to the aircraft, out of sight, to be hauled aboard by Mike Brand and Hockey.

Ben reported all tanks full.

"Right. Start Two and Three, Ben. Jerry, takeoff checks."

Ninety seconds later...

"Captain speaking. Here we go. I think we're in good shape—good luck to you all. I will call you again when airborne. Thank you."

The intercom buzzed. *"Door One closed, on Auto, Captain."*

"Thank you, Kate. Captain to crew—stand by for takeoff."

The five black throttle levers went forward steadily together, Delta Tango shuddering against the parking brake.

"Full power...EPR one decimal four...EGT 850 degrees steady...clear, Skipper."

"Thank you, Ben. Here we go."

We surged forward, slowly—oh, so slowly—over the grass and onto the concrete fairway. She was lumbering along, perhaps 40, 50 miles an hour, flaps half down, and I rammed the throttles through all the way.

"EGT's rising, Skip. Eight seven five...885...900 degrees..."

"Let me know when we hit red line."

"Seventy knots...80..."

"I have rudder now, Jerry. Keep those damned engines wide open."

"Bloody right. Ninety...95...Jesus God, she's slow...98...hundred knots."

Ben said quickly. "EPR 1.45...EGT 910 degrees...on red line, Skip!"

"Hundred and ten knots...V one, Skip."

Thank the Lord for small mercies.

"VR...rotate!"

"Rotating. Is there any runway left?"

"Damn little...120 knots...125. She's lifting...lifting!"

"Engineer here—Number Five EGT fluctuating like hell—way past red line! Nine five oh degrees!"

"Keep 'em all flat out.... Come on, you gorgeous old cow, you!"

Jerry said in a small voice, "Airborne."

"Gear up—fast!"

"Gear coming up...150 knots...100 feet...Come on, baby, go...go...go!"

"Anything ahead?"

"Clear, Skipper—we just passed between two trees on the coast."

"She won't climb, Jerry!"

"She'll go, Skip...she'll do it—200 knots, 140 feet...she's coming up."

"All engines past red line, Skip! She'll bloody well blow up if we don't throttle back!"

"If we throttle back, we go into the drink, Ben. Shut up and stop bitching."

"Two one zero knots...200 feet—I think we can come back to normal takeoff power, Skipper."

"Okay, Jerry. She feels better....Ben?"

"All coming back. EGT's dropping....Good grief, Number Five's gone right off the clock—it has to be that damned gauge again, Skip. All engines below red line and falling. Board all green, Skipper. Main gear up clean, no lights."

"Two four zero knots, 400 feet." Jerry sounded almost happy.

"Check. Flaps up to ten."

"Flaps up to ten. Holy cow, Jonah—that must have been a shocking takeoff to watch. I bet they were frightened to death down there."

"I've got news for you, fella. I had the same trouble."

And it was true....I was fighting to slow down my racing pulse.

"All right...starting a turn to port. Flap up all the way, Jerry."

"Flaps coming up. Seems odd, having no radio procedures to follow. First way point set into Number One INS. Speed coming up to 250...1100...flaps up."

"Fine. Jeez...my mouth's dry. Soon as we get the climb established on course, I'll call Kate. Switch off the No Smoking sign, Jerry, and light me a cigarette. I'm bringing her round to due south before I cut in autopilot."

She nosed delicately round the shallow turn, still feeling ominously heavy through the controls, despite the power circuits. I was on instruments almost immediately—there was no horizon, the overcast now really black and solid, and there was now a dank, sooty, unhealthy odor in the air, reminiscent of burned-out bonfires soaked with morning rain. I wrinkled my nose in disgust; it would be far worse when we got into that layer of slok. I checked my watch: five minutes past noon. It was almost dark, and I could hardly believe it.

"I'm locking in autopilot now, Jerry. What time did we leave the ground?"

"Noon—give or take a few seconds. If everything goes like

the timing for takeoff, we're laughing. Autopilot in, board all clear."

"Back to climbing power, Ben. Who has a cigarette?" I slumped back in my seat—and as quickly leaned forward again; I was wringing wet, perspiration channeling down my back, cold and clammy against the leather seat back. I dragged deeply at the Lucky Strike Jerry passed over. We were climbing steadily southwards, passing through 7000 feet, drawing closer every minute to the nauseating layer waiting for us. I began to wonder if I should not tell those people back there of the waiting danger—and realized they almost certainly knew: perhaps ignorant of the fact that we might have to fly eighteen hours embedded in the crud, but aware that we had to climb up through it.

"Well done, Jonah.... Here—you've earned it." Kate's coffee was like her smile—warm, sweet and acceptable.

"Thanks, love. Everything all right down back?"

"Fine. Except during takeoff. Did you keep her down low to gain speed?"

"Kate, you must be off your tiny shelf. She just wouldn't come up—bloody well sat there at a hundred feet dragging her arse through the waves."

She grinned. "I have to say it, Jonah—half the people back there thought we wouldn't make it. Cue for joke."

"Yes—I know. Half the people up here too. Well—we damn well did make it. Are they all right? Or do you think I should speak to them?"

"I would, Jonah. Just—don't tell them too much about...that mess up there. Do you know how thick it is?" Kate asked.

I shrugged my shoulders. "Your guess is as good as mine, Kate. If we are to believe Doc Rabin, our chances are not very good if we have to breathe that muck for a whole day— it's probably hotter than a stolen Rolls-Royce. Right off the clock."

"And if we can't climb up through it?"

"We have no choice, Kate. We have to make the height to make the distance; there is damn-all margin for error even if things go well. If we fly below 25,000 feet—we don't make McMurdo."

I sat there in silence for what seemed to be a very long time. Had anyone ever been faced with a situation like this? I wondered. That damned black quilt of incinerated ashes...One of two things was happening. Either the layer of debris was sinking into itself, consolidating as the heavier particles fell through the lighter (in which case the top could be within climbing distance) or—and I hoped to God I was wrong—the whole of the miles-thick belt of gas, hydrocarbons and rubbish was sinking bodily as it cooled. Cooled, that is, speaking thermally and not radioactively—it would not "cool" in that sense in my lifetime.

I stubbed out the cigarette, keyed the PA system microphone.

"Ladies and gentlemen, this is the Captain. I don't have to tell you that we have made a good start. The takeoff went very well...."

I caught Jerry Chambers grinning into his palm and scowled; the grin switched off like a light. I went on:

"We are climbing on course to our cruising altitude. With our present heavy load of fuel, that will be about 34,000 feet, but as fuel is used, we'll get up to 39,000. We'll show some cartoon movies, soon, for the children—brought along specially from Lajes. I would advise you all to rest as much as possible, reserving the last two hours of the flight for landing drill. It will be daylight when we get there—the sun shines most of the day at 80 degrees south latitude. Settle down, put out the lights and rest as much as possible. We will serve your first meal in about four hours—four o'clock Azores time."

I stopped short, assessing the best way to say what I had to say. "We shall enter cloud shortly—in ten or fifteen minutes. It may be smoky, difficult to breathe. Hold a handkerchief to your mouth, if so—and see the children do likewise. If possible, tear up linen to make a mask for each one. There is not much else we can do—we must maintain height. If the winds are favorable for us, we should land at McMurdo Base around six A.M. tomorrow—about eighteen hours' flying. It is a long flight, and Miss Monahan, the Chief Stewardess, has worked out a program of exercise which you must all follow, to avoid getting cramps. It is not difficult—a fifteen-minute walk around the deck every two hours...."

"I think that is all. If you have any questions, the crew will help. Good luck once more, and thank you."

I switched off the PA, slid the microphone back onto the clamp and stared round defiantly. "Well?"

"Super, Skip. Do we get to take a walk too?" Ben queried.

"Say the word and I'll even open the door for you. Swimming is better exercise than walking anyway."

I checked the instruments. Sixteen thousand feet... climbing steadily. The Machmeter had started to indicate, needle tracking slowly around the dial, even though the Indicated Airspeed was still held accurately at 240 knots by the autopilot. As we gained altitude in the less dense air, the airspeed indicator underread more and more; our true airspeed was certainly approaching 500 knots, equivalent to almost two-thirds of the speed of sound, shown by the Machmeter needle at Mach .75. Soon the meter would reach .84, our best climbing speed with the loaded aircraft, and the autopilot would hold that indication, ignoring the erring Airspeed Indicator. At 40,000 feet, Indicated Airspeed would be as low as 175 knots—approaching the stall, in fact, and I would have to handle her very gently.

It was almost totally dark now, the flight instruments showing luminously in serried ranks and groups. Far aft, the five great engines labored near top speed to lift 300 tons of aircraft up through 8 miles of sky, singing a steady song; each one hurled sternwards hundreds of pounds of water, burned hydrocarbons and other byproducts every minute.

Kate brought forward half a dozen new white handkerchiefs: "Out of Lajes PX—with the compliments of the U.S. Air Force," she said simply. "We'll need them, I'm thinking. You need anything more to drink up here?"

"No, thanks, Kate. We'll be in it soon—best go back aft now."

"All right, Jonah"—and that was that. I heard the door close softly.

"Twenty-two thousand, Skipper," Ben chipped in. "All engines on line, no snags, and I'll give you your first fuel check at the top of the climb. I want to see how my calculations worked out.... Thirty-five thousand the best we can do?"

"We'll soon know, Ben. It's no use pushing it—we could probably scrape another thousand feet or so by losing 20 or 30 knots. But she'd be too close to stall—she would fall out of the sky below 150 knots, with this load aboard."

"What worries me a bit," Jerry said hesitantly, "is the slow rate of climb. I know we're heavy—but look at her!"

"Not long now," I said. "Passing 25,000 feet." Almost as I spoke, Delta Tango gave a great lurch, and I grabbed for the wheel, fearing that the autopilot had dropped off line.

But the invisible man at the controls juggled aileron, elevator and rudder to establish equilibrium again, and she straightened up on course, shuddering a little in the heavy turbulence of the cloud bank.

"My God," Chambers said shakily, "if we have eighteen hours in this crap, she'll shake herself to pieces!"

"Shut up and start praying," I told him. "She's still going up, we're all in one piece—and that's a hell of a stink, isn't it?"

Chambers retched a little and clapped a handkerchief over his nose. The air was rank, smoky, thick and turgid, a mixture of unspeakable cremations, loathsome ashes of disgusting origin; I heard Ben heaving helplessly into some container or other, and I tasted the rising bile in my own mouth.

The nightmare went on and on....The flight deck was filled with the reek of sulfur fumes, acrid and noisome vapors clotting on the tongue, stinging the eyes. It seemed not to matter that the ordure we were eating was radioactive and lethal—we sat helpless, steeped in nauseating filth, while our airplane staggered and vibrated in heavy turbulence. I got my seat belt fastened, which helped, and put on the Fasten Belts sign—belatedly. Conditions back in the main deck were impossible to imagine.

Time dragged by.... The linen at our mouths stained black within minutes, and did little to filter out the fetid smut. Fighting every inch of the way, Delta Tango passed the 30,000-foot level, on up towards her ceiling; and at last, one hour and five minutes after takeoff, we leveled out, let the speed settle. Jerry managed to get three or four way points into the INS—the Cape Verde Islands, a position abeam Recife in Brazil, and an ocean position far to the south.

The blackness outside, darker than a moonless midnight, battered and rocked us, forcing us down 500 feet, up 700, in sickening lurches, and the time dragged on...and on. I checked the time...13.45. We had been in this mess only half an hour...thirty sodden beastly minutes, and another thousand to go. I realized, within five minutes of entry, that enduring seventeen hours of these conditions was quite impossible.

Yet what in hell could I do?

She was so close to the stall, with so little a margin of airspeed left on the clock, that it would be suicide to try to climb any higher. My imagination tried to conjure up an image of myself trying to recover this enormous contrivance from a spin in cloud, at the same time fighting back nausea—and eventually losing the battle. It did not bear thinking about.

There was no other alternative; if I descended into smoother, cleaner air, we would run out of fuel somewhere over the ice cap. And all the while, we breathed in the poison.

I looked across at Chambers. He was holding a chart, folded in the form of a cone, vomiting a dreary yellow fluid, tears staining his cheeks. Ben—Ben crouched at his desk, face buried in a pile of shirts and underwear, dragged willy-nilly from his flight bag.

The long minutes dragged by. I sat dully, staring at the instruments, and eventually the Machmeter moved up a notch. Some fuel had been used: the same power pushing less weight produced more speed. I found the electric trim button on the stick, eased it back a shade, and the Rate of Climb Indicator showed a scanty 50 feet per minute—but upwards, thank God—upwards. Thirty-four thousand feet. And a hundred. And a hundred more. Get up there, you wonderful old bitch...go, go, go! And 500...600...700...by the Almighty, she was going to make 35,000. And she did...started the next long slog around the clock.

Time passed—I do not know how much—and suddenly I was blinded! A vast glare of yellow light, arrowing through every window; in real pain, I clapped my hands to my eyes, cupping them to form shades. I opened a tiny gap between my fingers, let the glorious light pour in and screamed in sheer animal delight.

"Sun! the sun! Look, you miserable bastards—get up and see—the sun!"

We were all out of our seats, staggering round the flight deck, bumping, laughing, cheering and crying a little. Soon I was able to cope with the glare and got my face close up to the side window; looked down upon a hideous gray layer; grimaced and looked up—into the depths of the most beautiful blue sky I had ever seen. And above us, almost overhead, the blessed wonderful golden sun, huge, clean, blazing down upon the remnants of mankind. I felt Ben and Jerry at my side, and looked at their stained, tired faces. They were weeping unashamedly, and we locked together in a tripod of thanksgiving, arms around shoulders, heads bent, listening to the thunder of cheers and rejoicing from those behind, delivered at the eleventh hour from the jaws of hell itself.

19

Five minutes later, when the euphoria had subsided, I called the Antonov on 121.5 megacycles.

"Jonah to Valentina...Jonah to Valentina...do you copy?"

"This is Valentina. Over."

"What is your position and altitude, Val?"

"We are climbing through one thousand meters, Jo-nah. All is well with you?"

"Yes. Valentina, listen carefully. The fallout layer is down to about 7600 meters and it is very dangerous. The top is at 10,000 meters and we are a thousand feet—600 meters—on top. It is very bad to breathe, and very rough."

She came through again quite quickly. *"I understand, Jo-nah."*

"Okay," I said slowly and distinctly. "Strap everything down, and do not enter the fallout cloud until I say it is okay. Now. With your load, what is the best height you can make?"

"Wait.... We can fly to 9000 meters, Jo-nah."

"Understand 9000 meters. Not enough, Val—you will still be in the fallout. You need at least 10,000 meters. If you fly just below the cloud, at 7000 meters, how long before you burn enough fuel to make the top—at 10,000?"

"Please wait, Jo-nah. I will make calculation," the quiet voice said.

Waiting, I asked Ben to call Dr. Rabin forward. The small, tubby man was in poor shape; he had kept moving throughout the turbulence and dense smoke, helping where he could. His clothes were torn, tie missing, and his hands were stained with blood and vomit. I had Jill Stewart fix a hot drink for him while he washed in the flight-deck lavatory.

"Feel better, Doc?"

"Yes, thank you, Captain. That was very bad while it lasted."

"That," I said slowly, "was what I wanted to talk to you about. Did you have a chance to take any Geiger readings when we were in the cloud?"

"Yes," he said tiredly.

"Okay. What's the message?" I asked.

He hesitated, took another pull at his coffee, took off his spectacles and cleaned them.

"How much do you know about radioactivity, Captain?"

"Not much," I said. "Enough to detest the goddamn stuff. Keep it simple, huh?"

"Yes. Well, from nuclear explosions we have violent emissions of X-rays which react on the atmosphere to cause enormous heat. From the explosion come alpha particles, protons, neutrons—very heavy particles which travel in straight lines, through the human body. They collide many times with the lightweight particles which surround the cell nucleus. Water in the cell is turned into hydrogen and oxygen, which produces hydrogen gas or hydrogen peroxide. These compounds in turn attack the molecules of the cell material, forming very quick-acting poisons. You understand?"

I wiped my face with a white USAF handkerchief. "Just about. Go on."

"So. These effects are most severe in a neutron-bomb explosion, as we saw in Lajes. Now—no one can compute how many bombs have been exploded, nuclear missiles launched. Nor do we know of what types the bombs were. Certainly, I believe more were used than anyone could ever have imagined. Many people have written books on the possible effects of a nuclear war...but this layer, this belt of radiation products is far beyond even my expectations."

He carefully set his spectacles back on the bridge of his nose. "However—we do know that as many as two hundred radioactive compounds may have been produced, and it is these which form our present great danger. You know what is meant by 'roentgen'?"

I nodded. "Measure of radioactivity, isn't it?"

"Yes—basically. Now, in this fallout, three things become very important. One—the species and amounts of radionuclides. Two—the half-lives of the compounds. Three—the length of time for which we were exposed. The common radioactive materials are carbon 14, with a half-life of 7500 years, cesium 137, 35 years, and strontium 90, at 27 years. A large number of compounds have half-lives much shorter."

I stared at the little man. "And there's no way of identifying what we were breathing?"

"Not without extensive laboratory tests and special equipment, Captain."

"Marvelous," I said grimly. "That's all?"

"We were in the cloud about thirty minutes, Captain—and I managed to get a reading of the radiation level, converted to REM—Roentgen Environmental Man units.

"Come on, Doc," I said wearily. "Don't bugger around—let's have it."

"For short-term exposure," Rabin said flatly, "from the normal background level of radiation of 0.13 REM up to 200 REM, chances of survival are good, but women may become sterile. From 200 to 400 REM, the chances are poor, if exposed any longer than one hour. From 400 REM upwards, effects are usually fatal even for short exposures."

"Go on," I said irritably. "Was that layer hot?"

"The two readings I took were both about 350 REM."

"So—we're all dead, sitting here talking—is that what you mean? Goddammit, Rabin, you are the most evasive bastard I ever met. For Christ's sake—will we make it?"

He stared at me. "Oh—yes, of course. I am almost certain. Another half-hour, I would have said 'no.' But the body can excrete noxious substances—you know this? Good. The people must drink plenty of fluids—and they must stay away from all other sources of radiation for many years to come."

I looked at Rabin and tried not to show that I was sick to my guts. "One last point: suppose an aircraft had to fly in that layer of crap for, say, five or six hours?"

Rabin shook his head positively. "The people in the airplane would be as well to crash, Captain. To die quickly."

I turned round, sat hunched up in my seat, gazing down onto the endless miles of the fallout belt, thinking about the old Antonov bumbling along, so many miles behind. I stirred at last.

"Jonah to Valentina. Do you copy?"

"Yes, Jo-nah. I have calculation now. We are flying just below overcast, at 7000 meters. We cannot fly to McMurdo at

this altitude. We cannot rise to 10,000 meters—we have too much weight. Over."

"Valentina, you must not fly in the fallout layer more than thirty minutes. How much weight must you lose before you can reach 10,000 meters? Over."

"Wait, please."

Minutes later—

"Jo-nah, this is very bad. We must lose 4500 kilograms minimum."

I pressed my forehead to my crossed arms, laid across the control yoke, to curb the jabbing pains in my head. It would do no good to rail against the workings of Fate—those fixed and ice-cold equations, those natural rules of the Universe, which had this day decided to wipe from the board one Valentina Borofsky, Russian, pilot, aged twenty-six; her copilot, Elena, and two hundred and fifty men, women and children. I could call her—and tell her she must return to Lajes—but it would make little odds; they would die just the same. No power on earth could enable her airplane to fly higher than its load determined—or make the fuel last the full distance, flying in the lower and denser air below the fallout.

They had, I told myself, two options only. To fly in the "hot" layer and die slowly, from radioactive poisoning, or to fly below it and crash on the ice cap, without fuel, a thousand miles short of McMurdo.

Valentina came back on the air, voice flat and neutral; she sounded oddly withdrawn, remote. *"Valentina to Jo-nah. We have found a way. It is necessary to drop everything possible to reduce the weight by 4500 kilos. We have dropped clothing, food—everything we can take from the aircraft. Elena says we have lost 1250 kilos, but we must lose 3000 more. With fifty people less on board we can fly to 10,000 meters. Elena, she has explained this to the people."*

I sat quite still, trying to understand what she was trying to tell us.

"Val...you don't mean..." I stammered.

"Yes, Jo-nah. We are together two hundred and fifty-five. The people are coming forward now—the old, the unwell, those without families, who know they must soon die but not to waste their death as all Russia has been wasted. They say it is good that a few shall go, to make sure the rest shall live."

Great God in Heaven...They couldn't do it. Surely Val would not let them do it. She was speaking again.

"Jo-nah, we have hatch in the tail, for dropping loads by parachute from altitude. We will come down to 4000 meters, open the tail hatch for a short time. Then we climb back up, through the fallout, into the sunshine. Please...not to talk anymore. I will call again—when it is done."

I believe we were all, in Delta Tango, too shocked even to comment. The airplane hummed on, cruising at nine-tenths of the speed of sound, 8 miles above the deep Atlantic, and we were afraid even to look up, for we might see mirrored in other eyes the horror and enormous sense of loss we felt.

I sat woodenly, watching the instruments; we climbed very slowly, the Rate of Climb Indicator barely registering. But the electronic digital readout on the radio altimeter clicked up a handful of numbers each minute.

We had been airborne for two hours, give or take a few minutes; somewhere astern, 800 miles back, under the fallout layer, lay the Azores. Ahead, slightly to port, the Cape Verde Islands; I did not believe we would see them, unless the cloud layer below began to break up. And that, I estimated, would not occur until we had penetrated far to the south, on towards the Tropic of Cancer.

I began to think about the global wind circulation; it was essentially a simple system, of warm air rising at the Equator, forced up by cold air from the north and south undercutting it. The warm air flowed towards the poles, where it descended as it cooled, turning once more to drive towards the Equator—two huge circulating systems. If the Earth did not rotate, the lower winds would flow directly north and south, into the tropics—but rotate it did, generating the Coriolis force, which not only deflected the winds but caused the spiral flow of drain water from countless millions of baths and basins.

When Valentina called again, I missed it, sunk deep in some reverie. Chambers leaned over, nudged me. I keyed the switch.

"Sorry, Val. Jonah here. Say again."

"It is done, Jo-nah. We are climbing through the cloud. I will call you when we see the sun."

"I copy, Valentina."

Silence washed over the flight deck once more. My mind was one vast paradox of conflicting thoughts; I knew a great swelling joy that Valentina might yet be saved, and a surge of guilt—because I had killed all those people. In my haste and greed, I had talked Val into taking many of my passengers—so that I could reach safety myself. Recently, I had pondered on the feelings of the murderer: now, I knew. I could feel the eyes of Chambers, Ben Price, Capel, Nickie Bassett, staring, accusing, burning on the back of my head. And in the midst of my own personal trauma, I found myself utterly confused in trying to understand how even one person could find the courage to step into a 3-mile chasm and certain death. And not just one—fifty....I tried to imagine those last terrifying moments; the long farewells, the ordeal of those who had been forced to watch. My mind kept thinking, How—how could they do it, in cold blood...?

There was the classic example of Oates—Captain Oates of the Scott Expedition in 1908; when he realized that he could go no farther on the trek back from the Pole, he made some excuse to leave the tent—and was never seen again. That I could understand. But the odds against finding fifty such heroes in a single aircraft—it was beyond belief! What unknown reservoir of courage had those simple Russian women tapped? Words like "faith," "belief" and "spiritual strength" kept flooding through my mind, and I felt a deep sense of shock and uncertainty, as if the very foundations of my being were under attack.

"Jo-nah...! Jo-nah...!The sun! We are in sunshine. The cloud is below. We are coming quickly now. Over."

I tried twice to reply. Then—

"Jonah here. Wonderful, Valentina. Wonderful. Can you maintain 10,000 meters now? Over."

"Jo-nah, yes, yes. We can fly 10,000 meters easily. It was very bad, the climb through the cloud. Many are sick. But we are through in twenty minutes. All well now and working together in love."

I pressed the key again. "We are all very proud of you and Elena. Over."

She did not reply for a long time and I thought perhaps she had not heard. But at last, we heard her voice, unsteady and distorted.

"Jo-nah—Elena is gone. She went back to the tail to be with the people...I said she could go. Sergeant Ivanovich, she goes back with Elena also, to help lock the hatch. Ivanovich says Elena opened the hatch, took the hand of the woman beside her, and again until a great chain is made. Elena has smiled and said, 'Come, my friends...a wonderful world awaits us

*out there,' and she walked out, head held high, and the long
chain of women falling down the sky like the wild geese flying
south...*"

Valentina's voice cracked at last, and we heard her break
down; some neighborly hand must have switched off the radio,
for the transmission ended, and it was some hours before we
spoke again.

The two great airplanes, carrying all our hopes and all
our sorrows, flew on into the South, across the endless wastes
of water.

20

Crew fatigue tends to rise steeply towards the end of the stage length, and for the average six-to-seven-hour flight we had become accustomed to dealing with the problem. It is not that flying is such hard work: modern airliners are virtually fully automated, with duplicated and triplicated systems: the crew is there for the most part to deal with landings and takeoffs (always the most difficult and hazardous sectors) and to monitor aircraft performance and navigation in flight. This flight would set some kind of record for the type of aircraft, although military versions, carrying complete crews in reserve, had certainly exceeded it. Time hung heavy on our hands.

Delta Tango swept away the long sea miles under her tail at the rate of 9 every minute, yet such is the vastness of the earth that she would fly for most of an entire day at more than 500 miles per hour. Each way point came up on the INS readout with immaculate precision; the data output was of interest only to flight crew, in that an extraordinary process was taking place for those with eyes to see. The longitude indicator varied but little: it took many hours to cross from the east to the west side of the 30°W meridian, which we followed into the South Atlantic, while the latitude readout dwindled steadily from 30°N to 20°, 10° and finally the Equator, before starting the long haul from 0° to 90° south latitude.

Some three hours after takeoff, we passed to the west of the Cape Verde Islands; Valentina was building up speed, but was still more than two hours behind. She reported that she had no mechanical problems, except that the aircraft lacked heat, although pressurized, and everything possible had been jettisoned, including blankets, cold-weather clothing and food.

Jerry Chambers and I relieved each other each hour on the hour, and about half past five, well before the next waypoint check abeam Recife, I went down aft, into the bedlam of the main deck. I should have been warned by the rank odor of vomit and excreta welling up the staircase: the panorama of personal discomfort and disaster was worthy of Hogarth, and the noise was indescribable. Brand's soldiers were sweating, almost out of their minds trying to cope with frightened parentless children, for Madame Ferrière and her little team were almost exhausted. Less than half of Kate's girls were still on their feet; Hamish Bond had cleared a space for them far forward, away from the smell of Avtur fuel being laboriously hand-pumped, and they lay groaning and coughing, close together.

Small groups of passengers, I noted, were courageously keeping the exercise circuit going, pacing monotonously up and down the aisles, avoiding those few high-spirited children who had recovered, more or less, from the earlier upheavals.

I found Kate herself in one of the aft galleys, heating a bottle of milk with one hand, cradling a six-month-old baby in the other arm; her hair hung damply from a sweat-stained brow, and it seemed to me that she was appallingly tired and close to collapse.

"Here," I said firmly, "give me His Nibs and use both hands on that bottle." She nodded dumbly, and I gathered the wet, squirming bundle together. "Anything else I can do?"

"No, thanks, Jonah." She tweaked a rubber nipple onto the bottle, checked the temperature and passed it over. I stuck it in what seemed to be a logical orifice at the most likely end, and stood watching Junior sink his half-pint.

Kate said in a tired voice, "We'll have to hoard these throwaway feeding bottles. There's no more where they came from. How are we doing, Jonah?"

"Very well indeed, love." I tried to inject a world of confidence into my voice, and succeeded in sounding like the second lead in some fifth-rate repertory company. "Five hours plus gone, twelve plus to go. Weather—smashing. I see some of your girls have clapped out, Kate."

"Not surprising—after being almost killed on takeoff,

half-choked in a cloud of poison gas. I don't want any more
of that, Jonah—I couldn't take it. Not that any of us believe
we have a dog's chance among all that snow and ice—and
you know as well as I that we probably got a fatal dose in
that stinking cloud layer."

She foraged in my jacket pocket, looked at Junior and
nodded, lighted two cigarettes.

"According to old Rabin," I told her, with a great deal more
confidence than I felt, "we weren't in it long enough to do
permanent harm. It may take a year or two for our bodies to
get rid of the odd radioactive particles, and apparently we
won't die from it..." I hesitated.

"But—?" she said. "You do have a 'but' lurking in there
somewhere?"

"Well—Rabin said some women might not be able to—
that is—"

"Have a baby, you mean?"

"Yes, Kate."

"Um," she said finally. "I had that figured already. Men
too? I mean, will they be able to do their bit?"

"Apparently, yes. They have a higher threshold, or something."

She took the distended infant from me, set him on her
shoulder in an attempt to extract a B flat—or maybe an F
minor. "That's just great," she said bitterly. "So the Brave
New World is for fellas only?"

"Come off it, love. It's only a possibility, so far. You'll see—
we'll all produce hordes of nippers in due time."

She looked miserable, still. "But it's a nasty, dirty world
we have inherited, Jonah. I know a little about what's in
store for us. There may be houses and food—but it's going
to be bloody cold and desolate, and we have to live there all
the rest of our lives."

"Kate, love—not so. By the time our current crop of kids
grow up, there will be areas which have cooled down, the
radioactivity bleached out. Places like the Falkland Islands,
South Africa, Tasmania.

"And how in hell do we get there?" she snapped. "Walk?"

"Don't stir it up so hard, Kate. We're lucky to be alive—
and when the time comes, we'll find ways and means of getting back."

She absorbed this rebuff without emotion, laid the child
down in a nearby empty seat and picked up her cigarette

from the edge of the kitchen unit. Irrelevantly, she said, "How's your girlfriend?"

I told her—all of it—and wished I hadn't. She cried for a little while on my shoulder, and I believe it did her quite a lot of good. She moved away, started to straighten up her hair and said she was a bitch and she was sorry.

"Don't get me wrong, Jonah—I'm not jealous. Well, maybe just a little. Only—it was so quick . . ."

"It usually is, Kate," I said gravely. "But it doesn't mean I love you any the less. We've always had something special, you and I—maybe not rice-and-orange-blossom stuff, but it was good for both of us."

She smiled, reminiscently. "It was indeed, you lovely man. And I'm happy for you both. If half of what you say is true, she must be a hell of a woman."

"That makes two of you," I said diplomatically. "I have to go—way point coming up. Feeling better now?"

"Sure. I'll dance at yer wedding or me name's not Kate Monahan."

I grinned. "And climb into our bed if I don't spot you in time. See you later, Kate."

I worked my way slowly up the main cabin, speaking to people here and there. I told them the flight was going well, that we had no permanent problems with radiation, that the worst of it was over. Mike Brand, Lemaistre and Hamish Bond were near the forward stairs, handling queries and problems brought by soldiers and civilian passengers alike. Most involved a craving for information, and I had Jill Stewart, who habitually carried a portable typewriter, draft out half a dozen copies of a reassuring report I compiled with Mike Brand's help.

Back on the flight deck after an absence of more than an hour, my attention was drawn by Jerry Chambers to the sun: it was following a slightly unusual trajectory on its way to the horizon from the overhead point when we took off, gradually curving south. We had found a very comprehensive survey of the Antarctic in the Lajes recreational library, written by a man called Hatherton, and it contained an invaluable chart of daylight hours on the ice cap. I got it out, for a closer look. At 78 degrees south latitude, where McMurdo was sited, there was continuous daylight, with the sun permanently above the horizon, from the present time—early November— through almost to the beginning of March. It followed that during this fantastic flight, we would see the sun fall partially behind the southwest horizon, to rise again very soon as we flew under the base of the world, past the Pole and heading north towards McMurdo. Thereafter, the sun would always be visible—very close to the horizon initially, and rising towards the zenith in midsummer—December.

"Position, Jerry?" I asked.

"Almost abeam Recife, in Brazil, Skipper. Next way point Falkland Islands Dependencies, about 52 degrees south latitude. This is a long leg, Jonah—nearly seven hours."

I nodded absently. "Ben's down in the cargo hold, checking on the fuel transfer. You keeping an eye on his board too?"

"Trying to, Skip. Yes—it all seems okay."

"Maybe. But I think two of us should be up here all the time, Jerry. We can't afford any mishaps this trip. Take over at the engineer's board for an hour; then I'll go down and relieve Ben."

Settled down in the familiar leather seat, I put in a quick call to Valentina. She had nothing new to report; her fuel consumption was satisfactory, and she seemed much more cheerful. I started a long, close check on the aircraft. We were already at 39,000 feet, and the autopilot was holding her rock-steady on the same heading, 187 degrees, with Mach .81 on the Machmeter. Jerry read out fuel consumptions and checked with Ben, down under in the cargo bay, on the number of drums left. We gave the on-board computer a workout, and while I was not totally sold on the results, it seemed that fuel would not be a problem unless we ran into very adverse winds. I took the position, corrected airspeed and height, fed it into the computer. It burped and stated that the wind vector was 288 degrees at about 55 knots. It also told us that this wind, in terms of the tail-wind component, was probably helping us along by a welcome 18 knots, such that continued benefit of this nature would put us overhead McMurdo with at least forty minutes' fuel left.

I spent a few moments thinking about Val's last transmission; it was noticeably clearer and with less interference. Could this be the first true indication that we were outrunning the radiation?

Slipping off the headset, I leaned far over, stared down from the side window at the overcast layer below. The light was fading a little, as the sun dropped slowly, and this gave me the first real clue. The flat upper surface, almost a mile below, had lost its unnatural flatness; there were occasional shadows, cast by mounds and castles of cumulus, rising above the stratus layer and caught by the oblique rays of the sun.

I stared until my eyes ached—until I was certain. Vast areas of the cloud layer were irrefutably lighter, showing the milky translucency of unbreakable kitchen dishes between the darker valleys. What did it mean? It meant that in this sector at least, the clouds contained a proportion of water vapor, which had condensed out to form natural cloud; the next step, I was certain, would be actual clear patches through which we might even see the ocean itself.

John Capel poked his head around the corner. "Okay to come in, boss?"

"Sure, John. Put it there." I waved to Chambers' empty seat. "Look down there."

He looked. "Hot damn. You think it's clearing, maybe?"

"Could be. We're not far from the Equator—and almost in the center of the Atlantic, a long way from land. Things settling down back there?"

Capel produced a smile and said, "Sure. They're all eating. Most of Kate's crew are back on their feet. You hungry, Captain?"

"No—maybe later. I'll have one of those Yankee cigarettes of yours, though."

Capel said apologetically, "Sure thing. Say—I had nothing much in the way of personal things to bring aboard, so I slipped in a crate of Marlboros and a dozen boxes of stogies. You going to get mad at me?"

"No—'course not. What odds are you taking on flaking out from lung cancer before Old Man Roentgen gets you?"

"No takers, buster. But I'd figure it to an even shake. What the hell, anyway."

Capel sat for a while. "I read what you said down back, about radiation. We may not have stuck in that god-awful crap long enough to get burned, but it sure made a lot of people sick. If I barfed once, I did it ten times. Compared to that stink, New York is—was—a goddamn paradise."

We laughed a little.

"I reckon," I agreed. "I can't get over the way all those ordinary people just sat there and took it. They've had a hell of a trip. I bet they hate my guts."

Capel said, "Don't knock 'em, Captain. They're not stupid. They know what they got away from—and if they didn't before we got into that stinking cloud, they sure do now. Right now, they figure they have only one thing going for them: they're alive. And as long as they have a chance of staying that way, they'll take all you can dish out—and thank you for it."

I said, "They must be out of their tiny minds."

"And don't knock yourself, buster, either," Capel said with some annoyance in his voice. "You have a good crew—but there's no way they'd have got us here without you driving them on."

"Screw you too, Capel," I said, amused.

"Yeah. Well. Look out there—clear blue sky, fine airplane, somewhere to go, at least. I guess we never dreamed back in New York we'd finish up heading thisaway."

"Would you rather be back there?"

"The heck I would. Or in the U.K.—even as it was before. It may sound a little nutty, but I'm getting the biggest kick for years, riding along on this bucket. And if we make it, out of all the billions who didn't—maybe that makes me and you and all of us something special."

"It won't be easy, John," I said.

"I know it. I did a short hitch in the Army in Greenland, before I got to Nam, and I found out one thing—you get to be very careful in sub-zero temperatures. Things tend to drop off when they freeze up."

"With luck," I said, "we've got all the comforts in the world at McMurdo, John."

"Is that so? Say—where in hell is this place, anyway?" he asked.

The Antarctic chart was in the copilot's stowage. John fished it out and I spread it over the center console, so that the fading daylight made it readable.

"Here's our track." I pointed, followed it down with a pencil. "We're about here—off the west coast of Brazil. It's about 500 kilometers out that way"—I pointed away to starboard. "We head due south, near enough, into the Antarctic Ocean, past the Falkland Islands Dependencies and down into the Weddell Sea—here. We cross the coast—or rather, the Filchner Ice Shelf, which covers Berkner Island, down over the Pensacola Mountains and past the South Pole."

Capel stared at the map. "We don't pass over the Pole?"

"No, John. To starboard of it. We cross the Queen Maud Mountains, past the Beardmore Glacier and across the Ross

Ice Shelf here. McMurdo Base lies on McMurdo Sound—Mount Erebus is on the far side."

"Mount Erebus?"

"Right. Antarctica's only volcano."

Capel was entranced. "Well, I'll be. Say—I heard you say there's already some Americans there? At McMurdo Base?"

"About sixteen or seventeen, John. All that was left behind when the U.S. evacuated the base last year. Sailors and Marines."

"And supplies?"

"Plenty. No problem there, John. In fact, I think our biggest obstacle may be getting back to better latitudes, once this damned mess has been allowed to cool down. We're going to be two, three thousand miles from anywhere at all. But I'm not about to worry about that now. Just let me get this beast down in one piece and we've a fighting chance. All I want is about two months' sleep—straight."

"I'm thinking," Capel hazarded, "that the base people may have ideas about getting back home sometime. Say—they're going to be pleased to see us."

"Pleased? You better believe it, Capel. They've been there two years or more, maybe, and never seen a girl in that time. We have about twenty loose in this airplane—and Valentina has about fifty ex-Army girls on her aircraft."

"Yeah," said Capel with satisfaction. "And some of them aren't bad, at that. Maybe I can pull one myself."

"Which reminds me," I said. I checked we were still on 121.5 Hertz and called the Antonov.

"Calling Valentina...Jonah here—do you copy?"

"I copy, Jo-nah. You are all right?"

"Fine. Fine. And you?"

She sounded almost happy. *"Our fuel position is very good, Jo-nah. We have given our people a little food—all there was left. There will be food at McMurdo?"*

"No problem, Valentina. I will call McMurdo when we get closer. When you land, all will be ready. What is your position now? Over."

I laid off the position she gave me on the map, made measurement adjustments for latitude and felt much better. She was right on the button down our vapor trail, and making good speed. I got back to her.

"Valentina, Jonah here. That checks out very well."

"That is good, Jo-nah. Please advise the weather—is the cloud still below?"

"No, Valentina. Very thin now and breaking into normal cloud. We are about 750 kilometers ahead of you—you will see a change in an hour or less. Are you tired, Val? Is there no other pilot on board? Over."

"No, Jo-nah. But I have autopilot. Also, one Army girl is flight engineer before she transfers to Army—she watches while I rest. Do not worry, Jo-nah. All is well."

"Well—okay, Val." I still wasn't convinced, but it sounded a little more under control back there. "Take care. Jonah out."

The long hours passed, and the sky darkened, a million stars cool and uninvolved in balcony seats, watching humanity's death convulsions. The sun was half-concealed below the southwest horizon. Shortly after midnight, we saw our first— and perhaps last—sign of civilization: a pitiful group of scattered lights from some remote island. Jerry and I changed the guard regularly; in an attempt to fight boredom, we held open house on the flight deck for anyone who wished to visit. After one A.M. the quiet of sleep enveloped the entire aircraft, and we flew on steadily. At intervals, Ben came back on deck for a brief rest; Mike Brand and his minions were coping competently with the refueling, but Ben was rarely far away from the cargo bay. Below the main deck, the hold was an inferno of sweating soldiers, empty drums being passed up for storage aft, full drums passing hand to hand down the line ready for use. Each one was broached, slipped into position, hand-pump suction pipe inserted and transfer valve opened. Each time I went down to see progress, the stench of fuel hit me like a hammerblow, yet Ben and Mike Brand insisted one became used to it after a while.

It seemed to me also that the stack of full drums aft was dwindling alarmingly fast. But the engineer assured me that all tanks were being kept as full as possible, so that when the last drum went into the system, he could wrap it up, seal off the cargo hold and fix the troops with food and drink.

Other groups of men may have worked harder—but I doubted if ever some 50 tons of fuel had been shifted by hand pump as quickly. Just over ten hours after takeoff, with eight to go, Ben came up, sweating but very pleased with himself. "That's it, Jonah." He sagged into his seat and produced a lopsided grin. "All transferred. We have virtually full tanks, and what do you make it—less than eight hours to go? It's a breeze."

"No—it's incredible, Ben. And she's all the better for it—we've picked up 0.02 Mach in the past hour."

I looked round at John Capel. "John, can you rustle up some coffee and grub for Ben? And while he's eating it, I want you to get a load of clothes—cold-weather stuff, anything you can find—and make him up a bed in the corner behind me."

"Sure thing."

Ben protested. "No—really, I'm okay, Skipper. Just coffee—really."

I stared at him balefully. "Am I going to have trouble with you—after all these years?"

"Well..."

"Well, nothing. Here—have a smoke. Coffee'll be up in a shake."

Jerry was somewhere aft, and I left it to Capel to get the weary engineer bedded down. In my own seat, one of Capel's Marlboros going, I relaxed in the subdued light of the flight deck. There was enough light coming in from the sun to make cockpit lights unnecessary, but hardly enough for reading. Here, in the Southern Hemisphere, the sky above Delta Tango was truly remarkable; the southern constellations in all their beauty outlined the vast section of the Milky Way, fading only partially in the lighter arc of light around the sun, now a flaming red disk a few degrees above the horizon, slightly west of south. Time seemed to have stopped, and it seemed to my fatigued brain that the 797 hung motionless, suspended between the sky and the earth. All at once, the staggering immensity and primeval savagery of the Earth and the Universe penetrated my brain with cataclysmic impact. I conjured up a brief mental image of the gigantic underside of the earth, and the puny handful of creatures flying around its flank, chasing the sun, the mother of all life.

I shook my head, as if to shake myself out of some trance; I felt deeply disturbed, disoriented even, after the most shattering spiritual experience of my life.

"Skipper? You all right?" It was Jerry Chambers, face troubled and upset.

"Huh? Oh—sure. I'm okay. Must have dropped off for a moment. What's the problem?"

"No problems, Skipper. Come to relieve you, that's all.

Why don't you get back in the VIP section—there's a spare seat, and Jill Stewart'll fix you something to eat."

"Jill—still awake? She's got no more sense than... than...well, never mind. Still—okay. She's all yours."

I looked down at the ground below.... Ground? I checked my watch: just after four in the morning....I'd slept for almost three hours—and left no one at all to keep an eye on the airplane. For a hundred and seventy minutes, she had thundered on across the Weddell Sea, and we were now over the ice cap.

"Hold it, Jerry—look at that INS latitude scale...we're going away from the Pole! We have about two hours to go, that's all. Look at that damned sun—it has hardly moved in three hours; it's bloody uncanny."

I stretched mightily. "Well—time we got things moving. I'll have that coffee now"—and the radio interrupted me.

"Valentina calling Jo-nah...calling Jo-nah...please answer...please." Val sounded worried.

"Jonah here—go ahead, Valentina."

"Jo-nah! Jo-nah! I am thinking you are dead. I have called many times. You have trouble? Over."

Suddenly I began to feel very guilty. "I'm okay, Val. Sorry—I've been asleep. Luckily, there were no problems. We are two hours from McMurdo—I shall be calling them soon. Are you still okay? How is your fuel? Over."

"I am very well now. But when we are landed, Jo-nah, I will be very angry with you. I am made to be very frightened. Is not good. I do not like you, Jo-nah Scott, when you do these things."

I sighed. "Okay, Val—I'm sorry. Really. I'll make up. You'll see. Must go now. Love you."

She made no reply. I shrugged and settled down for action. I buzzed the intercom for Kate.

"Yes?"

"Who the devil is that?"

"Ah—Captain. Corporal Mellor here. Anything I can do?"

"Yes—yes, there is. Tell Miss Monahan—the senior stewardess—that we land in less than two hours. I want everyone awake, with a hot drink inside them, and fully briefed for landing, within ninety minutes. Can you remember that?"

"Yes, sir."

* * *

"How long to letdown point, Jerry?"

"We can start a letdown in five zero minutes, Skip."

"Okay. Stand by—I'm calling McMurdo. Delta Tango calling McMurdo Base. Delta Tango calling McMurdo. Do you copy? Over."

"Delta Tango, this is McMurdo. We read you faint but clear. Thank God you've made it. Welcome—welcome!"

I transmitted again. "McMurdo, thank you. It has been a long haul. We are about two hours out from you at this time, oh four hundred hours. We are leaving cruise altitude 39,000 feet shortly. This is Captain Jonah Scott."

"Delta Tango, this is Commander Elkins, in charge of the base. It's sure good to hear your voice. We spoke a long time ago to a British naval officer in the Falklands. He told us you might be coming. What is your estimated time of arrival?"

"Scott to McMurdo—we estimate you just after six A.M. We are going through our emergency drills now. We have about five hundred and eighty people aboard, all in good health. Also two babies born at Lajes, aboard second aircraft two hours behind us. Over."

"Okay, Scott. Fine. I figure the first thing is to get you safely down on the deck. How are you doing for fuel? Over."

I made a quick check with Ben Price, a man obviously better for the short sleep. He nodded. "Forty minutes' fuel margin, Skipper."

"Scott to McMurdo—we are okay for fuel. We need two items urgently—your surface wind direction and strength, and the position of the nearest strip of flat snow a mile long or better. Over."

"Stand by, Delta Tango."

Kate, on the intercom: *"Jonah, everything under control here. Everyone has had a hot drink, and we've gone through emergency drills. We'll be pushing out the snack meal in about five minutes. All cabin crew on line except one."*

"Right. Well done, Kate. I'll keep you informed. We're in touch with McMurdo."

Jerry Chambers said quietly, "Descent time now, Skipper."

"Right, Jerry. Power back to 1.2 EPR. Flaps ten."

"Flaps ten. Reducing power."

"Autopilot going out. You have control, Jerry—keep her

on this heading and descend at 2000 feet per minute. Airspeed Mach 0.75."

We started cautiously down the hill. I checked our position against the chart and the INS readout. The Queen Maud Mountains were twenty miles behind, and we were now over the southern end of the Ross Ice Shelf.

"McMurdo to Delta Tango—we have your information. Are you ready to copy?"

"Go ahead, McMurdo."

"Roger, Delta Tango. Our Meteorological Officer is here with the wind data, and so is every other man on the base. The atmosphere here is like July fourth. Reference your landing area: our Survey Officer advises he has a suitable location but would like to know if you want to land close to base—we have transport available if you want to land farther out."

"McMurdo from Delta Tango—as close as possible, please. We have a large number aboard including two hundred plus children. Believe airplane will cool down very quickly on ground—time is of the essence."

After a short wait, we heard Commander Elkins again.

"Understand, Delta. Okay—the surface wind is from the northwest at about 30 knots gusting to 50 knots. Sky clear but sun very low. Visibility is driving ice and snow particles— approximately one mile at ground level. How do you want details of your landing threshold? Over."

I thought about that one. If I flew overhead and made a normal approach, I could miss the threshold altogether in visibility of only a mile. I stared ahead: there was not yet the faintest hint of light upon the horizon. The sun would have risen before we landed, but it was going to be a difficult approach. I made up my mind.

"McMurdo, how accurately can you give me coordinates of touchdown point?"

"Stand by . . . We can use latitude and longitude in degrees, minutes and seconds. Otherwise, a magnetic bearing and distance from a known position, but this is not recommended. Over."

"Lat and long ideal, McMurdo," I said happily. "We will set it into our INS system and make a straight-in approach from a position about 8 miles downwind."

"Understand. We copy. Stand by to receive coordinates . . ."

Elkins read off the latitude and longitude, and I repeated

back. I got out the best Antarctic chart I could find, but the scale was useless.

"McMurdo, Delta Tango. Can you give similar coordinates for a position 8 miles downwind from the landing point? Also the suggested touchdown heading. Over."

"McMurdo here. Yes, Tango. Stand by. Your Point Alpha coordinates as follows"—Elkins read them slowly—*"and your suggested approach heading 135 degrees magnetic. This does not include wind correction. Is this roger?"*

It sounded first-class to me. I set the two positions into the INS, together with the approach heading, and locked in the autopilot. The latter would fly me, under the direction of the Inertial Navigation System, to Point Alpha, at whatever height I selected.

The altimeter digital readout said 18,000 feet: no sweat. I set the altimeter bugs to control our minimum height to Alpha at 2000 feet. McMurdo, I knew, was virtually at sea level, but unless they came up with a pressure setting—wait a second: they had a Met man there!

"McMurdo from Delta Tango. We have coordinates locked in. I will require a pressure reading, preferably in inches of mercury, for touchdown. Can your Met officer oblige?"

Elkins came straight back. *"Affirmative, Delta Tango. We will pass to you as soon as we have it. Say—how far will that thing slide on touchdown? We want to position transport close to your stop point—but not too close."*

I smiled grimly. Elkins was a man of many reasons. I decided to make a last check with Valentina. I told him I thought we might slide a mile or so. Then—

"Jonah to Valentina. Do you copy?"

Her dear voice came back strong and true, without interference. *"I copy, Jo-nah. I hear you talk to McMurdo. He is a ver' nice man, I think."*

"I think so too," I said, amused. And that wasn't for Elkins' benefit, either.

"Jonah to Valentina. We are descending into McMurdo now, passing 13,000 feet at this time. Conditions seem okay, Valentina—and the light will be better when you get here. If you are okay, I am going back to talk with McMurdo now. Will call you from the ground when you are inbound. Is this roger?"

"Yes, Jo-nah. Everything is good here. But we all have

much hunger. Please ask the nice man at McMurdo that we can eat when we land. Good luck, my Jo-nah."

"Okay, Val. Call you back."

"McMurdo to Delta Tango. Who in tarnation is Valentina? Over."

I laughed aloud. "McMurdo, you aren't going to believe it. Second aircraft is an Antonov 10 flown by Lieutenant Valentina Borofsky, carrying approximately two hundred fifty passengers, mixed Russian and European/American. Probably last aircraft to leave Russia. We joined up at Lajes. Will give additional information on the ground. Sorry to come in such numbers. How are you fixed for accommodation? Over."

"McMurdo here. Well, I'll be...I don't know if your Valentina can hear us yet, but they are very welcome. Yes, we are okay for accommodation and food. We make total approximately seven hundred, including about two hundred fifty children. Is that roger?"

I tried to remember how many Valentina had on board—without success. I said:

"McMurdo, that is approximate. We brought about two hundred kids out of New York before the balloon went up, and the Antonov has about forty more aboard."

There was a long silence from McMurdo, and I had time to check that the descent was progressing steadily through 11,500 feet before I heard Elkins again.

"Delta Tango...I don't know how to say this. Commander Elkins here. My wife lived in Newark. I lost touch about a year ago. Up to that time, a friend of mine from Brooklyn Navy Yard called in frequently—until he was moved to the West Coast. The mail stopped dead about that time. I had two kids— Mark aged seven, Hayley age eight. Have you...could you...?" The transmission stopped. Elkins' voice was overloaded with emotion.

I turned to Ben. "Go find Madame Ferrière—quick. Ask her if she has two kids on her list name of Elkins. If she has, get her up here right away. I'll talk to McMurdo."

"Delta Tango to McMurdo. We are checking on that now. Will advise. We estimate you in twenty-five minutes, passing 10,000 feet at this time. We will call you at Point Alpha."

I began running through in my mind the sequence of events in the next half-hour. The various emergency drills were laid down in the Aircraft Operating Manual and included emergency landings—but not the arrival for which we were planning. Indeed, it was doubtful if such a contingency as a belly landing in very deep snow had been seriously considered. In the case of an emergency wheels-up arrival on land, the occupants would evacuate the aircraft via the seven doors on each side of the fuselage, using the canvas escape chutes provided. Would the same procedure be possible at McMurdo? I thought not. In fact, it was unlikely that it would be possible to open the doors, once on the ground, against the weight of snow outside.

An added complication was the temperature. We were likely to find it below freezing at ground level; the longer we kept the cabin sealed, the better.

Fire? Without being overoptimistic, I thought it was very unlikely. I would shut down all electrics just before touchdown, and activate all engine fire extinguishers. Engines would fill with packed snow instantly, and the snow itself would be as effective as foam itself in blanking off vital areas from the outside air.

A soft hand touched me on the shoulder, and I turned to greet Madame Ferrière.

"Captain—I will keep you only a moment. The children you asked for—?"

"Yes—any luck, Madame Ferrière?"

She nodded, eyes shining. "But yes! They are here—and both well. I have told them that their father will be waiting when we land. They do not quite believe it, I think—but they are very happy."

I said, "Are they okay? Physically, I mean?"

"As well as anyone can expect—they lived alone in New York for seven months until the American Army found them six weeks ago. They are very thin and anemic—but good food and rest will restore them." The Red Cross woman's smile was broad and confident.

"Okay, Madame Ferrière—thank you. Best go back to your seat now—we will be landing in about fifteen minutes. Good luck."

"And good luck to you, Captain—but I know you will not need it: you have brought us safely through many problems. I know we shall all sleep safely tonight."

I nodded and turned away.

"Okay, Jerry—take her for a while. We have about twelve minutes to Point Alpha. Altitude 2000 feet set into the INS. You have control."

Chambers nodded, hitched his seat forward and began monitoring the INS. I decided to call McMurdo first.

"Delta Tango to McMurdo. Commander Elkins there?"

"Go ahead, Tango. I'm here."

I took a deep breath. "Good news, Commander. We have the articles in question aboard. Both in good condition—a little skinny, but nothing a good meal or two won't put right."

When the answer came back—and it wasn't Elkins himself, because I figured he was not fit to speak to anyone at that time—I could hear the screams and shouts of rejoicing behind the speaker's voice. *"Goddamn it, Delta Tango, that did it! The place is jumpin'! The Commander can't talk to you right now—but I'm speaking for all of us when I say that is the greatest thing I ever heard! This is Phil Harris, radio operator. Over."*

I couldn't have been more pleased if it had happened to me. I could imagine how Elkins, marooned on the ice cap for more than a year, might feel. It was nice, very nice, to be able to pass news like that.

"Okay, McMurdo—we feel pretty good about that too. We are due at Point Alpha in seven minutes, seven minutes. Will advise. Delta Tango out."

There was one other important job to be done. I keyed the PA system.

"This is the Captain. We shall be landing in a little more than ten minutes. This will not be a normal landing, as you know, and I want you to listen carefully. First, your cabin crew has shown you how to sit, how to brace yourself. Do exactly as they say and you will come to no harm. The landing itself will be in deep snow, only a few hundred yards from McMurdo Base. There should be very little impact shock, but it will be in two parts—a gentle brief shock as we touch for the first time, and a long steady deceleration before we come to a stop.

"Normally, you would be able to leave the airplane via the seven doors on each side, using the escape chutes. The snow will prevent the doors being opened, and of course we don't want to get outside until our transport has arrived—it is a little cold down there."

I gave them time to think on what I had said and to translate for the benefit of those who spoke no English.

"When we stop, I want you all to remain seated and keep quiet. You can loosen your safety belt when you are told. It may take a while for the people on the ground to reach us and open up an exit. In emergency, of course, we can always open the forward roof exit. Check your seat belt is fastened, put your head on your lap and please try not to worry—this is a straightforward landing and conditions are good. Thank you."

The visibility ahead was a little better: I could see clearly the flat plain of the Ross Ice Shelf below, with the rounded peak of Mount Erebus off to the starboard side of McMurdo Sound. The sun was on the horizon, and my watch said it lacked about ten minutes of six A.M. McMurdo Sound showed like a black wedge driven into the ice shelf, and now I could make out the scattered buildings of the base, close to the shore; beyond, the rough coastline ran almost straight into the distance, and there were massive cloud banks all along the northwest horizon. There was a massive rise of high ground inland, to port, and I began to plan out our approach. The INS was taking us down on the seaward side of the base, so that a standard left turn from a downwind position would bring us in line for an approach on a southeasterly heading.

"I think everything looks good, Jerry. Ben—fuel still okay?" I said.

"About thirty-five minutes left, Skipper. No sweat."

"Fine. Jerry, reset those altimeter bugs: we want to run downwind at 1500 feet on radio altimeter—McMurdo is as near sea level as makes no odds. Let's start the approach checklist. It's not going to be much like a standard check—but let's do it."

I looked ahead once more. McMurdo was about five miles, slightly to port, and we would pass just to port of Mount Erebus.

"Okay. Ben—approach checks complete?"

"Check complete, Skip."

"Radio check?"

"Still on 121.5," Jerry confirmed.

"Landing bugs?"

"Set on altimeter and airspeed as requested. I set approach and landing speeds as for Lajes, Skipper. Touchdown on 140 knots, full flap, gear up."

"Okay. Fine. Landing lights on."

"Landing lights on."

I turned for a brief look at McMurdo, drifting down our port side. I could see a finger of black smoke beyond the cluster of black buildings, on the northwest side. Could be someone had had the bright idea of marking the touchdown point. The INS readout was still clicking away steadily, making only small corrections in terms of seconds and minutes.

"Okay. Looks good. Flaps twenty."

"Flaps to twenty...set."

"Engineer, all main tank pumps on, crossfeed open."

"Pumps on, crossfeed open, Skipper," Ben Price reported.

"Fasten seat belts, no smoking light—on."

"Lights on."

I settled down in the seat, feeling the tug of the lap strap. "Okay...fine. Set landing heading 135 degrees on the flight director, Jerry, will you?"

He leaned forward. "All set, Skipper."

We were tracking steadily downwind now, perhaps a mile or two out from the jagged icebound shore, McMurdo falling back behind our port wing. The autopilot moved the control yoke firmly into a port turn; the nose of Delta Tango began drifting through the 180-degree turn, taking a full minute to complete. I checked the INS; we were very close to the imaginary Point Alpha, and the base was visible dimly some six miles ahead. I disengaged the autopilot for the last time.

"McMurdo from Delta Tango—we have you in sight. We are inbound from Point Alpha. Leaving 1500 feet at this time. Over."

"We read you, Delta Tango. All the luck in the world, fella."

"Thank you. Will call before touchdown."

The big bird felt alive and vibrant under my hands. Part of my conscious mind was absorbing into my memory the sights, the sound of thrumming engines, the feeling of immense power, and the responsiveness with which she answered the smallest demands on the controls. How long I would have to get along on my memories, I had no way of knowing—but they would be there for as long as I lived.

"Power back to 75 percent!"

We began losing height gently, at no more than 500 feet per minute. I took a long look ahead and made out a row of steel drums lined up across our approach path, filled with something that burned with heavy black smoke—possibly old engine oil, I thought.

"Full flap, please." I wriggled into a more comfortable position.

"Flaps down," Jerry confirmed. "Heading 135, 400 feet, 160 knots reducing."

The smoke was moving slightly seawards from the drums a mile ahead, and I kicked on a trace of right rudder to offset the drift.

"Three hundred feet, 150 knots!"

"Captain to aircraft—we are about to land. Brace yourselves."

"Two hundred feet, 145 knots!"

"McMurdo, we are about to land!"

"We see you. Good luck."

"One hundred feet, 140 knots!"

"Brace yourselves...here we go!"

I eased on a shade more power, and we slid in over the row of drums at no more than 20 feet. I dragged all five throttles back hard, heaved back on the yoke to keep the nose up.

"Shut down all engines! All fuel off! Blow all fire bottles! All electrics off!"

She wanted to go down badly by the nose, and I held her off, feet planted firmly on the pedals, hauling back all the way on the yoke. I felt the tail touch once, twice, and she settled down luxuriously into the deep snow; instantly the whole of the windscreen was obscured in glaring white.

It was grotesque, as unreal as Salvador Dali: she swam through an ocean of white softness as if suspended in cotton wool, and I began to lose the sensation of movement. Vertigo hovered around the picket fence of my consciousness, hammering for access, and the slide went on. I got my feet up onto the instrument panel, my head down on my forearms on the yoke, for I believed that the final deceleration could be hard and savage. We heard distant sounds of tearing metal, and the slide went on—straight as a die, because I felt no side accelerations, and incredibly smooth. We slowed, coasted to a stop in a silence broken only by the hiss of melting snow and ice against hot metal, farther aft. I began to note absently the metallic cracking noises associated with rapid cooling of metal.

Through the closed door of the flight deck, I heard the dull roar of cheer after cheer, but we sat there, Jerry, Ben and myself, sagging in sheer fatigue, breathing deeply and savoring the sensation of doing absolutely nothing. I stared at my hands, lying useless in my lap: they were locked with nervous tension into curved claws, and shaken by occasional fits of trembling. We sat quietly, breathing deeply, letting the healing silence of the ice cap penetrate deep into the whirling kaleidoscopes of our brains, oblivious to everything but the end of noise, stress and tension.

21

Mike Brand surged through into the flight deck ahead of a motley crew which included Karen Waldheim, Volkel, Sven Olaffsen and Doc Rabin. John Capel, Nickie Bassett and Jill Stewart were close behind, and the flight deck became confusion exemplified. All showed a hysterical reaction to the release from fear: broad grins, unintelligible speech, arms and hands flying around indiscriminately. My hand was shaken again and again; I was dragged forth from my seat, to be kissed comprehensively and often by the girls. Vaguely, I was aware that Ben was receiving more of the same, that Jerry Chambers and Nickie were locked together so tightly I feared we would need a crowbar to separate them.

Eventually—"All right...all right." I managed to make myself heard. "So far, so good. We are very close to the base, but we are also in very deep snow. I want everyone dressed and well wrapped up—it's going to be damned cold out there. Everyone back to their seats, please. Move on out!"

When the excitement had subsided and we were left in comparative peace, "Thank God for that," I said, satisfied. "Now all we have to do is wait for the base people to get here."

"Super landing, Skipper," Jerry said warmly. "I bet there is hardly a scratch on the old girl."

I said, "In the sense that we're all going to walk away from it, the landing was okay, I guess. But she's bound to be twisted up around the flap area—I heard them ripping. Anyway, it's academic—she's not going anywhere, period. Shut up—I want to listen for the McMurdo people."

"Skipper"—Ben sounded puzzled—"it's a big airplane. How in hell are they going to find the door?"

He was absolutely right, of course. I should have thought of that—there could be as much as ten feet of snow on top of the aircraft.

"Point taken, Ben. Look—find me an anorak and some gloves. Jerry—can you get that roof emergency exit open? If I can get out on top of the snow, I can put them in the picture."

What appeared to be five tons of loose snow cascaded onto the flight deck when Jerry unlocked the hatch—and he collected most of it on his head. I told him to stow the bad language and move out of the way. By dint of getting a foot on the back of each pilot seat, I clambered through the hatchway, got both feet on the edge and slowly stood up until the hood of the anorak met a dome of snow. Balancing precariously, I looked upwards; the refracted light seemed brighter, and I formed the opinion that the depth of snow overhead was not excessive. I pushed gingerly, felt a hint of movement with my head and shoved upwards as hard as I could. My head and shoulders burst through into the upper air, and I gasped in shock; the stark coldness bit deeply into my lungs, and within seconds my face began to stiffen. I brushed away nearby ridges of loose snow and stared round.

A hundred yards away to my left, the first of a column of massive Sno-Tigers rumbled towards me—weird boxlike structures mounted on four caterpillar undercarriages, with enormously wide steel tracks which kept the vehicles suspended magically near the surface. Each had a raised plastic dome at the front of the roof; in the lead Tiger, two bearded men in fluorescent orange anoraks were waving frantically. Across the front of the odd-looking contraption were painted the words U.S. NAVY.

I grinned madly, waved back and damn near fell back down into the airplane. I waved the lead truck off to the right, around the front of the aircraft; the driver stopped fifty feet away and they scrambled out, white teeth flashing in bearded faces. I felt the flow of warm air from the airplane flooding up past my face, and I knew we had to seal off that hatch quickly.

"Hello there—Captain Scott, I presume?"

"It sure as hell," I said, "isn't Dr. Livingstone—not in this climate!"

"Great. Great. I'm Elkins—Base Commander. Say—that was one sweet landing, Captain. But we can talk later. Just one thing—about the kids. You weren't—joking? They are on board?"

"Large as life and tickled pink, Commander."

"Goddamn..." he breathed. "Okay—where the Sam Hill do we start?"

I thought for a moment, pointed down and to my left.

"There is a main entrance door about 20 feet behind me and about the same distance down to floor level. If your people can dig a sloping ramp down there parallel with the fuselage, we can walk straight out. You'll have to make room for the door to open—it swings forward, flat against the skin. Can do?"

"Consider it done. Anyone hurt at all?"

"No," I said seriously. "We were very lucky."

Elkins grinned. "Bullshit—begging your pardon, Captain. You don't get to drive things that size around the world by relying on luck. You staying in there?"

"Yes. I want to close the hatch—we're losing heat," I said.

"Right. You just learned the first rule of survival here—preserve heat. Anyway, that top snow layer isn't compacted—you'd need snowshoes to get out here. You get back in the warm. Let's get to it."

Getting the hatch closed was a frustrating and time-consuming job, but we succeeded in the end. I herded everyone off the flight deck and closed the door, because the forward end was knee-deep in snow. I went down aft, amid the noise and bustle, smiling and trying to avoid the hundreds of hands wanting to shake mine. The kids were delirious with excitement, racing around the deck pursued by the young SAS men, but not too seriously; there was an air of carnival aboard, and every light burned brightly.

"Priorities, Jonah?" Mike Brand and Hamish Bond were islands of sanity in a sea of jubilation.

I scratched my chin thoughtfully.

"Well—kids first—and have Commander Elkins' two up at the front. You heard about that?"

Brand nodded. "Quite incredible. If I'd read it in a book, I wouldn't have believed it. That's them—hanging on to Madame Ferrière."

"Okay. Next—have we anyone sick?" I asked.

"About half a dozen, but nothing serious, Jonah. Residual sickness from breathing that shitty air back there; took me an hour or two to get over it myself. I understand Doc Rabin says there should be no aftereffects?"

I said I thought that was right. "Perhaps you can get a line organized, Mike—kids, followed by sick cases; women and families next. All crew to wait till last. That sound okay?"

Slowly, the beginnings of an orderly queue were to be seen, starting at Gate 1 Port, stretching back down the aisle and back up the starboard side. The cabin was becoming warm and stuffy, and I began to worry about supplies of air. I sent Ben Price back to the flight deck to open the hatch again: fresh air was more important at this stage than keeping warm.

A voice outside Gate 1 yelled, "You all set in there?"

Ben Price snapped the door catch open, pushed hard and admitted a blast of icy air and the gray light of day. The massed banks of children in the aisle bellowed a welcome, and a bulky figure in snow boots and anorak came in.

Commander Elkins wore, behind that frosted beard, a sunburned face fractured by a thousand wrinkles, concentrated around a pair of keen blue eyes under shaggy brows. His hair was iron gray—prematurely so, because I guess he was only in his early forties.

I walked forward slowly. "Captain Scott. I have someone here who would like to meet you, Commander."

He looked down from his seventy-five inches upon two small figures, standing on either side of the motherly Madame Ferrière, and slowly went down on one knee. "Mark? Hayley? Is it really you?"

They hurled themselves forward into his arms, and he wrapped them in a grizzly bear of a hug; he kept pushing them away, saying, "Well, I'll be..." and grabbing them again as if afraid they might disappear in a puff of smoke. I am not a sentimental character, in the normal way of things, but when he stood up at last, eyes brimming, and shoved his hand out towards me again, I would not have been human not to feel deep emotion.

"Anything I can ever do, Captain...anything. Goddamn—and I thought they were dead..."

I picked up the boy, he the girl, and we walked slowly up the snow ramp into the Antarctic daylight. A dozen or so burly figures leaning on long-handled spades produced a remarkably loud cheer—there was no doubt about our welcome. Elkins led the way along a hard-trodden path to his Sno-Tiger, climbed in and helped his driver settle down the children. We managed to pack in twenty, plus Madame Ferrière and two of her team, and I stood up front between Elkins and Joe Kelso, his driver, watching with intense interest. The Tiger was driven by two gas turbines, each of which drove two undercarriages via a gearbox. The engines roared briefly and settled down to produce quite an amazing thrust; the cat made a steady 20 miles per hour, riding the snow humps with ease.

"Joe, I want you to drop Captain Scott, the kids and myself at my office. When you leave the others at the base Mess Hall, find Olsen—have him report to me p.d.q."

"Aye aye, sir."

The Tiger drew up alongside a snowbank in which a doorway stood in sharp relief. We clambered out, watched the truck clatter away, and Elkins set his daughter down, stamped over to the door and entered. Inside, I found myself in a six-foot-square cubicle, the walls of which were fitted with coat hooks and hangers. Several of these supported anoraks and other items, and snow boots stood neatly in pairs. Shucking out of his outer clothes, Elkins explained.

"It's always below freezing in here—so we don't thaw out clothes. That way they don't get wet. These are thermal boots. Feet tend to sweat badly, and wet socks can be dangerous when temperatures get very low. So we keep the insulation dry, and the sweat can't escape. You get used to wet feet—and wet socks. We change them daily, and once you get used to walking in wet feet, it's fine."

We went through another heavy insulated door, into a warm, comfortable world of pale-yellow walls and ceilings, shining floors in nonslip blue vinyl, and discreet fluorescent lighting. A warm, gentle draft blew down the corridor, entering through ventilator grilles located at intervals in the upper walls; each had a louver control and a shiny plastic streamer. A door opened farther along, and a figure in Navy blues, shaped remarkably like a Rugby football, came bouncing to meet us.

"Captain," Elkins said, "this is Olsen. He is supposed to look after me. Unfortunately, he spends half his waking hours sleeping and the other half eating; any spare time available he spends running the base poker game."

Olsen absorbed the friendly insult with the ease born of long practice and grinned. "Hi. You must be Captain Scott. Say, you're just a kid—and flying those big airplanes..."

I stared at him. "I can give you ten years or so, friend."

Elkins laughed in a deep, chesty fashion. "Blame it on your beard—or lack of it, Captain," he suggested. "We've not only seen no new faces for years—the sight of a clean-shaven face we are not used to. Not yet."

He turned to Olsen, who stared at him blandly.

"You will have your little joke, Commander," said the fat man.

"If the little joke doesn't listen carefully," his commanding officer said, "he will find I'm not amused. These are my children, Olsen. You heard about that? You did. Okay—take them along to my cabin, fix them up with a bath, a meal and a bed. They need rest more than anything—rest and good food. And you stay with them until relieved. Do I make myself clear?"

"Aye aye, sir. In your usual pedantic way," Olsen said drily. "Okay, kids—welcome aboard. You call me Klaus until you grow up and learn the names your pappy usually calls me."

"This way." Elkins walked ahead into his office, got out of his coat and hung it on a homemade hatstand in the corner. "The discipline may be a little slack around here, Captain," he apologized, "but the way things are now, what the hell? It doesn't matter a damn—but we keep up appearances, just so we don't get on each other's nerves."

He waved me into a chair, opened a wall cabinet and worked for a while on a bottle of bourbon and two glasses. Behind the back wall of the cabinet, he opened a hatch directly into a cavity hacked out in the ice and took down a plastic tray of cubes.

"We have a good iceman," he chuckled. "No shortage on cubes. That okay for you? Well—what can I say, Captain? Have we a future to drink to?"

I considered for a moment.

"I think we have—but I don't think any of us can imagine what it will be like. Suppose we drink, just this one last occasion, to old times?"

"Yeah," he said broodingly. "Why not? To old times."

The bourbon ignited a bush fire south of my breastbone, and I got up, topped up the drink with water from a jug on the desk and sluiced down the flames a little. I stared round. The office was decorated and furnished after the style of a moderately successful businessman, with fitted carpet, a polished oak desk with no lack of character, a swiveling leather chair in which Elkins sprawled, and subdued lighting. With the exception of his uniform cap, on the hatstand, and the American flag occupying one corner, we could have been in a second-story office on Main Street, U.S.A.

The big man refilled his glass, slid the bottle along the desk towards me. "Don't think we're always hitting the bottle here," he said. "But if this isn't an Occasion with a capital O, I'll be a monkey's uncle. Not only because of the kids—I'll suddenly start believing they're really here and lose my marbles completely. No—it's kinda strange, watching history being made. You know—in six, seven months, the only people still alive could be right here on the ice cap. There are maybe twenty, twenty-five other bases still manned, with almost every nationality you can think of—maybe a thousand or more people. We could finish up with no more than two thousand survivors."

He drank deeply again, wiped his mouth, sighed.

"Captain—we know *what* happened out there. But not how. When the comsats started failing, we stopped getting regular news. How the hell did it all get started?"

I stared at him. "You really want to know?"

"Just the bones," he said softly. "Just so I know who to hate."

It took most of fifteen minutes to tell. I believe he was more interested in the conditions in New York than in the holocaust itself.

"I think the worst part," he said at last, "is not knowing what happened to my wife. I know things got pretty rough back home—but not as bad as you tell. Maybe when the kids settle down and I can talk to them sensibly, I may get to know a little more. Just now, I couldn't trust myself to be with them very long without breaking down."

I fixed another drink for us both, and he sat, lost in reverie, for long minutes, until he jerked back into action.

"Say—that second aircraft!"

"No sweat," I said. "Valentina won't be here for more than an hour yet." I gave him the story. When I got to the weight problem they had met—and solved—he shook his head in total disbelief.

"Incredible...those crazy goddamn people...I never heard of anything so tragic—and wonderful. Yet in this lunatic futile world, it makes some sort of twisted sense. There was only one way out—and they took it. Captain, I just hope I can be half as brave as those old Russian women when the time comes." He lit a cigarette with hands that shook more than a little. I got up, reached for my coat. "I'd like to use your radio, Commander—to call Valentina. And see if there is any way we can help."

"Why, sure thing. Anything I can do?"

"Those smoke drums," I said, "were a hell of a big help—but if she comes in at the same place, she could slide into my old bus. Could we have them shifted over a few hundred yards?"

"Leave it to me." He opened the door, yelled, "Chief!"

Chief Petty Officer Miller was a revelation. He wore immaculate blues and a chestful of decorations; his iron-gray hair was cropped close, his shoes shone glossily and his shirt could have graced a ceremonial inspection. He shook my hand, smiled through his beard—a neatly trimmed Vandyke—and listened carefully.

"Aye aye, sir. About an hour? We'll be ready. I'll pull two drivers off the cats—they can operate one-man, this close to base."

The radio shack was built on the roof of the office block, entered via plain wood stairs from the main corridor; even so, the snow was almost level with the triple-glazed windows. Here I met Phil Harris, radioman. His beard was immature, straggly; eyes pale blue; fair hair long and untidy. He stood up as we climbed up through the floor aperture.

Elkins said, "We still on 121.5, Phil?"

"Yes, sir."

I settled down in the seat at the control desk, slipped on the headset. Harris pointed under the desk. "There's a foot operated switch, sir. Leaves both hands free."

"Jonah to Valentina. Do you copy? Over."

The channel was not totally free of interference, but the background mush did not affect her transmission: her voice came in clean and sweet.

"Valentina to Jo-nah. Is so good to hear you again. You have landed?"

"That is roger, Valentina. What time do you estimate McMurdo?" I glanced at my watch perplexed: it said five minutes after seven. Impossible!

"Jo-nah, we arrive McMurdo at eight hours fifty. One hour forty-five minutes. Over."

I bit my lip thoughtfully. She was taking longer than I had estimated. I keyed again.

"Val—are you all right? Have you any problems? Over."

"No problems, Jo-nah. Our fuel is very good, but we have difficulty keeping passengers warm. When weather is good, we come down to six thousand meters. Is a little warmer, but we do not fly at best speed. Over."

Relieved, I sat back, transmitted a little more slowly. "That's fine, Val. Good. Here is the situation at McMurdo. We landed safely, no injuries, aircraft being evacuated now. Weather is good, light is improving. Sky mostly clear but cloud building up southwest. Visibility on the approach about 6 kilometers until you get down low; on final approach, about 1 kilometer. Do you copy?"

"Yes, Jo-nah. Go ahead."

"Right, Val. Your landing direction will be to the southeast, southeast. The landing area is 1 kilometer inland from the base, surface level and plenty of room, but covered with soft snow. Suggest you overfly the base, turn northwest onto downwind leg for approach on 135 degrees. Is that roger? Over."

"Wait...yes, we copy, Jo-nah."

"Fine. Now, listen, Val. On final approach you will see a line of smoke drums. That is the start of your landing area—land past the drums. Suggest you make a wheels-up landing. McMurdo is at sea level, near enough. Over."

Elkins passed me a cigarette while we waited. He leaned over. "Captain, you won't mind if I leave you to it. I want to get back to my kids—you understand?"

"Of course, Commander. And—thanks."

Radioman Harris stood to one side, staring without a trace of rudeness at my face, and I began to appreciate that it was part of the burden of isolation to see no fresh faces, month after month.

"How has it been down here, Phil?" I asked.

"Rough, Captain. Rough. But better, now you're here. Say—the scuttlebutt says this Russian plane has a load of broads—begging your pardon, sir—some women on board?"

I laughed. "That's right. We got together at Lajes, in the Azores. There are about two hundred women aboard—most of them older people, many with children. But also quite a few Army girls. They don't speak English."

Harris said dreamily, "Girls...real girls. Say, they don't have to speak, Captain. Just stand there, that's all. You know we thought we'd never see a woman again?"

"Are there none on the other bases?" I said curiously.

"Shoot, I guess there are a dozen or so—but don't get confused by distances here, sir. Those bases might as well be on the moon. Hey—what happened to those guys up there when all this started?"

I told him that as far as I knew, they were up there still, and almost certainly running out of air and supplies.

"Tough," he commented. "I guess we felt the same, when we saw how things were going. You know there were twenty-four men here last week? Only sixteen left now, plus the Commander."

I was almost afraid to ask what had happened. "We lost eight men from suicide, sir. Leastways, six for sure. Maclean and Haggers, they took a Tiger and went south. Left word they were going right over the ice cap to Graham Land, across to the Falklands and up through South America back home."

"Will they make it?"

"Jeez, no way, Captain. You see any of that territory on the way in?"

I said I had seen it, and it looked very rough.

"Right—and they had enough gas on board to make the Beardmore Glacier, at most. And yet—maybe they did the right thing. I dunno."

"What happened," I said gently, "to the rest of the men?"

"Rather not talk about it, sir."

It was best to leave well enough alone, I thought grimly. Young Harris was like the rest—apparently well and adjusting adequately, but not far from breaking up completely. I asked him if he could fix me a ride back to the landing strip.

He used the base radio to call Chief Miller. The petty officer had finished moving the threshold marker drums and was bringing in the last load from Delta Tango. He would collect me at the Administrative Block in ten minutes.

I got up, shook hands with the radio operator.

"I wouldn't let things pile up too much, Phil," I told him. "Things will get better now. You'll see."

"Sure they will, sir. It's just that—we were a big, close family. I had five brothers and four sisters—and Maw and Paw. They all lived in Washington, except my older brother. He was a torpedo mechanic in the *Appomattox*. That's a nuclear submarine."

That I knew—only too well. But this wasn't the time to tell him. I went down the ladder, along the corridor into the freezing lobby, put on my anorak and gloves.

Chief Miller kept his word. "Hi, sir. C'mon up next to me. Where to?"

"The second aircraft will be here soon." I squeezed myself into the right-hand seat, took off my gloves and blew into frozen fists. "Can you get out the other side of my old beast, somewhere near where they'll end up?"

"No problem, sir. Say—that's a hell of a coincidence—bringing in the Commander's kids. He with them now?"

"Yes. It was a pleasure seeing someone happy for a change. How do you get along here—after what happened?" I asked casually.

He looked at me, shrugged and concentrated on getting the rig moving straight, working hard at the big power-operated steering control. We ground down the hill, past the Mess Hall and the USO building, and I began to appreciate how big the base really was—it was a small town in its own right. We passed Sick Bay, (how Doc Rabin would love that!), a cinema, gymnasium, accommodation blocks, office buildings, stores, warehouses, transport yards.

Farther along the shore, a massive concrete building could only be the nuclear power station. We were perhaps only a hundred feet or so above sea level, positioned just inland of Delta Tango, deserted now and lying with half-exposed back as the heat of her structure melted the snow piled haphazardly around her. The massive vertical stabilizer, bisected by the mighty engine that had served us so well, rose above the snow plain like some monument, and I speculated how many hundreds of years it would stand in memory of the folly of man. Miller kept the turbines idling to maintain the inside temperature of the Tiger, and I stared out upon the nightmare landscape which I must call home.

The immediate vicinity, reasonably flat loose snow, covered an inland strip perhaps 3 miles long, a mile wide. Farther inland, the land, under the permanent blanket of snow and ice, rose in shallow waves and ridges, a harsh and forbidding panorama. Behind us, and to the north, the Ross Ice Shelf lay like some great wedge aimed at the Pole; the seaward boundary formed a solid ice wall, stretching along hundreds of miles of sea. Had there been no ice, the shelf would have been a great inland sea fed by the rivers of the Queen Maud Range; under that ice lay Roosevelt Island, off Cape Colbeck—as big as the Isle of Man, or Malta, but concealed under the ponderous sheet of ice forming the shelf.

I could see the rugged black promontory, with the cross at the summit, erected in memory of an earlier Scott venture; the sound itself was littered with broken pack ice, and the mountains on the far side were shaded blue and white in the sunlight.

The stark naked savagery of the land appalled me, and I shook my head in despair, denying the twist of Fate that had brought me here, away from home, from civilization. This land was never meant for men. Or animals; I knew there were none on the ice cap, and thought of a world peopled only by men.

"Gets you, doesn't it?"

"Huh?"

Miller waved a gloved hand. "Out there. You think it's terrible now, Captain? Wait till you've had a year, five years. I tell you, sir, if you hadn't brought these people in—especially the girls—there would not have been a man left this time next year. Did anyone tell you we lost—"

"They told me," I said, disturbed because this man had seen that on my face which I would prefer no one to see. Not fright; nor horror—but despair.

After a long time, the base radio channel came to life.

"Chief, you got Captain Scott there?"

"That is affirmative, Phil. Go ahead."

"Captain, we just had a call from the Antonov. She's about 10 miles out, descending, has the base in sight."

"Can I speak to him, Chief?" I said urgently.

"Sure. In fact, if you want to be patched into the channel, he'll do that."

I took the hand microphone. "Captain Scott here. Can you patch me in, Phil? On 121.5?"

"No sooner said than done, Captain. There you go."

"Valentina from Jonah—do you copy?"

"Yes, Jo-nah. We hear you very good. We have the base in

sight and we are passing 1000 meters. Oh—I can see where you have landed. Over."

"Fine, Valentina. I am in a ground vehicle near the 797. Call overhead base."

Miller and I leaned forward, staring up, fascinated. The huge Antonov droned inbound from our left, whistled overhead, propeller disks burnished silver.

"Overhead now, Jo-nah."

"Okay, Val. I see you. Turn northwest now, go downwind and turn inbound to port. Your approach heading 135 degrees. Are you all ready for landing?"

"Yes, Jo-nah. We are prepared."

"Fine. You have a slight crosswind from starboard. Surface wind is about 30 knots. Visibility about...2 kilometers on final approach. Land beyond the marker line. Can you see it? Over."

"Jo-nah—yes. We see. You will be there when we land?"

"I'll be here, Val. Good luck."

We watched apprehensively as the Antonov drifted crosswind, turned slowly inbound and began to settle down into the haze. I was beset with the same fear that all pilots harbor, watching some close friend flying an airplane in an emergency: we tend to forget that the pilot is perhaps as experienced as ourselves and certainly in control of the situation. And with Valentina handling the monster single-handed...

It sank into the ground haze of windblown ice spicules and was gone. I sat frozen, imagination working overtime, eyes glued to the line of smoking drums a mile away.

The big transport appeared quite suddenly, skimming the threshold marker, dropping feather-light towards the snow. A wing dropped momentarily as the landing flaps showed stark black under the wings; lifted again, and she brushed the first snow dune daintily, soared a few feet and was down, propellers slowing and stopping, feathered and immobile. Puffs of gray smoke swirled briefly behind the wings before they sank into the snow plain: good girl—she had remembered the fire extinguishers.

Down, down until only the tall black fin, the obsolete red star were visible in the swirling wake of snow, slowing, slowing and coming to rest, pointing almost directly at our Tiger, clouds of fine snow settling like some dust cloud around her.

"Get going!" I screamed, and Miller, cursing, jammed in

the drive, boosted the turbines and sent the fifty tons of Sno-Tiger lurching across the snow.

The Tiger was still moving, Chief Miller blaring a warning, when I banged open the side hatch and bailed out into waistdeep snow, rolling into a tight ball, finding my feet and fighting my way towards the Antonov, forcing my way against the clammy weight of snow. The forward hatch flew open, swung down and locked, compacting the snow beneath. Valentina hurled herself into my arms, and I staggered back, fell into the deep white mantle. We were laughing madly, half-crying, rolling over and over in mock combat until I found her lips, like cold flames.

22

Epilogue/Prologue

By the beginning of December, almost a month after we arrived, we were beginning to make changes, adjusting to a way of life stranger than we could ever have imagined. In the beginning there was chaos, and this understandable, in relation to accommodation and meals, priorities and ratings. I could not place specific blame: the Russians, in the main, were peasant stock from a small Black Sea fishing port, and it became generally accepted that theirs was the most difficult task. Acclimatization to life in the Antarctic would have been difficult even for well-educated people, as we were finding out, but for the simple Russians, it was impossible even to persuade them that the outdoors could be lethal.

They knew all about cold weather, they told us. In Mother Russia it became so cold that the breath froze when inhaled and was stacked ten meters high waiting for the summer sun to melt it. It was so cold that if one was breathed upon by a careless friend, one was likely to stay encased in a block of ice until some kind passerby brought along a blow-lamp.

So they went out. And they suffered. They lost fingers and toes and earlobes and eventually it sank in that this was a different environment, requiring scrupulous care.

There was trouble, too, persuading them that this was

summer. This they could not believe. They invited us to observe the snow, the ice, the sun low upon the horizon: how could this be summer? No, soon the ice would melt, the grass would grow and life would begin again. When Karen Waldheim got around to mentioning that come April the sun would set and remain out of sight for several months, they got up and walked out, disgusted that such an educated woman could be so deranged.

So the Board of Management—the closest we cared to approach to a government—got tough and enforced the safety rules. The board was an odd assortment of motivated characters which included our Four Wise Ones, Mike Brand, Elkins and John Capel, and they tackled the language difficulty with methods that were at once simple and Spartan. Each Russian group or family lived with an equal-sized group of English-speaking people—and the future language of the land was English; any objectors could like it or lump it.

Valentina—elected against her great reluctance because of the need for people with linguistic qualifications—paraded the whole Russian population in the Mess Hall at an early stage, behind locked doors. She confessed later, in our quarters, that she had sworn at them in angry frustration.

"I cursed them," she said defiantly, "for ignorant peasants. I told them to forget Mother Russia—that there was no Russia, no Soviet Union, no Sukhumi. I told them they had to forget their belief that one day they would return home. I said we had been welcomed here and it was not good to say bad things about other people. I said they were to learn English because here there were ten English-speaking people for every Russian. That this was our land now and there were no more Russians, no more English, no more Americans—just people."

"I know it is hard, Valentina." I knew only too well how she felt. "You know, I think what you said a long time ago—was it only last month?—is right. There is only this land left. And even if we are all from different parts of the world, speaking different languages, we are bound together for all time. You understand?"

"Yes."

"So very soon, we must find a name for this land. We have to stop thinking of ourselves as American or English or Russian. It is as if we have all emigrated to a new country, which

will be ours until we die, and our first task is to learn the
name of our land. Any ideas?"

"What ideas, Jo-nah?" she said, amused.

"What to call this damned forsaken place!" I said, irritated
beyond reason.

Valentina curled up on the single bunk we found more
than adequate. "In university," she said dreamily, "I am
learning a poetry—"

"A poem, Val."

"*Da*—a poem. It is by very famous English poet—Coleridge. You have heard of this man—yes?"

"Vaguely. I mean—yes, Val—I have. Go on."

"So..." she stared at me suspiciously, as if she suspected
I was laughing at her. I kept my face straight with an effort
and tried to look attentive.

"The poem begins:

> *In Xanadu did Kubla Khan*
> *A stately pleasure dome decree:*
> *Where Alph, the sacred river, ran*
> *Through caverns measureless to man*
> *Down to a sunless sea...*"

She paused, glanced at me under drooping lids. "You know
this poem—yes?"

I wrinkled my brow. "From something called 'Kubla
Khan'—isn't it?"

"Ah. So—this man with whom I live has a little knowledge. Yes, is true. I think about this thing too, Jo-nah. I look
at this terrible place and I think that here are the caverns
measureless to man—somewhere under all the snow and ice
is a land which could grow and be good. Maybe, somewhere
under the ice, the sacred river Alph does run."

I said slowly, "I see what you mean, Valentina. We should
call this place 'Alpha'? That is the first letter of the Greek
alphabet, you know."

"Yes. Is true. And this is the first land where all people
are the same. I know we speak different tongues, eat not the
same food—but that is now. Think, Jo-nah—in twenty,
thirty years, when we are all speaking and thinking the same,
we are one nation. Alphans."

It would make some crazy sort of sense—not to us, but,
yes, to those who would survive in this land and eventually

some other place. The supplies available here would not last forever: in the end, men would have to go out in flimsy boats through the dark seas to find a new home.

Valentina came to sit beside me, slim and beautiful in a white shirt, green drab trousers presented by some proud Marine. "It will take many years, Jo-nah. The old ones—they will never change. And the little ones—now they speak Russian and no English. The next generation, they speak English first, Russian second. And *their* children will speak English only."

I rubbed my forefinger gently over the back of her hand. "It may not take as long, Val. We brought sixty soldiers; there were seventeen Americans here. And there is John Capel, Ben Price, Ed Burns—some of these will find a girl among your Russian girls."

She looked at me under half-closed lids and smiled. "Yes, is true, I think."

"What I mean is that we're pushing hard, Val, all the time. To bring us all together. Kate Monahan and her girls are getting up a party next Saturday night in the Mess Hall. Listen, boys are boys and girls are girls—there'll be more than one who'll have to call herself a woman, come Sunday morning."

She laughed, delightedly. "Is not good, my Jo-nah, that we have no priest. We live together—but we are not married."

"Does it matter? Really?

"Yes." She pouted. "But not too much. For you and me, is all right. But for these young girls—wedding is important. Is very serious—a good girl does not give herself before marriage."

"You did," I pointed out.

"Yes. Am ashamed. You were very bad. Before I know where I am, you are loving me. Is correct?"

I grinned broadly. "Well—that's not the way I heard it— but I'm not complaining. Come to bed and I will tell you a fairy story about a Russian princess who fell from her carriage into the snow one day..."

She looked at me sternly—but her mouth was twitching. "I know why you want me to bed, Captain Scott. But is still daytime. You must wait until the sun goes down!"

"What—until next March? Here—come over to the window." I grabbed her arm and dragged her—but she didn't resist too much, screaming quietly in mock terror.

"There—look at that—the sun is..." I broke off suddenly, staring. That was very odd....I knew the sun rose a little higher higher each day until midsummer, before falling again into the six-month night—but it had not been as high yesterday....On closer inspection, it seemed larger, too. Brighter—more orange than red, and with a glare I could not remember seeing in the last three weeks.

"Got to go out, love," I said urgently. "Go crawl into your sexiest nightdress and climb in—I won't be long."

I kissed her quickly, and got into the heavy U.S. Navy anorak presented by a grateful Elkins, and went looking for Professor Volkel, Olaffsen and Doc Rabin. I knew they shared a cabin and bathroom in the former Officers Quarters, about a quarter of a mile away. It was quite late, local time—after ten P.M.—but something was gnawing at my guts that would not stop until I checked a certain fact with the team. The wind blasted away at the flap of the anorak, trying to penetrate beneath the hood, and the driving snow gleamed in long streams in the raw light.

I pushed on hard past the accommodation blocks. In one room, a class of Russian women were learning to sing "Greensleeves"—disjointedly, and interrupted frequently for demonstrations on the pronunciation of particular words. But it sounded very good to me; we had brought little enough of Britain with us, but I was glad that the old song, preserved since Shakespeare's time, was part of it.

I kept staring at the red sun, shining fitfully through the white haze. Was it my own damned imagination?

The external door lock was frozen, and I had to shove hard with my shoulder to open it. Inside, with the door closed and my outer clothes on the peg, I slipped out of the snow boots and found a pair of the loose felt slippers provided. The warmth was insidious, like getting into a hot bath on Christmas Day; I started yawning, climbing the stairs to the second floor.

Many of the rooms—set aside for bachelor men—were empty, as people had started doing what came naturally and gone flat hunting. In the early days, we had thought to warn people about the hazards of radiation poisoning, the effects on genes of irradiation, but we could have saved our breath. I could not blame the SAS boys, the strong, hardy Russian girls, for wanting something permanent in a shifting world. The girls had been accustomed to an annual contraceptive injection, but we had neither booster nor renewal facilities. There was a strong feeling that if the race was to survive, and some of the kids might have a spare head or six fingers on each hand, or webbed feet—well, we'd love them just the same. Maybe more, because in our shrunken world, every human being was a precious, irreplaceable commodity.

I knocked on the door and walked in without waiting for an invitation. All three were there—sitting around the table, drinking hot chocolate and deep in a conversation which stopped dead when I walked in. It didn't taper off, or die away: it stopped. Bang.

At last—

"Captain Scott! Sit down. What can we do for you? Chocolate?"

"No thanks, Sven. I could find room for a drink, though— it's a bit chilly out there. Whiskey? Fine. Shove a drop of water in, Doc. Thanks."

They sat around in silence, three old gentlemen with probably more brains than any twenty others on the base chosen at random. I felt their eyes staring, finished the drink and sat back in the chair.

"Well, Captain?"

"Professor—you'll probably think I'm as mad as a hatter. But—well—have you noticed anything odd about the sun, the last few days?"

I struck oil, first go. The old coots exchanged glances and hitched their chairs closer to the table, all together, as if I had said something of real interest.

Volkel took off his glasses and started polishing. He usually did, when he got started into something good. "What about the sun?"

I said, "I thought it seemed—higher today than I'd seen it before."

"Go on," prompted Volkel, polishing faster than ever.

"Well—that's it. Again, it seemed brighter, too. And bigger."

Sven Olaffsen said gently, "But the sun always rises a little higher each day through the Antarctic summer, doesn't it, Captain? Until midsummer?"

"You're the goddamn experts," I retorted. "You tell me."

Professor Volkel put his double glazing back in place, apparently satisfied that he could see me clearly enough to point his nose in the right direction.

He said carefully, "Have you spoken to anyone else about this, Captain Scott?"

"No. Only noticed it a while back."

They sat for a very long time in silence. I got the impression each was waiting for the others to make a move, and I said irritably, "What's wrong? Cat got your tongues?"

Volkel got up, found an open book on the desk and brought it back to the table, under the main center light. He kept his thumb in a page, laid it in front of me and sat down again, lit a cigarette.

It was a reference work on the Antarctic, and the page was headed "Sun Azimuth Angles—Antarctica." It was a simple curve on squared paper, plotted against "degrees azimuth" on the ordinate and months of the year on the base line. It showed the variation in hours of daylight, the time during which the sun was wholly above the horizon, and the part of the curve under the base line which corresponded to the six-month-long period when the sun was not visible.

I looked a little closer. Someone had drawn in a modified curve, from the end of October as far as the current date in early December. The new line diverged steadily, rising above the standard curve sharply, and I began to extrapolate it, in my own mind, over the next few weeks. I didn't like the trend it appeared to indicate.

"This line—you've been taking azimuth sightings?" I asked Volkel.

"For the last twenty-one days. We are not one-hundred-percent certain yet—" he began.

But Olaffsen interrupted angrily: "No more doubts, Karl. Face the issue."

The old professor sighed. I was afraid we were in for another polishing while he pondered the situation, but he looked up at me finally.

"You are perfectly right, Captain. The sun is rising a little higher than it should each day. Not a lot—perhaps a fourth or fifth of a degree."

I lit a cigarette from the packet on the table. My fingers felt swollen and numb, and I absently wondered why. I blew a smoke cloud at the overhead light.

"Go on."

"You know we believe that thousands of bombs, including thermonuclear weapons, exceeding the 50-kiloton range were used?" he said slowly.

"Yes. Why?"

"Where were the majority dropped, do you think?"

That was an easy one. "Northern Hemisphere?" I put to him.

"Correct. And all within a very short period of time. You know, of course, that the axis of rotation of the earth is tilted?"

"Yes. About 19 degrees to the plane of the ecliptic, isn't it?" I said.

"Nineteen and a half degrees. And the ecliptic, of course, is the plane in which the planets revolve around the sun. Good. Next question, Captain. What do you know about gyroscopes and their properties?"

Lordy—that was a rough one. I had to go back to my training days and dredge through memories of interminable classes, sitting at my seat near the window and watching the white sails and slender yachts moving on the Hamble River. I jerked my mind away hastily and found what I was looking for in some dusty filing cabinet of the brain.

"Gyros... One property is rigidity. The axis stays put in reference to a point in space."

"Good. That is correct." Volkel sounded, dammit, like my old form master in Southampton. "The other?"

Oh, God. Back to the dredger.

"Precession?"

"That is correct, Captain. Let me refresh your mind. Apply a force to the rim of a gyroscope which is rotating—and the force appears to be exerted at a point on the rim 90 degrees around the gyroscope in the direction of rotation. You remember now?"

I grinned, got up and refilled my glass. "Now I'm with you."

Volkel scowled and said without humor, "So. Now, consider the Earth as a gyroscope, rotating on its axis. We apply a huge force—say, five hundred hydrogen bombs—at the 90-degree line of longitude, which passes through New Orleans, Memphis, St. Louis. As in any gyro, the force is moved to a point 90 degrees in the direction of rotation—on the Greenwich Meridian, passing through London. You understand?"

I said, "Yes. Please go on." This bearded old man was beginning to frighten me.

Volkel said, "That force is exerted on the earth's axis in a spatial direction, remember. We proceed. In six hours, the earth turns through 90 degrees. London is now where St.

Louis was and is bombed in turn. Again, the force, precessing through 90 degrees, is applied to the axis *in the same spatial direction*. That is the vital point. Yes?"

I said, "Yes, but—"

"Wait—we are not yet finished. After nine more hours, the 45-degree meridian is now where St. Louis was—the line passing through Armenia, the Caucasus and Central Russia. At this time America becomes able to launch a retaliatory strike, and perhaps the Chinese too—and for the third time, an enormous blow is concentrated upon the *same* point relative to the axis of the earth. Now do you see?"

The building seemed to sway about me, and I realized that my mouth was dry as a stick.

"You mean," I said hesitantly, "that we—moved the axis of the earth?"

Volkel pushed his glasses up onto his forehead; his eyes were red-rimmed and dull.

"Yes. Our azimuth readings confirm the movement—there is no possibility of error. There was a time when I would not have believed it possible—because of the rigidity of the earth's axis, its resistance to deflection. But I had not reckoned, firstly, upon the massive weight of detonations which happened and, secondly, upon the sheer misfortune which must have timed the blows, as I have shown, to be applied along the same spatial direction. Had the timing been different—to give a degree of cancellation between strikes...Well, that is what happened. It is the only way in which we could find the amount of axis movement we have recorded."

Sven Olaffsen got up stiffly from his seat, found a match for his pipe. Dr. Rabin did sensible things with the bourbon bottle; Karl Volkel sat immobile, watching my face. I believe they knew that this news was mind-bending, nerve-shattering, and that I needed, more than anything else, time in which to absorb it.

At last—"What—what is going to happen to us, for God's sake?" I said.

Volkel tapped gently upon the open page of the book.

"That," he said simply, "is where we cannot agree. There are three possibilities. One—that the change in axis angle will slow down, stop in a new position. Two—that it will reach an upper limit and return to the original position. Three—that the change will continue indefinitely, so that the Earth will continue rotating around the axis, and the axis itself will continue a rolling movement relative to space. If my own calculations are correct—and I believe they are—our present position will, in a way, move up almost to the Equator, return part of the way, move north again and eventually stabilize in a semitropical latitude. The new Equator line will run through South America and South Africa."

"Let me get this straight," I said, confused. "The ice is going to melt? It will be warm, so we could grow crops—have a chance to survive?"

"Possibly," said Karl Volkel cautiously. "There are—difficulties. First—my own calculations may be wrong: those of Sven and Moshe may be right. If we are embarking on a period of constant change in the axis angle, the Earth will in effect be rotating around two axes simultaneously, and we shall have a condition of total instability: the polar caps will melt and be unable to freeze again, and we shall see a huge rise in water levels—perhaps hundreds of feet—which will flood many low-lying parts of the world. Volcanic activity, too, will occur on a vast scale."

I stared dumbly at this man, who could discuss the end of the world with intense but totally abstract interest.

"Soon, we shall know. Each day we take azimuth readings against elapsed time. We establish the rate of change in axis alignment relative to space. If this rate is maintained, or increases—we are finished. If it decreases—we establish the periodicity of movement—like a pendulum—and calculate where the axis will finally come to rest."

I had trouble in lighting a cigarette. My hands felt stiff and clammy.

"How long, Professor? Before we know—for sure?"

Volkel said quietly, "We expect a trend to be revealed by Friday, Saturday at the latest."

I said sourly, "Looks like being a lousy weekend."

What a damned awful way to end up, I thought. All the way along the line, I had hung on grimly to a half-formed belief that as long as we could stay alive and keep fighting, we would get through this thing somehow. And when we'd got here, to relative safety and comfort, I'd thought we had it made, that all we had to do was sweat it out until things cooled down a little. Looking back, I began to understand that it had been this—hope, belief, whatever one wanted to call it—which had kept me going. I began to wonder how in hell I could tell Valentina and Kate and the kids we'd taken under our wing—Timmy and Jean. What a mess...a futile, tragic mess.

Karl Volkel leaned over, laid a hand on my arm. "I would suggest that we keep this to ourselves, you know. At least until we are certain, one way or the other. Just a few days..."

I stubbed out the cigarette clumsily in the ashtray. "Okay. That makes sense. But I think some people are going to catch on. The sun just now is brighter, warmer than at any time since we got here. Before long, the snow and ice will start to melt—"

"Not before the weekend," Volkel reassured me. "I think there is every chance we shall establish the trend within forty-eight hours."

"Talking about chances," I said bluntly, "what do you make them? Fifty-fifty? One in ten? Or worse?"

"For myself," Karl Volkel said, "I am certain. My friends here believe my calculations are in error—that I have made one or two unwarranted assumptions on the basis of the limited data we have available. The problem needs extensive computer time—which we do not have. We are making, in effect, an *ad hoc* experiment, and making the observed data fit one of three hypotheses. And we must wait—and see. I would say this, Captain: if I am wrong, I will regret it most of all because of the wonderful efforts you made to bring us here safely. It would be a great pity if it had all been in vain."

I looked at Olaffsen, sucking absently at a pipe once more unlit; at little Moshe Rabin, whose eyes mirrored the crushing weight of guilt, that his nation might have lit the fuse of annihilation; and at Karl Volkel, perhaps the sanest man still living because of his utter detachment from reality.

"We had it coming," I said slowly. "It took us only about three hundred years to wreck something that took maybe three hundred million years to build. And whatever happens to us now—we had it coming. In spades."

I went away from that place, out into the icy wind, head bent against the buffeting and hustled along by a giant hand in my back.

For the first time in my life I wished I knew how to pray. But I didn't know how.

Or to Whom—or What.

23

The main Mess Hall at McMurdo was a nostalgic fairyland of lights, shining through the driving snow particles traveling almost horizontally on a 50-knot wind, giving the scene an odd air of Christmas festivity. Within, streamers and hand-made decorations spanned a packed and sweating crowd, which gyrated and shuffled, chattered and giggled, screamed and shoved. Val and I walked in, the noise and warmth staggering in contrast to the cold frozen outdoors; it was about seven P.M. local time, but the window drapes were drawn to exclude the red sunlight, and a quadri-stereo belted out music from four vast speakers, so that we seemed to be standing in the midst of groups, bands, synpops—those weird extravaganzas composed by computers, played upon electronic synthesizers and containing no traceable vestige of humanity but vast quantities of percussion.

Commander Elkins met us at the door—and with him, to my delight, Kate Monahan. But such a Kate as I had rarely seen! Her long red dress of plain material had started its life hanging before some window. It was open to the waist, and if Kate realized that each lean forward exposed high, firm breasts with painted white nipples, she gave no sign. Her skirt was slashed to the waist, like a cheongsam, up the left side, revealing a total lack of underwear—and much more besides, when she swung round sharply.

Elkins put an arm around each of us and hugged hard. "Glad you came along, Jonah—Val. Welcome to the Saturday hop."

"Glad to be here," I told him. "Kate, that is some dress. You'll have to fight 'em off with a big stick tonight."

The big American grinned. "Over my dead body," he said complacently. "I have plans for this little lady here."

I stuck out my hand. "Couldn't happen to two nicer people. Keep fit and do your duty," I said—and dragged Val away hastily before Kate let fly.

Here was John Capel, looking sharp and oddly younger in a Hawaiian shirt and white slacks; here were Ed Burns and a radiant Jill Stewart, Tim Hockey with Carol—I figured I had all but lost my crew for good, but I didn't feel so bad about it, holding Val close to me. The crush allowed us enough room to hold each other tight and move enough to enjoy it. She rested her head on my shoulder, long hair streaming free, flexing her body lazily and experimentally against me, with devastating effect: I would have to ease the situation, one way or another, before many minutes passed.

Four full days had passed without sight or sound of Karl Volkel and his colleagues: they were eating in their quarters, keeping to themselves. After each sleep period, I looked ever more anxiously at the sun, climbing higher and higher; temperatures were rising steadily, and there were times, when the wind dropped, that the snow on roofs and vehicles began dripping and the icicles grew like translucent stalactites, and the kids out of school in the USO block fought mock sword fights until authority intervened.

Perhaps only the American base team, veterans of two Antarctic summers, suspected that anything unusual might be happening.

The previous morning, after taking Timmy and Jean to school, I had met Elkins outside his office block.

"Early in the day for dark glasses," he commented.

"Is it? Maybe. I think I got too much sun glare yesterday—went out to the aircraft on a salvage trip," I said carefully.

"Yeah—I guess it was kind of bright," he agreed. "I don't recall days like this last summer. Maybe you brought good weather with you.... There sure seems more land exposed along the shore this year. Wonder why?"

"Flash in the pan, I suppose. Next week we'll be neck-deep in snow again," I said casually.

He gave me a long quizzical look, stared at the sun again, shook his head and stalked off. I thought it wouldn't do much good trying to fool a man like Elkins.

Familiar faces passed in the crowd—not without difficulty. Mike Brand, still in uniform but minus all badges, decorations and the like—following his own edict (as a board member responsible for security) that all such military trappings be abandoned. He was dancing with a slim laughing Russian Army girl in white shirt and olive-drab skirt, which she had trimmed to the current six-inches-above-knee level, thereby displaying wonderful legs. I couldn't have interposed a microgauge between those two. Certainly, I could believe we would have no worries about the language problem.

The music stopped in mid-bar. Elkins climbed up on the dais, red-faced and jovial, holding arms outstretched for attention. It took a little time, but he finally established some sort of silence, interrupted with ribald remarks.

"All right—quiet, please. Thank you. Thank you. Look, will you guys knock it off and let a guy get a word in? Thank you." He took a deep breath and bawled, "Now hear this! Professor Volkel has an important announcement to make. Perhaps Mrs. Scott would come forward to translate for our other friends here?"

Valentina walked forward, slim and poised, head held high, and flushed at the subdued cheering and applause. Volkel climbed up beside her on the rostrum, adjusted the microphone stand nervously and tapped it experimentally. He extracted an echoing "boom-boom" and nodded, satisfied. He clutched a roll of notes in one hand, but managed to get through what he had to say without recourse to them.

He stared around the hall, spectacles reflecting the overhead lights.

"What I have to say, ladies and gentlemen, is perhaps the best news you have ever had."

He paused while Valentina translated fluently.

"When we first came here, thanks to Captain Scott and Valentina"—he had to wait long moments for the applause to subside, and I began to feel acutely embarrassed—"we believed that if we were very careful for five, six years with the supplies available, we could possibly return to more temperate latitudes when the radioactivity fell to acceptable levels."

He waited until Valentina finished.

"Some of you may have noticed that the sun becomes brighter each day, that it climbs farther into the sky. You may also know that this happens during the summer, when the sun never falls below the horizon at all for many weeks."

The vast crowd was quite silent, listening with rapt attention. I lit a cigarette with trembling fingers: all I could remember was his "best news you have ever had."

"What I have to tell you is that it is not the sun which is moving—it is the Earth. Let me explain as simply as I can. Before the bombs, the axis of the earth was tilted about 19 degrees, and it was this tilt which caused the seasons—summer and winter, spring and fall. Because of the tilt, we can see the sun, as I say, for many weeks."

Valentina finished with a long sentence, listened carefully again to Volkel.

"Now a strange and wonderful thing has happened. Because of the hundreds, thousands of big bombs, the Earth's axis has tilted. What does this mean to us, here at McMurdo Base?"

After Valentina translated the question, I could hear only the remote howl of the wind.

"It means," Volkel continued, "in effect, that this location, on McMurdo Sound, is slowly traveling north, towards the Equator. Or—if you like—the Equator is moving slowly towards us here. There will be a little overshooting, a little overcompensation, before we settle finally into our new position. Our calculations indicate that this will be in the subtropics, with a climate similar to the South Pacific islands—Honolulu, Hawaii."

The storm of cheering and hysteria broke over his head like a tidal wave, and the old man's face opened at last into a shy smile. It must have been three or four minutes before Valentina could translate his last statement, but I believe the Russian people knew, in some way, long before that time.

Karl Volkel began to clarify the situation.

"We calculate that a number of years must pass before the seasons stabilize. At first it will become very hot—and the ice cap will melt entirely. The sea level will rise, and we shall have to move to higher ground. Luckily, the nuclear power station is well above sea level, but there is much work ahead. The weather will be unpredictable—I believe we shall see much fog, cloud and rain. But eventually, we shall live in a warm and pleasant land, bathed in a climate brought to us by the tilt of the earth. Out of evil cometh good, the Bible says. Out of cold shall come warmth, and out of the north shall come salvation. I can tell you no more than that. Thank you."

He stood before the microphone, a frail, bespectacled little creature in a creased and stained suit, clutching his notes as if they were some talisman, drowning in the deafening outburst of pleasure and rejoicing. The crowd pressed forward around the dais to shake his hand; I saw people laughing, kissing, embracing, crying and smiling. And in a corner away to the left, a small group of Russian women in dark, old-style dresses knelt in prayer.

Valentina hurtled through the carnival towards me, eyes starry and tear-filled, a smile as broad as McMurdo Sound on her dear face. I met her halfway, lifted her with hands under her armpits; she rested her hands upon my shoulders, laughing down at me between those proud breasts.

She slid down, drew my head gently towards her, and we kissed as we had never kissed before; not with passion, or lust, but the simple human welding of body and spirit, as if we had only now met, and in the knowledge that a lifetime of sweetness could lie ahead.

By the year 2000, 2 out of 3 Americans could be illiterate.

It's true.

Today, 75 million adults...about one American in three, can't read adequately. And by the year 2000, U.S. News & World Report envisions an America with a literacy rate of only 30%.

Before that America comes to be, you can stop it...by joining the fight against illiteracy today.

Call the Coalition for Literacy at toll-free **1-800-228-8813** and volunteer.

**Volunteer
Against Illiteracy.
The only degree you need
is a degree of caring.**

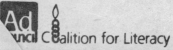

Ad Council   Coalition for Literacy

LV-2